Red Rabbit on the Run

by

Jodi Bowersox

Rendered:September 12, 2021 8:39pm -06:00— Ms. Modified:

Special thanks goes to Dr. Jack Westfall for his medical knowledge and expertise.

Books by Jodi Bowersox

Interiors By Design
Horses, Adrenaline, and Love

Anonymous Series
Cinnamon Girl Explains It All
The Diamond Diva Vendetta
Red Rabbit on the Run

Rocky Mountain Series
Rocky Mountain Angels
Rocky Mountain Sunrise
Rocky Mountain Redemption
Rocky Mountain Destiny
Rocky Mountain Calvary

Lightning Riders Series
JOLT
JUMP
JIVE

Tripping on Mars Series
Mars Madness
Beware the Eyes of Mars
The Mars Heir

Ephesians: The Plan, The Purpose, and The Power
Chosen and other productions, programs, and skits

Books under the name J.B. Stockings

A Tale of Two Kitties
The Stubborn Princess

Red Rabbit on the Run

Chapter 1

"Will, I think I found her!" Dani Harper had opened a cabin door at the third brothel they had raided to find a redhead sprawled across the bed, face down and naked, her long hair spilling over the edge to the floor. The room reeked of alcohol from a bottle of something that had tipped over on the small settee on the opposite side of the room, whose opulence clashed with the rustic interior. From the strength of the smell, she'd bet it had happened more than once.

Dani moved swiftly to the side of the bed and pulled a sheet over the young woman she believed to be Tiffany Morrow, then strove to find her face under the hair. The girl was out. *Not all the alcohol was wasted on the couch.*

Will Yarnel appeared in the open doorway in that beat up Aussie hat of his, his longish, brown hair curling under the edges. "Is it her?"

"I think so," she said, hooking her own limp blonde hair behind an ear, her blown-in volume a victim of the Amazon's heat and humidity. "Come see."

Two long strides put him by her side in the small space. "Well, she is a ranga." He crouched down to get a better look at the girl's face.

"A ranga?" Although Dani was starting to be able to interpret Will's many Aussie-isms, this was one she had never heard.

Will pulled a photo out of the breast pocket of his navy t-shirt—a change for the man who usually wore army green. "Redhead," he said simply. After comparing the two, he nodded. "It's Tiffany, all right. That freckle above her lip matches even if the make-up doesn't." Then he gently slid his fingers under her wrist, and Dani realized he was checking for a pulse. She hadn't even considered that she might not be alive.

She held her breath, waiting, and finally Will blew his breath out in obvious relief. "Thank God!" A smile split his red mustache and beard as he pushed up to standing, and in his exuberance, he threw an arm around Dani, giving her a sideways squeeze. "Thank God we found her!"

They were both hot, sweaty, and just plain gross from spending hours in the rainforest, but Dani felt a zing of electricity move through her anyway at his touch. She shook her head, blaming it on the nonstop adrenaline of the day. Now was not the time for self-analysis, and she'd spent too much time lately feeling guilty about her fiancé back in Kansas City.

Will scratched at his bushy beard as he assessed the situation, oblivious to the theatrics going on in her head. "Is she. . . " he began.

"Not a stitch," Dani provided. She looked around for clothes, but only saw a thin silky robe on a hook.

"No clothes is how these mongrels keep them from running." He turned for the door. "Well, we've got clothes in the van. And I'll get Vi to help you get her dressed. In her current state, it's gonna be like shoveling wet concrete into a tube sock."

The clothes had turned out to be a police uniform that was two sizes too big for her, but she was covered up, and the belt did its job to keep her from exposure, even if Will had to punch a new hole with his pocket knife to make it tight enough.

When he scooped her up to carry out, Tiffany roused enough to lift her head, but nothing changed in her zombie-like expression. "It's all right, love," Will whispered to her as he took her out and down two steps where the thick jungle nearly blocked the midday sun. "You'll be right as rain soon enough."

Dani certainly hoped so. No woman should have to endure what this young girl had before her twenty-first birthday.

This fun Brazilian vacay had turned out to be the education of a lifetime on the depravity of man and the depths that men would go to subjugate women and men alike for their own vile and perverted pleasures. They'd freed victims from three brothels hidden in the Amazon rainforest, but according to Will that was just a tiny corner of the trafficking trade in Brazil.

She knew what she had experienced had changed her forever, and she'd never be able to go back to the posh life she'd settled into with her rich fiancé and take up right where they left off as if nothing had happened. And then there was the side of him she'd seen when Rita had disappeared that had given her pause and plenty to think about.

As they reached the van, Vi opened the back and climbed in, ready to receive Tiffany's upper body as Will gently shifted her in on the floor of the utility vehicle.

Vi, a fifty-something strawberry blond and former employee of Stafford Investigations, had left her Rio cat café temporarily to help Logan, Will, and Rod locate Rita after Formosa had driven away with her. She then took on this undercover job with Dani to find Tiffany Morrow, a Denver college student whose boyfriend had drugged her and sold her to Justin Miranda in the States. He had, in turn, sold her to Perez in Rio de Janeiro, and Perez had handed her over to Perigosa, the scum who ran the brothels they had just shut down near Rio Branco.

As soon as Tiffany was settled in the back of the van, Dani climbed in too, adding yet another rip to her favorite summer dress. She thought of Tiffany who had far more than clothes taken from her and counted her blessings. Shifting her gaze to Will, still outside, she saw Justin Miranda limping their direction.

She couldn't help noticing how rumpled, bruised, and just plain filthy the man was. His handsome face not only bore the scars of the evil diamond smuggler Lourenco Formosa on his forehead, but he'd earned some actual battle scars today, helping them take down a small part of the industry that had made him rich. He had been the one to deliver Tiffany to this living nightmare, however—not to mention hundreds more just like her—so in Dani's opinion, he hadn't repaid his debt with one afternoon of fighting with the good guys.

"Is she all right?" he called out as he drew near. Was that real concern in the man's voice?

Will turned. "She's alive. We won't know the extent of damage until she's had a medical exam, some blood work, and a psych eval."

Miranda nodded solemnly as he looked in the back of the van. "God, she's probably lost ten pounds."

Will didn't say a word, but Dani noted his scowl as he backed up and closed one side of the van doors. Miranda closed the other, then the two were getting in the front, this time with Will in the driver's seat.

They were at least ten minutes down the rugged narrow trail that almost couldn't qualify as a road, following the police vehicles out, when Miranda spoke again. "I worked very hard to never think about what happened to them later. Men like Perigosa—" he paused, and Dani could see his tight jaw working from her spot in the back. "I never hurt them," he said, his voice husky with emotion.

"Yeah, and Bin Laden didn't fly the planes," Will ground out. "He turned to look at Miranda with a fierce look Dani had never seen on his face. "Doesn't make him any less responsible."

Miranda turned to look out the side window, and Dani was left to wonder if the man really understood his culpability, or if he was content to still push the evil of his deeds aside to focus on someone worse. And she wondered how someone so good-looking and charismatic had ended up trafficking women anyway. Why didn't he have a beautiful wife and children? If he'd just been all about money, surely he could have been a Wall Street exec or a hedge fund manager. That was at least a legal way to steal.

Tiffany's head lolled right and left with the next bump, and she let out a groan. Will put on the brakes and looked over his shoulder, and before anyone knew what was happening, Miranda was out the door, disappearing into the jungle.

Will's eyes flew wide, and a string of curses filled the van as he threw it in park, unbuckled, and jumped out himself. Trying to go extra slow for Tiffany's sake had put Will way behind the police convoy, who wouldn't have a clue that they had stopped. Dani didn't have Capt. Artez's number, but surely Will did. Crawling to the back door, she opened it, ignoring Vi's admonitions to just stay put.

Not a soul was in sight, but she at least knew Miranda's starting point. She ventured into the leafy mass of green, searching for Miranda's pale melon polo shirt. It was Will's voice, though, that actually pulled her the right direction.

"Miranda, put it down."

"What are you going to do if I don't, Will? Shoot me?"

Dani tread carefully in her completely ruined flats, hoping not to step on a lizard or a snake or some other rainforest creature.

"After your bravery today, don't tell me you're a coward after all." It was Will again, and not too far ahead.

Dani lifted a palm-like frond on front of her and sucked in a breath. Miranda was holding a pistol to his own dark-haired head. His eyes registered her presence, and his scarred brow puckered as his gun hand started to shake. "Go! Go back, Dani! You don't need to see this!"

Will glanced back, and she noticed he was holding a gun as well. Evidently, Miranda did understand his guilt and planned to perform his own execution. She supposed she should be happy to see him blow his brains out when he had destroyed so many lives, but she had seen things in his eyes she never expected to see several times over the last few days. Things that made her think that even this "blue-eyed devil" might be able to change.

She stepped through the leaves to stand by Will. "I won't leave, Mir— Justin," she amended, hoping to make a more personal connection that could pull him out of this jungle suicide plan. "Now that you understand—now that you've let yourself understand, you don't have to end like this; you can begin again."

He gave a mirthless laugh. "I'm going to prison, beautiful, maybe for the rest of my days!"

Dani supposed that could be true, but he had been a really big help in finding these women. In fact, they never would have been found without him. "Maybe you could cut a deal, Justin. There are more traffickers to bring down, and I'm sure you know connections in the States, the same as Brazil." She wiped away a bead of sweat running down the side of her face. "You could make amends."

He seemed to actually consider her words before taking his gaze back to Will. "Is that true? You said helping you here might get me a shorter sentence, but could I actually avoid prison altogether if I agree to help more?"

Will slowly shook his head. "I don't know. All I can do is put in a good word, but she's right; it is a possibility."

Miranda licked his lips and lowered his gun, and Dani blew out a breath, hoping the day had at last lowered the curtain on drama. She was pretty sure that Rita would have delivered several great headlines over the course of the day, but all her weary brain could come up with was "Case Closed."

* * *

"To Tiffany!"

Will and Rod clinked their champagne flutes to Dani's. "To Tiffany."

They all sipped the bubbly stuff that Dani had insisted on ordering after putting away more food than two men and one petite woman should be able to. It had been a hell of a long day, but with Tiffany safely checked into the hospital, and the news that Lourenco Formosa had been caught and Logan and Rita were safe, Will finally felt as if he could relax.

"So," Rod began, still picking at the custard he obviously had no room for, "did I hear you tell Capt. Artez that Justin Miranda just stepped out of the van and decided to kill himself?"

With the mention of Miranda, that relaxed feeling fled. He lifted his glass for a bigger gulp.

"Yeah," Dani said with wide eyes, "he seemed to actually feel bad for Tiffany. I guess he suddenly grew a conscience."

Will didn't buy it. "He just knows that he's too pretty for prison. Even with those new scars."

Although Will had tried a scar-reducing treatment on the man's forehead in exchange for his trafficking contacts in Brazil, the "LFF" that Formosa had carved there was probably never really going away. It was doubtful that the feds would care to continue the treatment.

With all the hubbub and confusion over Rita Miller's true identity, FBI agents from the States had belatedly shown up to assess the situation for themselves, and Will was all too happy to unload Justin Miranda on them for the return trip. He had enough to worry about with getting Tiffany home. Dani had agreed to go with him as a female chaperone, which had him feeling both elated and… tense.

"So you don't believe he's changed even a little bit?"

Will looked to the pretty blonde, more dolled up than he'd ever seen her in what was probably a designer dress paid for by her rich fiancé. "Defo. Remember, the bloke's a conman. That's what he does for a living. He's sheepy as hell." It nettled him that Dani could still be taken in by the guy. He drained his glass and poured another, topping off Rod and Dani's as well.

"You might be right," Dani agreed. "Sometimes I think I can't read people at all." She lifted her own glass to her lips, her eyes implying something he wasn't sure how to interpret.

Rod leaned back, stretching with his hands clasped behind his sandy-haired head, oblivious to whatever Dani was not saying. "That Perigosa was something else. Absolutely didn't know when to stop talking."

Will dragged his attention back to Rod, who was now stifling a yawn. "Yeah, he was rabbitin' on about 'his successful business' even as they loaded him into the paddy wagon. That bloke is one stubby short of a six pack, not to mention a purebred mongrel, and I'm proud to have given him his shiner." He looked to Dani, whose cheek was bruised from that dog's slap. "Had he been my only reason for being there, I would have thrashed him within an inch of his life."

Dani held his gaze with an intensity that surprised him. Or was it just the extra eyeliner? She wasn't the only one having trouble reading people. Right now, she was a mystery he just couldn't solve. He looked to the big diamond ring that, this evening, seemed to define her in a way he hadn't experienced. How did extravagance and fancy clothes fit with the woman who risked her very life several times over the last two days to rescue trafficking victims in the heart of Brazil?

Rod yawned again and pushed back from the table. "Sorry guys, but I'm done. I'm heading back to the hotel."

Will nodded, thinking Dani would probably want to do the same, but she didn't move. He smiled. "You're not tired, possum?"

She shrugged. "I got in a short nap after my shower this afternoon." She tilted her head toward the champagne on ice. "And it's not gone yet."

Will hitched a brow as he reached for the bottle once again. "I suppose this big ole thing won't fit in those little tiny fridges they give us." He poured out two more glasses, and she lifted hers to her lips. "So I guess you like champagne. I suppose that fits."

"Oh, really." She set the glass back on the table. "Fits in what way?"

Will twigged he'd probably spit out a clanger with that line. "Oh, just that you're looking very schmick tonight."

"Schmick?"

"Stylish, classy."

"And why do I get the feeling you don't approve? Either of my clothes or the fact that I like champagne?" She drank another sip.

God, now he was in trouble. "No, I didn't mean anything... You look... lovely." More than lovely, but seeing her mussed and sweaty in the jungle had nearly stopped his heart. Now she seemed... too sophisticated. Unreachable. He quickly grabbed his own glass and guzzled a third. *She should be "unreachable," you drongo. She's engaged.*

She drank the rest of hers as though it were a challenge, then waved down a passing waiter for another bottle.

Will leaned forward over the table. "Dani, you've had a pretty traumatic day. Maybe you should go easy—"

She matched his posture, her eyes radiating her irritation. "You're damn right I've had a dramatic... traumatic day, and if I want champagne, I'm going to drink champagne. You are welcome to go to bed without me." She waved a hand at her very own clanger. "I mean, go to bed with Rod."

Will couldn't help smiling. She was well on her way to drunk already.

"Don't laugh at me!" she insisted crankily as the waiter showed up with their next bottle. "You know what I mean."

Will sat back slowly, running a hand over his beard as he tried to suppress a laugh. He wasn't sure where this mood was coming from, but he suspected that the danger she'd put herself in this morning was finally hitting her, and he wasn't about to leave her to drink with the flies.

After the waiter unwrapped and popped the cork, Will took it and poured two more glasses.

Chapter 2

Dani woke with a groan. She hadn't drunk so much since college, and she obviously couldn't handle it anymore. She slowly got out of bed in an over-sized nightshirt and made her way to the bathroom, tripping over her discarded dress and high-heeled pumps on the way. *What was I thinking, anyway?*

She'd been freaked out, that's what. The nightmare she'd had during her short afternoon nap of Perigosa pinning her down and tearing at her clothes had sent her fleeing the feelings of helplessness and desperation her little undercover job had brought out. The expensive dress, the glam make-up, ordering the champagne had all been a way to escape the terror—to return to the safe place that Keith had made for her where women weren't bought and sold like cattle.

The cold tile bathroom floor shocked more than her physical senses. It sent that lie right out of her. Trafficking happened everywhere, and living a high society kind of life didn't make you safe; it just made you blind.

Once in front of the mirror, she groaned again and quickly opened a pack of makeup remover wipes. She went to work on the mascara she had neglected to remove the night before as she made her way across the room to start the shower.

She started it running, then deciding she needed something for her pounding head, turned it off again and went back out to her purse to find some ibuprofen. One eye scrubbed, she set the blackened wet wipe on the bureau to use both hands in the search. There was a light tap on the door, and a soft Aussie-accented, "Dani, are you awake?"

Dani blinked and looked around the room for a robe but didn't see one. "Umm, just a minute." Despite her aching head, she scurried to the bathroom, but no robe could be found there either. *I guess a robe isn't a perk of this place.* She looked down at her big nightshirt and decided she didn't really care what Will thought of it.

She undid the lock and opened the door to find him standing with a glass full of orange, fizzy liquid, looking concerned. "I thought you might need a Berocca this morning."

She hesitantly reached out a hand. "A what?" She took it and stepped back, allowing him to come in.

"Berocca." He closed the door behind him. "It's a Down Under cure for what you're feeling this morning."

"Oh?" She squinted her eyes. "And how do you know what I'm feeling this morning?"

He lowered his voice and leaned toward her. "I know what you're feeling this morning because I was with you last night."

The way he said it started her brain cells firing, although the engine was still slow to start. *Did we…* She didn't remember anything more than talking. But then again, she didn't remember getting into bed.

He chuckled, easing her panic. "Nobody your size can put away that much booze without a hangover the next day."

She stared at the glass he had handed to her, fighting for memories.

"Go on, drink it down, possum. It really will help."

She took a tentative sip. "Mm, wow, that's strong."

He shook his head. "You can't just sip it, love." He smirked. "Drink it down like you chugged that fourth glass of champagne."

Her eyes went wide, and his narrowed. "You don't remember much about last night, do you?"

Her stomach picked that moment to turn over completely, and she quickly ran into the bathroom. Abandoning the Burnt Wookie, or whatever he called it, by the sink, she sank to the floor over the toilet. She tried to swallow the sick feeling down, sensing Will behind her, but it wouldn't be tamed, and in another few seconds she was puking up her stomach's contents along with her dignity.

As the spasms subsided, she flushed the toilet and realized he was crouched behind her, his hand at the back of her neck, gathering her hair away from possible defilement. She sat back on her heels, and he released her hair, sliding that hand down her back in the gentlest of touches. "Sorry you're feeling crook. Hang on a tick until your stomach's settled, then drink the Berocca, and you'll start to feel better." He rose. "I'm heading over to the hospital to check on Tiffany and see when she might be released. I took a chance and got us booked on a flight out tonight."

"Is Rod coming too?" she asked, still feeling a bit queasy.

"He's on his way back to São Paulo as we speak. He's got another case to get started on."

"It never ends, does it?"

"I'm afraid not." He turned toward the door. "I'll come back and get you for lunch." He looked back at her, his mustache twitching with a near smile. "If you're feeling up to it by then."

"Is it that late?" She pushed up from the cold floor.

He looked to his watch. "It's 10:30. I've been waiting for you to get up for a while."

She caught a glimpse of herself in the mirror. Mascara still ringed her left eye, and she reached for the makeup wipes and went to work, mortified that Will had seen her once again looking horrible. "How did you know I was up?"

He nodded toward the shower. "The walls are pretty thin." His gaze shifted to the other room. "No secrets are kept in this place."

She decided that was a good moment to take on the bubbly drink, grabbing the glass and gulping it down. It wasn't that bad—sort of like drinking a glass of Flintstone vitamins. She handed him the empty tumbler, wishing she could remember their evening of drinking. Will left with a promise to be back around noon, and she turned again to the shower.

She'd been fighting feelings for Will for days. She hoped she hadn't made a fool of herself last night, saying things she'd regret. She needed to see Keith again—talk to him about everything that happened in Brazil and between them since she'd come to Brazil—before she made a decision about their relationship. As she reached in to check the temperature of the water, her eyes caught on her sparkly diamond ring, and memories came back to her. Not of the night before, but of Keith.

Keith, who had sent her a dozen roses every day for a week after their first date. Keith, who was always delighted in showing her off to his friends and colleagues. Keith, who bragged on her cooking and laughed at her bad jokes and wanted her to be his wife.

Pulling off her nightshirt, she stepped into the warm spray, wondering if she'd been too hard on her fiancé of late. He was under a lot of pressure with his congressional campaign and worrying about her in another country. *Stress does weird things to people.* She thought about her stupid behavior the night before, trying to drown her anxiety in champagne. *Maybe I'm the one who's been a jerk.*

After washing her hair, she watched the shampoo suds course her legs to the drain, wishing she could wash away her doubt, uncertainty and confusion as easily.

* * *

Will raked a hand through his slightly shaggy hair before setting his hat on his head, overheated before stepping outside into the bright Brazilian sun and sultry air.

What Dani's designer clothes could not do for him, that simple rumpled night shirt had, and getting out of her hotel room as soon as she seemed okay had been imperative.

He smirked. The mascara around just one eye wasn't her best look, but damn, she was still pretty, despite it. It certainly wouldn't have been a deal breaker had she pulled him into the other room and— His cab pulled up to the curb, and Will was grateful to be diverted from that line of thinking while he gave his destination to the cabbie.

What he'd learned about Dani last night in her inebriated state was that she was one mixed up sheila. At the age of thirty-nine, she was having some kind of mid-life crisis, questioning everything she'd done with her life so far and where she wanted to go.

It seemed that she had known exactly what she wanted not that long ago—she had started a business called Up-cycled Treasures, lighting up when she talked about it and how as a nonprofit, it made money for the homeless. *She isn't all that glitz she put on last night. She's as down-to-earth as a bilbie.*

And damn it, he'd felt himself falling in love.

It would have been the simplest thing in the world to take advantage of her in that state, especially once the tears had started, and he had felt the need to console her through them. But that wasn't the way he rolled. And once she had started blubbering about her fiancé—most of which he couldn't understand even when he caught actual words—he'd walked her back to the hotel and to her room. There were some things she was going to have to figure out for herself. Being the shoulder to cry on in that situation could only lead to heartache.

His.

The cabbie pulled up in front of the hospital, and Will strove to put Dani out of his mind. Tiffany was still his mission, and he needed to keep his focus there.

With the help of a nurse, he found the right floor, raised voices assaulting his ears as soon as he stepped off of the elevator. He followed the sound past an empty nurse's desk to a room at the end of the hall. He peeked in the not-quite-closed door to see no less than four nurses trying to hold his thrashing, screeching ranga down. He stepped in to the foot of the bed. "Tiffany, love, you're safe. These ladies are only trying to help you."

She paused in her struggling, staring at Will like he was a cypher, then she collapsed back, muttering and mumbling what sounded like numbers while her eyes darted over the ceiling.

The nurses used the lull to strap her arms and legs down. Will frowned. "Is that necessary?"

One of the women gave him an incredulous look as the others flew around the room picking up cups and pillows that he assumed had hit the floor during this fracas. "Did you not just see how many of us it took to keep her in bed?" She walked toward Will and lowered her voice. "She is strong for one so small. And she has done nothing but utter curses and numbers when awake." She glanced over at the still muttering girl. "I think she needs a priest more than a doctor."

Will rolled his eyes. Brazil was rife with superstition.

"Thanks for the medical opinion. Would the doc be around?" Will didn't like to see Tiffany restrained. After what she had been through, how could it not send her into a panic? And she obviously wasn't in her right mind yet.

She gave him a look up and down. "Are you the next of kin?"

Will pulled out his Stafford Investigations ID. "I'm responsible for getting this girl back to the States just as soon as I can."

She handed it back, then tried to wave him to follow her out. All the other nurses had already left. "The doctor will be available soon. If you will just—"

"I'll stay here, if you don't mind."

The expression on her face said she did.

Will was losing patience. "Check your chart, sheila. I'm listed as the responsible party, and I'm staying right here until the doc arrives."

The woman seemed ready to take him on. "It's Sofia, not Sheila, and—"

The door opened, and a white-coated, dark-haired man came in, just old enough for a few gray hairs at the temples. Seeing Will, he put out a hand. "Mr. Yarnel," he said with hardly an accent at all, "I am told you are responsible for all my extra work." He broke into a smile. "Thank you for rescuing the victims of prostitution."

Will gave his hand a firm grip. "Well, I didn't do it alone. It took a small army." Will looked to his ID for a name. *Dr. Dan Trent.* He turned to look at Tiffany. "What can you tell me about my girl here? Is there a compelling reason for her to be strapped down?"

Trent nodded solemnly. "We didn't want to use restraints, but it proved to be the only way to keep her in bed. Blood work would indicate some hallucinogenics are in her system, and we wanted to give her a chance to rest until they wear off."

"So how soon do you think I can get her on a flight home?"

Tiffany was quiet now with a blank stare. The doctor walked to her head and shined a penlight into each eye. "It's hard to say. As far as her physical well-being, she is obviously underweight with a number of bruises." He switched it off and slipped it back into his pocket. "But nothing is broken, and while her liver could use some rest from alcohol, she is in remarkably good shape. How long was she kept at this brothel in the jungle?"

"More than a month."

"Not too long then."

Will looked to her thin face. "Even a day is too long, doc."

The doctor nodded wearily. "That's certainly true. I only meant that some fare much worse."

Will knew they did. He'd seen them. He nodded grimly. He hated the thought of her strapped down, but what he hated even more was the thought that they might not be able to leave that evening. Could he and Dani handle her? If Tiffany was still acting like a fruit loop, would they even be allowed on the plane?

Dani hadn't been trained to deal with any of this and had only offered to help out of the goodness of her heart. Maybe he needed to send her on home to Kansas City and hire a nurse to see Tiffany back to Denver.

He had the strange, twisted up feeling that that was both the right and the wrong thing to do.

* * *

"It took four nurses to hold her down?" Dani watched Will take a bite of what the waiter called a "bauru," Will had called a "sambo," but what she would have simply called a roast beef sandwich. She was sticking with a kind of broth soup that was still probably too spicy for her stomach at the moment.

"She's evidently stronger than she looks, although a hefty dose of the right kind of drugs can do that—give you an energetic boost that comes off as strength."

"You'd think it would be wearing off by now." She sipped her maté through the silver straw. "Not that I know anything about it. I drank my share of beer in college, but I never did any drugs."

He smiled as he bit into a mandioca fry. "So when did you switch to champagne?"

She felt herself blushing and looked down at her soup. "Will, I'm sorry about last night. I was trying to drown my… my… my…" she couldn't find the right words.

Will helped her out. "Your out-of-the-country, out-of-your-comfort-zone, out-of-all-rational-behavior experiences of the last few days." He reached across the table to give her forearm a squeeze. "I know. I've been there. It's been a while, but I've been there. On my first free weekend in the RAR, I got soused on a six-pack of Carltons. It wasn't champagne, but the effect was the same."

He pulled his hand away to put it to use eating, and Dani missed it immediately. How could she be so mixed up about two men? Especially when she had no idea what Will really thought about her. Sure, he called her "love" and "possum," which she had learned was an Aussie term of endearment, but as far as she could tell, he treated all women that way. It didn't really mean anything.

"Well, I hope I didn't say or do anything embarrassing," she said, absently stirring her soup. "I'm afraid I don't remember much about it."

"Don't worry, your secrets are safe with me."

Her eyes snapped to his, and he winked. *Oh my, what did I say?* "You're just… pulling my leg, right?"

Will just grinned before tying up his mouth with a big bite of his sambo.

He knew he should stop teasing her, but he was enjoying it far too much, and the blush that had come to her cheeks had turned her into a goddess. He knew he was opening himself up to a world of pain, but he couldn't help having a bit of fun with her. The last few days had been nothing but serious and dangerous, and half of her vacation had been a nightmare worrying about Rita. The girl deserved some happy before going home. "How's your stomach? What's it up to doing this afternoon?"

She blinked. "I don't know. Probably not a roller coaster."

He leaned in. "With the heat today, how about a water park?"

The light in her eyes said he'd hit it in one.

He looked up options on his phone while they finished their meal, but before they could go anywhere, Will got a call from the hospital. Tiffany had seemed calm enough to release her restraints. Unfortunately, the doc had gotten a bloody nose and nurse Sofia a kick to the shin before the girl disappeared down the hall.

They were still looking for her.

Chapter 3

As their cab approached the hospital, Dani grabbed Will's knee. "Will, look!"

"I see her." Their ranga was running down the steps in what looked like scrubs. "I think she may have hidden in a supply closet for a while." He leaned toward the cabbie. "Follow that woman until we see which direction she goes at the crosswalk, then get ahead of her in the next block and park."

The cabbie followed the jogging girl, who looked over her shoulder every now and then, but didn't seem to suspect anyone in a vehicle. When she crossed the street without turning, he sped up and parked toward the end of the block. With no one following her on foot, she had slowed down considerably. Her scrubs disguise must have gotten her out without notice.

Will and Dani got out casually as if this was their destination, and Will played it cool, turning to talk a moment to their driver. "This gal," he said low, "has escaped from the hospital, and we need to get her back."

The cabbie nodded, and when she was nearly upon him, Will merely turned from the curb, took a few long strides, and grabbed her arm. She tried to pull away, but he held tight, flinging his other arm around her waist. "Tifffany, it's all right. We're not going to hurt you."

She swung a fist and caught him in the jaw. It was a damn good hook that nearly knocked his hat off. Dani appeared at her other side. "Tiffany! We saved you from the brothel! We want to help you!"

Dani kept her from swinging another punch, which Will appreciated, but then the girl started kicking. She had bare feet, but still managed a wicked strike at the back of his knee that nearly took them all to the ground. Regaining his balance, he pulled both women toward the still open cab door and turned to shove Tiffany in. “Dani, get to the other side!”

She ran around and got in, and he pushed down on Tiffany’s head while moving her decisively into the vehicle. She immediately started flailing like a frog in a sock, trying to scramble over Dani. Will reached in and pulled her hips to the seat, sliding in beside her. With one arm around her, he pulled the door shut with the other, then wrapped around her like an outback boa, pinning her arms down. “Go man!” Will yelled to the cabbie, and he pulled away from the curb, turning at the corner to make their way back to the hospital.

Tiffany tried to scratch his arms and bite his neck, but only got a mouthful of beard. That seemed to shock her, and she pulled her head back to stare at him with wild eyes. “You probably don’t remember me, love,” he said in a calm, quiet voice, “but I carried you out of that slave cabin yesterday. And my job is to get you back home.”

She turned to look at Dani, who had laid a hand on her leg. “We’ll take care of you,” she reassured. “No one can hurt you now.” The girl was calmer, although she was once again saying something under her breath. He leaned his head in to listen, but whatever she was rattling off didn’t seem to be directed at them.

They made it to the hospital without incident, and Will slowly pulled one arm away from the lock he had on her. She didn’t try anything—just stared straight ahead, muttering. He worked his phone out of his pocket and called to tell the front desk that he had her, and that he’d like to just check her out without bringing her back in.

Dani didn’t agree. “Will, are you sure we can handle her? Is she really okay to fly?”

Will studied the girl who was obviously still not quite in their world, but who was no longer trying to knock anybody out. “I think that would be preferable to having her strapped down again. That’s probably what set her to running—the feeling of being trapped.”

Dani still didn't look convinced. "Okay, if you think that's best. You certainly know more about this than I do." She took hold of Tiffany's hand with both of her own, and his heart squeezed at the compassion and courage that was just a natural part of Dani's being. Then it squeezed harder as his eyes settled on that damned engagement ring.

He snapped his head the other direction. "I do. We need to get this girl home." Nurse Sofia was heading down the steps with a clipboard in hand. He wished he was as sure about flying Tiffany out that night as he sounded, but there was one thing he was certain of. He needed to get Dani back home as much as Tiffany.

Back home and out of his head.

* * *

"They're coming for me! I know too much!" Tiffany ran her hands down her long ponytail over and over in between Dani and Will on their flight back to the States. "1 8 3 6 9 1 1 4 2 1 6 7. 1 8 3 6 9 1 1 4 2 1 6 7."

Dani wondered what the numbers were all about. Tiffany had been muttering numbers off and on for hours. She rubbed a hand on her shoulder while Will looked concerned but kept his distance. Once they had her back in the hotel room, she had seemed wary of him. Will hadn't been surprised. He said that men were probably not on her favorite-things list right now. "Honey, it's all over," Dani soothed. "No one is coming for you. We'll take care of you until you're back home again."

She began to rock. "He has the stick. He took it from me."

Dani frowned at the thought that they might have hit her with an actual stick. Perigosa seemed very proud of their "disciplina." He'd slapped Dani only a few minutes after her arrival at the brothel where this young girl had been forced into prostitution.

"No one has any sticks, love," Will said in a calming voice. "We'll keep you safe."

Wrapping her arms around herself, she continued to rock back and forth. "I had the evidence, but he took it."

"Shh, Tiffany," Dani turned and put her arms around her. "Don't worry about evidence, the police have all the evidence they need to put Perigosa and all his men behind bars, as well as Perez, Rocha, and Miranda. They won't ever bother you again."

"He funneled it into a shell," she mumbled. Or maybe she said something completely different. Dani wasn't sure. She looked to Will, who shrugged, looking baffled.

Tiffany quieted but didn't react to Dani's hug. She wondered if she could even feel it. She released her, and the distraught young woman rocked a few more minutes, then stopped, leaning oddly forward, her green eyes staring at the back of the seat in front of her with a glazed look that broke Dani's heart. Would this beautiful girl ever be the same again?

Dani looked once again to Will, who gave her a small smile and spoke softly. "This is a tough one, possum, but with time and the right help, she'll come out of it. It's a process."

"I hope you're right, Will," she whispered back. She turned to the window, although there was nothing to see but clouds. God, how she wanted to swing a bag of rocks at every one of the men who had terrorized this poor girl for more than a month. One of the victims said they were expected to "service" up to ten men or more a night. It was inhuman what they had been put through—used like sex toys.

Dani vowed she would not go back to her life of ignorance and carefree living that she had indulged in with Keith. She knew too much to ever be a part of their frivolous, wasted lives again. She wanted hers to count for something. She hoped that she could make him see beyond dollar signs or even political ambition. She supposed, as a politician, he actually could do a lot to help end human trafficking if he wanted to.

Dani just wasn't convinced he wanted to.

Getting on the plane had been easier than Dani expected it to be. Will was well prepared with all the paperwork, including police reports and an emergency travel pass for Tiffany since she didn't have a passport. Dani had been amazed that the government could work so fast on her behalf, but Will said that Logan always applied immediately to get the travel pass as soon as he started a case, so there wouldn't be any delay when the missing person was found.

They didn't have any clothes for her other than the scrubs she'd left the hospital in, but Dani had gotten her into one of her t-shirts, and although her jeans were a loose fit on the girl, a belt kept them up.

She had been pretty quiet getting on the plane, but shortly after liftoff, she had become more agitated. Will thought it was probably that feeling of being trapped again. It was a long trip home. Dani hoped she wouldn't feel trapped for the whole of it.

* * *

"I don't want to go home! You can't make me go there!"

Both Will and Dani tried to shush Tiffany who was acting as crazy as a kangaroo in the top paddock after Dani's reassurance that they would "soon be home."

She'd had other outbursts on the twenty-four-hour flight, but this one was by far the loudest. Heads were turning all over the plane, and a flight attendant was heading their way.

Will's head was pounding. With Tiffany's muttering, rocking, and intermittent outbursts, it had been the longest fourteen hours of his life, and they had ten more to go.

She had slept little so far, and Will had found himself wishing she'd spend more time in the catatonic state that overtook her at times, even though that was hard to watch. Right before this tanty, she had been rambling about secrets and lies and how she was going to be killed in the most horrific ways, and Will wished he had done more than punch Perigosa while he had the chance.

As the flight attendant drew near, her face etched with concern, Will leaned to pull out his wallet to retrieve his work ID and the paperwork signed by Tiffany's parents giving them permission to bring her home, along with a copy of the police report from Brazil.

He gave her a weary smile. "Ma'am, I'm sorry for the noise, but the girl's been through a lot. She's a trafficking victim, and we're just trying to get her home."

The woman took his ID and read it before glancing at Tiffany, who was now rocking and crying. "Sounds like she doesn't want to go home."

Will nodded. "That's actually not that uncommon. It's the trauma and the guilt they take on themselves. Coming back to herself is a process." He didn't tell the woman he'd never dealt with anything this severe before. He just pointed to the Morrows' signatures. "They know we're coming."

After the woman glanced through the police report, she handed everything back, giving him a small smile. "Bless you for retrieving her. I hope all goes well."

"Thank you, ma'am."

"I'll tell the others so they know what's going on."

Will nodded again as he put all the paperwork back in his pocket.

Tiffany looked at him with sad eyes. "They'll see the spiders in my hair." She continued her hand over hand slide on that pony tail. "They'll see the spiders in my hair, and they won't believe how they got there." She clenched her eyes tight. "The numbers, the numbers, I have to remember the numbers."

She started in reciting them again, and Will sighed.

Even though her hair and nails needed some care, and she was obviously too thin, her beauty was evident. He was sure those sea green eyes had captured more than a few men's hearts in the past, but now they flashed with unseen terrors or stared into an abyss so deep, Will wondered that she could find her way back out. He risked putting a gentle hand to her cheek. "Even though it may feel like it, there aren't any spiders in your hair, love. Your parents will help you."

Her face screwed up again in anguish. "No! They won't!"

He wasn't sure if the behavior she was exhibiting was due to trauma or drugs—who knew what kind of hallucinogenics or Amazonian mushrooms they might have fed her—but he'd never seen a more serious case.

After more than an hour of crying, sniffling, and moaning, Will knew they were on the last nerve of the people around them, and Dani looked worn through as well. He made a decision and pulled out his phone. "Tiffany, I promise we won't take you home tonight. Okay, love? Look, I'm calling your parents right now. They'll understand. You need more time."

He hoped with some sleep in a real bed, she'd be improved tomorrow. Her mother answered on the second ring. "Mrs. Morrow, we need to talk." He looked to Tiffany, who seemed to be holding her breath, and Will gave her a smile. "There have been some… new developments, and I think it would be best if we didn't meet until tomorrow."

The girl sagged back in her seat as if the weight of the world had been lifted, and he cursed again the bastards who had messed her up so badly she didn't want to see her own oldies.

She fell asleep then, her head sliding over to his shoulder. He looked to Dani, who gave him a weary smile. "What'll we do tonight? Just check her into a hotel with us?"

"I don't know what else to do. I promised her I wouldn't take her home tonight, and I won't be another bloke who lies to her."

Dani nodded, then shifted gears. "I hope we land before all the shops close in the airport."

He raised his brows, surprised she'd be thinking of shopping at a time like this.

"Will, we left Brazil's summer." Her tone insinuated he was a nilwit. "But we'll be landing in Denver's winter. I know Tiffany doesn't have a coat, and you only brought a small duffle bag." She quirked a brow. "You were judging how much luggage I brought, but I've got a winter coat stuffed in one of those suitcases."

"I never said a word!"

"You didn't have to. You squinted ever so slightly when you looked at the pile Wolf and CG brought me from Rio, and you pursed your lips, making your toothpick flip up."

Will blinked. "And you said you had trouble reading people. Heavens, sheila, I'd say reading people is your super power."

"So you admit it! You were judging my luggage."

He looked to her gleaming eyes—eyes that revealed her feisty spirit—and he grinned. "I promise to never judge your luggage again, possum. I will always assume it has exactly what you need in it."

He turned to face forward, easing both his and Tiffany's seat back a smidge. "Now I think I'll take a nap while Tiffany isn't reciting all the numbers in the universe." He tilted his hat over his eyes, wondering if Dani had already seen what he'd been trying to hide.

* * *

Dani was more tired than she could ever remember being in her life.

She sank to the edge of one of the beds in the modern-looking hotel called the Moxy that wasn't too far from the Morrow residence in a kind of ritzy area of Denver called Cherry Creek. She was almost too exhausted to change into her night shirt.

Tiffany had seemed a bit more normal after they'd landed, even picking out her own coat—or at least scowling at the black puffy coat Dani had picked out for her. She had reached for a navy pea coat, so Dani had grabbed a hat, scarf, and gloves to go with it, along with leggings and a sweater that was likely to fit the too-thin woman while Will tried on a brown ski jacket.

Will and Tiffany had worn their new outerwear out of the store and right out of the airport, then Will had loaded his carry on and her luggage set into the taxi's trunk after she pulled out her own short gray coat. The frigid air had been quite a shock after the heat and humidity of Brazil.

While she waited for Tiffany to come out of the hotel bathroom, she watched Will making his bed on the floor from extra blankets, nearly filling the short hallway to the door. "I hope I don't step on you in the middle of the night if I have to use the bathroom."

He looked back with a weary smile. "You and me both."

The Moxy hotel had an eclectic boho feel with bright mismatched pillows and throws on the furniture in the lobby and sleek, spare, almost IKEA-like decorating in the rooms. The padded headboards were covered with a dark blue tweed suspended by leather straps from a finished piece of wood above, and the heavy gray blanket that seemed to double as a bedspread was tucked in tight revealing a black platform with large drawers.

Gone were the usual hotel drapes. A high-dollar, retractable, textured roller shade was the only window covering. No big furniture held a TV. The large flat screen was mounted on the wall with pegs on both sides that held a folding round table, canvas chairs and baggage holders. One understated curved-back chair stood in a corner.

She looked back to Will, camping out in front of the modern bathroom with a sliding door. After their less than comfortable, extremely long airplane trip, she hated to see the man sleeping on the floor. "I'm sure I can sleep with Tiffany, and you can have this bed. That looks so uncomfortable."

"I've slept on worse, believe me," He sat back on his heals. "And the point is blocking the door. I can't do that in a bed."

"Hmm. I guess not."

She lay back and stretched above her for a pillow, sat back up and tossed it to him, unintended words spilling out. "You're a good man, Will Yarnel. Why are you single?"

He caught it and put it near the door without responding, then he sat and began to untie his boots. "I had a girlfriend once. We hadn't gotten around to the marital bliss, but we had our own bliss while it lasted." He kicked off one and started on the other.

Dani put her elbows on her knees, propping her weary head on her fists. "What happened?"

The bathroom door opened, and Tiffany came out, back in the hospital scrubs that actually would make pretty good pajamas, and crawled into the other bed. Even though she was still obsessed with the feel of her own hair, her improvement gave Dani hope.

She looked back to Will expectantly, but he was stretching out on his blankets. "Not gonna tell me, huh?"

"Not tonight, possum."

Her eyes slid closed, knowing she wouldn't have heard more than a few words anyway.

Chapter 4

"Dani."

She pulled her foot out of the grasp of the man who was daring to shake it. "Stop it, Keith," she mumbled before turning over. "I'm just gonna sleep in, okay?"

The next shake was on her shoulder. "Dani, I'm sorry, love, but I need you to wake up."

The Australian accent pulled her out of the haze, and she blinked up at Will, still in a mental fog.

"I need you to keep an eye on Tiffany while I take a shower."

She turned to see the red hair on the pillow in the other bed and finally found the time, place, and present company. "Yeah," she assured, sitting up and rubbing one eye. "I'll watch her."

Will grabbed his duffle bag off the floor where he'd left it near his makeshift bed and headed into the bathroom, and Dani shivered with how cold the room was. *We should have bumped up the thermostat last night.* She saw it on the wall but felt no motivation to get out and deal with it. Instead, she snuggled back under the pile of blankets. *Will can turn it up when he comes out.*

She thought a moment or two longer about the day ahead, before those thoughts ferried her back to Brazil, laughing with Will in a water park memory that never actually happened.

* * *

Will stepped out into the chilly room, berating himself for not turning up the heat earlier. The heavy blanket had kept him toasty all night, and his dreams of Dani in the bed so close had only added to the torridity that had awakened him in a sweat.

He had watched her fall asleep sitting on the edge of the bed with the light still on and had gotten back up to turn back her blankets, thinking that would rouse her. It didn't. Living up to her nickname, she had just tipped over like a possum playing dead and slept on.

Smiling, he'd pulled off her shoes, scooped her up and stuck her under the covers. He hadn't expected to be taking care of two women, but he could hardly blame her. That trip had been brutal.

Glancing now at the two lumps of women snuggled in so deep they could hardly be seen, he shook his head and strode to the thermostat, bumping it up from sixty-five to seventy degrees. He turned, rubbing his newly trimmed beard to give Dani a hard time for her confident, "I'll watch her," when an alarm went off in his head. The person-shaped lump in the other bed didn't look so person-shaped after all.

He strode toward it and cursed when his hand sank into one of the hotel's extra fluffy pillows where Tiffany's shoulder should be. He flung the blankets back, revealing what he already knew.

"Dani!" She sat up with a start, looking wide-eyed and disoriented. "Tiffany's gone." He moved to where he'd left his boots and sat on the edge of Dani's bed to put them on.

"Gone?" She looked around the room, but there was literally nowhere for their redhead to be. "Oh Will, I'm sorry!" She scrambled out from under the covers, still wearing the khakis and pull-over top she'd had on the day before. "I can't believe I fell back to sleep."

Will could believe it. He still felt knackered himself, but he was too narky to be gracious at the moment.

She grabbed her shoes off the floor then tossed them down again. "Sorry, I gotta pee."

She ran to the bathroom while he pulled his coat off the wall, noting that Tiffany's was missing. He slipped it on, grinding his teeth while walking to the bathroom door. "Dani, I'm going down to see if I can spot her. Her coat is missing, so I'm heading outside." He spotted their phones charging on the night stand between the beds and strode to retrieve his. "Come down when you're ready," he called out as he headed for the door. "And don't forget your phone," he added before stepping into the hall.

He closed the door and jogged to the elevators as happy as a tin of worms going fishing. He should have just taken her home last night. That's what he was getting paid to do—take her home. The elevator door opened, and he got in.

He was tempted to arc up about the whole situation, but he knew that wasn't fair. He could have hired someone else to make this trip. They had contacts they'd used before to get women home. It was his own fault he hadn't been able to let go of Dani yet, and she couldn't be blamed for not being up to a job she'd never done before.

The elevator door opened, and he stepped in. His first stop at the bottom was a quick trip past the small lunch counter/bar, but Tiffany wasn't among those seated. Turning, he headed back toward the spacious lobby full of cozy and inviting sitting areas. Those manning the front desk were busy with a complaining customer, so he just headed out the door.

The arctic blast had him pulling his gloves out of his pocket and his stocking cap over his still-damp hair as he walked past an outdoor sitting area he hadn't paid much attention to when they'd arrived. Covered in snow, it wasn't being used at the moment. He walked around the corner to where a sidewalk ran the length of the building along a busy street and strode to the other corner. Unfortunately, he saw no one who resembled their wayward ranga in any direction.

He circled the building, coming back to the main entrance as Dani stepped out into the cold. She still looked as shamefaced as a hound dog who'd got caught chewing his master's shoes. He stopped her before she could rabbit on about it. "There's no point beating yourself up. What's done is done. Now we just have to focus on finding her."

She looked around with wild eyes. "And how will we do that, Will? How can we possibly find her when we have no idea which way she went?"

He smiled. "Every missing persons case starts out that way." He paused, evaluating the best place to start. "Here's what we know. She doesn't have a phone." He put a hand to his back pocket. "The cash in my wallet is still Brazilian reals, so she got no help there. Did she take any of your cash?"

Dani pulled her wallet out, opened it, and rifled through the bills. "Yes. All my American bills are gone."

"How much did you have?"

"I think I had a couple of twenties and some smaller bills." She unzipped a pocket. "And she took my change."

"Okay, so there's a cab sitting here now. There may have been another, and she took it."

"Or there wasn't, and she's on foot," Dani put in. "Probably heading to a phone store. I know that's what I would want first."

Will tracked a passing bus as he nodded, his eyes going wide at the woman looking back at him. He grabbed Dani's arm and pulled her toward the cab whose light indicated it was available. "Or she may have taken the bus."

She allowed him to pull her along. "I suppose… so where are we going?"

He opened the back seat of the cab. "She was on that bus." He closed the door on Dani's surprised expression and ran around to the other side. After telling the cabbie that they needed to follow the bus until their quarry got off, he sat back, feeling at least hopeful they'd still get her back home today.

"Are you sure it was her, Will?"

He nodded. "She looked right at me with that blank expression she frequents." He gave her a crooked smile. "And that red hair is hard to mistake."

Dani sure hoped Will was right. Her guilt over falling back asleep when she was supposed to be watching Tiffany was eating her up. "Why doesn't she want to see her own family, Will?"

He sighed and scratched the shorter beard that Dani finally took the time to appreciate. Now that she could clearly see the shape of his squarish jaw, it was almost like seeing him for the first time. He answered her question, oblivious to her new infatuation with his face. "Sometimes victims come out believing that they are at fault for their predicament and that their family doesn't want them back. It was probably pounded into her by that dog, Perigosa. It's a kind of brainwashing they use to keep them from trying to escape, that only time and a good therapist can erase."

"What have you told her family? Will they be prepared for this?"

He nodded. "I called her parents last night while you were getting Tiffany a coat, and I also gave them the number for a survivor's organization I looked up here in Denver."

She was grateful for Will's expertise. She had volunteered to see the girl home, but she felt like a fish out of water. Nothing in her life had prepared her for this. Except for the sneak peek she had gotten into the sleazy trafficking trade when she had gone undercover as a "Miranda Girl," infiltrating brothels hidden deep in the rainforest. The treatment she had experienced *without* being forced to be a sex slave had been bad enough. She couldn't imagine the trauma that Tiffany Morrow had gone through in the time that she'd been in Perigosa's possession. *I'm pretty sure I'd be an alcoholic and a drug addict too.*

Her thoughts turned to Justin Miranda, the man who was responsible for putting Tiffany in Perigosa's hands. He might be back in the U.S. now too, although his escorts wore dark suits and dark glasses, and would make a case for a long prison sentence for the ridiculously handsome man with eyes like sapphires.

She wondered if he'd really be able to cut a deal if he turned into an informant. Her forehead furrowed with the memory of his arms around her, giving her one last whispered word of encouragement before he handed her off to be a part of the sting operation. He had been an unwilling participant in search of a plea deal even then, but in that moment, it was almost as though he truly cared about her.

She looked down at her diamond ring, her head shaking at how she had been admiring Will's newly revealed jaw line and even thinking about a good-looking sex trafficker when she was supposed to be engaged.

The cab slowed to a stop behind the bus, and they both leaned to see the departing passengers, unbuckling their seatbelts to jump out fast if they saw her. The bus started forward again. No Tiffany yet. Dani shivered, regretting the fact that she'd left her hat and gloves in the hotel room.

* * *

Tiffany closed her eyes against the onslaught of thoughts swirling like a tornado in her brain as her hands slid over a strand of hair. The feel of it grounded her, even though she recognized that the gesture she couldn't seem to stop meant she wasn't as well as she was before.

She had thought she only imagined the demon horse with glowing red eyes at the airport, since it looked like so many of the demon creatures that had haunted her in the past, but there was no mistaking the mountain view she had seen out the window this morning. She was really and truly in Denver.

She was home.

The nightmare of the jungle was over.

She had vague memories of the in-between. Men and women in white. Being tied down. The bearded man and the blond woman who had brought her here. She'd been trippin' hard for days, so most of that was like a fever dream that had frightened even her. And she wasn't frightened by much anymore.

She still didn't feel normal—the noise of the bus was clawing into her head—but she was much improved over... before. She really didn't know how much time had passed since she'd been carried out of that vile cabin in the Amazon. She did remember that—waking for a moment or two in the arms of someone strong—a red dragon. Whispered words she couldn't recall. Words that had struck her as kind.

So why did you run from them? God, you do the stupidest things.

The voices that had been nearly eliminated before she had awakened in a Brazilian hell had been her almost constant companion without the meds whose job it was to hush them to a whisper.

She knew it would do no good to answer the voices. They never listened to her. But she did know why she was running from those who had helped her. Aaron McCain had spoken with kind and beautiful words. Justin Miranda had too. Kind words were often a trap. Who's to say that those two weren't taking her from one hell to another?

There was another reason she had to get away. They were going to take her home, and even though a few things were still mixed up in her mind, she knew that home was not somewhere she wanted to go. She loved her parents, but no one there believed her about what she discovered before she was kidnapped. No one there took her seriously. They just gave her a pitying smile and asked if she was taking her meds. They always asked if she was taking her goddamned meds like she was a child. Yes, she had… issues, but she wasn't a child, and even though the embezzling scheme she'd stumbled upon at her family's business sounded paranoid, she knew she wasn't being paranoid. It was real.

The numbers proved it. And she'd kept them through it all.

"I know what you've been doing." She heard her own words echoing in her head. Words she'd spoken to Chase Owens. How long ago had it been? She didn't even really know.

She put hands to her ears as the laughter rang through her brain like a great clanging gong, and she strove to focus on remembering the details of that night. She might have to testify about their conversation.

"Tiff, this is the second time you've been caught messing around with company computers. You have to stop."

She hadn't bothered answering him. She had needed just a few more seconds for the files to download on her memory stick.

"What do you think you're doing anyway?"

She had looked up then. She remembered how the security lighting had given him an eerie glow, although his face had been mostly in shadow.

"I'm gathering evidence," she had told him.

The laughter started in her head again. Blowing out a breath, she recited the numbers and fingered her hair until the noise eased. Tiffany knew Owens was dangerous, even if her parents couldn't see it, and she was determined to show everyone who and what he was.

Forcing her hands to her lap and a smile to her lips, she turned to the guy across the aisle engrossed in his phone and asked if she could borrow it for just a minute or two.

* * *

Will's head was freezing even with the stocking cap on. He yanked it off, hoping that a bit of air—even blasted nippy air—might help it dry faster. At least the cab was fairly warm. He looked out at the snowy Denver streets, praying he'd be on a flight back to the godawful heat and humidity of Brazil as soon as possible.

There were snowy mountains in Australia too, but he had spent most of his time in the more arid areas of Oz. He could stand the heat a lot longer than the cold, and he was grateful for the gloves that Dani had insisted he buy at the airport. He'd picked a hell of a time to decide to take his beard nearly back to ground zero.

It had been a weird obsession that morning—a desire for Dani to see what he really looked like before saying goodbye. His hair was too long too—he had a real seventies vibe going on—but he hadn't been brave enough to take the trimmers to his scalp.

As if the universe were privy to his thoughts, fingers ruffling the mess on his head had him turning and grabbing Dani's slender wrist exposed below her coat. "What on earth are you doing, sheila?"

"Your hair needs to get dry," she said with big, innocent eyes, "or you'll end up with pneumonia." Will gently pulled her hand down to the seat and gave it a pat, trying to pull words back into a brain that was stuck on the feel of her fingers in his hair.

"It's all right, love, you'll just get your hands cold. You made me buy gloves; where are yours?"

"In my rush, I left them in the room."

She clutched her hands together in her lap and began to spin that big rock around her finger. She'd been spinning that thing for the last two days, having put it back on after their undercover work was done, bursting the little reverie he'd briefly entertained where she was free and available.

He turned back to the side window, watching the snowflakes start to fall and trying to slow his breathing. Dani was a big help on the plane, and God knows he'd miss her, but now he needed her gone. He rolled his head around, stretching out the tension in his neck. *We'll get Tiffany and take her home, and Dani can be on her way. The girl has to get off that bus somewhere.*

"Stiff neck?"

He looked over to see Dani studying him. "Yeah." He blew out a breath. "It's been a hell of a few days, hasn't it?" And it would be a hell of a few more until her sweet face faded from his memory.

The cab turned the corner and slowed again at another stop. They unbuckled again and leaned to see around the bus, but again, Tiffany was a no-show.

They both sat back with an expelled breath and refastened their seat belts as the bus and their cab pulled forward again. He wondered how long they'd be mucking around with this little wild goose chase in a town he'd never been in before, and he pondered where Tiffany might be running to. Mates? Other rellies? She probably didn't have a boyfriend, or she wouldn't have been dating the creep who handed her off to Miranda.

His eyes were once again drawn to Dani's nervous ring spinning. "When's the wedding?" burst out of him before he could stop it.

Dani looked up with startled eyes blinking, cramming her hands into her coat pockets. "I… don't really know. Keith is pretty mad at me right now, and I—"

The cab slowed, and they both went through their unbuckling routine. Will wondered how Dani was going to finish that sentence, but now wasn't the time to pursue it. The snow was really starting to come down, adding a new layer to what had been scooped to the edges of the sidewalk.

"There!" Dani pointed. "Isn't that her?"

Will slid toward her on the seat but couldn't see everyone who had gotten off. He gave Dani a little push. "Go! The cabbie will wait for us one way or another."

She opened the door and speedily exited the cab only to sink into the glacial mess at the curb, then fall forward when her feet refused to follow her upper body momentum. Will saw no fast way to extract her so slid back to his side to get out.

Dodging between the cab and the rear of the bus, he turned to survey the bus passengers who had gotten off, quickly catching sight of a long-haired redhead moving swiftly up the sidewalk in a short navy coat that matched what they'd bought Tiffany at the airport. He started forward, sending a "Sorry, love" back at Dani, who was still struggling to pull a lost shoe out of the snow drift. Turning to the fore, he broke into a jog to close the distance, shouting, "Tiffany!"

She spun in surprise, then turned and high-tailed it with a burst of speed to rival any wild hare he'd ever seen run in the outback. Will kicked into a higher gear himself, but he was no match for the little speed demon.

As they approached the end of the block, she cut across snow-covered church property to its parking lot. She ran through the few parked vehicles, and to Will's surprise, stopped beside one, opened the door and jumped in.

Will could only watch as the silver Mazda spun its tires on the slick lot, and was pulling out onto the street a good five seconds before Will reached the spot where it had been parked. "Bloody oath!" he puffed out, his lungs feeling frozen clear to the middle of his chest. He hadn't even been able to catch the license number.

He turned around, still breathing hard, to see Dani jogging his way. He slowly walked toward her, knowing he would not be heading back to Brazil today.

"What the heck!" Dani' bellowed when they met, her bewilderment hanging in the air between them as thick as her foggy breath. "Who? How?"

Will shook his head, his breathing almost back to normal. "She must have borrowed someone's phone on the bus and called in a ride."

"Did you get the plate number?"

He started walking back toward the waiting cab. "No. At least not all of it. What wasn't snow-covered looked like the bottom of a 2 and a 3, although the 3 could have been a 5."

"Well, we know, whoever it was, they don't live very far away."

"Or they just happened to be in the neighborhood when she called."

They walked back to the waiting cab, and he opened the back door for her. She paused a moment, looking up with concern, snowflakes catching on the fur around her hood. "So now what do we do? How do we find her?"

Will gave her a tight smile. "*We* don't need to do anything. You should just go back home. This is my problem."

She started to protest, but he left her to go around to the other side of the cab. Her stubborn streak was waiting for him inside. "I'm not bailing out on you, Will, when it's totally my fault she got away from us."

He'd been afraid she'd say something to that effect. He told the cab driver to take them back to the hotel, then faced Dani and saw his old girlfriend Renae in her determined expression. His heart clenched. "Let's talk about it over breakfast." He squeezed her knee then turned to look at the snow continuing to fall, not looking forward to the call he'd have to make to Tiffany's oldies.

Or to his boss.

Chapter 5

The tension in the Morrow residence felt as heavy as rain forest humidity.

The building was so huge and sterile, it really didn't seem right to call it a house, and it certainly didn't feel like a home. The upscale modern living room felt more like a ritzy waiting area for a Silicon Valley start-up than a comfortable space for a family. Dani took in the camel and celery silk shantung pillows adorning the cream furniture that did nothing to bring any excitement into the drab earth tone pallet that was anchored by a thick stone coffee table that probably took six burly men to move. The only color came from a bright abstract painting over the fireplace.

Mrs. Morrow sat across from Dani and Will, dabbing at her eyes. Even though her hair was much shorter than Tiffany's, it was only a shade lighter, and the family resemblance was obvious. She looked to be in her mid-to-late-forties, but sorrow tended to make a person look older, so Dani considered she might be younger. She wore brown slacks and a silky green top that fit right in with the colors of the room. If it weren't for the red hair, she might have been camouflaged.

Tiffany seemed to have gotten none of Mr. Morrow's genes except for thick hair and maybe, if she squinted, the shape of his jawline. His very black hair didn't yet hint at even a touch of gray, and she'd bet he'd look like he had a five o'clock shadow fifteen minutes after shaving. He was just never going to be rid of it.

He sat with a somber expression, absently rubbing a circle on his wife's back, wearing black slacks and a pale salmon polo shirt. Dani thought she could be lulled to sleep just by the lack of color in the room alone, even if she hadn't eaten one too many pancakes for breakfast.

Will had told them immediately that Tiffany had given them the slip this morning, and weirdly, they hadn't seemed surprised. "The girl can run," Will said, rubbing his hands nervously together. "I couldn't catch her before she got into a parked car, and the driver took off. A silver Mazda, but I couldn't read much of the plate."

Mrs. Morrow nodded with a smile full of pride. "Yes, Tiffany can run, and she has the track medals to prove it."

"She can run like the devil is on her heels," Mr. Morrow added. An intense sadness took over his expression. "And there have been times when we wondered if he was."

Mrs. Morrow's pride turned into panic. "She's been off her meds all this time. Who knows how she sees the world?"

Her husband patted her hand. "You know the things she was saying before. I'm not convinced the meds were working, and you know she wasn't handling college all that well."

Will looked as puzzled as Dani felt. "Meds? What meds? Logan never mentioned the girl was on any meds."

Mrs. Morrow's eyes went wide. "Well we told the Denver police when she went missing!"

"It's possible that bit of information didn't get passed on to Mr. Stafford, honey," Mr. Morrow placated. "It went from a missing persons case to a trafficking case to an international trafficking case. Some vital info may have been lost along the way."

Dani leaned forward, beyond curious. "What meds are we talking about here?"

Mrs. Morrow looked as if she might start crying again. "Tiffany has schizophrenia."

Dani sucked in a breath. "Oh my gosh, that would explain a lot. We were attributing her muttering and moodiness to the drugs she might have been given at the brothel."

Will ran a hand around his jaw. "That does complicate things. Especially if she may be hallucinating. I imagine that's why she was afraid to come home."

Mr. Morrow nodded. "She's exhibited a great deal of paranoia at times. The meds have helped, but… sometimes we were still a target for her wild conspiracies."

"Are there any siblings?" Dani wondered.

Mrs. Morrow shook her head. "No. Tiffany is an only child."

"I'll need a list of her mates and any other rellies—relatives—anyone who might have helped her get away today or that she might contact in the future."

Mr. Morrow looked to Will. "Of course, although she didn't have many friends. I can't imagine who she called today."

"She was living on campus for several months before she was kidnapped, Bret. She probably made some new friends in that time."

The man looked skeptical. "I suppose it's possible."

His wife sucked in a breath. "She wouldn't have called that horrible man who—"

"He's in jail, Min," Bret soothed.

Min put a hand to her head. "Oh. That's right."

Dani knew parents rarely knew as much about their kids' lives as they thought they did. "Did she keep a diary or a journal?"

Min blinked. "It's possible, although the police searched her room here and on campus when she first went missing. Do you remember them finding anything like that, Bret?"

The man shook his head. "No. And if she did, it would probably be unintelligible gibberish." He looked between Dani and Will. "Schizophrenia can make someone think that they are brilliant, and that they have the answer, the secrets, the codes, whatever, that will solve some larger issue. She has told us about numerous plots against the country, against us, against her." He sighed. "She's accused everyone we know of something nefarious."

Min seemed overcome, rising and walking to the window. Dani couldn't help feeling sorry for this mother, who obviously loved her daughter very much. "When was she diagnosed?"

Dani had directed her question toward Tiffany's mother, but it was Bret who answered. "Women usually don't start to exhibit symptoms until their late twenties, but Tiffany was that rare exception. We began to suspect something was wrong her senior year in high school."

"The sooner we get started, the sooner we can get her the help she needs." Will seemed suddenly raring to leave. "If you can give me that list of mates, we can start with that. Which college was she attending?"

Min turned from the window. "The University of Denver. We thought she was in art, but it turns out she was enrolled in mostly computer classes."

Dani zeroed in on the impressive abstract painting over the fireplace, but Tiffany's father quickly relieved her of any suppositions she might make about its creator. "That's a Kandinski." She turned back to find him looking to his wife. "Do we have any of Tiffany's art here?"

Min shook her head. "She took all of it with her when she moved to campus."

Bret gave them a thin smile. "Tiffany is very good, but her subject matter has always been dark, and during the worst of her illness, it was rather… "

"Ghastly," Min supplied, massaging two fingers on her temple.

Rising, Bret walked to her side. "Are you getting a headache?"

"Just the usual. I think I'll lie down." She turned to leave the room, and her husband walked along with her to the four steps that led to a platform where one set of curving stairs went up, and from what Dani could see, one curving set of stairs went down, each framed by a gleaming silver railing. Min started up, then turned back. "You'll give them a list of her friends: Audra, Mikaylee, Jerry… no, it was Jeremy, I think."

"Yes, although I'm not sure they consider themselves friends after—"

"It doesn't matter!" she cut him off. "They still might know something."

"You're right, you're right," her husband quickly appeased.

"And what about the new friend she connected with in the hospital. What was her name?"

"I don't remember. I doubt she'll be much help."

The woman moved slowly up the stairs, Bret watching her go a moment before turning back to the room.

Dani had an idea. "Do you happen to have her school yearbook? That would have all her friends in it, wouldn't it?"

While Bret moved to a bookshelf, Will leaned toward her. "Good thinking, possum."

Bret returned, holding out a rather thin royal blue book that said Rocky Mountain Cougars in swirling script on the front. The school's name ran across the bottom: Denver Educational Institute. The years on the cover were not what she had been expecting. "She didn't just graduate last spring?"

He shook his head as he sat back down. "No, she had a year off while she was being diagnosed and treated, so her graduating class may have flown the Denver coop completely." He looked toward the stairs and lowered his voice. "Tiffany alienated most of her friends before she graduated. I'm not sure they've been in touch since."

Will opened the book, and Dani leaned in, hoping to see the typical senior notes written on pictures, but there really weren't many, and what there were seemed to be pretty standard wishes of good luck. She did see an Audra, a Mikaylee, and a Jeremy, but those were devoid of even a signature.

Bret waved a hand toward the book. "As you can see, there's not much personal in there. By the time the yearbooks came out, she had lost her best friends with her conspiracy theories on how they were all talking behind her back and plotting Carrie-like pranks to play on her. One of them—Audra I think—lasted the longest, but in the end, even she cut her off. By the time Tiffany got some help and began to get back to some semblance of normal, her friends were off to college, and Tiffany seemed uninterested in reconnecting."

Dani flipped the page to staff pictures, surprised by a bold notation written in red: "Run, Red Rabbit, Run!" Dani read out loud.

"Her track coach," Bret explained. "Somehow, he kept her running all spring, even during the worst of her delusions. I suppose he thought it helped her somehow, as she was failing in every other area."

After flipping quickly through the rest of the book, Dani had to admit it wasn't much help.

Will set it on the coffee table. "The friends your wife mentioned—do you have the families' contact info?"

"I think Min does. I'll send it to you in an email."

"Could you round them up right now while we take a look around her room?" Will pressed, rising.

The man seemed to falter a moment, then quickly recovered. "Of course. I'll see if I can get to Min's address book without disturbing her." He stood and headed toward the stairs. "She really hasn't been herself since Tiffany's mental illness began to surface." He waved them to follow, then pointed down the stairs. "As Tiffany's paranoia set in, she moved herself down to the guest room. I'm sure you can find it."

Will gestured for Dani to go first, and when she reached the bottom, she seriously wondered if they *would* be able to find it. Huge spaces opened before them. She looked into another large sitting area one direction, then a frightening hall of mirrors kind of playroom. By the time she reached the biggest home gym she could have imagined, she was speechless.

She turned around to see that she had lost Will. Retracing her steps, she headed for an open door to what was probably Tiffany's room. He was down on hands and knees, looking under the king-size bed. Dani finally found her voice. "Can you believe this place?"

"It's something, all right." He looked up at her. "Not my cup a tea." Pushing up, he headed for the expansive closet. "Not sure why a family of three would need all this space."

"Exactly." Dani began to look through drawers, not sure what she should be looking for. "Can you imagine how all this could be better used? My God, if this house were turned into a shelter, that gym alone could house five or six people!"

Will chuckled as he ran his hands over every piece of hanging clothing, searching pockets if he found any. "I don't suppose a shelter would need some kind of Frank Lloyd Wright design. I'm sure that added to the cost of this place."

"It just makes me furious that some use their money so… so… irresponsibly!" She closed one drawer and opened another.

Will stopped and looked at her. "Am I wrong that your fiancé isn't exactly a pauper? From what Rod read online—"

She looked at him aghast. "You guys looked me up?"

Will blinked. "Back when Logan was trying to figure out who Rita was, he ran across your appeal to the media, and that led him to your boyfriend." He turned back to the closet. "A rich wannabe congressman."

She searched through the socks, finding nothing but socks. "Yeah, Keith is pretty. . . " —she hated to say it— "well-to-do."

"Well-to-do," he repeated back as he bent to inspect shoes and boots on the floor. "Is that above or below stinkin' rich?"

Dani quirked her lips, feeling uncomfortable with how this conversation was going. "Below." She closed the drawer and went across the room to a desk, opening the drawer there. "His house is probably worth a million, but this one—"

"Almost eleven."

Her eyes popped wide. "Million? Eleven million dollars? How do you know?"

"P.I., sweetheart, we like to know what we're dealing with."

She sat and sifted through pens, pencils, highlighters, erasers, and sticky notes, seeing nothing that seemed important. "Okay, Keith is rich, but these people are rich rich."

"Is that an official tax bracket in the U.S.?"

"Probably," Dani threw over her shoulder. "Or it should be."

She was about to close the drawer when Will stopped her. Waving her away, she rolled the chair farther back, and he pulled the drawer out until it stopped, then reached in, feeling under the desktop. "This is a prime hiding spot for drugs, diaries, etc." He pulled his arm out, his hand empty. "But not today."

Squatting down, he reached underneath the desk to the back of the drawer, but he came up empty again. "Well, it was a long shot," he said, standing again, "since the coppers already searched the place."

After a quick look around the bathroom, they headed back out and toward the stairs. "If she was as paranoid as her father claims," Dani speculated, "wouldn't she have had everything of importance with her on campus?"

Will nodded. "Most likely. Just didn't want to jump the pond and miss the frog."

Dani couldn't help smiling at another new Aussie-ism.

Bret was waiting for them at the top of the stairs. "I'm afraid Min has mislaid her address book at the moment. The stress of the last few months has taken a toll, but I'll keep looking for it." He looked past them. "I assume you found nothing helpful in Tiffany's room."

They both shook their heads. "I didn't really expect to," Will said, "but I would be negligent not to look myself."

Bret nodded and walked them to the door. Will put out his hand. "I can't tell you how sorry I am that we lost your daughter this morning, and I'll do everything I can to find her again."

Bret took it in a brief handshake before sliding his hands into his slacks pockets, looking solemn. "It was probably inevitable. Min thinks if we can get her back on her meds, everything will be all right, but truth be told, she wasn't completely right even on her meds."

After Will assured him that he would keep in touch, he called an Uber, and they left what could only be called a modern mansion. "You said that *you* would do everything to find her," Dani began, pulling on her gloves, "but you're forgetting, I'm not going anywhere until *we* find her."

Pulling his stocking cap out of his pocket, he pulled it over his unruly hair. "We're on a pretty cold trail, Dani. It could take weeks. You said your fiancé was mad at you already. Just wait until you spend a couple more weeks with me."

She turned to face the street. "It will be a good test then. I'm sure marriages have to survive more than this." She didn't tell Will that the thought of more time with him made her happier than she'd been in a long while.

* * *

While waiting for Mr. Morrow's e-mail containing Tiffany's contacts, Will and Dani walked around the upscale shopping center called Cherry Creek. He'd only looked at a few tags before deciding he probably couldn't afford a toothpick in the whole place even if there happened to be a shop so base as to sell something someone actually needed.

Dani window-shopped but didn't venture over the stores' thresholds, which surprised him. Didn't all women love to shop?

She paused an extra long time at a clothing accessories store window that displayed shoes no foot should ever have to endure, and he urged her on in. "Go in and look around. I should probably call Logan."

She winced. "Is he going to be angry? Feel free to blame me."

Will shook his head. "Not gonna happen, and while I assume he won't jump for joy, we've had runners before."

She nodded with resignation before turning and going into the store. Will moved toward the center of the wide hall near a flying birds art installation and worked his phone out of his pocket. Logan answered with a jovial, "Will, good to hear from you! Is the package delivered?"

Will's jaw tightened. Yes, they'd had runners before, but never had he been directly responsible before. "I wish I could say 'yes,' but she gave us the slip this morning."

"What? How did that happen?"

Will filled him in on her escape plus her erratic behavior on the plane, ending with, "We thought Perigosa was responsible for her soaring high as a kite, and while there were some drugs and alcohol involved, it turns out she's also off her meds. Did you know she's schizophrenic?"

"Schizophrenic! Are you kidding me? No, I had no idea!"

"Unfortunately, that could turn our search into a dog's breakfast. According to Morrow, she tends strongly toward the paranoid variety."

"Damn. I wish you were in San Francisco. At least there we have some connections."

"I hear ya, mate." He blew out a breath and ran a hand through his hair, wishing he had time for a haircut. "But if her oldies come through with some friends to contact, we'll sus it out."

" 'We'll'? Dani still there with you?"

Will turned back to the shoe store, making sure Dani was still occupied. "Yeah," he said with quiet intensity. "She blames herself for Tiffany's escape and says she won't leave until she's found."

"Why do you sound so stressed out about that? Do you think she'll hinder you in finding Tiffany?"

"No, no," Will reassured, "she's been a lot of help so far, especially with calming the girl down. It's just… I can't…" He stopped and blew out a breath.

"Oh," he said with a lilt to his voice. "It's like that, is it?"

Will ground his teeth. “Now don’t start a furphy. Nothing’s happening between us.”

“Yeah, but I think you’d like there to be.”

“Well I can’t crack on when she’s got a rock on her finger, now can I?” He blew out a breath. “What’s not happening is not what’s important. If you could fly out to help, maybe she’d see fit to go on home to her fiancé.”

There was a moment of silence before Logan simply said, “No, I don’t think so.”

“What do you mean, ‘no.’ That poor girl is out there, traumatized by Perigosa, probably acting like a fruit loop. Who knows what trouble she might end up in?”

“And I think you can handle it. I just got to Rita’s. I don’t think she’d take too kindly to me leaving again so soon.”

“Logan—”

“You were the one who told me to let Rita heal my battered soul. Well that’s what I’m doing, and she’s not done yet. Hell, she’s barely started.”

Will knew the man deserved the happiness he’d found with Rita, but he wanted this case closed yesterday. And while he didn’t think Dani would be a hindrance, he didn’t really know how much help she’d be either. Logan had more than a decade of experience in finding the missing. Dani had none.

“You still there, buddy?”

Will cleared his throat. “Yeah. I’m here.” He looked to the store and his new off-sider, who was admiring a colorful silky scarf. “I’ll do my best without you.”

“I’ll support you all I can from here. Just let me know if you need some doors opened, and I’ll get on the phone. Be sure to check the reciprocity laws for private investigators. And the gun laws.”

Will directed his focus down the hall. “Right. Well, I suppose you could contact the coppers here in Denver before I get there, so I don’t have to fight them for information.”

“I’ll get right on it.” Logan abruptly changed the subject. “What’s the weather like there? It’s colder than a brass toilet seat on the shady side of an iceberg here.”

Will smirked. “Sounds about right. I had to chuck a flannie on this morning. My wet hair turned into icicles. Dani tried to—" He cut himself off, not wanting to think about her fingers in his hair. "Well anyway, I'll keep you posted."

"You do that. I have confidence in you, Will, and you know that means something, right?"

Will knew it did. The man had control issues, and only Rita had been able to draw him away from his work. Back in Brazil, he'd had to make a choice, and he'd chosen to protect Rita rather than going after Tiffany. Now, he was choosing Rita again, which Will knew was a good thing. "Yeah. It's surprising as hell, but yeah."

"And Will…" Logan continued more slowly, "no woman is off limits until she says 'I do.' "

Will wasn't sure that was true, but it wasn't something to discuss in the middle of a busy shopping mall. And anyway, Dani was heading his way. "I gotta go. Hooroo." He ended the call with a press of his thumb as she reached him.

"Hooroo? I haven't heard that one yet."

He checked his text messages but didn't see anything from Bret Morrow. "Means g'bye," he said without looking up. *Who keeps a physical address book these days anyway? Wouldn't all her contacts be on her phone?* He blew out a frustrated breath, looked up and twigged that Dani wasn't carrying any shopping bags. "Couldn't find anything you liked?"

She started to move on down the hall, and he followed. "Oh, I found plenty."

She didn't elaborate, so Will didn't press. She'd probably blown her dough in Brazil. She unexpectedly swerved to look at something in a shop window, and Will couldn't help it when his gaze slipped down to her shapely bum in skintight jeans below her short coat. Sometimes window shopping was just the best course of action.

Chapter 6

Tiffany tried to carry on a conversation with the woman driving while her mind raced. She wasn't sure that Krista completely believed her about the sex slavery in Brazil. "I have been off my meds, but it's all true. Aaron McCain drugged me and sold me." She immediately regretted telling her that. It sounded too outrageous. When had the truth gotten more far out than her usual overdramatic life?

She looked at her reflection in the mirror on the visor for the ninth time but still didn't see herself looking back. Her brain continued to cycle through stored images, refusing to let her see herself, mocking her with taunts of "it'll be the next one, just wait." Slamming the visor up, angry that the devil in Brazil had seemingly stolen her face, she looked to the friend who had come to her rescue. Would Krista help her defeat the evil dark lord who would steal her future?

She closed her eyes tight, squeezing the bloated creature in her mind—shrinking it into the real monster—a slick, smooth-talking man whose monster qualities were on the inside. Brazil had taught her that. The real monsters didn't have spikes going down their backs or fangs or shaggy, matted fur. The real monsters wore a smile.

Her heart began to race, remembering how Owens had taken the memory stick with the evidence on it away from her—had physically fished it out of her jeans pocket while he held her trapped against him, insisting that he couldn't let her leave with company secrets. She ground her teeth, feeling again his lips pressed to hers after he'd shoved her against a wall.

"So… do you want me to take you to Dr. Schmidt's office?"

Tiffany blinked and shook her head, stroking her hair hanging over her chest, banishing the memory for the moment. "I can't risk it. They'll be watching."

"Who? Who will be watching? Traffickers? Then why don't I take you to your parents' place?"

"No!" Tiffany said too loudly by the startled expression on Krista's face. "Sorry," she said quieter. "But no. I need the evidence from Pragnalysis first. About the embezzling."

"Mm, yeah, you mentioned that." Krista licked her lips and adjusted her hands on the wheel, and Tiffany knew what she was thinking. She sounded paranoid, and even she wouldn't believe herself if she didn't know better. There were just some things in the world that warranted paranoia.

"We all know about your paranoia, Tiff. Even your father." Chase Owens was back in her head. *"So reporting this supposed embezzling scheme to him will only ruin the man's day."*

"I'm not afraid of traffickers." She announced to Krista, striving to stay in the present. "Almost no one knows I'm back. My parents hired somebody, I think, to bring me home. The one who was chasing me this morning—he's the one who will be watching." She had almost not recognized him without the big beard.

"I really didn't see anybody," Krista said a bit hesitantly. "You just said to 'go, go, go' with such urgency, I went." She paused a moment before giving her a small smile. "Makes me wish I'd done a better job cleaning off my back window."

There was a tense silence before Krista continued. "So why run from the guy who brought you back? Maybe he can help you with... whatever you need help with."

"They work for my parents, so no. Their job is just to get me home, and I can't go home without the evidence."

"About the embezzling."

"Yeah. I haven't figured out how I'm going to get it yet, but I will."

"Are there meds in your dorm room?"

Tiffany checked the visor mirror again, scowling at the old woman looking back. "Probably, but they'll be watching that too."

"Do you have a key? I could go look for you."

Tiffany turned the visor up. Her purse had been lost or stolen, and she had no idea if her spare key was still in her hiding place or not. "You could give me a couple of yours."

Krista shot her a look. "You know a couple won't do, and besides, we don't take the same drugs, remember? You totally flipped out on mine."

Tiffany had a hard time remembering those early days of her treatment, but she knew that much of that time had been a living nightmare that she had probably blocked out. That had been a useful technique in Brazil—the blocking out, the escape inside her head, the sweet fantasies of a better place, the out of the body experiences.

Reciting the numbers.

She had learned to use her illness to survive in Brazil. She had endured there without her meds. She could make it here.

"Just let me crash at your place for a couple of days while I work out my plans, then I promise, I'll get out of your way."

Krista reached over and gave her forearm a squeeze. "You're welcome for more than a few days, but we have to figure out how to get word to your doctor. That's my one condition."

Tiffany nodded, even though she couldn't shake the feeling that the good doctor's phones were probably tapped. "I'll come up with something."

Krista drove in silence for a bit, then glanced her way with a reticent look on her face. "I hate to bring this up," she started slowly, "but you know it's possible that your mind invented the embezzlement scenario while you were off your meds. Especially if you were under duress."

Tiffany pursed her lips. "Duress" was the sweetest little word for what she'd gone through, but she simply couldn't believe she'd made it up.

"Remember everything you believed about your friends in high school," Krista went on. "Some of that was reverse engineering of memories."

Krista pulled into an apartment parking lot and parked.

"I know what you're saying," Tiffany confessed, "but this is different." It had to be different—the numbers proved it. She'd kept the numbers from before. Or were they just "reverse engineered memories"? She got out and followed Krista to a nearby building and up two flights of stairs to apartment 23B, where two dragons awaited them flanking the door.

There had been a time when she would have been freaked out at the sight, but therapy had helped her separate out what was obviously not real in the playground of her mind. Her therapist had said it was a rare gift for a schizophrenic. Tiffany had considered it just another form of organizing—something she had always had a knack for. And it helped that her most frequent hallucinations were mythical beasts.

Tiffany hesitated for just a moment under their beady-eyed gaze, then charged past.

* * *

Dani didn't think she would be any help talking to the police, so she went to her hotel room while Will went to talk to "the coppers."

The bed had been made, or she probably would have talked herself into crawling under the covers and taking a nap. One short night's sleep hadn't really made up for the long uncomfortable plane trip. Will's stuff was gone. Without Tiffany to watch over, he'd gotten his own room across the hall.

She hung up her coat on one of the wall pegs and went to use the bathroom. Washing her hands, she blinked at the woman in the mirror. *Dear God, I look awful.*

She hadn't had time to put on any makeup before Tiffany's speedy departure, and even though she'd gotten a quick shower in before they had headed to the Morrow's, she hadn't had time to style her hair— not that that would matter when one was wearing a stocking cap most of the day. Her hair now had the volume of a flat tire. The lack of sleep had taken its toll, as well, creating dark circles under her eyes. *I look like I need a month in rehab.*

Soaking a washcloth in cold water, she wrung it out and held it to her face. *No wonder Will just wanted me to go home.* Her phone began a jingle, and she sucked in a breath. It was the ringtone she had assigned to Keith. She was tempted to just let it go to voicemail, but she knew she had to face him sooner or later.

Striding out of the bathroom and to her shoulder bag she'd slung on the bed, she dug out the still-playing phone and answered, her heart pounding with the message she had to deliver. "Keith." She took in a quick breath as she tried to find words that wouldn't send him through the roof. "How are you?"

"How am I? I'm missing you like crazy! When's your flight home?"

She licked her lips. "There's… been a… development. I can't come home today."

"A development! What do you mean?" She pictured his blue eyes sparking with fury. "I already checked the weather. There are no blizzards, ice storms, tornadoes or hurricanes between Denver and KC. Nothing short of a bomb threat should be able to keep you from getting on a plane!"

She sank to the end of the bed, a hand to her head. "Well, there is something else. Tiffany got away from us this morning, and it's my fault. I have to help Will find her."

"No. You don't. This isn't your job, Danielle." He laughed. "And what makes you think you have any skills in finding a missing person anyway?"

She hadn't told him about her undercover work in Brazil, infiltrating a brothel. She knew he'd be furious. "There's something else, Keith. We found out she's schizophrenic. So she's in Denver somewhere, a basket case because of what was done to her in Brazil and also because she's off her meds."

"So? Again, you don't have the skills, Dani. Come home and do what you're cut out for."

Dani felt her hackles rising. "And just what might that be, Keith? Cooking for you?"

"I meant the job I told you about in H.R. I can't hold it for you forever."

Dani rolled her eyes, pretty sure he'd only made up the job a week ago to lure her home. "H.R. is not what I was going to school for."

"Oh, excuse me, I forgot about you being enrolled in the police academy."

Dani hated it when he pulled out the sarcasm. "I meant my studies in non-profits, so I could help people, Keith. It's the 'helping people' part that's keeping me here. So I can help that poor girl get home."

"Why did she run? Sounds like home isn't where she wants to be."

"Did you hear me say that she's schiz—" She cut herself off, trying to calm down. "You know what? Never mind. I could explain all day, and you'd never really hear me."

There was a long pause where the tension crackled between them, then Keith finally spoke. "It's the guy you're with, isn't it," he said slowly. "That's what's keeping you there."

Dani swallowed. Was Will part of the equation? Had she just talked herself into staying to help so she could have more time with him? She thought of the moment they'd found Tiffany in the brothel passed out and knew she was ultimately there for her. The fact that Will was so likable was just an added bonus. "No, Keith, I'm here to help Tiffany. If you can't understand that, then... then I don't think you know me as well as you think you do." She rubbed her forehead, tired of the silence he kept interjecting that seemed more potent than words.

"Maybe you're right," he said, his voice flat, "but how will I get to know this side of you if you're never here?"

Dani narrowed her eyes. Was he really thinking about her feelings, or was this just another ploy to get her on a plane? Her phone beeped an incoming text that she assumed would be Will. "Keith, I've got to go, but please... just be patient a little while longer." She thought of what she had told Will earlier and tried to put a smile in her voice. "Just think of this as a little test of our relationship."

He did not sound amused when he said, "Every relationship has a breaking point, Dani."

"So... is this it? Are you breaking up with me?"

"No, of course not! Would I be going through all this if I wanted to break up with you?" His voice softened. "I love you, Dani."

She didn't know if she could say it back. She just wasn't sure anymore. "We have some things to work out when I get home."

"Yeah, sure. Whatever you say." The man was suddenly as pliable as play dough. "I don't know what I'd do without you." He laughed nervously. "Actually, I do. I've been without you for three weeks, and I'm falling apart. I can't sleep, and I really have lost weight without your good cooking. Please, Dani, come home."

Dani felt tears forming at the desperation she heard in his voice. She truly didn't want to hurt him. She just didn't know if they were good for each other anymore. And she just couldn't go back yet if she could help here. "I promise I will only be here as long as I need to be, and not a moment more."

Resignation seemed to settle into Keith's voice. "If that's your best offer, I'll take it."

After a few more words of reassurance on her part, they said their goodbyes, and Dani tossed the phone back in her bag. Feeling as if Keith had just sucked what little energy she had left out of her, she decided she didn't care that the bed was made and whipped the covers back to crawl in.

* * *

Will wasn't really surprised that Dani still hadn't answered his text by the time he was finished with both talking to the police and renting a car. She had looked knackered by the time they finished lunch.

Knackered and still a beaut.

He imagined she was sawing logs, although he really couldn't picture her snoring. He'd watched her sleep in the helicopter to Rio Branco. Held her while she slept. Will shook his head trying to dislodge the thoughts of how perfect she had felt in his arms. Cursing, he straightened in his seat, and turned the heat to cool, hoping to freeze the desire that had only grown since that night.

He forced his thoughts to the police discussion with Capt. Rand. He had confirmed what Will suspected— that no new case needed to be opened because they hadn't closed the old one yet. He was appreciative of the new information on Tiffany's whereabouts, but said their job was trickier now that she had run away on her own as an adult. The fact that she was a person "at risk" would keep the police looking for her, however.

Although Will's P.I. license was good in Colorado, his concealed carry gun license was not, and even open carry was illegal in Denver. It would take 90 days to get a concealed carry permit, so he'd just have to function without. He didn't really expect he'd need a weapon anyway.

His phone's GPS informed him of an upcoming turn, and he maneuvered into the right lane. He had finally gotten that list of contacts from Bret Morrow, and his text to Dani had been to ask if she wanted to go along. Since she hadn't replied, he was heading toward the first address by himself.

It was only around 3:00, but the sun was in his eyes like a bitch. He guessed the sunset came early on Colorado's front range in the wintertime and grumbled about the fact that his sunnies were back in his hotel room. Adjusting the visor, he squinted as a silver car sped around him, cutting in too close, then immediately slowed down. He hit the brakes and narrowly avoided a bingle. "Ya hooligan, learn how to drive!" he yelled with a brief tap to the horn.

His brain suddenly lit up as he twigged he was looking at the back of a silver Mazda. *What are the chances?* He looked to the license plate that was clear and quite readable: *ZRT 923.* He arched a brow.

The GPS urged him to move onto the off ramp, but he decided to follow the Mazda instead. It looked like a woman was driving alone, but it was still worth checking out.

She signaled that she was getting off I25 onto Alameda Avenue. Will let a car squeeze in between them and followed. His GPS rerouted, taking him basically toward his original destination. It didn't say a peep for a couple of miles before telling him of an upcoming right turn. It was what he saw on the left, though, that surprised him. He was back at the church parking lot where Tiffany had made her escape.

The Mazda was going on past, so Will ignored his GPS again and continued on, excited that this might truly be the person who had been nearby to get Tiffany's call for help. It wasn't long before she slowed and turned into a small retail center, parking in front of a little store called the Smart Smoke Shop.

He parked two spaces over and waited.

A woman got out in a puffy long coat, a cloche-style stocking cap on her head with a rose on the side. What little hair he could see was dark.

As she passed in front of Will's vehicle, he opened the door and stepped out. "Ma'am," he said in his most congenial voice, "would you happen to know Tiffany Morrow?"

The woman's eyes went wide even as she was shaking her head. "No, I'm sorry. I don't."

She was obviously lying. Will shut the car door and followed her brisk walk to the store's entrance, putting a hand to the door over her shoulder. "Please, Ma'am, her family just wants to know she's okay and get her the medical care she needs."

"Release this door, or I'll scream!"

Will removed his hand and stepped back, then followed her in. Thankfully, there were no customers at the moment– just a guy watching a small TV behind the counter. Will pulled out his Stafford Investigations ID. "Ma'am, I truly mean Miss Morrow no harm." He held it up, blocking her route to the back room. "I was bringing her back from Brazil when—"

Her eyes flew wide again. "Brazil! So it's true; she was sold to a brothel?"

This got the attention of the dark-haired man behind the counter that Will would put at around twenty-five. "Is that your friend who was missing?"

The woman seemed to just realize that they had both revealed too much. She didn't answer, but waved Will to the far side of the small space. She sighed, looking weary. "She's at my place, and we got her prescriptions filled—*incognito* I might add, for the benefit of the pharmacy security cameras. I watched her take them, but they won't really be fully effective for a couple of weeks." She lowered her voice to a hissed whisper. "She thinks she's fooling me, but I can tell she's on the verge of a psychotic event or acting out some pretty serious delusions. I think one trauma has led her to invent more drama."

Will nodded. He didn't know a lot about schizophrenia, but the plane ride was enough for him to believe she needed help sorting out reality. "Can you take me to her? I promise I won't force her to go home, but I need to at least talk to her, and if possible, take her picture and have her sign something that I can show her parents. They're worried about her."

The woman turned back to the counter. "Sam, I'm sorry to ask, but could you—"

"Go," he said without taking his eyes from the action movie on TV. "I need the extra hours anyway."

"Thanks. I promise I'll do my regular shift in the morning."

He waved. "No problem, cuz. Just get Olivia to go out with me."

She chuckled as she shook her head, and Will followed her out the door, hardly believing that this was going to be wrapped up before suppertime, and he could be on a flight back to São Paulo tomorrow. He immediately thought of Dani, and how hard it would be to say goodbye, but he knew it was for the best.

The woman gave him the address in case he lost her in the now rush hour traffic, but he managed to keep up with her anyway. They parked, and she led the way up the sidewalk. Will hunched his shoulders with the wind picking up. He couldn't wait to get back to a warmer clime.

"She could very well be watching out the windows," she said as they walked, "but I'm on the second floor, so there's no way out except the front door." She stopped and turned. "I doubt she'll ever trust me again, but I recognize the signs. She's due for a breakdown, and I truly hope she will agree to go with you to her parents' house."

She continued, and Will followed. "You seem to know a lot about her issues. Are you a therapist?"

She laughed. "No, I'm a schizophrenic."

"Oh!"

She looked back over her shoulder. "I'm a high-functioning schizophrenic. I was lucky to find a combination of drugs that work for me." They started up a flight of stairs. "I'm Krista, by the way."

"I'm Will."

"When Tiffany is on her meds," she continued her previous thought, "she is mostly high-functioning as well, although she has told me she doesn't think her chemical cocktail is quite as effective as mine. She did, however, develop some method for discerning reality. There were researchers who wanted to study her."

They turned a corner at the top of the stairs and went up another flight. A few doors down, she unlocked the front door and stepped in. They were immediately assaulted by a cold breeze from across the space. The patio door was standing open. Will charged across the room, but the balcony held only two empty chairs. A sheet was tied to the railing, and Red Rabbit was once again on the run.

Chapter 7

Dani was pulled out of a deep sleep by knocking. Will's voice followed. "Dani, are you okay in there? I've called a couple times."

She blinked and flung off the covers. Had she slept right through her phone ringing?

She made her way to the door and opened it. "Will. I must have fallen asleep. What time is it?"

He smiled as his eyes flicked to her hair, and she ran a hand over it, afraid to see what it looked like now.

"It's nearly 5:00. Are you hungry? That little lunch we ate disappeared an hour ago."

She turned to switch on the light in her room. "Sure. Just let me… I'll be ready in a few minutes."

He nodded. "I'll be waiting." He turned to go across the hall. "You won't believe my afternoon."

Dani opened the door wider. "Why? What happened?"

He gave her a teasing smile. "I'll tell you over supper." His stomach growled. "So rattle your dags."

She just stared at him.

"Hurry, possum. That means hurry."

Dani couldn't believe he wouldn't just tell her. Blowing out a breath of exasperation, she stepped back in and closed the door. She nearly shrieked at her reflection in the bathroom mirror and ran out to her purse to find some help for the mess on her head that now looked electrified. She dug out a hair clip, then ran back to the bathroom to throw on some mascara and brush her teeth. Her armpits didn't reek, so she stuck with the cable knit pullover sweater she had on, knowing she was short on clothes, and seven minutes later, she was pulling on her shoes and grabbing her coat.

When she opened the door, she found Will leaning against the wall across the hall, his hands in his coat pockets, pulling it open to reveal the green and brown flannel shirt that made him look a bit like a lumberjack. A muscular lumberjack with thick hair a girl could run her hands through and a masculine jaw that begged for— She swallowed and met his gaze. His eyes sparkled for just a moment with what seemed like attraction, but it disappeared as he pushed off the wall to meet her in the center of the hallway. She swept aside her crazy thoughts. *Probably just glad I was speedy.*

"So, what are you hungry for?"

She dared not answer with what just popped into her head. "Oh, I don't know. I'm not too picky. You're the hungry one, so you decide."

"All right then. I want a steak."

She laughed, buttoning her short coat. "Okay. Have you scoped out the steakhouses in the area?"

"I have."

They stopped at the elevator. "I'm not sure why you asked me what I wanted to eat then."

"Oh, I could've changed my mind if you'd had a good suggestion."

The doors opened, and they stepped inside. "So are you really going to make me wait until we get there to tell me what you did today?"

"Uh huh."

"You're killing me, Will."

He laughed as the doors opened at the bottom. "Well, at least until we get in the car, so we can have some privacy."

The hotel had no parking lot of its own, and Will led her to the crosswalk that would take them across the busy street to the parking garage on the other side. Once in the garage and on the right level, he led her to the ash gray Toyota Rav 4 he'd rented. "This isn't a car," she proclaimed, "it's an SUV."

He didn't just unlock the doors, he opened hers for her. "Technically, it's a crossover SUV. I wanted something good in snow."

After they were both in and buckled, he started it, making sure the heat was set at max. "You really hate this weather, don't you?"

"That's a fair dinkum. I've spent most of my life in the heat."

"Winter's not much different here than Kansas City, temperature-wise, although they probably get more snow here." She waited until he had backed out and was heading toward the exit before saying, "Okay, tell me already."

He laughed. "I had no idea you were so impatient, especially since you slept the whole afternoon away when you could have gone with me."

Dani was all at once peeved with herself. "Dang it. That's right. I got a text while I was on the phone with Keith, and he got me so riled up I forgot to look at it. That was from you?"

He nodded as he turned out of the garage. "I did send you one, asking you if you wanted me to pick you up before I went to the first house on Morrow's list."

She leaned toward him. "And did you go? What did you find out? Anything useful?"

"Actually, no, I didn't. Makaylee Prescott is going to school in Washington state, and the parents didn't think that she and Tiffany had been in contact for more than a year."

"Dang. So if that was a bust, what's your big news?"

He lifted his hand, spacing his thumb and index fingers an inch apart. "I came this close to catching Tiffany, myself."

"You're kidding! Where?"

By the time Will related his chance near "bingle" with the silver Mazda and the woman who had rescued Tiffany that morning, he was pulling into the parking lot of 801 Chophouse. "I drove around the apartment complex and the neighborhood for the better part of an hour, but never saw hide nor hair of her. Her friend said she didn't think she had any other friends close by, but who knows. She might have told some random person she was being followed, and they let her in."

"So what's our next move?" Dani asked as they walked up to the steakhouse.

"See if we can get into her room on campus, then check out the other contacts on Morrow's list." He opened the door for her and stopped talking while they were being seated.

Once the hostess left, he picked up a menu. "Krista mentioned something that the Morrows didn't. Tiffany worked last summer for the family business, so she may have made some friends there that she might contact in a pinch."

Dani looked through the food options, dismayed at the high prices. If she wasn't going to use Keith's credit card, she needed to be frugal. Despite her own hunger, she turned back to the salads.

"Don't worry about the price, possum," Will said without even looking up. "This is a business expense."

"Oh. Are you sure Logan won't mind?"

"If he had flown out here like I asked him to, he would be eating that steak." He looked over the menu with a devious smile. "Since you're my new off-sider—with his approval, I might add—you get it."

His quick wink left her feeling tongue-tied. She stared at the salad page a few more moments before casually flipping back to the steaks. "So just what is the Morrow family business?"

Will closed his menu and set it aside. "Pragnalysis."

Dani knew that name. "They've been in national news lately, haven't they?"

Will nodded. "Their data mining software is controversial. Not to mention the facial recognition technology they're developing. Their main business is security." He reached for his glass of water and took a long drink. "From what I've read, it's a company that keeps reinventing itself as new technology becomes available."

"Probably why they're so rich," Dani mused.

Conversation was halted while they gave their orders to the waiter, but when he left the table, Will didn't return to the topic of the Morrow's multi-million-dollar corporation. After his eyes wandered past her several times, she started to turn to see what he was looking at, but Will stopped her.

"Don't turn around," he hissed across the table.

"Why?" she whispered back.

"Is your fiancé a jealous bloke, Dani?" he said quietly, lifting his glass of water.

Dani's eyes blinked wide at this abrupt change of subject, and she recalled Keith's accusation in their earlier phone call that she was only staying in Denver for Will. "Sometimes," she said slowly. "Why do you ask?"

His eyes never moved from her face. "Do not look, but there's a man over there who was seated shortly after us who can't seem to take his eyes off of you." The corner of his lips twitched into a tiny smile. "Not that you aren't worthy of admirers, but he has the look of someone who is hired to watch people." Dani's mouth dropped open, but he went on, "He's not much of a looker," he said quietly. "The guy fell out of the ugly tree."

Will sat back as the waiter brought their hot beverages, finally seeming to notice her shock. "Just act normal, possum. There's nothing to see here."

Dani's heart dropped as she picked up her hot chocolate and blew on the melting marshmallow foam. Did Keith hire someone to follow her? Did he have so little trust in her? She lifted her cup, trying to ignore the real question she wanted an answer to—did Will truly want there to be "nothing to see"?

* * *

Even though they had chatted through their meal on a number of topics, Dani had been obviously nervous about the bloke watching her, making Will regret telling her about him. He'd missed their usual easy-going conversation and her ready smile that she had kept under tight control, knowing eyes were on her. Eyes that could amplify every look, every smile, every laugh in a report to a jealous boyfriend.

She sat quietly now on their drive back to the hotel, her take-out box with about half her meal inside clutched in her gloved hands.

Will had managed to finish his steak, baked potato, and a piece of apple pie, less one bite he'd fed to Dani against his better judgment. Why had he abruptly thrown caution to the wind to make it look like they really were a couple? He gripped the wheel tighter. *Because you want to be a couple, ya nong.*

His mind went back to how adorably disheveled she had looked when she answered her door and how quickly she had transformed into her usual beautiful self. He'd take either version, and any in between. He chewed on his toothpick.

How was he going to get through the next few days working so closely with her?

He'd been holding onto her words all through the meal: "I got a text while I was on the phone with Keith, and he got me so riled up I forgot to look at it." He glanced her way. *What did ole Keith say to rile you up, possum?* He ground the toothpick between his teeth until it began to splinter. He would not ask. *She had the perfect opportunity when I brought up the man's jealousy, and she didn't say anything.*

He turned into the parking garage and found a place to park. Dani's hand was suddenly on his forearm. "Do you think he followed us? Mr. Ugly Tree?"

Even though he found the name Dani had christened the man funny, Will cursed again his big mouth that had told her about him at all. "I don't know."

He did.

"Probably not."

He was.

"Maybe you should go home tomorrow, Dani." He couldn't help the irritation rising up inside him. "Home to Keith."

He gave her a tight smile and reached for the door handle. He waited for her at the rear of the car, her miff evident in the glow of the garage lights, and together, they made the journey back to the hotel, Dani never saying a word.

Will looked for any suspicious, slow-moving vehicles but didn't see any. The car that had been behind them had gone on past but would probably just circle the block or come back early in the morning to catch them going out. If the man was watching from some parking spot along the street, Will gave him no reason to believe anything was going on between him and Dani, keeping space between them and only doing her the courtesy of opening the hotel's door for her.

Once they were alone in the elevator, she suddenly had something to say. "I don't know who I'm more irritated with—Keith, myself, or you."

Will looked at her with eyebrows raised. She was breathing hard, and Will expected a tongue lashing, although he wasn't exactly sure what it would be for. Was she furious that he'd suggest she go home to the man she was going to marry?

Abruptly, she tossed her take out box to a corner and stepped toward him. He couldn't imagine throwing aside a good piece of beef. While he was wondering what kind of tanty he was in for, she yanked the ragged toothpick from between his teeth and sent it the direction of the steak. "What—"

Her arms around his neck brought his attention back to her just as she raised up on her toes and pressed her lips to his. It took a moment for his brain to catch up, but only a moment. His arms went around her, and he pulled her in, kissing back with all the pent-up tension of the last week. Her lips were even softer and more wonderful than he had imagined. He inwardly smiled as the term "tongue lashing" took on new meaning.

The elevator opened, and they broke the kiss, staring at each other, neither really knowing what to say. The doors started to close again, and Will reached over to push the "Door Open" button. He looked back to her eyes, searching. "Is the ring coming off? Permanently," he added, wanting to be crystal clear.

She hesitated only a moment before nodding. "I want you."

Releasing the button, he swept her up and carried her out and down the hall until he stood between their two rooms, his heart still pounding as he drank in her green eyes looking up at him. "Your place or mine?"

"Yours."

He kissed her again before dropping her feet to the floor so he could pull his key card out of his back pocket. Then he opened the door to something completely new.

Chapter 8

"Steve! Hey Stevo!"

The tall, lanky black man, wearing a thick pullover sweater rather than a coat, stopped in his tracks and looked around, his aviator sunglasses revealing nothing of his eyes, but Tiffany could still tell when he spotted her. Steve was a guy whose reactions filled his whole body.

He lifted his sunglasses as he approached her in the shadow of the Ritchie building, the home away from home for engineering and computer science students, and she took her big sunglasses off as well. With most of her hair stuffed under a stocking cap, he probably couldn't tell who she was. A smile spread over the man's expressive face, and he opened his arms to her. "Tiffany!"

She walked into his hug, her breath catching at the contact before the beast from Brazil snarled and roared in her head. She was dismayed to learn that it had followed her home.

"I can't believe it's you!"

She pulled back, her heart racing, as the ferocious scaly creature backed up into its cave. Had Brazil stolen this from her too? The ability to enjoy a man's arms around her? She looked up into the astonished face that was surprised by something other than a fanged beast.

"The news said that guy you were dating kidnapped you or something. God, I've been worried sick."

Tiffany couldn't help the smile that pulled at her lips with the news that Steve had been concerned about her. "Yeah, well, hanging out with him turned out to be a real bad decision."

"So you were—"

“Can’t talk about it now, Steve.” She reached for a lock of hair at her shoulder that wasn’t there, then nervously slid her hand down her arm. He looked at her for a few moments as if he could somehow read what had happened to her in just her eyes. She blinked and slid her sunglasses back on in case he could. “I suppose Mona thought I’d just been put in an asylum somewhere.”

Steve gave a low chuckle. “You know her too well.” He shook his head. “Nasty woman.”

Tiffany’s lips quirked up on one side. “I’m sure she’d be pleased to know I’m barely holding it together right now.”

He reached toward her upper arm in a gesture of understanding, but Tiffany balked and stepped back. That beast was just too close to the surface. He dropped his hand awkwardly. “Well, I’m here if you need someone to talk to.”

She looked past him, blinking back the tears that were threatening, and spotted a professor she recognized and didn’t particularly like. A small creature crawled onto his shoulder. “It’s a long story best told another time, but I do need your help with something.”

“Name it.” The grad student who had tutored her through her computer programming classes swung his laptop case in front of him and grasped the handles with both hands. “Will you be coming back to classes? You missed finals last fall, so I’m not sure how—”

“I don’t know about classes yet.” She forced out a smirk. “I need to stop seeing Dr. Lambert as a black knight with a tiny dragon on his shoulder first.”

Steve’s eyebrows flew up. “That bad, huh? But the fact that you know it’s not real is good, right?”

She nodded. “Yeah, I guess.” Although sometimes it felt like she wasn’t “mentally ill” at all, and she could just see things others couldn’t. A kind of sixth sense. “I started my meds again yesterday, so… anyway, I need your computer brilliance for something that’s pretty serious. I believe my family’s business is being robbed, and I need someone to hack through their security to find the evidence.”

Steve was so shocked by that, he took a step back. “Tiff, that’s crazy! Why don’t you just report it to the police?”

"They won't believe me without any evidence, and the man doing the robbing has undoubtedly worked very hard to plug the holes I found in his files while I've been gone. This time I'll have to get the fake receipts from the shell companies he created."

He studied her for a few moments, and Tiffany knew what was coming. His skepticism was written all over his handsome face. "Tiff, are you sure this isn't just another dragon on someone's shoulder? Let's wait till your meds kick back in and—"

"I can't hide out for two weeks, which is what I'd have to do. People are searching for me, Steve, and I can't go home until I get the evidence." The numbers started marching in her head.

He leaned in. "Who's the embezzler?"

She hesitated. "I… shouldn't say yet."

She saw the doubt in his eyes and felt her own in her heart, hating herself for it. Had she made it all up in Brazil like Krista had suggested? But if her memories weren't reliable, she couldn't go around disparaging people without evidence. Even someone as loathsome as Owens. That's why Steve's help was so important. "If you help me, you'll see for yourself."

She'd hidden out last night at a shelter for battered women, claiming an abusive husband. She still had bruises to make the story quite believable. The police were going to be there at eight this morning to take her statement, which is why she'd sneaked out at seven. She used Dani's cash to take a bus to campus, and she'd been waiting in the cold ever since, hoping to catch Steve Elway going to or coming from the computer science building.

He pulled his phone out of his back pocket and looked at it. "I'm going to be late for class. If I wasn't teaching this one, I'd skip it." He looked back to her face with real sincerity in his eyes. "Can you stay out of trouble for an hour? I'm free after that." She nodded, and he headed into the building, saying, "Be back here in an hour."

Being on campus was pretty risky, but hopefully Will would think she wouldn't dare to set foot in such an obvious locale. She chewed her bottom lip, wishing for some chap stick. Was her private room still full of her stuff or had it been cleaned out when she didn't show up by the end of the semester? She'd bet her mother wouldn't give up on her that easily, no matter who tried to tell her it was a lost cause. She'd pay the school whatever they asked to keep it for her until they had her back or word that she was dead. Did she dare try to get in? Would the spare key still be where she left it? Would the numbers be where she had hidden them?

She knew that would be the test.

If she wasn't completely bonkers, the account number would be where she'd left it, and she might need that bit of proof to get Steve to help her. Her stomach growled. She was hungry, too, and there were probably still snacks in her room, although she hoped someone had cleared out the fridge.

The Johnson-McFarlane Hall that she had lived in—known on campus as J-Mac—was not that far away. She power walked there in a matter of minutes, and a matter of seconds after arriving, remembered that she needed a key card to get into the residence part of the building.

She paced back and forth outside, wondering if it was worth the risk, when she caught a whiff of pancakes from the neighboring cafeteria, and her stomach nearly turned inside out with the growl it put forth. She'd hardly eaten since Krista's place, and they were probably still serving breakfast.

"Nothing ventured, nothing gained," she said as she strode toward the door. If her room was still her room, that meant her bills had been paid, and she still had campus privileges.

Campus pancakes.

She approached the front desk with a smile. "Excuse me, but I've lost my keycard. How do I get a new one?"

The fair-skinned girl with rainbow hair stood. "Do you have your student ID?"

Tiffany shook her head. "I lost my purse. Everything's gone." She let out a deep sigh. "It's been such a hassle."

The girl turned to a computer monitor. "Okay… what's your name?"

Tiffany hesitated for just a moment. "Tiffany Morrow."

The girl looked up with eyes wide. "Tiffany Morrow!"

Tiffany blinked and took off her stocking cap, letting her red hair fall down to the middle of her back.

The girl gasped. "It is you! My God, what happened?" She lowered her voice. "Were you really kidnapped?"

Tiffany gave her a tight-lipped smile. "It's still really fresh, you know? I don't really want to talk about it."

The girl leaned in with sympathetic eyes. "Of course you don't."

She turned back to the keyboard and clacked for a few minutes while Tiffany started to sweat. A few others were starting to point and whisper.

"With parents as rich as yours, it's a wonder you don't have twenty-four-hour protection," the girl observed as she typed.

"Yeah," Tiffany agreed. "I may have to look into that."

A tiny printer spit out a temporary ID, and she pushed it toward Tiffany over the counter. "You will need to get a permanent ID in the admin office, but this will get you by for a few days." She then produced the coveted keycard. "I'll have to report the old keycard as missing to Campus Safety, and they may want to talk to you."

Tiffany nodded, picking up the new card. "So… can you tell by looking if I'm all paid up?"

She smiled. "It wouldn't have let me issue you an ID if you weren't." Her smile slid somewhat as she reached to grab a colorful brochure out of her information rack and opened it purposefully before sliding it, too, across the counter. Tiffany read the page's heading: *Sexual Assault & Dating / Domestic Violence*, then looked up to meet the girl's misty eyes.

Her face became stark and angular as the space around her went out of focus. A blurry, dark green creature spread its webbed wings and leaped at a hazy student behind her, taking her to the floor and ripping her throat out with its six-inch fangs.

Tiffany gasped, and the girl's concern intensified. "I don't know if this applies to you," she whispered, "but if it does, it's a really good program."

Tiffany took it and mumbled a thank you, not sure if what she went through could be called mere sexual assault or not. She folded it and stuffed it in her coat pocket, still breathing hard as red glowing eyes stared her down and blood dripped off the monster's teeth.

Closing her eyes, she spun toward the door that required the keycard. Her stomach growled again, and she decided no hallucination—no matter how horrifying—was going to keep her from getting her pancakes. She took a deep breath before turning and sprinting out of the building, praying the scaly creature didn't follow.

* * *

Dani and Will walked through the University of Denver campus a foot apart. In Dani's opinion, Will was being a butt.

After they'd made love the night before, he seemed to expect her to call Keith immediately and break off the engagement. Dani didn't want to ruin what had been a beautiful evening with Will and had promised to call the next day. Will had handed her the phone as soon as she woke up. She wasn't about to call the man right before he had to go to work. And that's when Will said he wouldn't kiss her again until it was done.

He'd even rebuffed her attempt to hold his hand.

"You know I'm going to call, don't you? I would have never gone to bed with you if I didn't intend to break up with Keith."

"I don't know, possum, you had quite a time getting that ring off last night."

She blew out an exasperated breath. "You know that's because my knuckle had swelled, right? It's probably an altitude thing or something."

"Anyway, with our friend Mr. Ugly Tree possibly still lurking nearby," Will explained, "I can't be pashing with you unless you want a picture of us lip-locked to get to ole Keith before you get around to picking up the phone."

Dani still couldn't believe that Keith would actually spy on her. Had running for Congress really changed him that much? Or did she ever really know him? She had thought she was in love with him when she left for Brazil with Rita, but that trip and Rita's disappearance had brought out things in her fiancé that had nearly killed all feeling for the would-be congressman.

She looked to the man who spent his days searching for the lost and missing, dedicating his life to rescuing trafficking victims and reuniting families—the man who had loved her so very thoroughly the night before. *After one week with Will, I feel a connection I never had with Keith.*

They'd gotten a campus map at the administration building, along with a signed memo by the dean for permission to search Tiffany's dorm room, made possible by a call from Min Morrow. Will said he didn't hold out much hope of finding anything useful, but just like searching her room at the Morrow mansion, it had to be done.

It didn't seem quite as cold this morning, and looking around, she could see why students would want to go to school here. It was a beautiful campus with a great view of the mountains.

Will paused at an intersection of sidewalks for a moment while he studied the map, then made a turn toward a modern looking building with peaked, roof-high windows. "Wow," Dani breathed out as they approached, "I love a house with windows."

"Don't all houses have windows?"

She looked to his teasing smile. "There are windows, and then there are *windows.*"

As they neared the door, he put a hand to the back of her neck and leaned in. "More windows just means more shades to pull down," he sexily whispered.

She felt a shiver run down her back. "Be careful, Will. I may drag you behind a bush and have my way with you."

His eyes held something dangerous as he reached for the door handle. "Make that call, and you can have me any way you want me." He pulled it open and held it for her.

Blinking, she focused back on the task before them, wondering if the whole day was going to be like this. Would it be terrible to call Keith on his lunch break? She sighed. For a conversation like this, she needed to wait until he was home, and preferably had eaten. That meant waiting until around 8:00. With Will's constant nagging, alternating with flirting, she'd be the tense and ready-to-explode one by then.

They passed a small food and snacks store on their way to a desk, Will trying to drag his brain away from a Dani fantasy. He still could hardly believe what had happened between them the night before. Far more than a romp in bed, it had been a time of deep connection with someone he hoped to form a real, lasting relationship with. He tried to keep a grin from forming. It had also been a ripper of a good time.

A pretty girl with multi-colored hair greeted them as they approached. He slid the paper from the dean toward her, along with his Stafford Investigations ID. "G'day, Miss, we're here to give another once over on Tiffany Morrow's room—hope to find some clues to help us find the girl." At her shocked look, he pointed to the memo. "The dean has given his permission."

"But… but Tiffany was… was just here," the girl stammered, "I gave her a new keycard and a temporary ID."

Will's eyebrows flew up. "Well, stone the crows, I wouldn't have guessed— How long ago?"

"Maybe fifteen minutes."

"Did she use the keycard?" Dani asked. "Did she go to her room?"

The girl shook her head. "She looked like she was going to, but then she seemed to change her mind and ran back out."

He swept up the memo and ID and jammed them into a back pocket. "Thank you for the information." He turned, ignoring her further questions, then stopped and looked to Dani. "I'm going out to look around. You give her your phone number in case she comes back."

Dani nodded and went back to the desk as Will jogged to the door. Outside, he did a 180 degree sweep, surveying the area, but didn't see a ranga. *If she was smart, though, she'd be wearing a hat.* He scanned the landscape of snow and scooped sidewalks again. *And with a fifteen minny lead, she could be long gone.* But he had a feeling that she was still here. *She had intended on going into the residence side of the building but had abruptly changed her mind.* He sighed, remembering that she wasn't really in her right mind. Anything might have sent her in another direction.

He walked up the sidewalk a ways before turning to see if Dani was coming and noticed students eating at tables through the arched windows of the next building. *A cafeteria.* Will smiled. *How long has it been since you ate, sweetheart?*

He jogged toward the building, found an entrance and pulled open the door just in time to be a gentleman holding it for a whole crowd of girls. Will smiled, wishing the chatty group greater speed in departure. At last, he was able to enter and made his way into a kind of breezeway that ran beside a long dining hall with a high vaulted ceiling, and scrutinized the dwindling breakfast crowd from one of the arched doorways.

A female working on a stack of pancakes sat alone at the far end, eating while wearing her coat, hat, and sunnies. Even though no hair was showing, he recognized the coat and hat. Opposite him, more large, arched windows lined the other side of the hall, but he didn't see a door. She could easily move into the breezeway he was standing in further down and reach a door at the end before he'd be able to catch her. The smart thing would be to back out and call Dani to come in this way while he blocked the other way out.

He reversed course a step, reaching for his back pocket when Tiffany looked up, straight at him. She hesitated only a moment before throwing down her fork and leaping to her feet, the chair making a screech on the flooring before she raced to the other exit. Will knew from experience he couldn't outrun her. He yelled to those beyond her in the hall. "Stop that woman!" His mind flew. "She's a pickpocket!"

Evidently no one cared, as not a soul moved to intercept her. "Stop *him*," she yelled back, "*he's* a rapist!"

A small mob of departing jersey-clad blokes the size of small cars swiveled their heads from Tiffany to focus on Will. What happened next took place in a matter of seconds, although it felt longer to Will who was being backed up by what was probably most of the football team, muttering about taking him apart.

Through the big windows, designed to take in the view, he saw Dani approaching, followed by a guy that looked like Keith's spy coming up the sidewalk. At the same time, Tiffany was racing away from the building, her hat gone, her long hair flying behind her, and to Will's amazement, the spy stopped following Dani and took off after Tiffany. Dani only hesitated a moment and went after both.

He started to step sideways while still processing the happenings outside when he was stopped by several large, grasping hands. "Hold him while I call Campus Safety," was yelled from somewhere behind the group, and Will finally focused on the trouble staring him down.

Someone brought a chair from a nearby table, and a black man big enough to be a linebacker barked, “Sit down till the cops get here.” In reality, he had little choice in the matter as many hands helped him sit whether he wanted to or not. Not knowing what the bloke who had been following them was up to was killing him, but he had very few options at the moment. He couldn’t take on this university football team. Blowing out a breath, he crossed his arms and settled in to wait.

Chapter 9

Dani bent over, completely out of breath. Tiffany was long gone.

She turned to see if Mr. Ugly Tree was still behind her but didn't see his long, black wool coat anywhere. His pudgy body had been no match for either of the women, and Dani had outpaced him easily. Catching up to Tiffany had been another matter.

She realized that Will had been wrong; the guy hadn't been following *her*, he was following *them* to find Tiffany.

She had no idea what had happened to Will. She had assumed that he had flushed Tiffany out, but why wasn't he following? As she pulled out her phone to call him, a couple of uniformed men walked briskly past her in the direction she'd come from. She had a sudden bad feeling about Will.

Turning, she followed, even as she scrolled to find Will's number. When he didn't answer, she knew something was up. She followed the uniforms back toward the residence hall, although they turned before reaching it, veering instead toward the building that Tiffany had burst out of earlier.

Once inside, they went straight toward a group of guys all focused the other way, and it wasn't until the mob parted for the officers that she spied Will sitting calmly in the center. She didn't know why, but she found his unshakable cool to be extremely sexy. She pictured Keith in the same situation, yelling and flailing his arms, and nearly laughed out loud.

Will smiled pleasantly at the campus security officers as he passed them his Stafford Investigations ID, the police report on Tiffany, and the memo from the dean while he explained that he only wanted to reunite her with her family. The mob of well-muscled young men slowly began to back away, making excuses about needing to get to class.

The officers read everything, then handed them back, apologizing for the misunderstanding, and Will graciously put out his hand to shake theirs, thanking them for taking campus security seriously.

Dani felt weak in the knees and a little more in love.

Eventually, the officers turned to leave, and Will focused on her. Stepping forward, he ran his hands through his hair and blew out an exasperated breath. "I take it she got away."

Dani nodded. "That girl can run."

"And Mr. Ugly Tree. . . "

"Yeah," Dani put in, "what the heck does he want with Tiffany? Did the Morrow's hire someone else?"

"The Mrs. didn't mention anything when I talked to her this morning." Will looked past her out the windows. "I take it Tiffany outran him as well."

She snorted. "Even I outran him. But when I wore out, he was nowhere."

"Hmm, then she's probably in no immediate danger."

"Danger! Do you think the man wants to hurt her?"

Will shook his head. "I just don't know. If it weren't for him, we could probably just report that she is on campus and close the case."

"But now. . . "

He pulled out his phone. "But now I won't feel good about leaving until we know what that scrub-headed turkey is up to."

Dani waited while he talked to Mrs. Morrow. From this side of the conversation, it sounded as if she didn't have a clue about anyone else on the case. Will then called Capt. Rand with Missing Persons, asking them about their procedures and describing the man in question. He concluded with, "So you have no plain clothesmen assigned to her case."

Will nodded through the response. "All right, Captain, I'll come by later to work with your sketch artist."

After sliding his phone into his pocket, he angled his head toward the residence hall. "I think we should still check her room. Maybe we'll find something having to do with this mysterious bloke that the police wouldn't have thought important several months ago."

They turned toward the door. "Will, how would Mr. Ugly Tree know to follow us to find Tiffany?"

"He might have been watching the Morrow house and saw us come out. I only saw him last night, but maybe he was following us all afternoon. I couldn't tell much about the vehicle behind us last night, except that it was white, filthy, and small."

Will opened the cafeteria door for her, but she didn't go through. "Last night you said you didn't think anyone had followed us."

Will knew he was in trouble and gave her a wary smile. "Sorry, possum, didn't want you to worry."

Dani moved through the door, but he could see she wasn't happy with him. He fell into step beside her, not sure what to say. She helped him out. "I hope you won't do that again. I need you to always tell me the truth, Will, because you said a lot of things last night I want to believe in."

He stopped her and pulled her off the sidewalk and behind a tree. Putting his hands on either side of her face, he looked deep into her eyes. "I'm sorry I took liberties with the truth to keep you from fretting, but I meant every word I said to you last night in my room." Her still-worried expression had him dipping his head, his lips moving toward hers. "Every single word." His mouth met hers, and he poured everything he felt for her into a reassuring kiss.

When he pulled away, she broke into a grin, her arms around his waist. "I knew I could make you kiss me."

Will's eyebrows shot up as his mouth dropped open. Then a slow smile spread over his face. "I didn't realize you could be so sheepy." Taking her hand, he pulled her back to the sidewalk that led to Tiffany's residence hall.

"There's still a lot you don't know about me, Will Yarnel, " she sassed.

"I see that." He stopped her before opening the door. "I know it will take a while, but I want to learn every detail."

She smiled up at him, and Will wanted to forget Tiffany's room and take her back to his. He pulled open the door, thankful for a job to do that would keep them busy until she got around to making that call to Keith. She'd taken off the ring, but it wasn't a broken engagement until he knew she took it off. He didn't envy her the job, but it had to be done.

Upon entering the residence hall lobby again, Will was glad to see a new person at the desk, so he wouldn't have to explain searching a missing student's room who wasn't really missing anymore. The bloke read the memo before using a keycard to let them on into the residence hall. He escorted them right to her door and employed a master key to get in. "Please make sure the door is locked when you leave," was all he told them as far as instructions.

The room had a stale smell from being closed up for months, but all in all was extremely tidy. He gave the Denver Police kudos for not trashing the place in looking for evidence.

There wasn't much on the walls—just a bulletin board that held mostly track ribbons above the desk. No pictures of friends, family, or anyone. He guessed that nobody printed out pictures anymore—they were all on their phones. He was a little bit surprised that she didn't have some of her own art on the walls.

He told Dani to take the bedroom side of the small space while he looked through her desk, books, and papers. There didn't seem to be any kind of computer, which he thought was odd, but the police might have taken it to look through and then returned it to the Morrows rather than make a scene by taking it back to her dorm room. He'd ask about it later.

He glanced to Dani, who was going through the clothes in the closet, feeling the linings and hems and looking through pockets, and smiled. *She learns fast.*

He had a flash fantasy of going back to Brazil and working on cases together. Sitting down at the desk, he tried to push that line of thinking aside as he looked in boxes of granola bars and poptarts. They had barely started down the relationship road; their future together—should there be one—was still too cloudy to see.

After thumbing through all the books for notes and searching every inch of her desk, inside and out, he pulled a penlight out of his pocket and got down on the floor to look under the bed. He pulled out what looked like an art portfolio, and they looked through it together, agreeing with Min Morrow's assessment of "ghastly." Dark brooding colors created horrifying creatures straight out of a nightmare. Bodies torn asunder by the beasts was a recurring theme, with a black dragon found somewhere in almost every one. They weren't anything Will would want to hang on his wall, but her skill was apparent.

After he put them all back in the portfolio and slid it again under the bed, Dani asked about stripping the bedding.

"Yeah," he said moving to the small nightstand. "Shake everything out and do an inspection where the mattress meets the head and foot boards." He opened the drawer and found nothing but the typical things one would expect—chapstick, eye drops, ibuprofen and some change. He pulled out two prescription bottles. Krista had said she'd gotten new scripts the day before. *So why would she risk coming back to her room if she didn't need these?* He put them back, then turned to walk around the room once again, letting his eyes wander. *What was worth coming back for?*

His eye caught on the carpeting in the corner that looked as if it had been pulled up and not pushed back down completely. While Dani began to put the sheets back on the bed, he walked to the corner, squatted down, took a hold of it and pulled. It came up easily for about thirty centimeters or so, but there was nothing underneath. If it was once a hiding place for something, it wasn't any longer.

"What did you find?" Dani asked as she grabbed the pillow off the floor and flung it back on the bed.

"Dust," Will said, standing. "And maybe a spider."

Dani pointed at the bulletin board. "Did you see that?"

Will followed her gaze to a purple page containing a list of some kind. A closer inspection proved it to be a list of tutors. "I suppose they could be possible contacts."

Dani pointed to one name in particular. One that had a tiny heart drawn next to it.

"Steve Elway," Will read aloud. "I thought she was dating the guy who sold her to Justin Miranda."

"Could be an ex," Dani theorized. "Or just a wish. But whatever his relationship was to Tiffany, he might be a lead to finding her."

"Could be." He smiled as he pulled out his phone to give this computer science tutor a call. "You've got good eyes and good instincts. I'm not sure I would have even noticed that little heart."

Dani smiled back before going back to finishing up the bedding, glowing with his compliment, and he wondered if Keith hadn't been the complimentary type. A friendly voice told him to leave a message. Will didn't.

He slid the phone back into his pocket, and Dani looked at him questioningly. "No answer?"

Will shook his head. "And I don't want to leave a message. If she's with him, he just might tip her off and send her running again. I'll do some sleuthing first and find out where he lives."

He looked around one more time, checking around the edges for more signs that the carpet had been lifted, before deciding there wasn't anything more to see.

He thought about the little heart by the tutor's name as they left Tiffany's room. "I never wrote a heart by your name," he said as they walked down the hall, "but every time I heard it, my heart lit up."

Dani smiled up at him, and it lit up again.

* * *

Tiffany paced the hall outside Steve's classroom, once again using her hair as an anchor, letting the feel of it calm her nerves and help her think. Five more minutes before he'd be able to help her find a safe location. She could hide out in the women's restroom, but then she'd be trapped if that fat, black dragon came looking for her.

She paused her stride, closed her eyes, and forced herself to breathe. She knew it wasn't really a dragon. She knew that. But at the moment, that's all her mind would show her. A tiny smile graced her lips as she remembered glancing back to see the blonde out-pacing the rotund beast. *Dani.* The name came to her out of no where. *And the guy was Will.* She was glad that occasionally her brain worked right.

She recalled Dani's tender touch and Will's gentle voice, almost second-guessing her reasons for running from them, and her hands stilled. But if they were only paid to get her back to the States, why were they still so persistently following her? She felt guilty for stealing from Dani's wallet, but she'd seen that big rock on her finger. The woman wouldn't miss twenty or thirty bucks. And while Will seemed gentle, she had a vague memory of him subduing her with muscular arms. She wouldn't get away from him if he ever got a hold on her.

If they didn't know before, by now they had undoubtedly gotten word of her mental issues. There was no way they'd believe her about the embezzling. She took several deep breaths and forced herself to release her hair and put her hands in her coat pockets.

She remembered the plane trip as a jumble of triggered schizophrenic psychoses that she'd lost control of due to an overindulgence of alcohol that she suspected had been drugged by her last john. It had taken several days for that hallucinogenic haze to clear, but she had awakened in the hotel room clear-headed. Well, as clear-headed as she could be without her meds. She knew that once she was in her parents' house, they wouldn't let her out of their sight for months, and when she'd heard Dani snoring while Will was in the shower, she had made the abrupt decision to make her escape.

Lost in thought as she was, the door to Steve's classroom opening startled her. Students poured out, and she waited to the side for the handsome man she'd had a crush on from the first. She wished to God she'd never gotten side-tracked with Aaron McCain, no matter how persistent he had been. Especially since she had only been trying to make Steve jealous, and McCain's devotion had been merely a show.

He came through the door and smiled when he saw her standing nearby. Steve had the best smile. He stopped in front of her, both hands once again wrapped around the handles of his laptop case. "So where do you want to go to talk about… stuff."

"Probably off campus. There's a big dragon after me here." He hitched a brow. "Plus, I saw those people my mom probably hired. They seem to be following me too." She didn't tell him about the beast. There was only so much she could expect the man to handle.

"You had a busier hour than I could have imagined."

"I managed to wolf down some pancakes too," she said as he turned to head down the hall, falling in beside him.

"Good," he said with enthusiasm. "Your face is thinner than I remember."

Tiffany didn't want to talk about her weight or how she got so thin. "The dragon was really an overweight dude in a black coat, but for some reason, I can't dredge up his face."

Steve held the door for her, then they followed the curved sidewalk that led to two small reflecting ponds on the other side of the green. "Was he really chasing you, or was that just—"

"No, he was really chasing me. My imaginary dragons are never fat and waddling on two legs. I just don't know why he was chasing me."

He didn't say anything more, and their footsteps grew unbearably loud on the concrete. "Steve, I know what you're thinking, but I was two months without my meds, and in that time, I learned to distinguish the real monsters from the imaginary ones really well. The real ones wear suits."

She swallowed hard, shoving the leering faces and grasping hands into the closets of her mind. She did not want that beast to show up again. Even imaginary monsters could be unnerving.

He slowed to a stop at the edge of the lot, concern lining his face. "Where were you Tiff? What 'monsters' are you referring to?"

She grabbed his arm and pulled him toward his old blue Honda. She could not go into that now. Not if she wanted to stay focused on getting the evidence from Pragnalysis. If the beast got near her, it would eat her alive, dragging her down into a den of hallucinations she might not crawl out of for days. She couldn't let that happen; she had work to do. "Let's save that conversation for when I'm no longer seeing dragons, okay?"

He gave her a weak smile before opening the car door. "Deal."

She went around to the other side and climbed in, thankful for an ally and a friend, even if he never became anything more.

Chapter 10

After walking around the entire campus and seeing nothing of either Tiffany or the man Dani had dubbed Mr. Ugly Tree, she and Will grabbed a quick lunch before heading to the police station.

Dani was always amazed at the talent of police sketch artists, and she was doubly impressed by this one, who did her work on a computer drawing tablet. Her skill plus Will's eye for detail was really fleshing out the face that only a mother could love. Dani studied the pudgy man with small, wide-set eyes, a crooked nose and ears that stuck straight out on the sides of his balding head. She tried to "never judge a book by its cover," but surely the man could be up to no good. What could he possibly want with Tiffany when the news had barely broken on her return?

When Will declared it good, the artist saved the sketch in a database, then Capt. Rand, who was probably in his fifties with graying hair and a thick mustache, ran a program to compare it to arrest records. He said it could take a while, and he would let them know if they found a match. Will asked for a copy, and he printed one out.

By the time they left, it was mid-afternoon, and back in the Rav 4, Will was pondering what direction to take. "It's doubtful that she'd go back to her room now."

"Why did she go back to campus at all?" Dani wondered. "Did she think she could just jump back into her old life after being used as a sex slave, as if nothing happened—without ever going home or getting any counseling or anything?"

Will tapped a finger on his lower lip. "It's hard to know what's going through her head. Is she reacting to real life or delusions?" He started the car and backed out of the space in the parking garage.

"Where are we going?"

"Back to campus. You're right, it was crazy for her to go back to her residence hall this morning, so why would I think she wouldn't go back later? Maybe she's there now, having a snack in the cafeteria. And even if she's not, we need to tell the dean about this morning's events and ask him to alert his security team to Mr. Ugly Tree."

Will parked in a campus parking lot, then they began their trek toward the old stone building called University Hall. Will surprised her by taking her hand. She lifted them up. "I thought this wasn't allowed until I 'make the call,' " she said in an ominous voice.

"It seems clear that Keith wasn't spying on you after all, and since I've already broken my rule and kissed you, I can't do much worse by holding your hand."

She sighed. "No more kisses then."

He gave her a sly smile, then lifted her hand to his lips and laid a kiss on her knuckles. Just that small connection sent electricity through her, and she couldn't wait for what the evening might hold. Of course, after talking to Keith, the whole evening might be destroyed. She couldn't imagine him taking the news of breaking off the engagement well.

The dean was in a meeting, so Will wrote him a note and had his secretary scan the police sketch of the man they now believed might be a danger to Tiffany. He'd hoped to get a list of the professors she'd taken classes under last semester, but it was obvious that the secretary wasn't going to let go of that information without an okay from the dean.

As they walked back across campus hand in hand, Dani asked, "What now? Are we just going to stake out her residence hall and hope she returns?" She shivered. "I think the temperature has dropped a lot in the last hour."

Will released her hand and threw his arm around her. "Yeah, I feel it. No, I thought we'd loop around campus one more time, talk to the front desk at her dorm again and leave them a picture of Mr. Ugly Tree. Then I'm thinking we need to pay a visit to Pragnalysis."

"Because she worked there last summer?"

"Right. It seems more likely to yield leads than those old high school friends she fell out with."

They walked a while in silence, each keeping an eye out for their red-headed runaway. Now that Dani had had some time to think about her somewhat impulsive leap into a relationship with Will, she wondered about the future. Did he plan to go back to Brazil as soon as he felt that Tiffany was safe? Did she want to go with him? She knew that was a huge step, but she couldn't expect Will to be like Logan, who went home with Rita.

Aside from the craziness of Rita being mistaken as the Diamond Diva, she had loved her time in Brazil. Would she miss living in the States? Probably. Her family would most likely say she was going through some kind of mid-life crisis in leaving a wealthy man running for Congress to run off to Brazil with an ex-military Australian P.I., but she *was* nearly forty. She smiled. If she was going to do something rash for a mid-life crisis, she'd better get to it.

She squeezed Will's hand. "So what are your plans after this is all over? Are you still going to catch the first flight back to Brazil?"

He slowed his steps as he looked to her upturned face. "That depends."

"On what?" she asked, her heart beating faster.

He stopped completely and turned to face her. "On if a certain Kansan will go with me."

"What if that Kansan were reluctant to leave the only home she's ever known? How would you convince her?" She really didn't need a lot of convincing, but he didn't need to know that.

Will's smile was downright devilish. "You're a conniver, trying to get me to pash with you again."

She quirked her lips to the side. "I admit nothing."

Will laughed and kissed her forehead. "That'll have to do for now, possum." He leaned toward her ear. "But later," he whispered, "I plan on convincing you all night long."

Her shiver that time had nothing to do with the cold.

* * *

"Mr. Owens will be down in a few minutes to talk to you, Mr. Yarnel."

Will turned from the wall that illustrated the Pragnalysis success story in newspaper clippings, magazine features, and technology awards. "Thanks, love."

The short-haired brunette gave him another smile. Turning up the Aussie accent always seemed to open doors with American women. Before he had started to speak, the look she'd given him and Dani when they walked in the front doors could hardly be called welcoming. Her gaze had clung to his shaggy hair a few seconds too long before coming back down to his eyes. But once he'd turned on the Down Under charm with no-holds-barred Oz, she'd warmed up like bare feet on the beach.

Dani had started at the beginning of the billion-dollar business's history, but Will wasn't really interested in the details. He scanned the most recent headlines of how a private jet crash took the lives of Martin and Cecily Tuttle, leaving the business to their only daughter Minuette.

Footsteps sounded, and both Will and Dani turned to see a slender man who was probably only in his early to mid-thirties coming down the curved, floating staircase. He extended his hand as he approached, greeting both him and Dani. "I'm Chase Owens. Bret tells me you rescued Tiffany from a… a human trafficking situation. I can't even imagine what that poor girl must have gone through."

Will nodded. "It's never pretty, and now unfortunately we've lost her again."

Mr. Owens shook his dark-haired head in disbelief. "It's that condition of hers, isn't it? I mean, we saw some of it when she worked as a temp last summer." He lowered his voice. "If Bret hadn't warned us about a few things… let's just say I caught her poking around in places that would have gotten any other temp fired."

Will supposed that was her paranoia coming through.

"And the wild stories she could come up with… It's tragic, really. I hope when you find her, they can get her on a better treatment plan."

Will thought about the fact that she had been well enough to go to college. "Did she make any friends while she worked here? Anyone she knew well enough to hobnob with outside of work?"

“Do you mean someone she might be tapping now for a place to stay?”

The man was perceptive. “Right.”

He shook his head. “I doubt it.”

Dani jumped into the conversation. “Would you mind if we talked to anyone she worked closely with?”

He gave a little sniff. “Tiff was really just a glorified gofer. She delivered coffee, snacks, and mail.”

Will nodded, feeling a dead end forming in front of them.

Dani still had more questions. “So when you say you caught her ‘poking around,’ what did you mean? Poking around where, doing what?”

“I’d hate for any of this to get back to Mrs. Morrow.” He was practically whispering now. “She’s been through enough.” He paused a moment before going on, but not long enough for them to reassure him of a confidence. “Shortly before she disappeared, I caught her in an office, looking through some off-limits company files.” He raised a brow. “I don’t think the Morrows knew she’d be a security risk.”

Will cocked his head, trying to make this new information fit. “She hacks computers? We were under the impression she was an artist. We’ve seen a little bit of her work.”

The man brightened. “Oh, she is that! Her illustrations—mostly of monsters, dragons, and other beasts—are amazing. To tell you the truth, I didn’t expect the computer thing either, although the computer she was looking through belonged to one of our lazier employees. He might have just left the files open. He claims he didn’t but” —he shrugged— “it’s hard to find good help.”

Will wished he’d had more time with the girl to make any kind of assessment of what she was capable of. “So what is your position with Pragnalysis?”

“I’m the Executive Supervisor in Research and Development.” He looked at his very expensive watch. “And I wish I could be more help to you both, but like I already said, Tiffany wasn’t really too close to anyone for the few months she worked here.”

The brunette at the front desk coughed, and Mr. Owens seemed to take that as his cue to get back to work. “I wish you the best of luck in tracking her down." He shook their hands again, then turned to go back up the curving stairs.

Will and Dani turned to go, and Will threw a nod and a smile at the brunette. "Thank you. Have a nice day."

She rose and leaned over the counter, holding out some sort of brochure. "Here's the Pragnalysis story."

When Will hesitated, she pressed on. "You both seemed interested in the wall."

Will nearly laughed. Didn't everyone read the wall when they were waiting? What else were they supposed to do? He didn't really care, but Dani reached out and took it. "Thanks. It is pretty interesting."

The brunette nodded, and Will reserved judgment on Dani's taste in reading material as he pushed out of the building and held the door for her. "Was it really that fascinating?" he asked as they headed for the paid parking lot that held their car.

"Parts of it. I was interested in their shift to data mining. Seems pretty scary what these companies think they are privy to in our private lives."

"I doubt that little paper will tell you what you really want to know about it."

"Probably not." She opened it up as they walked. "Didn't Owens remind you of Morrow with that ultra black hair? They may as well both grow beards. Shaving just doesn't do it."

Will chuckled. "I suppose, although I can't really picture either one of them with much of a beard."

"Well, not like you had a few days ago, no," she said, flipping to the back of the brochure. She suddenly stopped moving. "Will look at this." He stopped to read the handwritten note in the margin of the brochure Dani had thrust at him. *"Meet me at 9:00 a.m. Sat. at Java Jive, 300 Filmore."*

Will looked back to the Pragnalysis entrance. "Do you think she wrote that?"

"Who else?"

He handed it back to Dani, and the two started walking again. "Huh. She must know something."

"Something she didn't want Mr. Owens to hear," Dani added.

Will felt a glimmer of hope but couldn't help wonder about the secrecy. "You don't suppose she's got Tiffany at her place, and she's promised not to tell anyone?"

"I don't know, but I do know one thing."

"What?"

"I saw a salon up the street, and you need a haircut."

Will knew it was true, but he couldn't resist teasing her. "Let a woman in your life, and they try to change you within a week."

"Not you, ya nong," she sassed him in classic Aussie style as they stopped at the corner, "just that marsupial on your head."

Will laughed, and broke his rule again, pulling her in for a kiss while they waited for the light to change.

Chapter 11

Tiffany looked over Steve's shoulder as he studied the Pragnalysis systems online. She had remembered enough about the company's security to get him into the first layers of programming, and she could tell they'd beefed it up since she'd broken through last fall.

"I'm not seeing an easy way in, Tiff," Steve said with what seemed almost like relief.

She hadn't expected him to give up so soon. "So how about a not-so-easy, yet do-able way in?"

He gave a little snort. "I value my freedom, Tiff. Prison wouldn't suit me."

She pulled a chair up next to him. "So just tell me what to do. I'll take full responsibility. My mother would no sooner prosecute me than give away her diamonds."

Steve pushed back from the kitchen table and walked to his fridge to pull out two bottles of water. "So daddy has nothing to do with it?"

"Nope," she said as he returned and handed her one. "When you're as rich as the Tuttles, there's always a pre-nup." She uncapped it and took a swig. "For both my dads. As I understand it, Raymond Garrett never wanted the job my mother offered him, and he left for California after only a year of marriage. Bret Morrow, on the other hand, took to it like a hippy to pot."

"Are you in touch with your real dad?" he asked before taking another few gulps of his water.

"Yeah, but he's never been terribly present in my life." She shrugged. "We email some."

"So your stepdad was good to you?"

Tiffany wondered about all this sudden interest in her family, but she had no reason not to answer. "Yeah, although he never liked my art—said I should draw 'happy things'—and once my schizophrenia manifested, and I confided that the black dragons of my imagination had somehow stepped out of my paintings and into the real world… well let's just say, there was always doubt in his eyes after that, no matter what I said." Tiffany had a sudden weird queasy feeling and put a hand to her belly, shifting in her seat.

Setting the now-nearly-empty water bottle on the table, Steve pursed his lips for a few moments before bringing his eyes to hers. "Can you give me some evidence that this isn't just another imaginary dragon? That paranoia hasn't set in because you were so long off your meds? I'm going to need that reassurance to dig into a company as big as Pragnalysis."

If Tiffany had evidence of the wrong-doing, she wouldn't need Steve, but she had known she'd need something to convince him to help her. She pushed down her own reoccurring doubts and the sick feeling that had unexpectedly come over her and pulled a folded piece of paper out of her back pocket. "This is kind of the opposite of a pre-nup."

He took it from her hand with slightly narrowed eyes, unfolded it and began to read. Then his brows shot up, and a hand reached out to grasp the back of the kitchen chair he'd vacated. "Holy hell, Tiffany."

"You could have your dream, Steve. Start your own 21st century school that 'creates the future.' " She used his own words to try and sweeten an already sweet deal.

He just looked at her, blinking.

"I meant every word I wrote. Nearly a half million had been embezzled out of Pragnalysis by last October. Who knows what the number is now, but I promise you at least that half mil if you help me catch the thief."

He pulled out the chair and sat. "A half million… You'll give me five hundred thousand dollars."

"That's practically pocket change to my family. If we can prove the theft, my mother won't think twice about giving it to you as a reward."

"I thought you were going to keep me out of it."

"Okay, to me. Then I'll give it to you." She pointed to the paper still in his hand. "I signed it and dated it. If I'd had the time and resources to get it notarized, I would have."

Steve shook his head. "I trust you, Tiff. I don't need..." He ran a hand around his jaw before standing and walking to the nearby living room. "I don't need money to help you. I just need to know that—" he stopped and took another step toward the window, looking more purposefully through the partially open vertical blinds. "That overweight black dragon of yours. Was it bald?"

Tiffany sucked in a breath as the man's true face flashed in her mind. "Yes! He was!" She leapt up and strode to Steve's side, hoping to see whatever he was seeing. They were on the ground floor looking straight out at the "fat dragon" who had chased her on campus, now looking up with binoculars. "You used to live on the third floor."

"Yeah. Directly above us. I just moved two weeks ago."

"I thought I lost him on campus, but he must have followed us."

"Why is he following you, Tiff?"

"I'm not sure. He might just be another P.I. hired to drag me home. Or he might be after me because of what I discovered at Pragnalysis." She looked up at Steve, trying to talk about Brazil without "feeling" Brazil. "I can't prove it, but I think there's a connection between that discovery and my kidnapping."

He stepped slowly to the side of the window and tilted the blinds closed, then escorted her back to the kitchen with a hand to her back. His touch sent both panic and euphoria through her—a knife of pleasure and pain.

Thankfully, or regrettably—she didn't know which she felt more strongly—he released her quickly and moved back to the chair in front of his laptop. He paused for a moment, taking a deep breath. Then he put his hands on the keyboard. "Let's get to work."

* * *

Dani listened to her call go to voicemail for the third time in an hour. It wasn't like Keith to ignore her calls if he could help it.

Maybe he had a late meeting. She tossed the phone to the bed and leaned back against the pillows just as Will came back into the room after working out in the hotel's gym downstairs. He'd given her an hour of privacy to talk to Keith, but it had all been for naught.

He came to the foot of the bed, his hands gripping the ends of the towel around his neck, looking sexy as all get out with his newly cut hair. She'd had the stylist leave her just enough on top to run her fingers through. "So how did it go?"

She shook her head, releasing an exasperated sigh. "I couldn't get a hold of him. He's not answering or returning my calls."

He turned toward the bathroom, obviously disappointed. "I need a shower." Dani heard him mumble, "A cold one," before he disappeared inside.

She pulled a pillow to her chest. As nervous as she'd been about making the call, this was worse. Both Will and Keith had shown her a lot about herself—who she wanted to be and who she didn't, the kind of causes she wanted to champion and those she wanted to leave behind, and she was ready to move on and get to it. She looked to the clock. It was only 8:00 in Colorado, but in KC, it was 9:00. She'd never known him to have a meeting so late.

Tossing the pillow aside, she was tempted to leave him a break-up message just so she could say she'd done her part, and Will wouldn't keep her at arms-length all evening, but she knew she couldn't do that. No matter their disagreements of late, Keith wasn't a total monster, and he deserved better than a "dear John" message.

Swinging her legs to the floor, she decided she would not let the evening be a pity party. While Will showered, she put on some fake leather skinny jeans and a red sparkly sweater, touched up her makeup, and added a few curls to her hair. Surely there was something fun they could do in the heart of Denver on a Friday night.

Will emerged with a towel around his waist as she was pulling on the new snow boots she'd bought after Will's haircut. He blinked at her. "Going out on the town, possum?"

She tried to put his half-naked body out of her mind as she turned back to the mirror to put in some hoop earrings. "*We* are going out on the town. I refuse to sit in here all night with us both… ticked off. Let's go out and do something."

A smile tugged at his lips as he moved past her and the second bed, toward his dufflebag on the small table in the corner. "All right. You lead, I'll follow."

"Hmm, I like that motto," she said trying to keep her eyes on herself in the mirror and not his naked backside as he dropped his towel and pulled on boxer briefs.

Will laughed, obviously in a better mood after his chilly shower. "Most sheilas do."

Dani gave in and turned to watch him finish getting dressed. "Why are women called 'sheilas' in Australia?" It was definitely a good idea to get out of their room. She almost wished she hadn't given up her own now that being with Will was to be a kind of torture until she could settle things with Keith.

"Shelah's Day," he began, buttoning his shirt "used to be celebrated after St. Patrick's Day. Pat or Paddy became a kind of label for an Irish man, while Sheila became the stereotypical Irish woman. In the beginning, it was a derogatory term for a wild or drunken woman, but later became a sweetheart or just any woman at all." He sat to put on his boots. "The evolution of language is a strange and interesting thing."

She laughed as she picked up her phone to find out where they could go for some fun. "Especially your Aussie-isms."

He stood. "You Americans have your own weird slang. You're just used to it."

They both donned coats and headed out the door. "So what American slang confused you when you first arrived?" she asked, scrolling through entertainment possibilities.

"Well, let's see." They walked down the hall to the elevators. "Stopping something 'cold turkey' didn't make a lot of sense to me. Neither did 'spilling the beans' or 'jumping the shark.' " They stepped in when the doors opened, and Will continued. "I had no idea what a 'raincheck' was, and when I told Logan we should 'table' a topic for discussion, he moved on to something else when I meant we should really talk about it."

"Huh, I guess you're right." The doors opened at the bottom, and they stepped out and headed through the lobby. "Although I think yours are stranger."

He opened the hotel door for her. "Stranger or just more interesting?"

She laughed. "They are that."

Will followed her out, "So where are we going?"

"There's a movie theater close by."

He groaned. "So you are trying to avoid being in our room together by putting us in a dark room together side by side?"

"Oh. Well. . ." She hadn't thought of that. "Do you have any ideas?"

"I could go for some dessert."

"Are you ever not thinking of food?" she asked with a grin.

"Occasionally. But we can't do what would take my mind off of it."

They started across the parking lot, when a horse snorting nearby had them stopping and looking around. Dani pointed to the street. "Look, it's a horse drawn carriage! I've always wanted to do that."

As they watched, it stopped along the street, delivering its passengers right to their hotel. Will grabbed her hand and pulled. Any man who ignored a hint like that didn't deserve a woman in his life. "Sir," he said as they neared, "do we need a reservation to ride?"

"I don't usually venture this far from the Cherry Creek Shopping area," he explained, "but I had a request for a special anniversary surprise. I'd be happy to take you to Cherry Creek, but I won't be returning this way."

"We can take an Uber back, right?"

Will looked down into Dani's sparkling eyes and pulled out his wallet. "How much is the one-way trip?"

Will settled up with the man, climbed in the back and extended his hand to Dani. As soon as they were under the big fur blanket, he realized his mistake. This was far worse than the theater would have been.

They hadn't gone far before they both realized how damn cold it was even under the blanket. They donned stocking caps and gloves and were still shivering. Ultimately, Will threw all his rules out the window and his arms around her.

"Sorry, Will, I didn't think about how cold this would be."

"Sure you didn't, possum," he teased. "You've been wanting to pash with me all day."

She tilted her chin up. " 'Pash.' I take it that means kiss?"

He leaned his cheek against her forehead. "Kiss, yes. With fire… passion."

They were silent for a few minnies, listening to the horses' hooves mingled with the traffic noise. Will was trying not to think about the woman in his arms, but his mind started a replay of their night together.

"Passionate" was a fair description, all right. Along with sensuous, seductive, and just plain romantic. The woman had crawled inside him with loving caresses and steamy kisses, and their coupling had been deeply fulfilling, like nothing he had experienced since Renae. He couldn't help it when his lips sought hers for a gentle kiss. One turned into more as her hand moved up his thigh, and Will did not have any willpower left to deny her. Lost to sensation, the rest of the ride blurred until the driver cleared his throat, and Will twigged that they had stopped. Dani wasn't easing up, however. If anything, she pressed in.

"I'm sorry, sir," Will heard the cabbie say, "but you'll need the couple's permission to take a picture."

A sudden flash of light had Will jerking away from Dani's hungry lips. A man with a pretty fancy camera turned and walked briskly through the parking lot. Will flung off the blanket and jumped from the carriage. The man started to run, but this time Will was the speedier of the two. The man ducked between cars, and Will latched onto the hood that hung behind him, pulling him up with a strangled yell. He reached behind and grabbed Will's wrist. Will grabbed his other arm and twisted it behind his back before slamming him against the car. "Stop before I take you to the ground and trash that expensive camera in the process."

The man released his hold on Will's wrist and stopped squirming. "I'm just doing my job, man, and if you hadn't been kissing the lady, there wouldn't have been a picture worth taking."

Will pulled his arm up higher, and he yelled again. "And just what job is that? Who are you working for?"

He didn't answer, and Will bent his thumb backward. "God, stop! His name is Keith Bisbee. He doesn't live here. He found me on the web. Said he thought his fiancée was cheating on him."

"I was going to break up with him." Dani had caught up. "He's not answering my calls."

He looked toward Dani. "That's not my problem, lady."

"Are there two of you?"

"Two of me?"

Will took over. "Are you working with an overweight bald guy with tiny eyes and a crooked nose?"

"No, man. I work alone. Now let me go before I yell for somebody to call the cops."

Will didn't let up yet. "That picture you took. You need to delete it."

He hesitated a moment before agreeing. "Sure, whatever. It doesn't matter. I already sent the others."

"What others?" Dani said with a hand to her mouth.

"Pictures of you two carrying on. I've been following you all day. Now let me go!"

Will released him and stepped back.

The man turned, holding his shoulder as he rolled it up and back.

Will pulled his camera forward and flipped it around. "Hey man!" He tried to pull it out of his hands and slide out of reach, but Will had him trapped against the car, next to the side mirror. He quickly brought up the menu of pictures on the digital camera's screen. Working backwards, he deleted the carriage kiss as well as a good ten more of him and Dani on campus and near Pragnalysis before releasing it and letting the man go.

Will turned to Dani, feeling sick. This guy had followed them all day, and he hadn't seen him anywhere.

"Will, are you okay?"

"No. I think we better just call a ride and go back to the hotel."

"He had a really long lens, Will." She seemed to know exactly what he was thinking, which only made it worse. "Don't blame yourself."

He couldn't bring himself to answer. He was too disgusted. Putting a hand to her back, he guided her toward someplace warm to wait while he called for a lift back to the hotel. He was no longer hungry for dessert, and he wouldn't have to worry about staying out of Dani's bed tonight. He doubted he'd be in the mood for any more pashing this evening after he called Logan to resign.

Chapter 12

Logan had just dozed off with Rita in his arms when his phone rang. As tempted as he was to ignore it, the ring tone was the one he'd assigned to Will and Rod.

Extricating himself from Rita, he rolled over to reach for his pants abandoned on the floor and pulled the phone out of the back pocket. Seeing Will's name on the screen, he answered with "G'day, mate."

Will's "Well, it started out good" had him swinging his legs off the bed and sitting up.

"What's happened? You sound like your dog died."

"I… I need to turn in my resignation. I'm not worth what you pay me."

Logan ran his hand through his hair. "Okay, start at the beginning." Will was one of his best. There was no way he was letting him quit without a fight.

Will let out a breath. "Dani and I… well we hooked up last night and—"

"Congratulations!" Logan was genuinely thrilled for the man. "Like I told you, no woman is out of reach until she says 'I do.' "

"Yeah, well, we still shouldn't have… I mean, she hadn't broken off her engagement yet, and—"

"So you two got swept up in the heat of the moment. It happens. That's no reason to beat yourself up." Sometimes Will's expectations for himself were higher than a Saint's.

"That's not why I'm resigning… Logan, Dani's jealous fiancé hired someone to follow us. He took pictures of us… kissing. He followed us all day, Logan, and I didn't see him."

He gave a mirthless laugh. "In fact, I suspected the whole scenario but got the wrong guy!"

Logan was momentarily speechless. It wasn't like Will to miss something like that, but it was probably understandable. He knew what it was like to have one's brain temporarily hijacked by a woman.

"So anyway, I'll be heading back to Brazil to pack up my things and—"

"No!" Logan wasn't about to let this Aussie nilwit quit over one distracted day. "Everybody has an off day, Will. Hell, I've had dozens. I don't accept your resignation."

"I can damn well quit if I want to," Will shot back.

"Do you want to?" Logan held his breath. He'd have a hard time finding a man with Will's skills, integrity, and passion for finding the lost.

There was a long pause. "It's not a matter of what I want. It's—"

"Been a bad day. Suck it up and get over it. How many bad days do the trafficked men and women have before we find them, Will?" He heard Rita shift behind him, and her arms slipped around his neck, showing her concern for the conversation she could only hear one side of. Will didn't answer, so Logan pressed on. "You've had your pride bruised today. *And* in front of Dani. I get it. Now you know how I felt when Formosa drove off with Rita. We were set up, and I didn't see it. We do the best we can, buddy, but we can't see everything. And there are too many out there who need us to let a few screw-ups stop us in our tracks."

There was still no sound coming out of Will.

"So don't make a decision tonight. You're tired and disappointed, and that's the worst time to decide your future." He smiled. "Snuggle up with that pretty blonde, and let her cure your blues. I guarantee you everything will look better in the morning." He plucked Rita's hand from his chest and brought it to his lips.

"Yeah, all right," Will breathed out in what sounded a bit like relief. At least Logan hoped he'd diffused the man's mental flogging.

"Okay… Not to make light of your personal stuff, but is anything happening on the Tiffany Morrow case? Have you gotten any leads?"

"Yeah. We almost had her several times, but that girl can run like the wind."

"Any idea yet why she's running?"

"No, and now we think there's someone else trying to find her. We don't know the why of that either, but we have a mysterious tee up with the receptionist from Pragnalysis in the morning, so maybe something will make sense after that."

Logan smiled. Will was obviously not quitting. "Okay, well keep me posted. Rita and I are hitting the art museum tomorrow, but I will always have my phone with me."

"Right. Well, uh… I'll call you sometime tomorrow. Hooroo."

"Hooroo, Will."

Logan hung up, and Rita tightened her hold around him. "What on earth was that all about?"

Logan turned and maneuvered her onto his lap. "Just the age-old story of the fragility of the male ego."

Rita laughed. "So he and Dani…"

"Yep."

Rita's eyes sparked approval. "Good. Keith's kind of a jerk."

Logan laughed. "More than you know."

Rita looked surprised, and Logan filled her in on the latest as they slid under the covers and into one another's arms for a night sure to cure any man's blues.

* * *

Dani and Will sipped cappuccinos in the coffee shop for their clandestine meeting with the Pragnalysis receptionist, but so far, she was a no-show.

They had slept in separate beds last night after he'd disappeared for nearly an hour to call Logan. He wouldn't even tell her if he really intended to quit Stafford Investigations or not. He admitted that Logan had made some good points, but he still hadn't made up his mind completely.

Dani wanted to slap him upside the head.

After another five minutes of silence, she couldn't take it anymore. "Will, do you regret our night together?"

"No," he said, setting his cup down, then leaning in. "Like I said, I've wanted you back in my arms ever since the ride to Rio Branco, and I meant it." He paused and licked his lips. "But I should have shown more restraint. I should have insisted that you make the call to Keith first."

Dani blinked. Will was making her feel like a wanton siren who played with men for sport. She matched his posture, her forearms on the table, her eyes narrowing. "You're probably right, Will, I should have told Keith it was over days ago because I knew in my heart it was, even if I hadn't been able to admit it out loud. But I didn't. There's nothing I can do about my lack of judgment now or the pictures that he has in his possession. It's not how I wanted things to go, but what's done is done. If I ever get to talk to the man, I will apologize, but it doesn't change the fact that I don't want to be with him anymore." She reached across the table to lay a hand on his forearm. "I want to be with you."

He turned his arm to grip hers. "And I want to be with you, but…"

"But what? Why is there a 'but'?"

His lips twitched with the words he couldn't seem to spit out.

"Will?"

"What I learned yesterday is that you… distract me. This is often a dangerous job. I can't let anything steal my focus. What if the man following us hadn't been pointing a camera at us? What if it had been a gun?"

Dani pulled out of his grasp and sat back. "But it wasn't."

"Could've been," he insisted.

"Logan seems to think he can do the job and have Rita in his life."

"And she could have been killed because he wasn't thinking clearly. He admitted as much himself last night."

She looked to the baristas busy behind the counter before bringing her eyes back to him, feeling suddenly lost and helpless in the face of Will's sudden turnaround. "So there's no room in your life for me. Is that it?"

"I didn't say that. I just want you to be safe."

She laughed. "Will, I went undercover for you twice in Brazil. That had to be more dangerous than what we're facing here."

"I just don't know what we're facing here. That's the problem."

Dani felt the heat rising in her face. Will's protectiveness was one of the things she loved about him, but it was galling her at the moment.

Someone showed up at the side of their table, and Dani lifted her mug for a refill, but to her surprise, it was not a barista with a carafe, but the Pragnalysis receptionist they'd been waiting for.

"I'm glad you guys are still here. I got caught in a traffic jam." She pulled out the empty chair and sat, cup in hand.

Will made a fast turn out of their relationship cul de sac to focus on the new arrival. "Nice to see you again, Miss..."

"Reynolds," she supplied, putting out a hand to shake Will's. "Amy Reynolds." She let out a sigh and dove right in. "I won't keep you long, but I caught some of what you asked about Tiffany yesterday and what Owens told you." She stopped to take a sip of her coffee, then reached for a sugar packet. "And it's just not true that Tiffany didn't have any friends. She usually talked to me for a few minutes every morning when she came in, and occasionally we did lunch together."

"Has she been in contact with you since coming back from Brazil?" Dani asked. If Will could turn on a dime, so could she.

Amy shook her head. "No. I was shocked when she disappeared and shocked again when it went around the office that she was back. I haven't heard from her at all, but we mostly had a work relationship. We didn't hang out after."

Will looked puzzled. "So... why the secret meeting with us?"

"Because there *was* someone who spent a lot of time trying to get to know her. Someone who Tiffany said asked her out more than once and that she could have probably reported to HR for sexual harassment."

"Who?" Dani and Will said together.

"You need to promise me," she said quietly, "that you will not tell anyone where you got this information. I'd lose my job for sure."

Will nodded. "Of course."

"You met him yesterday," she pronounced with a lift of her brows. "Mr. Chase Owens."

* * *

"Steve, I really think you should just cancel your appointments today. The semester has barely begun. Does anyone really need tutoring yet?" The beefy man in black was no longer in plain sight, but that didn't mean he wasn't out there somewhere.

Steve opened a closet by the front door and pulled a coat off its hanger. "It's a staff meeting, and I need to be there."

Tiffany couldn't be sure who her stalker was working for, but she had her suspicions. She had had plenty of time to think about Aaron McCain's role in selling her to traffickers—a man who had showed up in her life just a few days after Owens caught her on a company computer the first time. And Owens, himself, had introduced them at an office party—an event that had been only announced that morning.

If Owens was behind her kidnapping, he may have given up on a slow seduction and hired a complete thug this time who would just grab her and stuff her in a car. *Or just shoot me.*

Steve swept his laptop already in its case off his desk, and Tiffany forced herself to climb out of the deep well of thought she had fallen into. "He's going to be watching your car, you know." Her hands automatically went to the strand of hair in front of her shoulder, and she began the hand over hand motion that was almost a part of her.

"If he'd followed us yesterday, he would have seen us walk into this apartment. He wouldn't have been confused about where I live." She noted the way his eyes shifted to the movement of her hands, and she stopped them still as he walked toward the door.

Tiffany followed, forcing herself to release her hair and shoving them into her cardigan's pockets. "Yeah, but that's even worse. That means he's a man with access to information. He probably saw us together or maybe your license plate from a distance with his binoculars. From that he got your name and address, which isn't up to date yet. He may have found out that you're a grad student T.A., and he knows what buildings you frequent on campus and the classes you go to and teach!" Her volume was rising as panic set in. "Maybe he isn't out here because he's waiting for you there!"

The tall man turned, obviously concerned. "Tiff, it's going to be okay. The campus isn't deserted, and when I leave, I'll make sure no one is following me." A corner of his mouth quirked up as he put a hand to her shoulder, creating that pain and pleasure sensation once again, and this time she heard a low growl. "I promise I won't lead him back to you."

"It's not me I care about!" she blurted, and she watched those expressive eyes register what she had kept secret all the while he'd helped her with her programming homework. His mouth opened and closed again, and she turned away, unable to bear his pity. She'd seen that look enough since her diagnosis. "At least wrap a scarf around your face. I mean, it must be really cold out, or you wouldn't be wearing a coat."

"It is," he said, sounding like he was under water. "That's a good idea." The door squeaked back open twice as loud as it had before, and Tiffany put hands over her ears.

"Tiff, will you be okay alone? I shouldn't be gone more than a couple hours."

"Yeah, I'll be fine," she lied, then turned and forced a smile, crossing her arms over her chest to keep them from touching her hair. "I think my meds are maybe starting to work." That was another lie, as one prescription bottle had been lost almost immediately while exiting Krista's place via her balcony and the other must have fallen out of her pocket sometime the day before in her race across campus.

He wrapped a black scarf around his brown face above a black ski coat that probably came from Goodwill, then picked up his laptop again. "Look at me, I'm a skinny black banana."

She recognized the reference from his favorite Three Stooges episode he'd showed her on YouTube after one of their tutoring sessions, and even though they'd laughed hysterically then, all she could manage now was a tiny smile. "Watch out for the fat, black dragon."

He gave her a thumbs up— "I promise" —then turned and opened the door. "Be sure to lock the door after I leave and don't stand near the windows." The whooshing sound in her head grew louder, making his words almost incomprehensible.

"I will, and I won't," she assured him, barely able to keep her composure.

When he left, she turned the lock on the door knob and flipped the bolt lock before fastening the chain. Leaning her head against the door, she craved a drink, but she knew Steve didn't have any alcohol. He said he didn't even like beer. She hadn't been much of a drinker before Brazil, but things change when you're trapped in a living nightmare. There had been some days when alcohol was the only way to shove the creature with six glowing eyes back into its cave.

She returned to the sofa where she'd spent the night. She'd barely slept, and she knew that was fueling what she felt coming on. Curling up on her side, she put a pillow over her head and prayed for the noise to stop. Instead, it formed into words.

Echoing words that mocked her, berated her, and scolded her for having feelings for Steve. Words that blamed her and shamed her for what happened to her in Brazil. Steve didn't return her feelings. It was all there in his eyes. So what did it matter if all of Pragnalysis went down the embezzling drain?

What about her mother, she argued. Her mother was innocent. So was her dad. The words disagreed. Her mother wouldn't listen to her. Her dad mocked her. Maybe they were in cahoots with Owens. Maybe they were hiding the money so Tiffany would inherit nothing. And if they didn't feel that way now, they soon would after they learned what Tiffany had done in Brazil.

She tried to focus on the numbers, but they were flying around in her head, pulsing red and blue and purple, clashing, and exploding. Then she heard the roar, and she had nothing left to fight with. The great beast appeared suddenly, leaping over the sofa, snarling.

It caught her arm with its sharp teeth and dragged her to the floor, tearing her skin from her body. Tiffany tried to push it back inside its cave but she was too weak. She opened her mouth to scream, but no words would come out. Time stood still as she fought the teeth and claws that tore at her. How could she be alive when blood was pouring out of her body?

A door slammed somewhere and voices called out. Tiffany blinked at Steve's refrigerator, covered in magnets and take-out menus. She'd made it to the kitchen. She looked down at the knife in her hand. She'd gotten it to kill the creature—to hack off its grasping arms with long sharp talons and plunge it into its heart—but lucidity had returned, bringing with it the knowledge that the creature was inside her head.

To kill the beast, she'd have to kill the host.

Chapter 13

Will crossed his arms over his chest, narrowing his eyes at the Pragnalysis receptionist. "Why didn't Tiffany report Owens?" He never understood why women put up with sexual harassment. Especially in the workplace.

"Evidently, he was also a friend of the family. I guess she didn't want to make waves, and Owens seemed to know that." Amy Reynolds took a sip of her coffee. "Tiffany was smarter than everyone gave her credit for. I think it was the artist thing. People put her in a box. Even her parents. She told me she had a gift for computer programming, but she flunked out of her high school classes because they were boring." She dipped her biscotti in her coffee. "Of course there was the whole schizophrenia thing, but she had that under control when she worked for us, as far as I could tell. She said she sometimes saw or heard things that other people didn't, but that, for the most part, she had learned to tell the difference between what was real and what was not." She bit off the soaked biscotti.

"Do you think she really could?" Dani asked with a healthy dose of skepticism in her voice.

Amy shrugged. "Who knows? I wasn't inside her head, but she was able to keep her job all summer." She sipped her coffee before saying, "And even a few hours a week after she started college. She had moved into accounting doing data entry by then. She said it was dull as dirt, but it kept her away from Owens."

Will lifted his cup, twigged it was empty and set it back down. "Did she ever talk about any men in her life? Men she *wanted* to be around?"

Her brow furrowed. “I assume you mean someone other than that asshole who drugged her and sold her out of the country.”

“Yeah,” Will acknowledged grimly. “Maybe someone before him.”

She shook her head. “No, not really. And I saw far less of her after she was at the university.”

“She never mentioned a… Steve Elway?”

Amy’s eyes lit up as she finished chewing the last of her biscotti. “Oh, yes, I do remember a Steve, but I think he was her tutor or something.” She looked to her own phone’s screen— “Sorry I can’t be of more help” —and pushed back from the table. “I’ve got a nail appointment in thirty minutes, and I’ll never make it if I don’t leave now.”

They exchanged phone numbers before she left, with Will wondering if they had learned anything of value at all. He reluctantly looked to Dani, hoping she wasn’t going to take them right back to the argument they’d been having before Amy arrived, but she was looking thoughtful.

“Didn’t Owens say that Tiffany was a glorified gofer? When do gofers do data entry?”

Will ran fingers back and forth in his short beard. “Yeah. Why not mention her work in accounting?”

She leaned in. “Maybe he didn’t want us talking to the people in accounting.”

Will couldn’t fathom why. “Maybe it just slipped his mind.”

Dani laughed. “That is almost assuredly not true.”

Will didn’t really think it was true either, but he had no explanation for him withholding details.

Dani at least had a theory. “Maybe he was trying to keep us away from anyone who might report on his less than professional behavior toward Tiffany. If it was as bad as Amy said, surely others saw some things.”

Will wrapped his hands around his now cold, empty mug. “As much as I find his harassment reprehensible, if he’s keeping us from talking to anyone who might know where she is when he knows about her medical condition… well, that’s lower still.”

“Definitely,” Dani agreed. “Especially when he acted all concerned for her well-being. How would we talk to them without going through Owens?”

Will picked up both their empty cups and made to stand. "Not sure, possum. Maybe Ms. Reynolds could help us set something up."

Dani pushed back from the table and followed suit, picking up the used napkins. "So what's next? Did you try calling Steve Elway again?"

Will started to move toward the exit. "Yeah, he's not answering. Probably screens his calls just like everyone else. I found him listed as a Teaching Assistant in Computer Technology in the University Faculty Directory." Dani grabbed her bag and followed.

He made a detour to place the mugs in the self-bussing tubs, and when he turned, she was holding the door open for him. He smiled at her willingness to serve as much as be served, and he saw Renae yet again.

His smile slid into a scowl as they walked back to their vehicle. Not at the memory, but at the fact that his brain seemed to be doing everything possible to keep Renae in the forefront of his mind all of a sudden. Renae's memory had been pulling at him hard ever since their carriage ride, leaving him feeling more guilty than he would have thought possible. He thought he was ready to move on and love again, but now he wasn't sure.

He also scowled at the frigid air that didn't seem to be getting any warmer and pulled his hat out of his pocket and over his much shorter hair.

Dani interrupted his thoughts as they neared the car. "So does he live on campus? Actually, since he's old enough to be a T.A., he probably has his own place. Did they have a picture in the directory? Could we maybe run into him if we hung out around the Computer Technology building?"

"There were no pictures in the campus info, and we wouldn't have much luck on a Saturday anyway." He pressed the button on the key fob to unlock the doors.

"Oh that's right," Dani said, opening her door. "The days are a complete jumble. Is it even still January?" she said throwing up her hands before getting in.

Will opened his own door and slid inside. "Last time I checked. We've got ten or eleven days left I think."

Dani seemed to be pretending their earlier disagreement never happened. He knew they'd have to return to it eventually, but for now, he was glad to be able to set it aside and concentrate on finding Tiffany.

"So did you search elsewhere for a picture of our man, Steve?"

Will nodded. "I think I found him on Facebook." He started the car and backed out. "There are a lot of Steve Elways in the world, but I found one working at the university who seemed to be about the right age. He's tall, thin, and black, with a big smile."

"Oh," Dani said with surprise in her voice. "I don't know why I had any picture in my head at all with just a name, but it definitely wasn't that."

Will chuckled as they reached the parking lot's exit. "What did you picture?"

"I don't know. Reddish auburn hair like Tiffany's, I guess."

"So Keith is blonde, I suppose."

Her forehead pinched. "Hmm, actually he is. My lack of imagination is disturbing."

Will laughed. "I guess I helped you break out of your box."

She laid her hand on his thigh, her voice going low. "You certainly did."

He shook his head, smiling. "You may not want to distract me while I'm driving. The drivers don't seem to be much better here than San Francisco, although they're a tad better than Rio."

She pulled her hand back and clasped them in her lap. "Heaven forbid I should distract you."

He made a right turn. "Just save it for later, sweetheart."

"Oh. Will there be a later where I can distract you? Or will you spend the evening in the gym, the shower, and your own lonely bed?"

He blew out a breath. "Any word from Keith?"

"No. He's ghosting me, I guess." She changed the subject. "How do private investigators find peoples' addresses? Or do you just Google them like the rest of us?"

"Well, we usually start there. It works for most."

"So have you done that yet?"

He nodded as he changed lanes for a left turn. "I did that last night when I… couldn't sleep." He pressed on quickly, shifting away from the topic of last night and listening to each other not sleeping. "I've got an address to check out that's close to campus."

"Oh! Why didn't we go there first?"

"If I'd known the receptionist was going to be late, we would have, but I didn't want to risk missing her." He stopped for a red light. "I guess it wasn't a complete waste of time."

She nodded. "Not only did we discover that Owens is 'sheepy,' as you say, we also learned that Tiffany was remarkably normal before her abduction, which doesn't line up with either Owens' or her father's assessments."

Will pondered that for a moment. "Hmm. I don't know about Owens, but her father may just have higher expectations. She may still seem different to him. Her friend Krista seemed to think that Tiffany's meds weren't a perfect fix for her. Although she, like Reynolds, also mentioned that the girl had some method for bridging the gap and discerning reality." She glanced to Dani with a thin smile. "That doesn't mean she didn't seem different to her own oldies."

"Maybe," she mused, "but I sure would like to ask her about it."

"You and me both. Especially if that means we're in the same room with the sheila, and she's not running."

The light turned green, and in a half block, he was turning into the parking garage across from the Moxy. "Why are we stopping here?"

"I uh… I need to use the dunny before we go."

He parked, and she unbuckled. "The dunny?"

"The American equivalent would be the john, I guess," he clarified.

"Oh! Okay. Another new word to add to the list."

Will felt guilty again. Although he really did need to use the dunny, he was also hoping to talk Dani into staying there while he went to check out Steve Elway's apartment. They still didn't know why that scrub-headed turkey had been chasing Tiffany, and just how dangerous the man was. He may have stumbled onto the same information they had and was now ahead of them rather than behind. When Will wasn't able to carry a gun, he'd feel better if Dani was safe in their hotel while he checked out Elway's place.

"Are you just going to use the lobby's *dunny*? Shall I just wait here?"

Will hadn't expected that. "Oh… it's… too cold. Just come on in. I need something from the room anyway." He'd have to come up with what that might be on the way up. As they approached the wall of windows on the front of the hotel, a man rose from a seat in the lobby, and Dani stopped and stared.

"Oh no," she said barely above a whisper. "It's Keith."

* * *

As soon as Dani saw Keith, she knew she wouldn't be going with Will to Steve Elway's apartment. Will couldn't afford to wait for her to break up with Keith, and she owed the man at least one more decent conversation before she said goodbye for good.

After an awkward moment where Keith refused to shake hands with the man she'd walked in with, Will looked to her, the question of whether she wanted him to go or stay clearly in his eyes. "You better just go," she said softly, and he gave a small nod, turning and heading out without using the bathroom at all. She couldn't blame him. This wasn't going to be pretty.

She focused back on Keith, who really did look a few pounds lighter than when she'd left for Brazil three weeks ago. His face held a weary desperation that didn't bode well for an easy chat, and she couldn't believe that he'd dropped everything to fly to Denver. "Shall we sit down?"

He looked back to where a number of people were chatting in the space that felt more like a coffee shop than a hotel lobby. "Here?" He faced her again with a kind of sarcastic disbelief. "A bit of privacy might be nice. Why don't we just go up to—"

"No, that wouldn't be good." The last thing she wanted to do was take him up to a room she was sharing with Will. She thought up a quick excuse. "It's probably about time for housecleaning." She pointed down the hall. "There's a little self-serve food nook that might be empty this late in the morning."

He scooped up his coat from where he'd been sitting, and she started down the hall with him behind her, her heart taking up a rapid-fire rhythm. Dear God she hated break ups.

The space was deserted, so she led him to the end of a long table and sat. He shoved his coat onto the chair beside him, but Dani left hers on. She hoped this wouldn't take long. They sat and shared a few tense moments where neither knew what to say. Dani didn't need to ask why he was there. She knew that. She decided to just start with the worst—an apology. She took in a breath, but he beat her to the punch.

"I'm so sorry Dani," he said with what seemed like sincerity. "I was a jerk about Rita going missing."

"Oh. Well. I appreciate that but—"

"I'm not done. I was self-centered, unsympathetic, and just plain horrible." He reached for her hand, and Dani, lost in the puzzle of did he get the pictures of her and Will or not, didn't pull it back. "I promise to do better—be better—in the future. Can you ever forgive me?"

This was not the conversation she expected to have with the man. She thought of the way he'd stiffed Will over the handshake. He had to know about them. She looked to their hands and slowly began to pull hers away. "It won't do any good to pretend that nothing's happened. I know I told you a few days ago that I wasn't here for Will—and I wasn't—but—"

"Don't say it, Dani. If you can forgive me, I can forgive you. We can start again. You've just been through a traumatic event with a stranger. That's basic Psychology 101. You bonded somehow because of it, but you've known him, what? A week? Two? What do you even know about the man. We've got eight months of history together."

It was hard to argue that point, but it was also hard to believe she and Will had only known each other for a week and a half. They'd been through so much together in that time, it felt much longer. She struggled to form a reasonable argument that wouldn't sound like a love-sick teen with a crush on someone she just met. "I know I haven't known Will long, but I was drawn to his heart almost from the beginning. I mean, he rescues people out of slavery and forced prostitution. He—"

"Ah, there it is," Keith interrupted.

Dani couldn't help her irritation. "What do you mean?"

"You've just fallen for what he does—you think that's your new purpose. And your mixed-up emotions—"

"My emotions are not mixed up, Keith! Yes, I love what he does, but I've found that I love the man who does them even more."

Keith snorted in derision. "It's not possible to 'love' him after a such a short time, Dani. You're just infatuated with that Australian accent and a bit of adventure."

She blinked at him. "You said you loved me from the first moment you saw me. Was that a lie?"

Keith turned pink as he sputtered, "Well, that's really just something you say…" Her eyebrows rose, and he pushed on. "I mean, people say that to mean they were attracted from the beginning. They aren't really 'in love.' Love at first sight is an illusion."

While Dani was inclined to agree, she was happy to let Keith squirm under her gaze. She hadn't been particularly attracted to Will at first glance. She had been pulled to his heart once she saw it in operation. The rest of him had grown on her with every shared moment. She knew it was time to say hard things. "I'm sorry, Keith, but I've seen things in you over the last couple of weeks that I don't like, and I don't think I can live with, and even if I never connected with Will, I was probably going to return your ring and get my life back on track."

"So pulling you out of that dump of a business was somehow pulling you off track."

She felt the slap of that insult, and her jaw dropped. "Yes, Keith, it may have looked like a dump to you, but I had poured my soul into that place, and when I closed the doors for an easier life, I left my soul behind. I think I've been looking for it ever since."

"Dani, please, just—"

"No, Keith, you need to listen to me. I had stars in my eyes when a good-looking rich man started paying attention to me, and I let you sweep me into your world. I admit, I enjoyed it for a while. Heck, I loved not having to worry about money every waking minute, but what I discovered in Brazil is that some things are more important than financial security. A purpose has infinite worth."

Keith's pink face was turning red. "It's obvious that man has… has… beguiled you in some way with that fakey Australian bit. He's taken you in, but he can't give you what I can." He reached across the table to grip her upper arm. "I love you, Dani."

Dani felt her feathers ruffle. She didn't know where to begin to dismantle all the untruths in that discourse. *Time to end this.* "Keith, I know you hired someone to follow us and take pictures. Does your apology include that as well?"

He sat back slowly. "I needed to know what was going on out here. I—"

"Then you should have answered your phone when I called!" Dani forced a few deep breaths. "I've known for three weeks now," she began again slowly, "that things between us weren't good, but I thought I needed to give you another chance. So even though I started to have feelings for—"

"Don't say it!" He sat back, his tired eyes flaming. She watched with wide eyes as he attempted to rein in his anger, forcing a very unconvincing smile. "He's hypnotized you, sweetheart. Can't you see that? He's just a nobody with an accent."

Dani had had enough. This was still another side of him she'd never seen before. Another side she didn't like. She pushed back from the table. "I'm sorry that things didn't work out for us, and I'm sorry for the way you found out about Will and me, but you and I are through." She dug through her purse until she found her wallet and pulled out Keith's credit card. "Here, this belongs to you. It might take me a while, but I promise I'll pay you back for everything I spent while in Brazil, and even the flight." He picked it up and stared at it, looking as if he might cry. She pressed on. "Wait right here, and I'll go get your ring."

She rose and took a step, but he grabbed her wrist. "You need to give me another chance, Dani. Just tell me what to do to win you back. I'll do anything."

She turned, calling his bluff. "Drop out of the congressional race."

His shocked expression and subsequent silence told her all she needed to know. She pulled her hand free and walked briskly through the room and down the hall, bypassing the elevators to take the stairs. She needed both the exercise and the exertion to blow off steam. The whole round trip didn't take more than ten minutes, but Keith wasn't where she'd left him when she got back.

She looked around the lobby and even walked around the building but didn't see him anywhere. She looked down at the little black box in her hand and cursed the man who wouldn't let her make a clean break.

Chapter 14

Will glanced around as he walked to the address he'd given to the cab driver. He'd seen no sign of Mr. Ugly Tree, but it never hurt to be cautious—especially when he had no idea what the man was about. So he'd cut across back lots near the hotel and was hoofing it a couple of blocks to get picked up.

A cold wind whipped around the building as he turned a corner, and he tugged his stocking cap down farther over his ears. God in heaven, he hated this Colorado weather. It made him wish he'd never trimmed his overgrown beard or let Dani talk him into a haircut. His feet beat out a rhythm on the sidewalk as he recalled the new sparkle that had shown in her eyes when the salon stylist had spun his chair around to get her approval. *All right,* he admitted to himself, *I'd do it again for that look.*

Last night with her in the other bed had been torture. *Thank God she's finally settling things with Bisbee.* As much as he'd been beating himself up for losing his concentration on the job, he did not want to lose her. She already felt a part of him.

His protective instincts had wanted to watch over her while she said goodbye to Keith, but he knew breakups were best done alone. She'd never given him any indication that she was afraid of Keith, so he tucked his mother hen nature away and let her handle it. She was a strong woman, and Keith...

Will realized he actually knew very little about the man except that he was "well to do," as Dani had put it, and that he was running for political office. She had avoided talking about him before that surprise kiss in the elevator, and Will had neglected to ask any questions after. All he had cared about was that the ring was off. A smile pulled at his lips. *And only a complete nilwit asks about an ex in bed.*

With his blond hair, blue eyes and pleasant face, Will doubted Bisbee had trouble turning women's heads, and with money, he probably could have his pick. Add on political ambition, and he became a regular chick magnet. Will wondered why the man hadn't been snatched up before now. He must have some deficiencies if a nowhere-near-rich Aussie P.I. with average looks can win out over all that Bisbee had going on. *It can't just be the accent.*

His thoughts went back to their night of revelation—their bodies entangled and moving together as one, their hidden thoughts and feelings emerging and blooming like a flower in the dessert. Her eyes had held his with trust. Her hands had caressed him with the gentle promises of the future. And her words—when she'd used words—were all about the pull of his caring heart. *Ole Keith must have a few deficits in that area.*

He had no delusions about Dani's relationship with Bisbee—it sounded as if she'd been living with him, so of course she was sharing his bed—but he hoped somehow it wasn't the same—that what he and Dani shared was different and special.

Once again, Renae was as close as his frosty breath, reminding him that he had loved her with his very soul. That he would have gladly given his life to save hers. Was it possible to love two in one lifetime with that kind of love?

Would Renae let him?

He shook his head as he reached his destination, trying to free his brain of both women so he could concentrate on what he needed to do and how he needed to do it. Pulling out his phone, he checked the app for the cab company, hoping he wouldn't be standing in the freezing wind for long.

* * *

Steve was having a difficult time concentrating on the dull-as-dust staff meeting. *Yeah, thanks for telling us every detail of the snow removal issues. Could have been sent in a memo.* And he had not a care about meal vouchers for visiting professors. *I'm barely getting paid, dude. I bet they can afford a meal.*

His mind wandered back to Tiffany's expression right before he left and the passion with which she seemed to care about his safety. Did she have a crush on him? He relived the moment he recognized her on campus—the sheer relief that he felt knowing she was okay. He realized his heart was pounding, and it wasn't due to the rising cost of paper products.

Of course he'd appreciated her beauty from the first moment he'd laid eyes on her—what male in his right mind wouldn't—but he'd never considered there could be anything between them. Had he just been trained by the culture to "stick with his own kind?" *This is the 21st century, for Pete's sake. Mixed race relationships aren't news.*

He considered their age difference. She was barely twenty; he was twenty-seven. She just started on her bachelors; he was a grad student. Did that matter? She'd always seemed older than her years. He breathed out a sigh, knowing any real reticence on his part came from her mental condition—the schizophrenia.

That was a biggie.

He had an aunt who suffered with the affliction, which is probably why he was more understanding with Tiffany than some of the others. It was why he hadn't pulled away or put up walls when he found out. But there was a big difference between befriending someone with a serious mental issue and getting romantically involved with one. And now she had gone through some kind of kidnapping. There had to be trauma associated with that even if she wouldn't talk about it. Even if she was pretending she was okay.

So intent was Steve on the topic of Tiffany, that it took a few moments to realize that her name was being spoken from the front of the room.

"What she went through was a tragedy, but it has only served to spur us on to greater campus security for our students and an education that includes the warning signs of dangerous relationship red flags. Tiffany is still considered a missing person by the police as she has not gone home and even gave those bringing her home the slip. I can't discuss the reasons as to why she is considered a person at risk, but please, if anyone sees her, call Campus Security."

Her picture from the university directory was projected on the screen along with the number to call, and Steve hoped no one could see his big secret all over his face. Tiff always said his expressions were like "reading the book of Steve." He thought about how he had been completely unaware of any feelings she might have for him. She was as good at hiding as he was bad at it.

At long last, the meeting was wrapped up with an announcement of a policy change that would lead to a committee to discuss the politically correct verbiage to include in the student handbook, and he was slipping back into his coat to go out again. He hadn't seen the guy that Dani referred to as the "fat dragon" on the way to campus, but he didn't want to take any chances. He took a moment to wrap the scarf around the lower half of his face.

A slap on his shoulder had him turning to find Prof. Thomson, a professor in the computer department. "What's this? Steve Elway is actually dressed for the weather?"

Steve laughed and pulled down the scarf to speak. "It's still not Lake Michigan cold, but I hate to flaunt my ability to withstand the single digits in front of the older set."

This time Thomson laughed. "Be careful, Elway, or I'll give your classes to Amal."

If Steve didn't need the money, he'd let Amal have them. It would give him more time to work on Tiffany's Pragnalysis embezzlement claims. He had a comeback on his lips that froze with the remembrance of her offer of half-a-mil to help her break through Pragnalysis security. "You know what?" he shifted. "I really could use next week off if he wants to step in. I've had some… family business come up that I should take care of."

Thomson looked suddenly sober. "Nothing serious, I hope."

He shrugged. "Serious, but not deadly." At least he hoped that was the case. Embezzlers were probably not Sunday School teachers.

"I'll give him a call this afternoon and let you know. Just the week?"

Steve nodded, hoping that would do. "Yeah, I think so. I really appreciate it."

Thomson nodded, and the two walked together out of the conference room and the building, chatting about some of their more challenging students. "Hey," Thomson said as they both headed toward the parking lot, "weren't you a tutor for that Morrow girl?"

Steve swallowed and pulled his scarf back up. "Yeah, she was struggling, but she had quizzed out of the lower-level classes."

"Hell of a deal to be sold to a Brazilian brothel."

Steve blinked. "A what? A brothel?"

Thomson hit the button on his key fob, and the lights blinked on the man's car. "That's what I heard, although it could just be a rumor."

Thomson said a final goodbye before getting in his vehicle, and Steve walked to his car, feeling sucker punched. He sat a moment in the cold car, Thomson's words going around again. He shook his head, suddenly angry with himself. *What did you think happened to beautiful women who were kidnapped, Steve? They usually end up dead or trafficked.*

Sexually trafficked.

He ground his teeth as he started his car. Tiffany hadn't been the only one pretending she was okay. He'd been doing it ever since she'd gone missing.

* * *

Tiffany was trembling as the knife clattered to the kitchen floor. For now, the monster that looked like her worst nightmare was gone.

She walked on shaky legs back to the living room and the patio door. She needed some air, but she didn't dare go outside. Carefully parting the vertical slats a smidge, she peeked out, scanning the area. There was no sign of the fat dragon, which didn't give her any sense of relief. If he wasn't here, he could be following Steve. She fingered the trac phone Steve had bought her the day before in the pocket of her sweater, tempted to just send a little text to make sure he was okay.

That thought fled as a yellow cab parked near the sidewalk, and a man got out that she recognized. *Will.*

Stepping back quickly, she let the slat fall back in place and thought about her options should he knock on Steve's door. She decided the best plan was to sit tight. Will probably had the same old information about Steve's address as the fat dragon. And even if he did knock on the door, she doubted that he would try to break in, and if he was that persistent, Tiffany would know exactly where he was and could go out the patio door and do what she always did—run.

She circled the small space several times, her arms folded over her chest, before stopping in front of the large screen TV mounted on the wall, staring at her reflection in the black. "How did Will make the connection between me and Steve without seeing us together?" she muttered aloud. "Are they giving out that much information in the university records office?"

She began to circle the room again, this time giving in to the compulsion to put hands to her hair. Once he found out from the people upstairs that Steve hadn't lived there for a few weeks, he'd dig deeper. How long until he figured it out? She supposed that depended on how good of a detective he was. She stopped and stared, this time at a movie poster on the opposite wall. "Well, he did find me in Brazil."

Moving to the patio blinds once more, she risked another look, and her heart leapt at the sight of Steve heading up the walk. She sucked in a breath as Will's backside came into view from around the building walking straight toward her friend. Will slowed as Steve came closer, and Tiffany knew that her "skinny black banana" had been recognized.

She ran across the room to the closet and pulled out her coat, sliding it on as she went out the door. Crossing under the stairs, she made her way quickly to the other side of the building while Will was tied up talking to Steve. She hoped he wouldn't just say, "Sure, I've got Tiffany in my apartment. Come on in!" and would stall just a bit, even if his honest face would never be able to keep the secret for long. A voice in her head was second guessing her decision to run from Will yet again, but she had no choice; she didn't know if she could trust him.

She paused a moment, scanning the landscape, wondering where she could hide until he was gone.

* * *

Even though the man approaching Will had done a fair job of disguising his face with the scarf, hood, and sunnies, Will could still tell he was a tall, thin, black man. Maybe Steve Elway hadn't moved out of the complex—just the upstairs apartment. Will smiled and tipped his chin. "G'day, Steve."

A mumbled hello came from below the scarf as he passed by.

Will's smile only grew with the response, and he walked on a few more steps before looking over his shoulder. The man turned into the alcove before the stairs, meaning his apartment was behind one of the two doors under the stairs. He walked carefully back that direction, and found no sign of him in the alcove when he got there. *Now which door.*

The door on the left led to an apartment with a patio that viewed the parking lot. If Tiffany was in that one looking out, she had surely seen him arrive. If she was in the one on the right, she probably didn't have a clue he was anywhere around. If she had been watching, she easily had time to slip out while he was talking to the tenants on the 3rd floor.

Determined to not be outmaneuvered again, he backed up and pondered how to have a look around without being seen out any windows. A wall at the back of the property might provide him cover if he could find a way to the other side.

He didn't have to backtrack far to get around it to a sidewalk along the street. Jogging to the other end, he began to make his way across the back of Elway's building from the other direction, glad that the icy wind had died down. Now it was merely cold, not frigid.

Movement near some bushes caught his eye, and he stopped. If it wasn't Tiffany, it was someone with hair just like hers. Someone hiding in the bushes. She was obviously expecting him to be coming from the other direction. He approached slowly, now wishing he had Dani here to herd her his way while he hid behind a bush of his own.

He wasn't more than twenty feet away when she turned, leaving him no option but to make a plea. "Tiffany, don't run! I'm here to help you!"

His admonitions fell on deaf ears, and she took off. Will gave chase, following her as she turned right at the end of the building and headed toward the parking lot, even though he knew he didn't have a chance in hell of catching her.

She quickly outdistanced him, but near the end of the lot, a large, dark figure charged out from between the vehicles, and although Tiffany tried to run around him, he got a hold on her arm.

Mr. Ugly Tree.

Even though he was wearing a stocking cap on his bald head this time, Will had no doubt it was him. Will saw him drag her back the way he'd come, fighting him all the way, but the petite woman was no match for the beefy man's strength.

With bursting lungs, Will put an extra kick in his sprint, catching up with them as the bastard turned from pushing her into the back seat of a dark blue mid-size car. As Will dodged a punch, he saw that Tiffany was handcuffed to the grab handle inside.

Will backed up, daring the guy to come out into the open. Instead, he closed the door on Tiffany and moved to the driver's door. Will went back at him— "Oh, no you don't, ya mongrel!" —and shoved him beyond the door. "You're not taking her anywhere!"

The man spun with a gun in hand, and Will leaped and rolled over the hood of the car parked next to him. Ducking down on the other side, he took several steps as he unzipped his coat and reached for a Glock that wasn't there. The Denver gun laws had bitten him in the butt after all.

He heard the car door opening, and he frantically looked around for anything he could use as a weapon. An empty beer bottle wasn't much, but it was all he had. Springing up, he threw it as hard as he could at the man getting in.

It hit his shoulder, and the man yelled out as he brought his other arm around, firing through the car, shattering windows and barely missing Will.

Squatting down again, he made his way to the back of the car, stopping for some idiot driver zooming through the lot like it was a Nascar track, then slamming on the brakes to come to a sliding stop right in front of him. The dark face of the driver turned to look at Will, eyes full of panic. Steve Elway had just blocked Tiffany's kidnapper from backing out.

That kidnapper wasn't about to be deterred by Steve's junker, however, and rammed it. Will yelled for Elway to get out, then heard sirens. Someone watching from an apartment had evidently called the cops.

The man pulled his car forward, and Steve crawled out the other side, coming around but staying low to squat next to Will with wide eyes. "What do we do?"

Will didn't answer due to the squeal of tires and crunch of metal, this time pushing the car a good ten centimeters. "He won't get out before the cops get here." He put a hand to Steve's shoulder. "Good onya, mate."

"Why were you chasing her?" Elway asked as the guy pulled forward again. "Are you the man that brought her back?"

Will nodded. "Will Yarnel, Private I. I don't mean her any harm, and I won't even take her home if—"

He cut himself off when he heard a door banging into the car they were hiding behind. Will cautiously peered over it. Mr. Ugly Tree had obviously heard the sirens too and was making a run for it. Despite being armed and proven to be dangerous, Will could not let him get away. "Stay with Tiffany," he threw back at Steve, staying low and moving as quickly as he could through the parked cars.

The overweight man jogged the distance from the center lot parking and through the vehicles on the side of the lot. Will followed, stopping and crouching a moment behind the cars to watch the man's path. He was making his way diagonally across the lawn, obviously not wanting to be exposed to the street and the approaching black and whites. Will followed behind the row of parked cars, staying with him. He watched him head between two buildings, slower now, and as soon as Will saw which way he turned at the end, he sprang up and sprinted around the building from the other side, hoping to catch him unaware.

As he neared the corner, he looked around for something he could use as a weapon, moving decisively when he spied a nearly empty firewood rack on a nearby patio. Dumping off the few sticks of wood, he picked up the heavy, metal rack by the side poles and carried it to the corner of the building to wait. It wasn't long before he heard the panting, large man, and Will tilted it, gripping the poles, estimating the strength he'd need to utilize it.

The man's beady eyes peered around the corner, and Will swung the rack with a power yell, propelling it and himself around the corner of the building. The man in black was slammed into the wall, his gun shooting wild as he stumbled sideways, and Will sent a frantic prayer heavenward that it hadn't hit an innocent bystander.

The fat man hit the ground with an "oof," and Will planted the heavy rack on top of him, pinning him to the ground. The wincing man with blood running down the side of his head aimed the gun at Will again, and Will grabbed his wrist while putting a knee on the rack. The man's eyes bulged as his grip weakened, and Will pulled the gun from his hand.

"Drop your weapon and put your hands on your head!" sounded behind him, and Will tossed the gun out of the kidnapper's reach, taking his weight off his chest as he did. Turning slowly, he found two coppers with their guns trained on him. "I'm a private investigator—Will Yarnel. I helped stop this man from kidnapping Tiffany Morrow back at that demolition derby in the parking lot."

They seemed to be unimpressed. "Please move away from the man on the ground," one of them projected loudly his direction.

"Gladly." Will moved a good three meters away, his hands still on his head.

One patted him down while the other checked on the man he'd sent to the dirt, tipping the firewood rack off of him. He didn't move, and Will started to worry. The jack paused a few moments then squatted down to pick up a limp wrist. Rising, he spoke into the radio on his shoulder. "Yeah, we're gonna need an ambulance. Probably the coroner."

Will closed his eyes, his chin dropping with a breath blown out as his hands were pulled in front of him and cuffed.

Chapter 15

Tiffany and Steve were giving their statements to a police officer when Tiffany noticed Will being escorted back to the parking lot, handcuffed. Despite the fact that she had been trying to avoid him for days, and that there was a large, ugly creature watching her from the shadows, breathing flames out with each exhaled breath, she couldn't let that stand. "Excuse me a minute," she threw at their officer, then jogged over to the waiting squad car. "Sir, there must be a mistake. This man saved me from being kidnapped."

"That may be," he said, opening the back, "but there's a dead man back there. We're going to have to go by the book."

She looked to Will in surprise. "Dead? The black dragon's dead?"

Will nodded grimly, then narrowed his eyes. "The black dragon, huh? So you know who he is?"

"Inside," the policeman interrupted.

"No," she admitted as Will made to get in the back of the car, and the cop pushed on his head like he was a child. "That's just what he looked like to me. Sometimes my brain changes what I—"

"Miss," the policeman interrupted. "I need you to go back to officer Laird."

Tiffany's temper was swiftly lit. "Do you have any idea who I am? Or who he is?" All her guilt for running from the man who had rescued her out of a disgusting Brazilian brothel suddenly came to the surface. She'd had to give her name already. There was no hiding now. "I'm Tiffany Morrow."

The man quirked an eyebrow, and his mouth formed an "O," but Tiffany wasn't done yet. "And this man rescued me from slavery in the Amazon, so give him some respect."

The beast crawled out with measured steps, staring, waiting to spring. Its crinkly wings expanded. Tiffany's heart was in her throat, but she turned and stared it down. Could she send it away this time, or would it take her to the ground in front of everyone here? It leapt, and she roared, startling both men. It dissipated in mid-jump.

She looked back to their stunned faces, knowing she'd just killed any chance she had at credulity, but damn that felt good. She'd handled that mutant dragon in Brazil; she could handle it here.

The police officer took a step back. "Talk to him all you want, Miss."

Will jumped in first, ignoring what could only be seen as bizarre behavior. "I'm right stoked to know getting you out of that brothel was something you appreciated, but I gotta ask—why did you run? Your parents just—"

"My parents will put me under lock and key, and I just can't have that right now." She couldn't explain the details in front of the cop. "I've got too much to do."

Will gave her a concerned smile. "I know you've lost some time, but—"

"Oh I've lost more than time, Will." She couldn't think about that if she wanted the beast to stay in its cave. She focused on the future. "And I'll lose a lot more if I go home right now."

He spread his handcuffed hands in his lap. "Tell me about it."

She gave a side eye to the cop, then a tiny shake of the head to Will. "Can't."

Will licked his lips, looking thoughtful. "Well, you two shouldn't stay here. It's not safe. If Mr. Ugly Tree knew you were here, you can bet whoever he was working for knows."

"Mr. Ugly Tree?"

He smirked. "Your black dragon is our Mr. Ugly Tree." Steve appeared at her side. "I'm serious, though," Will went on, looking between them, "you two pack a bag and head back to the Moxy and find Dani. 'By the book' means that they're going to have to take me to the station until they look through your statements, my documents, and verify that the gun isn't mine. It's a pain in the arse, but I should be out in a couple hours."

Tiffany pondered this new proposition. Could she really trust them? Ignoring her roar to no one meant he knew about the schizophrenia.

"I promise you we won't make you go home," he said, "but maybe we can help with whatever else is going on here."

She still hesitated, unable to read his sincerity and unwilling to put herself in what might turn out to be a trap.

Will wouldn't give up. "Tiffany, when I told you I wouldn't take you home the first time, did I break my promise?"

She slowly shook her head as the cop moved toward them, butting in again. "If you won't be safe here, Officer Laird can transport you anywhere you need to go."

Her hand went to her wrist that was still sore from pulling on the handcuff. "All right," she finally conceded.

Will gave her a reassuring smile. "It's going to be okay. You've got a team now."

Steve's hand pressed gently to her back, bringing a sudden rush of tears to her eyes. *A team.* It had been a long time since she'd been a part of a group that she felt was totally on her side. She looked up at Steve, who was looking down at her with something she'd never seen before. Of course, in her current mental state, she couldn't really trust that what she was seeing was true, but she'd savor it nonetheless.

* * *

Will had a lot to think about on the way to the cop shop. First, he was amazed at the change in Tiffany from their exhausting flight back. She almost seemed completely normal. Well, he would have said that if it weren't for that bizarre roar aimed at the bushes. Still the difference over a few days ago was significant.

Second, even though he was grateful that Mr. Ugly Tree hadn't gotten away with Tiffany or put a hole in his head, he was still pissed off that the man was dead. There was so much red tape involved when a P.I. injured somebody, and knocking them completely off their perch could waste half the day at the police station. He didn't want to think about it, but all it would take is having the wrong man in charge at the time—someone who didn't appreciate a private investigator from another state, for instance—and he could land in jail until Logan could bail him out.

And then there was the fact that he couldn't question the man—couldn't find out why he was after Tiffany or who he was working for.

Will didn't feel any guilt for the man's death—not an ounce of grief. He'd been in this business too long for that. Men who tried to abduct women didn't deserve his grief. This man was a hired hunter—probably a killer. His was a life wasted, but he'd waste no one else's life now.

His mind turned to Renae—a life wasted by a bullet from a man who considered himself to be "just enforcing the law" when a protest had turned ugly. Life could be short and well-lived or long and a complete waste of time. Personally, he hoped for long and well-lived, but no one really knew.

He'd been right there when she'd fallen beside him—gone before she'd hit the ground—and without warning, their future together had shrunk from infinity to none, with no more time to say the right words or do all the things they'd planned.

Time wasn't a promise the universe gave us. Anyone still breathing had an opportunity to use whatever time they had to do what they loved most. That's what Renae had done. And that's what Dani wanted to do.

With him.

Are you going to give her less of a chance than you gave to Renae to stand by your side, even if it's risky?

Losing her had nearly killed him.

He leaned his head back and stared at the ceiling of the squad car. He didn't have an answer yet, but he knew he'd have plenty of time to think about it while the cops processed the paperwork on the man he'd sent to the morgue.

* * *

Tiffany and Steve walked briskly across campus toward J-Mac as the sunlight was fading over the mountains, hoping to slip into her room without being noticed. She had turned down the cop's offer of a ride when they found that Steve's car, though dented on the side, still ran.

Steve had wanted to drive her to the hotel like Will had suggested, but she couldn't without knowing if she was operating with all pistons firing or not. Her room would tell her if her memories were real or imagined. And she really did need the meds that she hoped were still there.

The spare key was where she'd hidden it, jammed behind the door frame, although it took Steve's jack knife to pry it out. Taking a deep breath, she turned the door knob and pushed in. It felt like an eternity since she'd been there, concerned with homework, art projects, and trying to fit into college life when her brain sometimes fought her for reality.

"Are you… going in?" Steve's voice behind her shook her out of her thoughts, and she realized that she had stopped just inside the door.

She blinked and went straight to the corner of the room by the closet and squatted down. She tried to pry up the carpet but couldn't get a hold on the short pile. She looked over her shoulder to a silent but obviously curious Steve. "Let me have your knife again."

He dug it back out of his pocket. "You keep your meds under the rug?"

She took it and pointed across the room. "They should be in that nightstand drawer."

While he walked that way, she nervously used the knife to pry up the edge of the carpet, pulling it and the pad beneath it back a foot from the corner. There was nothing there. She yanked it farther but still found nothing.

Rising and going to her desk, her heart was pounding as she pulled open the drawer and pawed through the contents. She remembered the white notecard clearly. It couldn't have been just her own paranoid mind making it up. Could it? And if she made that up, what else had her defective brain dreamed up? The whole embezzlement? Downloading the evidence? Working for Pragnalysis?

Steve held out the pill bottles. "Here are your meds. What are you looking for, Tiff?"

She barely heard him as she moved to another corner of the room, using the knife to pull up the carpet there. Finding nothing, she crawled into the closet to do the same in there. The numbers started to go around in her head. *I didn't make it up. I couldn't have made it up!*

Steve squatted down behind her. "Tiff…"

She turned, feeling tears forming. "I am a basketcase, Steve. It's not here. And I remember it so clearly."

Taking the knife from her hand on the floor, he folded it closed, then rose. "Come on." She got up off the floor, and he waved her over to the bed. He sat, and she sat beside him, feeling hopeless. "What do you remember?" he asked calmly. "Something you put under the rug."

She nodded slowly, unable to look at him. She should have never contacted him until she was sure. She should have waited until her meds had brought her mental function back to what it was before. Now he would never look at her with anything but pity.

She stood. "Let's just go."

His surprise was evident. "Where?"

"I may as well go home."

"Home, as in your parents' home? I thought you couldn't— What about the embezzling? Pragnalysis?" She moved out of the room and into the hall, and Steve closed the door, making sure it was locked. "Why not stay here in your dorm room and get back into classes?"

She stopped at a water fountain and held out her hand. Steve knew what she wanted and placed the pill bottles there. She opened each and popped the pills, chasing them with a slurp of water from the fountain. Then she held up the bottles. "It'll take a couple of weeks to… to find a world without dragons" —she turned and shoved them deep into her coat pockets this time, so they wouldn't fall out— "or monsters or created memories."

He fell into step beside her. "What did you hide under the rug?"

She didn't look at him, afraid of what she'd see in his expression. "The account number where they were hiding the stolen money, but it wasn't there, so…"

A group of girls came out of a room, laughing and chatting about their Saturday night plans, so they moved silently down the rest of the hall and through the lobby. Once they were outside, Steve began again. "So you think you made it up."

Tiffany nodded in the dark. "Yeah, it's the only thing that makes sense."

"You know what doesn't make sense?" They turned onto the sidewalk that would take them to the parking lot and Steve's poor, old car. "Your fat, black dragon. Why was he after you?"

She blinked. In her cyclone of thoughts, she'd almost forgotten about him. "I don't know. Maybe he was a pal of McCain."

"How would McCain even know you were back? I don't think he was released on bail. He was considered a flight risk."

Tiffany deliberated as they walked. She allowed her thoughts to turn to Brazil for just a moment. While there were men who had claimed her as their favorite "wildcat," she doubted that any of them would know where she lived. She couldn't see how this new kidnapper could have anything to do with them.

They reached the car, and she waited while he unlocked it and crawled through the passenger side. The driver's side was too crunched to open. "I don't know what that guy was about," she admitted, getting in after he cleared her seat. "Do you really think I'm not crazy then?"

Steve laughed. "The jury may be out on that one, but you didn't make up that man who grabbed you and handcuffed you to his car, and would have driven off with you. That was real. And there has to be some explanation for his persistence. He wasn't after just any pretty woman. He wanted you."

Tiffany felt buoyed by his words. "You think I'm pretty?"

Steve looked at her with comical surprise that even she could read quite clearly as he backed out of the parking space. "Of course I think you're pretty. Only a blind man would say you weren't." He stopped before pulling out onto the street. "So where to ma'am? Until we get this figured out, I can't go back to my place. That P.I. really seemed to want to help you, Tiff. Maybe we should trust him."

Tiffany caught the word “we.” She had dragged Steve into this and couldn’t just abandon him when it may not be safe for him to go back to his apartment.

“Okay,” she breathed out. “They’re at the Moxy in Cherry Creek.”

He turned out of the lot, and Tiffany hoped she was making the right decision.

Chapter 16

"Come on, Will, pick up!" Dani walked back and forth in front of the TV in their hotel room. It was getting dark, and even though she didn't want to be accused of being a "distraction," she had decided to call him and find out what the heck was going on.

Her call went to voicemail, and she let out a frustrated breath. "Dang it, Will, did you find Steve Elway or not?"

She went to the window and looked down, although she didn't know what she hoped to see. Their window didn't face the parking garage he usually parked in. And from the fourth floor, she didn't know if she'd be able to make Will out even if it were. *So is this how it will be?* she wondered. *If Will and I are a couple, will I just spend my life pacing the floor, worrying about him?*

She decided she needed to do something to relax, or she was going to come completely unglued. Getting down on the floor, she bent one leg in front of her, stretched the other out straight behind her, then leaned over until her forehead touched the carpet. *Why couldn't Keith have arrived a few minutes later, so I could have gone with Will?*

"Or," she said aloud, "why couldn't Will have just pulled into a fast food place to use their 'dunny,' then I would have missed Keith altogether."

She knew that probably wasn't true. Keith would still have been waiting when they got back, even more peeved with the man responsible for her absence.

As she pushed into the burn of her stretch, she felt all kinds of emotions concerning her ex-fiancé. She was still angry with his childish disappearing act that had negated her efforts to give back his ring, but he was right about the way things looked. She had only met Will eleven days ago.

Sometimes you just know.

Shifting to stretch the other leg, she scoured her memories for the way she had felt about Keith in the beginning. He was a good-looking guy, besides being rich, and when he'd called her after the charity auction, she had been flattered. He'd wined and dined and wooed her with charm and wit and what had seemed like caring, but looking back, a lot of that caring now felt like manipulation.

He had maneuvered her out of her business, her career choices, her education, her wardrobe, and even her apartment. The latter, she wasn't sorry to leave, but it had been the final tie to her old life.

Once in Keith's house, she became a part of his social whirlwind—parties and gatherings several nights a week where he tried to get his name out as running for Congress. Then it wasn't long before he had her planning their own events, meeting with power players in the city and the state.

And of course, there was a lot of shopping involved, Keith sparing no expense to fill her closet with the most stunning clothes she'd ever owned. It was like a fairytale. And she'd been swept away for a time.

Then Brazil happened.

Rita's disappearance, Dani's sudden education on human trafficking, and Keith's heartless communication had been like a bucket of ice water down her back, shocking her out of the frivolous life she'd been living the last eight months. Feeling hollowed out, she had vowed to live a life of purpose once again, which is how she ended up going undercover and helping Will find Tiffany.

And how the comparisons began. At nearly every turn, Will showed her what she wanted in a man and what was missing in Keith.

Shifting again, she did a cobra stretch, feeling more anxious than ever. Now that she was worried half out of her mind, she wondered sarcastically if Keith's predictable life might have been the better choice.

Sound at the door had her looking over her shoulder, and in another couple seconds, Will was walking in, looking wrung out.

"Will Yarnel," she scolded, scrambling up off the floor, "what have you been doing all afternoon? I called, but—"

He pulled her in, cutting off her rant with a fierce hug. Finally, his hold on her eased. "I know you've got questions, and I have at least a few answers, but first, did Tiffany and Steve show up here?"

"Tiffany and Steve? No! Did you see them today?"

Will blew out a breath as he leaned his forehead on hers. "I had hoped that she trusted me after I saved her again."

"What? Will, start at the beginning."

After shedding his coat and hanging it on a peg, he pulled down one of the folding canvas chairs and popped it out. She sat on the end of the bed, so he sat in the chair and begin filling her in on his eventful afternoon. She listened with wide eyes and a racing heart. What they had done in Brazil was obviously dangerous, but she hadn't been flat out in love with Will at the time. Suddenly, it all seemed different. She tried to focus on something other than the thought that Will could have been killed. "Wow, I can't believe that... Mr. Ugly Tree is dead."

"It turns out he was actually Charles Meisner. He had a number of outstanding arrest warrants in Florida."

"Florida? What the heck was he doing here?"

"That's the million-dollar question. And how is it he was targeting Tiffany from almost the moment we got her home?"

"If he wasn't here already, he would have been flying in at almost the same time we were. And why? None of this makes sense."

Will nodded. "Putting aside the 'why' for now, who knew she would be here?"

"Her parents, obviously."

"And the Pragnalysis crew seemed to be in the know by the time we got there, but who knows when they were first informed," Will added.

"The police department in Brazil knew our flight plans and destination," Dani brainstormed along with him, "but I can't imagine this Charles Meisner being connected to them, and why would they want Tiffany anyway? And if they did, they could have sent someone to the hospital in Rio Branco while we weren't around."

"Yeah," Will agreed," I think that's a dead end. "It had to be someone here."

"So why do you think Tiffany just won't trust us to help her?"

"I don't know. She…" Will hesitated, looking as though he were searching for words. "She's got more going on in her head right now than us."

"You mean the schizophrenia."

"Yeah."

"So are she and Steve a couple? Will he help her?"

"Well, he gave his car to save her this afternoon." Will chuckled. "Not that that rust bucket was gonna last too much longer anyway."

"So what do we do now? Charles—no, I can't call that horrible man Charles, as if he were going to have tea with the queen…" Her eyes lit up. "*Chuck* is dead, and the police will tell Tiffany's parents they've seen her and talked to her… What's left for us to do?"

"Nothing, I guess, although I'd bet a Benjamin she's not out of the woods yet. *Chuck*," he said with a smirk, "was almost certainly not calling the shots. He was working for somebody, who will probably just hire someone else to grab her another time." He blew out a breath. "But the girl's been found, she's acting on her own, and we can't help her if she doesn't want our help."

They sat in quiet contemplation for a few minutes with Dani wondering if that meant Will would be going back to Brazil soon. Maybe as soon as tomorrow. She really wasn't even sure where they stood. At the moment, she didn't feel very close to his heart. "Will, you were gone all afternoon. Couldn't you have sent me a text to let me know what was going on?" She blinked back tears. "And that you were all right?"

He reached out to put a hand on her knee. "Sorry, possum. They took my phone until I was cleared, then I was so lost in the mystery of who might want to harm Tiffany, I just forgot." He gave her a lop-sided smile. "I haven't had anyone to report my well-being to for a while." He rose and headed to the bathroom. "You called as I was just getting out of the cab here in the lot," he said on the way. "No point answering when I'd be up here in a few minnies."

He disappeared behind the sliding door, and Dani sat, stunned. Was this the caring man she'd just broken her engagement for?

Springing up from the bed, she pulled her coat off a peg and put it on in a fury. Then she stomped to the small table in the corner that was now holding Will's duffle bag, took up a pencil and scrawled a note to Will on the Moxy Hotel pad of paper. *I need some air. See you later. Da–* The lead broke, and she threw the pencil in a huff, grabbed her purse, and headed out.

* * *

Watching her on the ice, Steve would have never guessed Tiffany had any sort of mental difficulties, not to mention any recent trauma. She was as graceful as a swan, circling and twirling on her frozen pond, her red hair spilling down her back out from under one of his stocking caps. Gone was that compulsion to tug on her hair, as if the ice let her be her true self.

Before heading to the hotel, Steve had taken her to get a bite to eat, then talked her into going ice skating. He had reasoned that they needed to make hay while the sun shone and take advantage of the time when probably no one knew where she was. Plus, if Prof. Thomson was right, she had been through hell and needed to have a little bit of fun. He hadn't expected to be mesmerized by her skill.

Having grown up near Lake Michigan, he expected to be the ice skating expert, but Tiffany would definitely not require his assistance. He knew he shouldn't feel disappointed by that, but he kind of did.

So much had happened in the last two days, he wasn't sure what he thought about much of anything, but when the door of possibility had opened between them, he hadn't shut it. He had only stepped back. And now, against his better judgment, he found himself wanting to step forward. He couldn't deny the fact, though, that she wasn't yet back to normal—that weird roaring thing she did back in his apartment's parking lot testified to that fact.

She skated literal circles around him, smiling in a way he hadn't seen since she'd been back. "Show off," he yelled as she zipped off again, but he was thrilled at the joy he saw on her face. *She'll get there,* he told himself.

She caught up with him again, but didn't zip past this time, settling into a rhythm beside him. "Do you know how to ice dance?"

"I was ice dancing before you were born," he teased.

She laughed. "I kind of doubt that, but show me what you've got."

He reached for her hand, but she quickly swung around in front of him, skating backward. "The thing is, you can't… touch me." Her smile was crooked. "I'm hoping things will get better when the meds kick in, but right now I've got a lingering, persistent hallucination that followed me back from Brazil." She glanced back over her shoulder, and Steve didn't know if she was checking for that hallucination right then or concerned about running into someone, but they pretty much had the ice to themselves on this decidedly brisk evening. When she brought her gaze back to his, even her weak smile was gone. "And I can't even talk about it without possibly setting it off."

Steve searched her eyes for some hint of what she'd gone through, but she kept a tight lid on her emotions. If she wanted to dance with him—even without touching—he'd do his best. "Okay, so dooo weee just keep doing this?"

She put her hands up, palms toward him. "Like a mime mirror routine, only we can also shout out a move, and we'll do it together… just a little bit apart."

This was a challenge Steve could not resist. They did this "mirror skating" once around, then Tiff said, "Twizzle," and they did the simple turn together.

Then Steve called out, "lutz," and Tiff took a position beside him so they wouldn't run into each other on this leaping turn. They continued for the better part of an hour until they didn't even have to shout out the moves. They could tell by each other's feet and arm positions what they were about to do.

After a camel spin that nearly sent Steve to the ice, he sat on a bench and shouted to Tiffany, who was still spinning like a top. "I think this old man is worn out."

She brought her leg down and straightened, then skated over and sat on the bench beside him, though she left a good foot. “Me, too. That was fun, though.”

He began to unlace his skates. “It’s been a while for me, but I guess it’s like riding a bike. It comes back to you.”

She started unlacing too. “I’ve always loved ice skating, and I don’t really mind the cold that much. God, Brazil was awful. The heat and humidity were un—” She stopped, and Steve looked over at her. She seemed frozen with her eyes closed, her hands motionless on her skates.

He sat back, putting a hand toward her, but stopping short of touching her. “Tiff?”

She came back to him slowly, as though she were thawing out. “I’m sorry,” she said in almost a whisper, “I have different triggers than I had before. I nearly stepped on a trip wire, but I managed to back away.”

Everything in him wanted to throw his arms around her, but he put his hands back to work on his laces. He didn’t know what her triggers were and where the trip wires lay. “How long until the meds start working?”

“Shouldn’t be more than a couple of weeks, and some things, like hallucinations, should become less frequent sooner than that.”

He nodded, slipping off his skates and sticking his feet into his hiking boots. If she was right about the Pragnalysis embezzlement business, they’d be busy trying to find a way past their security. And he’d be too busy to think about her in any way other than a student, a friend, and a partner in crime.

There was that damned disappointment again.

* * *

“Well, there it is,” Steve said, as they came upon the very modern-looking Moxy Hotel on Josephine Street, “but I don’t think they have a parking lot.”

Tiffany pulled her thoughts away from the ice and pointed off to the left. “There’s a parking garage.”

Circling to the third level, they found a spot, and Steve pulled his battered car in and turned off the engine. He looked to her expectantly—the door still didn’t work on his side—

but Tiffany couldn't bring herself to move. "Are you sure we should do this?"

"Tiff, I don't think we can do this on our own. Let's just see if they can help."

She nodded and opened the car door, wishing she could live in an ice skating fantasy world with Steve forever and forget about everything else. *Really, truly forget,* she thought, as they made their way to the elevator, riding it down to ground. She wanted to ice dance with Steve the way it was supposed to be done—swirling, leaping, touching. If she could forget Brazil ever happened, the mottled green beast would be gone. Roaring it down here, now, was not the same as in her little cabin in Brazil. Her company there thought it was part of their fun. Present company would think it insane.

They were nearing the front door after passing under the curved pieces of wood that was the most artistic "awning" she'd ever seen, when a man's voice shouted from the other end of an outdoor patio strung with lights. "Tiffany!"

She looked up, searching the shadows, but Steve grabbed her arm and pulled. A shot rang out as he yanked the door open and shoved her in.

Chapter 17

Will came out of the bathroom with a towel around his waist, scrubbing his hair with another one. He hadn't really intended on taking a shower right then, but once in the bathroom, he had caught a whiff of himself and wondered how Dani hadn't keeled over from the stench. A dead fish on a hot beach smelled better.

He headed for his duffle bag, then stopped when he twigged that Dani wasn't anywhere in the room. Continuing on, he assumed she'd stepped out for ice or to work out in the gym downstairs. He pulled out a clean pair of boxer briefs, and a pencil flipped out of his bag with them. Then he noticed she'd left him a note, hastily scrawled. *"I need some air. See you later. Da—"*

She had obviously broken the lead on the "n," then threw the pencil. He looked to the door. *Dani's narky.* He huffed out a breath through his nose as he clenched his jaw. He knew she had every reason to be.

He'd spent too much time that afternoon on police business, and in between, bouncing around in his own head, listing all the reasons why she shouldn't want to be a part of his crazy P.I. life. And those reasons had formed a wall. He'd made love to her two nights ago, and tonight he didn't even kiss her hello.

He finished dressing, vowing to lay everything out and let her make her own choices, when he heard what sounded like a gunshot. If Dani had been there with him, he probably would have just reported it to the cops, but since she wasn't, and he had no idea where she was—*Did she really go out for some air?* —he strode across the room, grabbed his coat off the wall on the way and headed out the door.

There was what looked like a group of tourists waiting for the elevator, so he opted for the stairs. He took them two at a time.

* * *

The woman at the front desk of the Moxy looked up with wide eyes as Steve pushed Tiffany into the building. "Was that a gunshot?"

"I believe so, yes," Steve answered, pulling Tiffany past the desk and down a hall by her coat sleeve. "You should call 911." Tiffany couldn't believe his calm.

The woman yelled after them. "Are you checking in?"

"Unknown at this time," he yelled back. "We're just visiting friends at the moment." He dragged her around a corner and to a door marked stairs.

Once on the other side, Tiffany pulled back. "Will was the only person who knew we might show up here, Steve! We've been set up!"

Steve shook his head. "I don't think so. Why would he work so hard to save you this afternoon, only to shoot at you tonight?"

Tiffany didn't have an answer.

They heard someone coming down the stairs in a big hurry, and Steve stepped protectively in front of her.

Will appeared around the corner of the stairs and started down the last set, smiling when he saw them. "I didn't think you two were gonna show."

Tiffany stepped out from behind Steve. "So I guess you didn't just shoot at us."

"Did you really think I would?" Will said with a hand to his heart.

Tiffany licked her lips. "Maybe. I don't know who to trust anymore."

Will put a finger in the air. "First things first. Number one, was that shot definitely fired at you, or are you just assuming."

"Oh, no," Steve interrupted, nodding with too much adrenaline. "It was fired at her. The man yelled her name to get her to turn around."

"Okay. The mystery deepens." He glanced to the door, looking torn. "You didn't see Dani out there, did you?"

Tiffany shook her head. "We weren't out there long, but no."

Reaching into his back pocket, he pulled out a key card. "Go on up and let yourself in. Sit tight and don't open the door for anyone except me or Dani."

"Is your friend missing?" Steve asked, holding his laptop in front of him as he often did.

"Naw, she just… went out for some air. I wouldn't worry except…"

"Yeah, go, man," Steve urged. "We'll find it." He looked at the card. "418."

Will nodded and turned for the door. Steve and Tiffany started up the stairs. "How is it possible that someone was waiting here for me?" she wondered aloud as they moved ever upward. "Am I broadcasting my thoughts somehow? Is that a little-known side effect of schizophrenia?"

"If you could control it, that would be seriously cool, but I've never heard of that one. Not even from my aunt, who seemed to have all possible symptoms."

Tiffany stopped, flabbergasted. "Are you telling me your aunt has schizophrenia?"

Steve turned on the step ahead. "Didn't I ever mention that?"

"Dude, no, you never said a word." Tiffany started forward again, feeling unexpectedly weird about everything. "So that's why you're so nice to me."

"That… may… be… why I'm not wary of you," he stammered out slowly. "You're a nice person, so why wouldn't I be nice to you?"

"Maybe you're just nice to me because you feel sorry for me—the poor girl with the defective brain trying to make it in college." She fought the urge to reach for her hair.

He shook his head as they kept climbing. "Tiff, my schizophrenic aunt has nothing to do with our friendship. It just gives me understanding that some of your other friends don't have."

They reached the fourth floor, and Steve put his hand to the door handle but didn't pull it. "Are we good, or do I need to disown my aunt so we can still be friends?"

She couldn't help the laugh that sputtered out of her, and before she knew what was happening, he had put a hand to the back of her neck and his lips were on hers. Her breath caught, but seconds later, claws tore down her back, and a roar ripped through her head. She stumbled back with her hands over her ears, her eyes clenched tight.

Steve's "Tiff, I'm sorry. I didn't think," could barely penetrate the noise in her head. She heard a muffled, "Ah hell," and then she was floating.

* * *

Dani had been knocked out of her pity party with a shout of "Tiffany!" and a gunshot. From her spot in a dark corner of the hotel patio wrapped in a fur blanket from the lobby, she looked up to see a couple disappearing inside the hotel, then to the raised patio, where it seemed the shot had come from. She couldn't see anyone there.

She let out the breath she'd been holding, grateful that they had made it inside, then slowly rose, throwing off the blanket, and tip-toed forward until she was against the wall of the raised patio. She followed it until it sloped with the stairs and she was able to peek around the corner into the now-deserted space. With her heart beating like a galloping horse, she quickly moved around the stairs and to the far side to look over the low retaining wall the shooter must have been hiding behind and caught a glimpse of him disappearing quickly across the back lot of a neighboring business.

She sized him up as she slipped over the wall. He wasn't as tall as Will. He was a few inches shorter—probably more like Keith's height.

She knew following him was dangerous, but if they were going to solve some of the mysteries surrounding Tiffany, they needed to know who that man was. She tried not to think about the fact that he had a gun as she started after him, heading northeast.

At the corner of the neighboring building, she stopped and cautiously peered around it. The light was much dimmer here, and he was dressed in black, but she still detected a moving figure heading north between the businesses. If it had been her, she would have parked right in this back lot for a quick getaway, but what did she know about it? *He might have been in danger of being towed while he waited.* As soon as she saw the man turn left, she started after him, walking as lightly as she could.

Her mind went back to the girl that so many people seemed to want out of the way. Evidently Will had gotten through to her, after all, about trusting him. *Or maybe Steve.* It was definitely a tall black man she'd seen with her.

Dani's earlier temper had definitely cooled, but she couldn't say she was feeling much better about her relationship with Will. *Maybe Keith's right. Maybe I just bonded with Will in a crisis situation, and there really isn't enough beyond that to build a relationship.*

Her phone buzzed in her purse, and she veered to behind a dumpster, fishing it out and silencing it as fast as she could. If she talked to Will now, she'd lose the guy and put herself in danger. *And besides,* she thought with no small amount of spite, *let him worry about me for a change.*

* * *

Once outside the stairwell, Will pondered his direction. He decided to check the snack bar first, in case Dani had changed her mind about actually going out.

The room was full of people, but he didn't see his blonde, so he turned back to the lobby, pulling out his phone and scrolling to find her name as he went. He paced the lobby that looked like it had been decorated by hippies, waiting for her to answer. When the call went to voicemail, he hung up with a slow sigh and headed for the door. The shooter had been in the front but no doubt had fled the scene by now.

As he strode past the check-in desk, the woman tried to stop him. "Sir, we believe a gun was discharged out there just a few minutes ago. You shouldn't—"

"Thanks, but I'm aware." He would feel better with his firearm, but if the guy had yelled out to make sure he got the right girl, he probably wasn't shooting at just anybody. The frigid evening air made him suck in a breath. *Surely Dani wouldn't want to be out here long.*

He paused and scanned the outdoor patio but saw nothing other than snow-covered tables and chairs under the outdoor party lighting. Donning stocking cap and gloves, he strode the few steps to the corner of the building. Nobody was on the sidewalk that ran along Josephine Street, although he could see the flashing lights of cop cars in the distance, heading his way. He continued on the sidewalk to the intersection, but there was no sign of her down that side of the building either.

As the police cars parked along Josephine, he deliberated as to whether he should tell them what he knew of the situation or not. They would undoubtedly want to talk to Tiffany, and with her trust issues… well he just didn't know what to expect. Would she just run again? He had a feeling that Steve had talked her into coming to the hotel. If she wanted to report that the shooter had called out her name, he guessed she could do it herself. Plus, it could tie him up for a while, and right now, he had to find Dani.

He stood a moment, mad at himself for making her feel the "need for some air." Renae was dead. This woman was alive and wanted to be with him. It was time he got that straight. He pursed his chapped lips. *Where would she go?* The bright lights of the Cherry Creek Shopping Center shone a few blocks away, but he wasn't about to walk that distance in this cold. Crossing the street, he made his way back to the parking garage and his car.

* * *

Peeking over the trash bin after silencing her phone, Dani no longer saw the gunman. Afraid she had lost him, she moved swiftly to the next corner. Looking discretely both ways, she spotted him to her left, leaning against the building close to the other end in the shadows. He seemed to be waiting for something. Or maybe some*body.*

After a few minutes, with Dani watching and shivering, a car turned onto the street, and the guy pushed off the wall to move toward it as it slowed to a stop. *He's getting picked up.*

The car was probably some kind of classic, although Dani had never paid that much attention to cars. At any rate, it wasn't new. She'd guess it to be a model a good thirty to forty years in the past. It seemed in good shape, though—at least from what she could tell under the streetlights.

After he was inside, and the car started forward, Dani stepped out of hiding, trying to look like she was just out for a walk. As the car passed, she turned and ran toward the curb, focusing on the license plate. The car squealed around the corner as an arm with a gun swung out the window.

Dani hit the ground as a shot rang out.

Chapter 18

Steve struggled with the key card while carrying Tiffany, and he finally had to drop her legs to the floor to be able to manage at all. Her eyes were open, so she hadn't fainted. He recognized it as a kind of catatonic state that sometimes overtakes a schizophrenic.

When he had it open at last, he pushed on the heavy door while half dragging her inside, holding her tight against him. He reached the end of a bed and lowered her down to sitting. Then he took a step back. It seemed counter-intuitive to do so under the circumstances, but touching her—kissing her—had sent her into this state. Holding her hand would probably not get her out of it.

He squatted down to her eye level, studying her face. God, she was beautiful. Even with her current blank expression, those green eyes called to him. And that freckle above her lip... He mentally kicked himself for that kiss. "Tiff, if you can hear me, I'm sorry. It was an impulsive move, and I promise I won't touch you again." She sat unblinking, and Steve knew there was probably nothing to do but wait.

Rising, he took in the spare styling of the room, then let out a heavy sigh as he sank into a simple folding canvas chair. So much had happened in the last two days since Tiffany had popped back into his life, his head was swimming. And he had no idea what to do with the new feelings that were growing for the lost creature sitting on the bed. If he hadn't known her before—known how normal she had seemed before she was kidnapped, he'd probably walk out the door and not look back.

But he did know. He remembered the night they'd watched the Stooges after her tutoring session when she said she'd never seen an episode. He remembered her laughter and the way her eyes sparkled. And now that he allowed himself to think of her as more than just a student, he remembered that she had made him his favorite cookies that night and just happened to have brought his favorite soda along as well.

He ran a hand around his tired face. *This is just a blip. As soon as her meds kick in, she'll be back to—* He couldn't really say normal, but she'd be back to what she was in the fall, anyway. Pushing up, he strode to the window and looked out the side of the shade, trying to push all his other misgivings aside. They came shooting into his brain anyway.

What if whatever happened in Brazil broke her in a way that can't be fixed?

He turned to look at her still sitting and staring ahead, and "whatever happened in Brazil" swiftly took center stage in his brain. Her inability to be touched seemed to give credence to his professor's idea that she'd been sold to some kind of sex slave operation. He wondered why that whole thing didn't repel him, but it didn't. He just wanted to know how to help put it behind her. *How long will that take? And will she ever really get over it? Will she never want me to touch her?*

He remembered that she'd told him once that schizophrenia researchers wanted to study her because she had the unusual ability to compartmentalize her illness and think about it more objectively than most. She could generally hold onto a baseline of reality with which to judge her perceptions by.

He wondered if she had done that with the whole Pragnalysis embezzling business, or if things were so rough in Brazil, her baseline had shifted. There was no doubt that someone wanted to harm her; he just had no idea if it had anything at all to do with her family's corporation. Especially after she couldn't find the evidence she was so sure of in her room.

He peeked out the window again, hoping Will had found his friend. Now that he'd talked Tiffany into coming here, he was really hoping for some help.

Finally feeling warm, he shed his coat, then rid Tiffany of her winter wear as well, pulling off her hat, gloves, and coat, being careful not to touch her skin. Then he turned on the TV to find some comedy to counteract all the drama of the last few days. He didn't know if it would help Tiffany, but it sure would help him.

* * *

Just as Will neared the parking garage, he heard another gunshot and sprinted past it to the corner and looked both ways. His heart nearly collapsed when it looked as if someone was on the ground, down the block to his right. He didn't wait for the light to change. Dodging a car or two, he sped across the street.

When he was still half a block away, the figure started to get up, and Will slowed his pace slightly in relief. Then the person turned. *Dani.*

She seemed to recognize him and started forward. He slowed enough to not take her back to ground as he reached her, pulling her to his chest. "Are you okay?"

She nodded against him, wrapping her arms around his waist. "I wasn't hit. I'm fine." Her voice sounded a bit shaky.

He loosened his hold just enough to look down at her face. "What were you doing, possum?" He couldn't help the exasperation in his voice. "Tell me you didn't follow the shooter all by yourself."

She shrugged. "I had to. No one else was around to do it." Her voice was gaining strength. "A car picked him up, and I got the plate number."

Despite wanting to thrash her for doing something so dangerous, he couldn't help the smile that slipped out. "You did?"

"Big deal."

He was surprised by her attitude. "Well, it is a big deal, Dani. I mean, I don't want to congratulate you for putting yourself at risk when you knew he had a gun, but… getting the license number might solve this thing."

"No, you goof. The vanity plate said 'BIGDEAL.' "

"Oh," he said with real surprise. "Okay then. We finally have something to go on." Will turned her around for the walk back to the hotel. "Now do you want to hear my lecture?"

She pulled her arm out of his grasp as they walked. "No, Will, I don't. I did what had to be done, and I took precautions. If I were Rod or Logan, you wouldn't be lecturing me."

"That's because they've been trained."

"I wasn't 'trained' to go undercover in Brazil either, but I did it. I got a few bruises, but I did it, and I helped free those women. I'm not as fragile as you think."

Will made her stop. "Dani, no one who saw you take Perigosa's slap with barely a whimper would call you fragile, but—" he paused, his throat going tight. "Watching it," he began again, "was like a knife to the gut. And hearing a gunshot, not knowing where you were, nearly turned me inside out."

She searched his eyes. "Why, Will? Earlier, you just seemed—"

"Because I love you," spilled out of him without thought as he put his hands on either side of her head, his thumbs caressing her cheeks. "I love you, Dani Harper," he whispered out on a breath.

Her confusion turned into a shaky smile. "I… I think I love you too, but—"

He took her arm and started walking again. "No buts. At least not until we get back to the hotel. It's freezing out here."

She veered left toward a dimly lit alley. "This will be faster."

"So you've just gone complete 007 on me now, have you?" He tried to keep his tone light even if his guts were still churning with the thought that she could have been killed. "Sneaking through dark alleys, shadowing hit men."

"Do you really think it was a hit man?"

He shrugged. "Steve said that the gunman yelled out Tiffany's name, so he was looking for her."

"That's right, he did. He was behind the wall on that upper patio, and I was down below where he couldn't see me. But I heard him call her name just before the shot. If not for Steve's quick reaction, she probably would be dead."

A bright flashlight up ahead reminded Will quite abruptly that they shouldn't be sneaking around in dark alleys when coppers were combing the area.

"Stop! Police!" was shouted their direction.

Will and Dani froze, putting their hands in the air, and Will wondered if he'd be taken downtown for the second time that day.

As the policeman closed the gap, Will whispered instructions out of the side of his mouth. "Don't tell them about Tiffany."

It seemed to Dani that they should tell the police everything, including Tiffany's second narrow escape of the day, but Will was the P.I., so she left the girl's name out of it when she retold what she had seen from the patio.

After she was finished, the officer shook his head. "I appreciate the fact that you got the plate number, but in the future, do not follow an armed person through dark alleys, Miss Harper," the man reprimanded in no uncertain terms. She looked to Will, who cocked an eyebrow in agreement.

"If I hadn't," Dani insisted, "we… I mean *you* would have no leads whatsoever."

"Nevertheless," —the man closed his notebook and slid it into the interior pocket of his coat— "your life is more important than that information."

Dani nodded, if only to shut the man up. At length, the two were allowed to go back into the hotel. Will seemed to want to pull her straight through to the elevators, but Dani needed to understand where *they* stood as a couple before they had to deal with the young couple upstairs. She slowed. "Will…" He stopped and looked at her expectantly. "Is there time to talk first?"

He nodded and allowed her to pull him toward a sofa full of pillows. They settled in, but neither removed their coats. It would be a while before they were warmed up. "I know you were cheesed off with me upstairs," Will began as he threw an arm around her and drew her in. "And you had every right to be. I… I was a real nong, letting a ghost build a wall between us."

"A ghost?"

He nodded. "Yeah… Renae—the woman I was in love with long ago. There was a time when she was my heart. My reason for living. Her death sent me spiraling, and that's how I ended up enlisting in the RAR, doing stuff I didn't believe in for people I didn't trust to do the right thing." He huffed out a derisive breath. "Just like our ranga upstairs, I just ran. But I could never outrun her memory or the hole her death left inside me. The only thing that helped fill it even a little was helping someone else. Logan's search and rescue of trafficking victims gave me a reason to live again." He shook his head. "But that hole was still there." He looked over at her, his hazel eyes meeting hers. "Until you."

She felt both touched and confused. "So… why the wall?"

He gave her a crooked smile. "Fear. Having that hole filled for even a few days made me afraid to lose you—afraid to have another hole form." He wrapped both arms around her. "But when I heard the first gun shot and didn't know where you were, none of that mattered. Whether you were lost to this world or only to me, the resulting hole in my heart would be the same. That's just the price of love."

Dani turned to slide her arms around him, laying her head against his chest. She understood his fear. She'd felt it that afternoon when she didn't know what had become of him. Was that the way their lives together would be? And if he wouldn't let her work with him, the fear would be all hers.

She pulled back abruptly with the idea that just popped into her head. "Train me."

"What?"

"You said you wouldn't lecture Logan or Rod because they're trained. So train me. I want to do what you do—find the lost. Reconnect families." Her insides lit up with a new revelation. "I want to be a P.I."

She could see him thinking as he straightened her floppy stocking hat that had gone eschew. "Sooo does that mean you're coming back with me to São Paulo?" The question in his eyes wasn't nearly as flippant as his voice.

She leaned in to give him a tender kiss that immediately ignited into a passion too often denied the last few days. She moved her lips to his ear, breathless. "Yes, Will, I'll go back with you, and as glad as I am that Tiffany and Steve finally showed up, I sure wish we could be alone in our room right now."

He rubbed his cheek against hers. "Oh yeah." Without warning, he straightened, rose, and pulled her up with him. "But we better get up there before they fly the coop again."

They walked toward the elevator, their fingers entwined, as he called Capt. Rand to fill him in on the latest in his missing person case.

* * *

The pulsing sound of waves filling Tiffany's head all but drowned out anything that was happening around her. Of all the schizo symptoms, this was the worst. She was frozen with her racing thoughts, circling, spinning, zigzagging in all directions until she wanted to scream. But she couldn't. It was a living nightmare that was impossible to get out of. It was a weighted net that held her in place while the sea hag stole her voice.

She was utterly helpless and so despondent that she knew she would gladly kill herself to get out of it, but even that was denied her. The mutated dragon would be welcome now if he would swallow her whole and put her out of her misery. A new terror seized her with the thought that she'd still be in this state inside the beast—another layer between her and the real world. Another barrier between her and… Steve.

His name swirled in her head, and she tried to see him, but a hundred other faces blinked on and off in front of her. A thousand pairs of lips came toward her until one face froze, sneering. *Owens.*

The memory of the night he'd caught her red-handed with the evidence whooshed through her brain at triple speed. The lips that had crushed against hers brought a sudden feeling of nausea as he morphed into a dragon.

Clawed dragon hands began to undress her, and panic set in anew. Then they left her, and in place of a physical assault, she experienced an assault of sound. The pulsing distortion was a kind of torture, but slowly another sound broke through. It was like… wind chimes.

She strained to make sense out of it, and gradually a face came to mind. Steve's face. And she recognized the sound. Steve was laughing. Not his usual belly laugh—kind of a small laugh, as if a big laugh just wasn't possible. *Steve's frozen too.*

And with that realization, she turned her head. She didn't know how long it took before he came into focus, sitting on the end of the bed, watching TV. It could have been minutes. Or hours. But as soon as he did, she was free. She blinked her dry eyes. "Steve," she whispered, and he turned to look at her in surprise.

He started to rise, then stopped himself and sat again. "Tiff, are you okay now?"

She rolled her head around and shrugged her shoulders. "Yes. I think so." She put her head in her hands, feeling as if she could cry—wanting to cry, but no tears would come. "God, I hate that."

"I'm so sorry."

The crack in his voice had her looking up again. "It wasn't your fault."

He gave her a crooked smile. "It kind'a was."

She shook her head. "No. This was McCain's fault. This was Miranda's fault. This was Perigosa's fault." Her volume rose as she stood and stepped toward him. "This was hundreds of men's fault that I don't even know—that I hope to God burn for all eternity in hell for what they did to me!"

The door opened, and she spun to see Will and Dani coming in. "Well, sheila," Will began in his Aussie accent, "I'm hoping the same thing, right along with you."

Tiffany didn't know why she hadn't seen it before—it had to be the damned schizophrenia—but the sincerity in his eyes reached inside her and gave her new understanding. She'd been afraid that this man could restrain her and take her home against her will. Now she saw that his intention all along had been to fight for her, not against her. It was a shift in perception that maybe meant her meds were starting to work, but frankly it scared her. She sank to the bed. *What else have I been wrong about?*

Will took off his coat and sank into the canvas chair. "I hope you realize, Tiffany, that we only want to help you." He shook his head as Dani sat on the bed near him. "You don't want to see your oldies, that's okay. We've only hung around because we thought you were in some kind of danger."

She nodded. "I know that now." She felt like an idiot. "And I'm sorry I've made things so difficult for you." She paused a moment before speaking again. "Do you know about the… the schizophrenia?"

He nodded. "Yeah, we should have had that news earlier, but we got it."

"So what I'm going to tell you, I warn you will sound as if I'm paranoid." She glanced to Steve. "And the jury's still out on if I've made it all up, but—"

"But someone is obviously after her," Steve butted in, "so I lean strongly toward believing her story." Tiffany's heart warmed with his support.

"So what is your story?" Dani asked sincerely, leaning forward. "And what were all those numbers about?"

Will put up a hand. "Before we get into that, let's see if Tiffany knows anyone with a black classic car."

"Oh, right!" Dani agreed. "And a license plate that reads BIGDEAL."

Tiffany's eyes grew wide. "Why do you want to know?"

"I followed the man who shot at you, and he was picked up by someone driving that car."

Tiffany looked to Steve with something that felt like victory before taking her gaze back to Will and Dani. "Yeah, I know who owns that car. Chase Owens."

Chapter 19

Will and Dani were once again in the Morrow mansion after a late night of listening to Tiffany's accusations against Chase Owens.

According to her, he was more than an HR nightmare; he was an embezzler, had probably organized her kidnapping, and might have even hired Mr. Ugly Tree. Will had to admit, the fact that his car was involved in the previous night's events certainly gave her theories more credence.

Rand had verified Owens' ownership of the car early this morning, but Owens claimed that it had been stolen while he was out. With his claim of theft, they would have to prove that he was actually the one driving, and he insisted he had an alibi for the whole evening, even though the lady refused to put her name to a statement.

Will didn't really know what to think about any of it, but something was definitely amiss, and the connection between Owens and McCain certainly seemed suspicious as well. McCain had ratted out Miranda to the cops, though, so why not Owens, if he was the mastermind?

They'd been let in by someone he supposed was a maid, and they'd been sitting for at least twenty minnies even though Will had called ahead to tell them they were coming. Dani had gotten restless after five and had gotten up to look at the abstract painting over the fireplace, then spent time perusing the books on the shelves. He'd gotten so bored, he'd pulled out a toothpick to chew on.

He had been grateful that Tiffany and Steve had showed up, but it had still been another night without Dani beside him. He'd bunked with Steve while she slept with Tiffany. There was obviously something between Steve and Tiffany that neither were talking about—at least not in front of him and Dani—even if Steve avoided coming too close to her in their now-quite-crowded hotel room.

Eventually, footsteps were heard on the stairs, and Mr. Morrow appeared coming down in what looked like golf attire. The temp was up from last night, but it still wasn't golfing weather. Will supposed he got his swings in at some posh indoor golf club.

Will rose and moved to shake his hand, wondering that the man somehow entered the house from the upper level. "Mr. Morrow, we've got good news." He pulled out the signed affidavit out of his back pocket. "I'm pleased to tell you that we know where your daughter is, although we couldn't convince her to come with us today."

Morrow took the page and unfolded it. "She is… well?"

"As well as can be expected, I think," Dani threw in as she joined them. "Her meds aren't at what Tiffany called 'peak performance' yet, and of course, she's dealing with trauma from Brazil, but she seems remarkably coherent." She glanced at Will. "Especially compared to what she was like on the flight here."

Mr. Morrow nodded with almost a smile. "Good. Good." He let out a sigh. "It's been a rough few days worrying about her all over again."

Will couldn't help the brow that lifted, although he supposed different people handled anxiety in a variety of ways. Some, he supposed handled it by improving their golf game. He wondered at the absence of the man's wife. "Is Mrs. Morrow here? We thought she would be especially thrilled with the news of Tiffany's safety."

Morrow looked to the stairs. "She's having one of her bad days, I'm afraid." He looked back to them with a smile. "I'll be sure to tell her the good news later." He refolded the page. "And you're right. She will be thrilled." He stood a moment with a thin smile as if to end the conversation. When Will didn't move, he went on awkwardly, "Do you have my bill?"

"Logan will send it."

"Ah. Well…"

Will crossed his arms. "Mr. Morrow, you need to know that there's something going on with your daughter."

"Oh? Something other than her psychosis?"

His flippant response was unexpected. Dani jumped in before Will could. "Don't you watch the news? Tiffany was nearly kidnapped again yesterday by some man from Florida, and she was shot at last night."

Mr. Morrow brought a hand to his chest. "What?" He shook his head, looking dazed. "No, I didn't watch the news yesterday. I worked all day here on a board briefing. But... Tiffany's all right?"

"She's fine," Will assured, then squinted. "We kept her name out of the news after the shooting last night, but the kidnapping incident was another matter. I couldn't help with that one. I was... tied up for a while with the fallout. No one called you to ask about it? Friends, relies, employees..."

Morrow licked his lips. "They might have. I turned off my phone yesterday so I could get my work done, and I forgot to turn it back on until this morning."

He dug it out of his pants pocket to look at the screen, as if to make sure it was still working. Will assumed the man was frazzled by their news and pressed on. "Tiffany believes something shady is going on at Pragnalysis. She says she told you and Mrs. Morrow last fall, but you didn't believe her."

What sounded like a nervous laugh gurgled out of him as he slipped the phone back into his pocket. "Tiffany has accused everyone she knows of something corrupt or nefarious in the last few years. I'm sorry if I seemed uncaring about her condition. It is just very rough to have your daughter accuse you of horrible things."

"Tiffany didn't accuse *you* of anything, Mr. Morrow," Will clarified. "It's Chase Owens she says has embezzled thousands from Pragnalysis." The man opened his mouth, then closed it, blinking with what appeared to be surprise, but Will kept going. "I understand your concern about paranoia and false accusations, and I have to admit, I'm right there with you, but something is going on, and we can't say for sure that Owens was involved with last night's shooting, but his car definitely was."

Morrow put fingertips to his forehead as he seemed to be digesting Will's words. "His car?"

Dani nodded. "A classic black Grand Prix with a license plate that read BIGDEAL. I don't know who was driving, but I saw the shooter get picked up by that car."

"I know the car. I assume you've spoken to Chase. What does he say about this?"

Will flipped his toothpick up and down. "I haven't spoken to him personally, but according to the police report, he claims it was stolen while he was spending time with a woman at her house. She won't back up his story, though, as it seemed to be something she didn't want her husband to know about."

The man shook his head. "Chase can't seem to keep away from the women. Especially the ones who should be off limits."

Will wondered if he was also referring to his daughter.

Dani leaned in. "So Owens as an embezzler… Does it seem more likely now?"

Morrow shook his head. "Chase is one of my top men, and he's paid very well."

"Even rich men can be greedy," Will pointed out.

"True," Morrow agreed, "but I've known Chase for a good decade. He interned with us right out of college. He's a womanizer, yes—and I've spoken to him about that—but an embezzler… I don't think he has the ability to keep that kind of secret. The first time he was drunk, he'd spill it all."

"And you're certain no funds have been lost?" Dani put in.

"Not that anyone in accounting has made known to me."

"Would you consider an audit?"

Morrow shifted his gaze back to Will. "I suppose under the circumstances, that would be prudent. I'll see to it. Is Chase… under arrest?"

"No, not yet. So far there's not enough evidence that he was actually involved."

"And you're certain that Tiffany is in a safe place."

Will nodded. "We'll stick around until we figure out who put a target on her back and why."

"It's most likely someone trying to get back at me, *or*," Morrow said as if struck by a new idea, "it could be someone connected with that first man, McCain. More traffickers."

Will shook his head. "That's really not how trafficking works. Traffickers are men of opportunity. They don't go hunting for specific women."

"Maybe she… made enemies in Brazil," Morrow speculated. "She was very good at that the last few years. Maybe somebody big, with connections in the U.S." He paused, looking dazed. "I just can't believe it's Chase. He's… he's a family friend."

Will rose. "All the 'big somebodies' who had anything to do with Tiffany are in custody, and family friends have done worse." He put out a hand. "No matter your opinion of Owens, I'll want to talk to him again."

Morrow rose and shook it weakly. "Of course. Do you want me to set up a meeting?"

Will released his hand and turned to put it to Dani's back as they headed for the door. "I'll take care of it. Thanks."

Morrow followed. "Where is Tiffany staying?"

"She's with us at the Moxy." Will turned back at the door. "But she really doesn't want to be contacted yet."

He nodded solemnly. "I understand. It will be hard on Min, but we'll honor her wishes."

After they were outside and moving down the long, curved stairs, Dani again brought up how much she thought Morrow looked like Owens. "He said he was a family friend. What if he's just family?"

"What would be the point of that kind of secret in this day and age?"

"I don't know. Maybe he's the product of an affair."

Will was skeptical. "Morrow is in his late forties. Owens is close to thirty, if not a few years older. Morrow would have had to be pretty young, which would make Owens the son of a former relationship, but not an affair." They reached the sidewalk.

"So what if he's jealous of Tiffany as the heir of Pragnalysis? Maybe he'd be the heir if she were out of the way."

Will smiled. "It's not the 1700's. Parents don't have to leave everything to just one."

"Well, if you had read 'The Pragnalysis Story,' " she said with sass, "you'd know that the company technically belongs to Min Morrow. Maybe she doesn't want it to be passed on to a son who isn't hers."

They arrived at the curb, and Will reached for the car door but didn't open it. "So Owens was hitting on his half-sister?"

For the first time since she'd started down this mental path, she paused. "That would make things… kind of icky, but—"

Will laughed and pulled the door open. "I think you've watched too many soaps."

She sighed and made to get in. "You're probably right. It's most likely just a coincidence that they have similar coloring. People have told me I look like Michelle Pfeiffer. I suppose we all have a doppelganger somewhere."

He looked at her with clear disbelief as she fastened her seat belt. "You are way prettier than Michelle Pfeiffer."

She laughed. "Thank you, sir, but I doubt most of the world would agree."

"Most of the world is full of nilwits." He closed the door and ran around to the driver's side.

"By the way, " she said as he climbed in, "why did you tell Morrow that we were still at the Moxy?"

"I don't want anyone to know where we've moved to, possum," he said putting the key in the ignition. "Not even the Morrows."

* * *

Steve was clacking away on his laptop, cross-legged on the other bed when Tiffany came to the surface of a deep sleep to find she was alone in her bed with no sign of Dani or Will in the room.

She'd slept better than she had in a long while. Whether it was the feeling of relative safety or her meds starting to work, she couldn't say, but a small feather of hope tickled inside her.

Rolling to her side, she propped up on an elbow. "Whatcha doin'?"

Steve looked over at her and smiled. "Oh, nothing much. Just breaking into your corporation."

Her eyes blinked wide, as she sat on the edge of the bed in the scrubs she was still using as pajamas. "Seriously?"

He laughed. "Not quite yet, but I am seeing some things I didn't see before. A few holes in their security that I might be able to wedge a knife in. Metaphorically speaking."

"So… you think it's worth pursuing, even though I couldn't find what I thought I hid in my dorm room? Even if that memory could have been fabricated while I was gone?"

His expression said he obviously did. "Tiff, someone is clearly after you, and the embezzling is really the only line we've got on a motive for that. We have to check it out."

She smiled. "Thanks." His eyes held hers in a way that for once, she couldn't easily read.

"You're looking… better," he said, with what sounded like the hope she felt.

It should have been reassuring, but somehow it made her more aware of how "not better" she had probably seemed the last few days. She ran fingers through her hair and tucked it behind an ear. "Better than what? A whorehouse bimbo?"

His expression changed in an instant. The pain in his eyes had her shaking her head. "Sorry. Forget I said that… I don't know where that came from."

He set his laptop aside and turned to face her. "It obviously came from a place of deep hurt. I know you can't talk about it yet, but when you can, I'll listen." He slowly shook his head. "And I will not judge you."

She couldn't help her puzzlement. "Why? I don't know how you can even look at me, let alone…" She stopped short of bringing up the kiss. Did she really want to know that it had just been a spontaneous Steve thing that really meant nothing?

His forehead squinched. "How could I blame you for something someone else did to you?" The corner of his mouth ticked up. "You are one feisty woman, and I know you can run, so if you'd been able to stop it or get away, you would have."

Tears came to her eyes. "I ran, Steve. I ran so many times, but that jungle is not something you can run through, and they had machetes, and I didn't. They always caught me. I tried so many times that they eventually took all my clothes away except for one silk robe."

A low growl rumbled through her head as horror overtook Steve's face. "The jungle? They had you in the jungle?"

She nodded but knew she couldn't say anymore. She'd already said too much—felt too much. She abruptly stood and made her way to the bathroom, trying to keep the growling creature in its cave.

"Tiff?"

She disappeared inside and leaned against the closed door, practicing deep breathing, picturing herself outside the creature's lair with a sword. After several minutes, she opened her eyes with a small feeling of victory. She'd thought about Brazil. She'd spoken about Brazil, and the beast had not swallowed her whole. It hadn't even ventured out to stare her down.

That glimmer of hope grew.

She turned and looked in the mirror. She still wasn't seeing her own face, but since it was Steve's, she didn't really mind.

* * *

Dani leaned her head back and closed her eyes as Will drove them back to their hotel, feeling the effects of a short night.

After talking to the cops, they had listened to Tiffany's take on everything. Then Will had moved them all to the Days Inn, late, after switching out the RAV 4 for a deep burgundy Honda CRV at the rental company. She probably didn't fall asleep until 1:00. She hadn't realized that she had dozed off in the car until Will's phone rang.

She blinked her eyes open and sat up, wondering where they were.

"Yarnel, here," Will said into the phone.

He listened for some time, then glanced her way, looking horrified.

Dani put a hand to his arm. "What is it?" she whispered.

"Okay, thanks for the info. Hooroo," he said in what seemed like an absent-minded afterthought as he set the phone in the cup holder between them.

"Will, what is it?"

He adjusted his hands on the wheel as he gnawed on that stupid toothpick. "The car's been found, and you won't believe this, but the driver was… Keith."

"Keith! My Keith? I mean, not *my* Keith anymore, but… Keith Bisbee?"

Will nodded solemnly.

"Where did they find it? Why does he have it?"

"I'm trying to drive, possum. Let's talk about it when we get to the hotel."

Dani was starting to panic. "Will, just spit it out! Where did they find the car?"

He did a hasty turn into a McDonald's and parked. Then he turned to face her. "The car went off a mountain road, Dani, and Keith's in intensive care."

Chapter 20

By claiming to be Keith's fiancé, Dani was able to see him. He still hadn't recovered consciousness, and it was amazing he was alive, although his accident wasn't quite as serious as Will had led her to believe at first. She had pictured the Grand Prix launching off the side of a mountain and plunging a quarter mile, flipping and landing on its top. In reality, he'd gone down a small slope and was stopped by a tree.

Still, classic old cars don't have air bags, and he'd hit his head on the windshield, and had some massive bruises on his chest from the steering wheel. They said his blood alcohol level was pretty high, which probably wasn't surprising, given their conversation yesterday morning, but she was surprised that he'd drive while drunk. Especially in the mountains.

She stood by his bed, unable to take her eyes off his handsome face that was now bruised and bandaged. She no longer wanted to marry him, but she would never wish this on him. A tear rolled down her cheek, and she wiped it away.

Her shock over his accident was only topped by her confusion over why he'd been driving Chase Owens' car. She couldn't believe that he had stolen it, so how did he get it? *Or did jilting him send him over the edge? Did he blame Tiffany for my not coming home and thought to eliminate her? Did he steal Owens' car from his garage?* She shook her head, knowing that was way too much of a coincidence.

She knew that all the thinking in the world wouldn't solve this mystery. It would have to wait until Keith could explain it himself. She gave his hand a squeeze, intending to leave, but stopped when she felt weak movement in his fingers.

She leaned toward his head. “Keith, can you hear me?”

His lips parted as his head turned the tiniest bit, his eyes still closed. “Dani,” came out of him on what seemed like an exhausted breath.

“Keith.” She laid a gentle hand on his shoulder. “What happened? Why were you driving a stolen car in the mountains?”

She missed a few whispered words and leaned in even closer to hear, “ate my chips.”

“Ate your chips? Who ate your chips?”

He licked his dry lips and swallowed. “Bears,” he said in a weak voice. “Hundreds of bears.”

Dani straightened and blinked. The man was obviously not yet in his right mind. She tried again. “Do you know how you came to be in the Grand Prix?” He didn’t answer. “Keith, are you still with me?”

His barely perceptible “I love you” tore at her heart, and she couldn’t bear to ask any more questions. She stood there another few minutes, but he seemed to have fallen asleep again. When a nurse came in to take his vitals, Dani told her of his short period of irrational consciousness, then took her leave, still feeling dazed.

Will rose as she entered the waiting area, concern on his face, and a sob rose up in her throat. He opened his arms to her, and she walked into them as the tears flowed. Would Keith recover, or was he now brain damaged? She knew she wasn’t responsible for his drinking—that was his own choice—but she did blame herself for giving him a reason to come out here in the first place.

Will stroked her hair as she soaked the front of his flannel shirt with her tears. “I’m sorry,” she blubbed.

“Shh, apologies aren’t required, love. It’s been a crazy week, and I know that all feelings for a person don’t die immediately, even if the cords are cut.”

Dani pulled back to look in his eyes. “He woke up for a moment or two.” She shook her head with the sadness she felt. “But he wasn’t really making any sense.”

“He’ll come out of it,” Will assured. “His head just needs time to heal. It’s a process.”

“I hope so.” Dani had a sudden horrible thought. “What if he doesn’t remember that I broke up with him!”

Will looked confused “Why would—”

“He said—” Her throat clenched, and she paused for control. “He said he loved me.” She said it almost as softly as Keith had.

Will gave her a small smile. “Of course he does, possum. He wouldn’t need to have his mind muddled to remember that.”

“I wish he didn’t,” she admitted. “It would make everything so much easier.”

“I know.” He pulled her back to his chest, and Dani let him hold her, knowing that if the tables were turned, and she were crying over Will, Keith would not be as understanding.

* * *

“Damn!” Steve hit another wall in Pragnalysis security. This morning’s optimism was long gone. He’d hate to disappoint Tiffany, but breaking into the high-tech company’s accounting department was probably not going to happen.

“You just need a break,” Tiffany announced from the other bed, where she was leaning against the pillows, eating yogurt. “Feed your brain.”

He shook his head. “That’s not the problem. Their security is just too good.”

“I got through before,” she insisted.

He turned and swung his legs to the floor. “From inside the building, on a company computer. You said you were in your father’s office when you got through. He’d have access to every department. You just had to get past his password. I have to get past a number of encryptions just to get to his password.” He shook his head, blowing out a breath. “I just don’t think I’ve got the skill to do it.”

“Then we have to get back inside.”

He cocked his head at her. “Tell me again why we can’t just go to the police?”

“They’ll never believe a paranoid schizophrenic, Steve, and right now, I have zero evidence.”

He leaned forward, clasping his hands at his knees. “But with Owens’ car picking up the man who shot at you, maybe that would give them more incentive to investigate him.”

"Maybe." She set her empty yogurt cup and spoon on the end table between the beds. "But I doubt it. Especially if my dad insists that nothing is amiss like he did last fall." She swung her legs to the floor, facing him. "I wanted to try this way first, but there is someone at Pragnalysis who might be able to get us in after hours."

"Who's that?"

"Amy Reynolds, the receptionist. She and I were kind of like friends when I worked there."

He felt his own forehead furrowing. " 'Kind of like.' You said you thought someone at Pragnalysis sent Aaron McCain your way. Maybe it was her."

"No, I never told her about the embezzling. If anyone did it, it was Owens." She half smiled and rose. "And she disliked Owens almost as much as I did."

She went to the window to look out, and he watched her go. Her newly washed hair reached the middle of her back, hanging in what almost appeared to be long curls. She was wearing something new that Dani had left out for her this morning—a short cream sweater over yoga pants. He wasn't sure what all the yoga pants controversy was about. He certainly didn't mind looking at them. At least not on Tiff.

He dragged his distracted brain back to what she had suggested—practically breaking in to Pragnalysis. He didn't know if he really wanted to be a part of that or not. Doing something like that could get a black man shot. "Aren't there actual security guards that walk around with guns?"

She turned back to him. "You'd think so, wouldn't you? But that would mean they don't trust their own high-tech security systems."

He spread his hands. "So how are *we* going to get past their high-tech security systems?"

"We won't have to if we have a friend on the inside."

"That seems like a lot to ask of a friend. She'd be putting her job on the line. Maybe even her freedom if she was an accessory to a crime."

Tiffany didn't seem to like that answer and turned back to the window, changing the subject. "I wonder what's taking Will and Dani so long." She scanned the parking lot of the Days Inn

Will had moved them into. "They couldn't have been talking to my parents all this time."

Steve had wondered that himself. "I don't know. That's all Will mentioned this morning when they left."

As if summoned, they heard a key card being used, and the door opened. Dani came in first, looking like she'd been crying for a week. Steve jumped to his feet, not knowing what to say.

Tiffany, however, stepped toward her. "My parents often have that effect on me, but I didn't think they'd make you cry."

Dani shook her head. "Not your parents." She looked to Will, who had trailed her into the room. "Can you fill them in while I use the restroom?"

He nodded, and she slipped past him to get to the bathroom.

Will let out a sigh as he sat on the end of the bed, turning with one leg hitched up to face them. Steve sat back down on the women's bed, joined by Tiff, although she sat a good distance away from him. "So what's up with Dani?"

Steve and Tiffany listened to Will's story of the Grand Prix and how it had somehow ended up in the hands of Dani's ex-fiancé and then ultimately ended up as scrap metal, sending the driver to the E.R.

By the time he was finished, Steve's mouth was hanging open. "And the guy just flew in yesterday? That's crazy!"

"I know how it sounds, but Capt. Rand sent me pictures of the wrecked car and the license plate."

Tiffany sat in silence, and Steve could see wheels turning in her head. "So do the cops think this Bisbee guy could be working with Owens?"

Dani re-entered the room. "They were trying to make that connection, but I told them that was nuts."

Tiffany crossed her arms. "Why? How could he possibly have Owens' car unless the two were working together?" Her eyes got big. "Maybe he's the one who shot at me!"

Dani moved farther into the room, shaking her head. "No, no, no, slow down. I know Keith, and besides, I saw the guy who shot at you."

"You saw his face?"

"Well, no," Dani hedged. "He had on a ski mask, but—"

Tiffany rose. "And he was probably in a winter coat. How can you be sure?"

"Because I. . . " Dani faltered. She remembered noting that he was about Keith's height. She looked to Will. "There's no way it was Keith. Why would he be shooting at Tiffany? And he doesn't know Owens."

Tiffany wouldn't let it go. "How do you know? Pragnalysis sells its services to all kinds of big companies. What did he do for a living? You were wearing an awfully big diamond a few days ago."

Dani blinked and swallowed. "He uh. . . he is the CEO of Mystique, a high-end women's accessory franchise."

Tiffany nodded knowingly. "Owens was laundering the embezzled funds through other companies. Maybe one of them was Keith's. Maybe he used you as an excuse to come out here and get to me."

Dani couldn't believe it, but Keith had definitely hated the idea of her going to Brazil. *Was that because he already knew about the trafficking problem there? Was he a part of it?* She sank to the corner of the bed opposite Tiffany, remembering how angry he'd gotten when he'd learned she was chaperoning Tiffany home, and furious when she was staying longer to help find her.

"He. . . he did seem to be someone I didn't really know lately." She turned to look at Will. "Could I have been that stupid?"

"The shooter also shot at you, Dani. Would Keith do that?"

Before Dani could answer, Tiffany jumped in. "If it was too dark to identify Keith, it was probably too dark for him to identify you."

"This is all guesswork, Dani," Will reminded her, "until Keith can speak for himself."

She nodded but felt a sudden churning in her stomach. *Maybe he did recognize me, and that's why he got drunk.*

Chapter 21

Will sat at the small corner table of the room he'd booked for Tiffany and Steve alone, waiting for the coffee she was making. He couldn't guard their door as well as he would like with this arrangement—even though he and Dani were next door—but he recognized their need for privacy, as well as Dani's.

She was having a nap at the moment, although he wondered if she was really just staring at the ceiling, second-guessing everything that involved her relationship with Keith. He wasn't ready to jump on the blame train that Tiffany was on, but he had to admit, Bisbee in Owens' Grand Prix was pretty hard to explain.

Tiffany had wanted to talk about her "plan for getting the Pragnalysis evidence." Will was skeptical, but he'd give it a listen.

While the coffee dripped, Tiffany seemed to be preoccupied with her reflection in the mirror above the bureau, but not messing with her hair or make-up like most women did. She was just staring.

Suddenly she turned, catching Will looking at her, and blushed. She quickly grabbed the now full coffee pot and poured two cups. "I… Right now, I can't see my own reflection," she said as she brought the steaming mugs to the table.

Will cocked a brow in surprise. "What do you see?"

Sitting, she hooked her hair behind an ear. "Other people's faces." Her lips formed a slight smile. "I'm hoping it will improve in a few days." She sipped her coffee.

Will wondered how the girl was keeping any kind of hold on reality in these circumstances. He knew hallucinations could be involved with schizophrenia, but this was more like a merging of fiction and truth. He wondered if the trauma of Brazil had taken her schizophrenia symptoms to new heights. "Is the mirror the only place your brain… altars what you see?"

She shook her head. "When I'm off my meds, I see a lot of dragons." She brought her mug to her lips once more as Will remembered the artwork they had looked through in her dorm room. "You were a red one the first time I saw you."

The door opened and Steve came in, carrying a soda from the lobby's machine. Joining them at the table, he unscrewed the lid. "What did I miss?"

"Nothing yet," Will assured.

Tiffany set her mug down and looked to the man she had obvious feelings for. "I've been thinking about what you said earlier, Steve, and you were right about putting Amy in the position of having to choose friendship or her job. Getting us in after hours would definitely be risky for her, and us too as the evening security is obviously tighter. *But,*" she went on with a new mischievous look that made Will nervous, "I have an even better idea. We'll just walk in the front door."

She paused for what seemed like dramatic effect as she took another sip of coffee. Will lifted his mug, glad she wasn't advocating some kind of Mission Impossible security-breaching scenario, but he couldn't imagine Owens letting her just waltz in to a computer terminal and start hacking.

Steve beat him to the question. "So… then what? No one knows me, but they do know you."

"Ah, but they won't," she said mysteriously with a Latin American accent. "I will be Maria Montego, a rich Brazilian heiress in need of top security while visiting America." She had picked up a passing good accent, but both he and Steve must have looked disbelieving as she added with wide eyes, "You think that's a ridiculous scenario, but it's not, it's kind of a weekly occurrence at Pragnalysis. And all Amy would need to do is show us to either my dad's office or Owens' for a private consultation, and we're set."

Will set his cup down and reached for a creamer. "And what's your plan for keeping both of them away from their offices?"

She pointed a finger at him. "That's where you come in. You said you wanted to talk to Owens again. Just make it a long lunch that also includes my dad."

"Are you sure no one will recognize you?" Steve was obviously not buying it.

"Dark wig, designer clothes and a lot of make-up, and no one will look at me twice. We'll put you in an Armani suit and—"

"Armani? Where are you going to get the cash for that? I mean," he faltered, "I know you're stinking rich, but at the moment you don't really have access, so… "

She looked to Will, who had gotten up to retrieve a plastic spoon from the coffee supplies. "Any chance you—"

"Sorry, love," he said coming back to the table, "I'm already on my own resources now that you've been found. I've got to be cheap as chips."

"Okay, we'll… improvise. Use knockoffs. We'll only be seen by a few people anyway."

Will sat again, pondering her plan as he stirred in the creamer. "Just how long would this 'long lunch' have to be?"

She looked to Steve. "A couple of hours?"

He shrugged. "It's a complete unknown, Tiff. You said yourself, they probably changed the passwords and beefed up security since you got through."

Will thought of a problem with her plan. "How will it not look suspicious for you two to be in an office where the occupants are out to lunch?"

Tiffany's expression went positively devilish. "Don't worry. No one will suspect a thing. My father's office has a private elevator so he can come and go without being bothered if he doesn't want to be. If they're having lunch together, they'll leave that way, and no one will know that they're gone. Amy will put our meeting in the appointments so no one will even knock to find out."

Will couldn't help chuckling, amazed at the transformation in this woman he'd feared had had her brains completely scrambled. It was still a shame she had to deal with the schizophrenia, and he sincerely hoped this whole proposition wasn't a product of paranoia, but she appeared to have a mind that could work around the challenges. Even when she couldn't see her true self in the mirror. "So when do you propose to do this?"

"If we can get the shopping done, tomorrow or the next day."

He shook his head. "I don't like the idea of you out shopping. It's too out in the open."

She quirked her lips to the side. "Can Dani do it? She's not much bigger than me."

Will's brows shot up as he remembered the schmick dress Dani was wearing their last night in Brazil. "She might already have you covered" —he waved a hand toward Steve—"although I'm afraid I've got nothing for your tall, skinny friend."

"I actually have a decent suit my mother bought me for my grandfather's funeral last year. If you think it's safe to go back to my apartment."

Will nodded. "Give me your key, and I'll get it." He really didn't know if there was any merit to this charade, and Logan might think he was a complete nilwit for going along with it, but he didn't have the funds to hide this woman forever. They had to shake the Pragnalysis bush and see what fell out.

If nothing else, they could cross it off the list once and for all.

* * *

Dani heard Will come into their room and go into the bathroom. She had dozed a little, but it hadn't been a restful sleep. Dreams of following shadowy figures down dark alleys followed by Keith driving off cliffs *Thelma and Louise* style had jolted her awake more than once. What if Tiffany was right? What if she had nearly married a criminal? Could she trust her own instincts anymore? She felt as if she didn't know which way was up.

Will lay down on the bed behind her and wrapped an arm around her waist, pulling her tight against him. She hated the thoughts that ran through her head, but she couldn't stop them.

If she could be so wrong about Keith after so many months together, how could she have any confidence in her assessment of Will?

"Possum, you're as tense as a plank of wood. I think Tiffany's safe here. Why don't we get out and go see a movie or something? *Watch* some fiction instead of spinning it in your head."

"I'm not sure it is fiction, Will. The more I think about it, the more I remember things that fit."

He pulled on her hip, urging her to turn over. She did but didn't see agreement in his eyes. "What kind of things?"

"Well," she said, "sweeping her hair out of her eyes, "when we met, he promised me a job in his business, but then he always had a million excuses for not actually hiring me. Maybe he was afraid I'd find out what he was up to if I worked with him."

"Or," he said, sliding a hand from her shoulder to her elbow, "maybe he never really had a job in the first place and just used that to get you to close your store. Maybe he knew offering you a cooking and hostess job with no pay wouldn't cut it. He can be a jerk without being a crook."

"I know, but… his attitude about me staying to find Tiffany was so over the top. He had no sympathy for her at all!"

Will nodded. "Again, he could be the most selfish bastard on the planet and not be a money launderer."

"So how do you explain him having Owens' car?"

"I don't, possum. Not yet. We don't have enough information. Forming a conclusion ahead of information is just a good way to miss the evidence when it actually shows itself."

She supposed he was right, but she knew the possibility of Keith's duplicity would eat at her until she knew the truth.

He leaned in to give her a tender kiss. "There is something else we could do to take your mind off of… things," he said in a low, sexy voice.

Dani didn't want to make love with Will just as a distraction, and right now that is all it would be when she was feeling so unsettled. "I'm sorry, Will. I just… can't right now."

He kissed her nose then smiled. "I had to try."

She licked her lips, wondering if she'd really be able to concentrate on a movie. She supposed it would be better than stewing. "I don't feel like going out, but we could probably find something to watch here."

"All right, but we do need to do a couple of things first."

"What?"

He released her and got off the bed. "I need to set up a meeting with Morrow and Owens and go by Steve's place and pick up a suit."

"A suit? Why does he—"

"And you need to see if you have something designer-ish that would fit Tiffany." He walked to the end of the bed and waved a hand to her suitcase on a folding stand. "I thought maybe the dress you wore when you got drunker than a skunk in Brazil might work."

Dani sat up, feeling completely confused. "Are they… going out?"

"While I'm gone, why don't you go next door and let Tiffany tell you all about her wild hare to infiltrate Pragnalysis as a rich Brazilian heiress while I have Morrow and Owens tied up with a three martini lunch."

Dani blinked, and Will smirked, grabbing his coat off the hanger by the door. "See ya in a bit, possum."

She watched him go, then slipped on her shoes to go next door to find out what the heck was going on.

* * *

Keith had never felt so much like a big pile of shit in all his life.

It hurt to move. It hurt to breathe. It even hurt to look.

Thinking was as futile as catching fog. His memories of the last few days came in bits and pieces that rarely hung together for more than a few seconds.

He was obviously in a hospital, and a nurse had told him he'd been in a car accident. He didn't remember that at all. And did he see a police officer peeking in at one point, only to be shooed out by the nurse? Was he in trouble? Did he hit someone?

He thought he remembered Dani being there earlier, but that couldn't have been true because she was still in Brazil looking for that stupid runaway. He wondered if she even knew that he had been in an accident. Had his parents been told? Why weren't they here? And his sister lived in town too. Maybe they weren't letting anyone in to see him.

That had to be a good sign then. They let everybody in if you're dying.

He tried opening his swollen eyes but received a sharp pain knifing through his head for his efforts. He'd had at least one great dream. He was driving a beautiful black Pontiac Grand Prix with red interior. It was in primo condition—not a crack in the seat, not a a scuff on the dash... He couldn't remember why he was driving it. That part of the dream was lost. Maybe he'd look for one like it when he got out of here. He wondered how long that might be? How long until he didn't feel like a huge pile of shit?

He wished he could see. He wished he even felt like lifting an arm to call the nurse to find his phone for him. He needed to let people at work know what happened. This would probably not be good for his campaign. He needed to talk to Marion, his campaign manager. His brain caught on her face circling around a black hole of missing memories. They'd had a conversation recently. Something important. Something about an upcoming trip.

He blew out a breath of frustration and let go of what he couldn't quite grasp, feeling what he'd recovered shredding and swirling into thin strands, like streamers in a tornado. Resigned to sinking into the oblivion of sleep, he spared one more coherent thought for Dani, and hoped that when he woke again, she'd be there by his side.

Where she belonged.

Chapter 22

Steve knew he was grinning like an idiot, but that dress of Dani's looked like it was made for Tiff. An overlay of fabric was pleated into one shoulder seam and crossed her body to circle her waist before fanning out on the front of the skirt, accenting her curves without revealing her lost weight. And the rich teal brought out the color of her eyes. He liked her own wavy red hair more than the shoulder length, brunette wig she was wearing, but he was surprised at how good she looked, even in that.

She laughed. "I guess I look okay. You look like you want to eat me for dessert."

"Why wait for dessert?" he blurted, then hoped he hadn't said anything too provocative that might trigger an episode of some kind. "I mean… " *oh shit* "I probably shouldn't have said that."

She turned back to the full-length mirror on the wall. "No, it's okay. I… " She licked her lips, and Steve held his breath. "I want to know what you think." She messed with the wig, finger combing the bangs. "About me," she said softer. "I can't really see myself right now—inside or out. I just see my mother today. In a wig."

Steve felt as if he'd just entered a mine field. "You're… you're amazing. You're smart and… and resilient, and I'm proud to… to know you."

"Is that all?" She turned to look at him, a kind of yearning in her eyes he'd never seen before. "Why did you kiss me, Steve? I think you can tell me without… incident."

He slid his fingertips into his jeans pockets, forcing his shoulders up. Was he ready to admit his feelings? She had improved so much over the last several days, but there were still so many unknowns. And he wouldn't hurt her for the world. On the other hand, if he was as easy to read as Tiff said, she probably already knew. "I've never met your mother, but she can't be as beautiful as you are." He paused and swallowed. "When I was your tutor, I never let myself think about you as a woman I might want to… to date—teachers aren't really supposed to do that, but now…" He paused, weighing his words carefully.

"Now?" she said with a slight tremble to her voice.

"Now I… I do."

"So you actually meant to kiss me? It wasn't just a spontaneous, crazy Steve thing?"

He laughed. "Well, it probably was that, but" —he grew more serious— "I'd do it again if I could."

"Even knowing what happened in Brazil. Even knowing about the schizophrenia."

Her skeptical expression gave him a moment of pause. Could he do this? Should he do this? Her laughing face from last fall came to mind. Like Tiffany's baseline of reality, he had one too. He'd known her months before the kidnapping. He had to trust that she'd get back to that baseline again. He nodded. "Yeah," he said simply.

She stepped toward him, and Steve stepped back. "Tiff, this plan of yours requires *you.* Don't do something that will shut yourself down."

"I usually have some warning. Your kiss was just such a surprise last time, there was no time to step away." She paused for a moment, looking as if deliberating. "I want to try something." She put her hands up, palms toward him, the way they had for mirror skating. "An experiment."

He put his up to match hers, keeping several inches between them. Then she moved hers slowly to his. Their palms touched, and her breathing accelerated. He was tempted to pull away, but the perseverance in her gaze held him in place. He smiled. If anyone could beat this thing, she could.

After a minute, she pulled her hands away, and Steve lowered his. "Are you still with me?"

She nodded, but he could tell it hadn't been an experiment without cost. She was staring at his chest, fighting for some kind of control. He felt helpless as she fought dragons and monsters and who knew what else.

"Tiff?"

At last, her eyes found his, and she smiled.

He smiled back.

* * *

"So you have everything set up for tomorrow, then?"

Will nodded as he and Dani walked to the hospital elevators after being told that Keith had been moved to a room. "Yeah. Noon at The Capital Grille." He was glad they had an extra day to prepare.

"How did you get Morrow to come too?"

"That part was simple. He had actually offered to set up a meeting in the first place, remember? I just told him I'd reconsidered and would let him do it." He smirked as he pressed the up button. "Men like that love being in control."

After getting out on the third floor, Dani stopped, looking hesitant.

Will thought he knew why. "You don't have to see him, Dani. We can let the police ferret out the truth first."

She shook her head. "No." She started forward again. "I need to find out for myself."

He fell into step beside her. "I'm not saying that he's been lying to you for months, but if he has, why do you think he'll tell you the truth now?"

"I don't know, but I need to hear *his* explanation coming out of *his* mouth."

They found the nurses' desk, and Dani asked after Keith's room. After checking her computer, the nurse looked up, her eyes losing their smile. "Why don't you wait in the family lounge just down the hall and around the corner. I'll have the doctor come talk to you when she's free."

Will saw the panic form on Dani's face.

"Is there a problem?" she asked, taking a step closer. "I mean, they moved him from the ICU. He's improving, right?"

The nurse's smile seemed forced. "He just had a little allergic reaction to one of the antibiotics." She rose, evidently intending to escort them to the lounge she had mentioned. "I've sent a page to his doctor, so…"

She came out from behind her desk and waved for them to follow. Will put a comforting hand to Dani's back. Her emotions had been put through the wringer over this man lately.

The nurse, whose nametag read Cassi, opened a door and ushered them into a small room with comfortable seating, a TV, soda and snack machines. "It shouldn't be too long." She opened a cupboard. "There are cups, sugar, and cream for coffee up here."

"Thanks," Will said, heading straight for the stack of styrofoam cups.

The nurse left them alone, and he turned back to a sitting, stunned Dani. "Coffee, possum?"

She shook her head. "No thanks."

He got his coffee then sat beside her, cup in hand. "I can see that you're busy working on the worst-case scenario."

"I can't help it. I wonder if I've had two minutes of sanity in the last three weeks."

Will threw an arm around her. "I can think of at least one night where the world seemed right."

She looked up at him with a slight smile. "That was a good night."

They sat in silence while Will sipped his coffee, wondering himself what kind of "allergic reaction" needed a doctor's explanation.

With the coffee, he started to feel too warm in his coat. He had just gotten out of it and helped Dani shed hers, when the door opened, admitting a small crowd of people all talking at once.

"An allergic reaction!" a woman said with shock. "I can't believe it. Keith has never been allergic to anything!"

"Mom, that doesn't mean a thing," a younger woman was explaining with exasperation. "You can develop an allergy at any time. And besides, he may be on a drug that he's never had before."

"What kind of bullshit hospital is this?" An older man with his sunnies perched atop his shaved head was bringing up the rear with poor nurse Cassi looking as if she needed a break. "We need to get him back to KU Med, that's what."

Dani tensed against Will's arm. "Oh no," she breathed out on a whisper.

Will felt the room close in as well. He very much doubted that Keith had told his rellies about the break-up yet. For all they knew, Dani was still on track to being a part of their family.

"The doctor can explain everything," Cassi was trying to appease. "Please help yourself to whatever you can find in here, and—"

"I just want to see my son!" the woman, who must have been Keith's mom, said, looking as if she were close to tears. Then her gaze fell their way, and she threw her arms wide. "Dani! Oh, Dani!"

Will noted over his cup of coffee that she had one of those trendy haircuts that was shorter in the back, with a fair amount of brassy highlights. He wasn't sure it worked on a woman of her age.

Dani rose stiffly. "Lillian."

The woman wrapped her in a bear hug so tight, Will wondered that he didn't hear a rib crack.

"What happened, dear?" She pulled back, her hands still on Dani's arms. "We didn't realize that you two had planned a Colorado trip after your Brazilian… jaunt."

"It… wasn't really planned. I just—"

"Women these days!" the man Will was assuming to be Keith's dad butted in. "If you had left me for a month in the middle of my congressional campaign," he directed toward his wife, "we would have been through."

"Roger!" Lillian admonished.

Will raised a brow and rose to his feet, ready to move Dani out if he needed to.

"Dad, you never had a congressional campaign!" the daughter said, rolling her eyes.

"I'm just sayin'!" he threw back at her, moving to the snack machine.

"Well, you're saying too much!" The taller woman with short, brownish hair moved in on Dani for a hug. "I'm so sorry," Will heard her whisper over Dani's shoulder. "If I could have left them at home, I would have." She released Dani with a sad smile. "How are you doing?"

"I'm okay, Heather. I'm… just waiting for news, the same as you all."

She nodded before glancing up at Will with almost a double take that turned into an appreciative smile. "Hi, I'm Heather Bisbee, Keith's sister? Are you a friend of Keith's or Dani's?"

He said "Dani" while she said "Keith." He looked to her in surprise.

"I mean, Will is a friend of both of ours," Dani side-stepped.

Evidently, she wasn't about to enlighten the Bisbee fam about their relationship shuffle at the moment. He couldn't blame her, but he knew it would just be harder later. Best to rip the band-aid off now.

"Well, Will," Heather said with cheer that hardly seemed to fit the occasion, "it's very good to meet you."

"Nice to meet you too, Heather. I'm sorry about Keith."

He saw her pupils dilate and silently cursed his accent. *I've got to learn how to turn that off.*

"Oh, yes," she said as if Keith were the very last thing on her mind. Her face took on an almost theatrical concern. "We've been in shock since we got the call."

"Shock is hardly the word, dear," Lillian put in. "We've been absolutely devastated, and now this business about an allergic reaction…" The woman shook her head.

"Complete bullshit, if you ask me!" came from across the room where Roger was helping himself to coffee. "This lousy hospital is going to have a malpractice suit on its hands if it isn't careful."

Heather tried to guide her mother to a chair. "Mom, why don't you sit. Do you want something to drink?"

While Heather studied the offerings of the vending machine, Will and Dani sat back down. Dani's hands were in her lap, her right gripping her left, and he wished he could unclench them before she had a heart attack, but "friend" Will would not be allowed to hold Keith's fiancée's hand.

While Dad Bisbee was stirring multiple creamers into his coffee and Heather was trying to appease Mom Bisbee with a vitamin water and protein bar, Will leaned in and whispered, "Breathe, Dani. I'm right here. I won't let them eat you alive."

"You're here, but my ring isn't," she hissed through clenched teeth.

Will suddenly twigged that she was trying to hide her left hand. He leaned in again. "Maybe it's time to come clean."

She gave him a look that should have ignited him on the spot. He straightened and lifted his hands in a clear gesture of leaving it to her.

After getting a different flavor of bar for her mother, Heather came to sit across from Dani, eating the reject. "So there's something we're all curious about… Why was Keith cruising on a mountain road without you?" She put a quick hand to Dani's knee. "Not that we're not glad that you weren't in the crash as well, but it just seemed strange."

Will could well believe that was a topic discussed all the way from Kansas City.

Dani carefully shifted her hands until her arms were crossed over her chest, still keeping that naked ring finger out of sight. "Well… I… "

The door opened, and a small woman entered in a white coat, her brunette hair thrown up in what women often referred to as a "messy bun," and Dani was saved from answering as all eyes turned to the doctor.

"Are you the Bisbees?" she asked, pushing her blue-framed glasses up her nose.

Good ole Dad chimed in with, "That's us. Are you the quack that gave my son the wrong medicine?"

The doctor, who introduced herself as Dr. Loy, only paused a moment before launching into an explanation of how allergies are always an unknown until an allergen is first introduced to any given person.

Heather interrupted. "Yes, all reasonable people know this. Dad, will you shut up so she can tell us about Keith?"

The man pursed his lips and waved a hand for the doctor to proceed. Some of the things Dani had told Will about her ex put him in the jerk column, in his opinion, but evidently, he was an improvement over the previous model.

The doctor took a breath and went on. "Keith has had a rather severe allergic reaction to an antibiotic we gave him due to the lacerations on his face and head. This has only exacerbated the swelling in his brain due to the concussion. We have switched to a different drug and are administering steroids to both counteract the reaction and bring down the swelling. You can see him one or two at a time, but be prepared; he will not respond."

Lillian rose to her feet. "So he's in a coma?"

"Yes. With the reduced swelling, he should come out of it, but there's no way to tell at this point if any damage has been done to the brain itself. All we can do is wait and see."

Lillian's lips trembled as she fought for control, and Heather got up to put an arm around her. Even Roger's face showed more fear than rage.

The doctor went on. "By morning, we should have a good idea if this treatment is working."

Will tuned out the rest of what the doctor was saying as he focused on Dani, who was gripping his arm. He moved his hand to her knee and squeezed, not giving a wallaby's ass what anyone in the room might think of it.

As soon as the doctor was out the door, Lillian started to whimper, Roger let out a string of curses to rival anything Will had ever heard in the RAR, and Heather just sat, looking stunned.

And that's when the policeman showed up.

Chapter 23

Dani had been so sidetracked with not revealing that she was no longer engaged to Keith, she'd completely forgotten about the whole stolen car issue. The policeman's appearance brought it all back like a brick to the head, and since they never mentioned it, his family obviously didn't know about that part of their little "Colorado vacay."

Dani knew it was the chicken's way out, but she couldn't stay in that room a minute longer. She jumped to her feet before the cop had a chance to open his mouth, and started to put on her coat. "I... I'm not feeling well," she blurted. "I think I need to go back to my hotel."

Will rose and swept up his own coat. "I'll drive you."

The policeman put up a hand. "Are you part of the Bisbee family?"

"No! No, I'm not. Not yet, and it wouldn't be right for me to—"

Heather jumped to her side. "Of course you're family! All that's left is the 'I do.' "

Dani waved an agitated hand, even though it was hidden in her coat pocket. "Yes, well, I'm sure this is just about the car and the insurance, and I've already told the police everything I know about that anyway." She kept moving toward the door.

"Where are you staying, dear?" Lillian asked, and Dani turned back, wondering how she could ever get out of this mess. Will was right. The truth would have been better. But she couldn't start that now in front of this cop. And she couldn't tell them she was staying at a cheap Days Inn either. They'd never believe that Keith would agree to that. "The… the…" Her mind was a complete blank.

Will rescued her. "Castle Marne." He pushed her toward the door. "It's a Bed and Breakfast. She'll text you the address."

After they were out and down the hall, Dani shook off her shock. "Castle Marne? What the heck, Will? Did you just make that up on the spot?"

"No, it's a real place. It's not that far from where we're at, but it's a lot pricier, I'm sure. It truly looks like a castle."

"But I'm not at this Castle Marne. How—"

"You will be. At least I'm hoping they've got a room."

The doors opened, and they stepped in. "My credit card is just about maxed out, Will, and I gave Keith's back to him."

"It's okay, I'll take care of it."

"I thought you needed to be thrifty now that you're working on your own case."

"I do, but I've got some savings. I'll be all right."

They stepped out, and Dani couldn't believe what Will was willing to do. For a lie.

Her lie.

She shook her head as they made their way to the exit. "No, I can't let you do that. I'm going to have to tell them eventually. I guess…" She slowed to a stop. "Oh, gees, I guess it should be now."

She moved to a furniture grouping in front of an expanse of windows and sat in a pale orange vinyl chair. Will sat in another on the other side of the small table to wait with her, and she realized that she didn't just "think" she loved this man as she had told him a few days ago. She loved him with all her heart. And she also knew she had never loved Keith in the same way. She reached a hand toward him over the table, and he took it. "How did you know the Days Inn wouldn't do?"

He chuckled. "Honey, I saw that rock Keith gave you. And I've been amazed that you'd take it off for me." He laughed again. "Until I met that family."

Dani laughed too, knowing that she always wanted this crazy Australian by her side, and she'd trade any diamond for that privilege.

After waiting nearly an hour, Dani got a call from Heather.

"Oh gees, here goes." She blew out a breath and answered. "Hello, Heather."

"Dani, we're at the Castle Marne, downstairs. We thought to just check in here too, but they are full up, and they won't give us any guest information. They said if you're here, you'll need to come down to see us... And we need to talk to you. Did you know about the— All right, all right, mother, we need to talk in person... Anyway, are you feeling better? Can you come down to the uh... parlor, I guess?"

Dani had no idea how she and Will had missed them leaving the hospital, but she supposed there were other exits. "Oh... well... I actually checked out. It... just didn't feel right to be there without Keith." Dear God, was she lying again? She risked a glance at Will, who was giving her one of his looks. She saw his toothpick flip up and down even though he wasn't chewing on one at the moment. She rolled her eyes. Why couldn't she just tell these people the truth?

Roger's voice blared in the background, making the "why" crystal clear. "Are we just going to sit down and have tea in the *parlor* while my boy is not only in a coma but wanted by the police for auto theft? She knew that! She had to know that! That's why she ran out of the room! Something smells rotten. Does that woman realize that Keith's congressional bid will be dead when this gets out?"

Dani sucked in a breath and looked to Will, who had probably heard the whole tirade even without putting it on speaker. She hadn't thought about Keith's campaign. Then Roger's "that woman" registered in her brain, and a fire rose up inside her. She knew she could tell Heather about the broken engagement, but frankly, she never wanted to have a conversation with Roger again. She had had to put up with his rude behavior when she thought he was going to be her father-in-law, but now she realized she was free.

"Heather," she began with a new confidence, "I'll be glad to talk to you at the Days Inn, but you need to come alone. I refuse to talk to *that man*."

"All... right. What's the address?"

"It's very close to where you are. Just Google it." Dani blew out a shaky breath as she hung up with a fierce press of her thumb and put the phone screen-down on the table. Closing her eyes, she put a hand to her chest, willing her heart rate to return to normal. Did it race this fast undercover in Brazil? She felt a hand on her forearm, but hated to look up into what would probably be disappointed eyes.

"I'm proud of you for standing up for yourself." She looked over at him, surprised. "No one deserves what that man dishes out." He rose and offered his hand. "Come on, we'd better get to the Days Inn before they do."

"Oh my gosh, I didn't think of that!"

They moved quickly to the exit and stepped into the huge revolving door. Will grinned. "Never a dull moment."

She smiled. "Well, you can't say I'm boring."

"That's a fair dinkum," Will proclaimed as they exited and jogged through the parking garage.

* * *

It wasn't long before Tiffany started to feel like a caged tiger, their little motel room reminding her far too much of her tiny cabin in the jungle. She knew they shouldn't go out, but she was seriously afraid of the thoughts that had been torturing her for the past hour.

Touching Steve had probably been stupid, but she'd done it without an appearance by the six-eyed beast or going catatonic. She'd won that particular battle, but the war was another thing altogether. He had been glued to his computer screen since lunch, and while she wanted him to find a way through the Pragnalysis security, at the moment she was starting to crave a drink. She needed a diversion.

What that would be, however, she didn't have a clue. This cheapo motel didn't even have a microwave or mini-fridge, let alone an indoor pool or a decent gym. She understood Will's desire for a cheap hotel, but this one was beyond cheap. All they had was a TV and a lot of pay-per-view options.

After pacing back and forth for some minutes, Steve looked up. "Bored?"

She stopped and looked to his big brown eyes. "Yes. But that's not all. The walls are closing in on me today."

He closed his laptop. "How can I help?"

"I really don't know. We're not supposed to go out."

"I don't know how anyone could possibly know that we're here. We checked in around midnight, and Will paid for both rooms. They don't even have our names at the front desk." He rose from the bed and stretched his back. "A short walk outside would probably be okay."

That sounded like heaven to Tiffany.

He went on. "Stuff your hair under her stocking cap, or" —his brows lifted mischievously— "put on that wig."

Tiffany couldn't help smiling. "Got a little fantasy going on there?"

Steve was the picture of innocence. "I am only thinking about your safety."

She swept up the brunette pile of hair on the bureau and headed for the bathroom mirror. "Just give me a minute."

It actually took about five to get her hair all packed into the hair net again in such a way that it wouldn't look like she had a tumor. She wasn't seeing her mother anymore. Instead, she saw Celeste, one of the American girls trapped in Brazil.

Finally satisfied, she slipped on the wig and came out to find Steve already in coat and hat. She grabbed hers, as well as her big sunglasses, and they headed out, hoping Will wouldn't show up right then to spoil their outing.

The motel had balconies across the front and back of the building with stairs going down the sides. As they descended the last set, they heard angry voices. "Dad," a woman's voice was saying, "she said she didn't want to talk to you. She probably won't even come down if she knows you're here."

Tiffany and Steve moved to the corner of the building where a woman seemed to be arguing with her parents right in front of the Days Inn main entrance.

"Why wouldn't Dani want to talk to Roger?" the older woman asked as the older man pulled the door open and held it for her. "What has gotten into her all of a sudden?"

At the mention of "Dani," Tiffany and Steve exchanged glances. Then Tiffany followed them into the building, pulling Steve over to look through travel brochures while she tried to find out who these people were and what they wanted with Dani.

"It's not 'all of a sudden,' " the older man argued. "She was never right for Keith. And this proves it."

Tiffany's ears pricked again. *Keith. So this is Keith's family.*

The daughter, who had to be Keith's sister, tried to bring the conversation volume down by lowering her own voice. "I agreed to come alone, so if you two really want to know what's going on with Dani, you should wait out in the car."

He pointed toward the door. "If you haven't noticed, this isn't exactly a stellar part of town. We'll probably get mugged sitting out there. I expect our tires to be gone when we go back out."

The daughter rolled her eyes as the woman behind the desk asked them if they wanted to check in.

"Not on your life, sweetheart," the man dished out with attitude, then turned back to his daughter. "Just call her. Don't tell her that your mother and I are here."

The daughter looked like she was on the verge of disowning both of them, but she pulled her phone out of her purse, all the while giving her father the stink eye.

Tiffany would love to ask these people some questions about their son, but she knew it was unlikely that they would know if Keith was a money launderer or not. And if they did know, they wouldn't tell her.

Steve nudged her arm with his. She looked up, and he whispered, "Let's just go."

She supposed he was right. They weren't going to learn anything here. As they headed toward the door, the daughter spoke into her phone. "Dani, I'm in the Days Inn lobby. First let me just say that Keith would not expect you to check into something so… inexpensive, even if he's not with you. And second," —she sighed— "they wouldn't let me come alone. Just come down, and I'll try to control Dad."

Tiffany wondered how Dani was going to "come down" when she wasn't up. At least no one had answered their knock when she and Steve had gone past Will and Dani's room.

Steve pushed the door open and gently nudged her out just in time to see Will and Dani getting out of their car across the lot. Tiffany turned and headed for the corner of the building before Will could catch them in the act of "being in the open."

They walked briskly along the side of the building, knowing it would have to be a short walk now that their protectors were back. "Wow, Dani's lucky to be rid of that bunch."

"They did seem to be an explosive group," Steve agreed, "although who knows how we would act with a son in the hospital."

She supposed he was right, although she had a hard time feeling sorry for Keith, who could very well be in league with Owens. She wondered what Keith was like? Surely Dani wouldn't have been engaged to him if he was as obviously awful as his father, but maybe she really had only been with him for his money.

As someone with money, she knew the feeling of never being sure of your friendships or your boyfriends. She sniffed. *McCain was an idiot. If he had managed to marry me, he would have gotten far more than whatever he got paid to kidnap me.*

"What are you thinking about?" Steve asked as they turned left to go around the Days Inn property.

"Just wondering if you're only here for the money?"

He stopped and looked at her with his mouth hanging open.

She regretted her words immediately. "I'm just teasing, Steve. No amount of money could make up for my issues."

He started walking again, but his mood had taken a serious tumble.

"I'm sorry. Seriously, I was just kidding."

He shook his head with tight lips. "I swear I'll tear up your little proposal when we get back to the room. You don't need to pay me to help you. I want to help you."

Tiffany risked grabbing his arm. Without skin-to-skin contact, she felt no warning buzz—heard no low growl. "Why?"

"I told you earlier, I... I... care about you."

"No," she said, continuing to hold onto him. "You said you might want to date me. That you'd like to kiss me again. That's not the same as caring about me."

"Well I do."

They walked in silence for a while, then he said, "You know, you're not the only one who thinks about money. I think about it from the other perspective—from the poor college TA's perspective. Why would Tiffany Morrow want to be with me?

What could I give her that she doesn't already have?" He gave her a quirky smile. "Maybe she's only after my brain."

Tiffany laughed, and so did Steve, and without thought, she linked her arm with his.

* * *

Will knew this conversation was not going to be "sweet," but he was determined to keep it as short as possible for Dani's sake. He didn't want to cause trouble for the motel, and it actually wasn't that cold out, so he suggested they all step outside.

As soon as they were out and away from the door, Roger went on the attack. "So you didn't want to talk to Lil and me, huh? Well, I've got some questions that—"

Will stepped toward him. "Put a sock in it, Bisbee. Either you bite your bum and let Dani say her piece, or I will personally escort you to your vehicle. We don't know why Keith was in a stolen car or why he was driving on mountain roads at night, so don't even ask." He looked to Dani. "Okay, love, tell them what needs to be said."

She let out a deep breath. "Keith and I are no longer engaged. I broke up with him several days ago. Before the accident. That's why I wasn't driving with him."

Their faces all showed their shock. Even Roger seemed surprised.

Dani pressed on. "He left me late morning on Saturday and it was about that same time on Sunday morning that we got news of his accident."

Heather stepped toward her. "Oh, honey, whatever disagreement you've had can be fixed. You're so good for Keith and—"

"He's not good for me," Dani countered.

"How?" Roger asked with eyes blazing. "How could having a man who bought you anything you wanted—including a trip to Brazil—not be good for you?"

"Some things can't be 'bought,' Mr. Bisbee," Dani shot back. "I'll admit he's not the asshole that you are, but he still falls short of what I want in a husband."

"It's like you said, Roger," Lillian said quietly, "Keith was going through a mid-life crisis. It started with her, and it ended in a stolen car in the ditch."

Dani sucked in a breath, and Will had had enough. “All right, onya bike. Tell your story walkin’.”

He tried to herd them away from the building, but Roger stood his ground, crossing his arms. “I’d like to see you try and move me anywhere I don’t want to go.”

Will was sorely tempted to give the bastard a black eye, but he truly didn’t want to end up back at police headquarters. Instead, he stepped back and threw an arm around Dani. “Are you ready to go up?”

She was breathing hard. “More than ready.”

They took several steps toward the side of the building and the stairs before Heather called after Dani. She stopped and turned to look at the woman who truly didn’t seem to belong in this horrible family. “So you and… ” —Heather flicked her head toward Will— “him.”

Dani gave a small nod, and to Will’s surprise, Heather smiled. “I can see it.”

* * *

Will, Dani, Tiffany, and Steve were all going over the next day’s plans when there was a rather urgent knocking on the door. Will got up and moved cautiously toward it. “Who is it?”

“I’m on staff.” It was a male voice. “We’ve received a bomb threat and are evacuating the building.”

Steve immediately closed his laptop, and everyone jumped to their feet, grabbing coats and hats.”

Will opened the door to the cold late afternoon air. “I assume this is a credible threat,” he said to the young man already moving to the next door. He could hear knocking above and below.

“Yes, we believe so.” He knocked on Steve and Tiffany’s door.

Will pointed a thumb behind him. “They’re in here.”

The man moved on, but projected back at Will the need for them to get out and move out of the area. “We’ll send you a text when we’ve got the all clear.”

Will stepped back in to find Dani right behind him, holding his coat. She had her purse, and Steve had his laptop. His wallet and the car keys were in his pocket, so he guessed that's all they really needed. "All right boys and girls, let's head out."

He took Dani's hand and turned right, striding toward the end of the building to the stairs. They had to wait a moment for a small crowd moving out ahead of them. "Never a dull moment," Dani said when they finally started down from the fourth floor.

"Yeah," he said with what sounded like disbelief. "Color me skeptical, but I don't believe there's a bomb."

"Why not?" Steve asked as they trotted down the stairs.

"Tiffany, stuff that red hair of yours under your hat," Will answered in his own way.

"You think this is a ploy to get Tiffany out of the building?"

"It could very well be. I'm not taking any chances."

"How did they find us?" Steve sounded as exasperated as Will felt.

"I don't know."

"Well, what can we do?" Tiffany managed to keep moving down the stairs even while twisting her hair up on top of her head. "They're not going to let us stay here."

"We'll have a little time before they check all these stairs." They reached the bottom, but he didn't go through the metal door that would put them on the south side of the building. Instead, he urged them to the side so others could pass. "I'll go get the car and bring it along here." There wasn't any parking on this side of the building, but there was room for a car to drive by. "Stay here until I get back."

He went out with the crowd and made his way to his rental car in the small lot, keeping a wary eye out for movement around the edges. It wasn't dark yet, but it soon would be. Before getting in, he retrieved a small, locked case from the trunk. Once in the driver's seat, he pulled out another key ring out of his pocket that held a small key and opened it. He no longer cared about Denver's gun laws. He would protect those in his charge. He slipped the handgun in his coat pocket and started the car.

Before he could back out, however, there was a rap on his window. He looked over to see Roger Bisbee glaring in at him. *Bloody hell.*

He lowered the window a couple inches. "This is not a good time for a conversation, mate. There's been a bomb threat in the motel."

His eyes went wide. "Well that would be a benefit to the city to be rid of this eyesore, and it's all the more reason to get what belongs to Keith before the place blows sky high."

Will saw red. "If you are referring to Dani, she—"

"Dani?" The old man huffed out a breath of derision. "You can keep that bimbo. I just want the ring. It's not among Keith's possessions, so she must still have it."

Will couldn't believe what he was hearing. Did he actually expect Will to go back in and get a piece of jewelry in the midst of an emergency evacuation? "Mr. Bisbee, you've lost the plot here, and I don't give a rat's ass about your precious ring right now. My job is saving lives." He put the window up and the car in reverse, his jaw clenched at the audacity of the man, but a pounding on his trunk had him squinting at his rearview mirror.

Will threw the gear shift back in park and exited the car with way too much adrenaline building. "Bisbee, if you don't get out of my way right now..."

The man stepped directly into his way. "I just need the ring. Bomb scares are usually just that—scares. But if you're too chicken to go back in, give me your key card, and I'll do it. You probably have no idea what that ring is worth, but I do!"

For a brief second, Will wished the building would blow and turn that rock into dust. "I'm not giving you my key card. Now move out of my way."

Bisbee folded his arms over his chest the way he'd done earlier in the day, and this time, Will was more than willing to show him that he could indeed make him move. He came at him hard, shoving him a good six feet.

Roger recovered his footing before going down, a bit of the confidence gone out of his eyes, but sheer stubborn still squared his jaw. "Is that all you got?"

Will's chin ticked down and to the right as he strode toward him again. The man swung a fist this time, but Will went low, putting his shoulder into the man's chest, pushing him between two vehicles on the other side of the lot.

It was the explosion behind him that took them both to the asphalt.

Chapter 24

The three left waiting at the bottom of the stairs on the side of the Days Inn jumped with what sounded like an explosion, stepping away from the building and turning to look up.

"Was that inside?" Dani asked in a panic.

Tiffany turned and put her hands to the door handle. "We need to get out of here!"

Steve grabbed her arm. "I don't think that was inside the motel." He tried to herd them back away from the door. "It didn't sound right."

He turned to look out the prison-like bars that defined the stairwell. In the dwindling late afternoon light, he couldn't really see anything other than people rushing off the property. There was a police car parked on the edge, and he pulled back before their hiding place was discovered. He looked to the two antsy women. "Will said to stay here." He tried to put the kind of authority in his voice that Will had. "So that's what we're going to do."

Even he was getting nervous as the smell of smoke reached them and the sirens started. He looked out several times over the course of the next tense minutes, but he couldn't see anything from their angle. "I wonder if it was a car bomb," he mused out loud.

Dani was beside him in an instant. "Do you see Will?"

"No, I can't see anything." He reached for the handle. "You two stay here. I'll see what I can find out."

"I'm going with you!" Dani insisted.

Steve shook his head. "Somebody needs to stay with Tiff."

Tiffany wasn't having it. "Let's all go."

Steve blew out a breath. He knew he'd get nowhere with these headstrong women. "Fine, but I go first." He reached out and tucked a wisp of red hair under her stocking hat, then turned and slowly pushed the door open.

There was a regular cacophony of sirens now, and even though a crowd of people had fled the scene, a new crowd seemed to have gathered and were being pushed back to make way for the firetruck. Keeping to the building, he quickly moved to the corner before they were boxed in. He couldn't see the tall Australian anywhere.

Dani tugged on his sleeve. "Let me get on your back so I can see over everybody."

Steve squatted down for her to climb on. Once he was standing again, she levered higher with her hands on his shoulders until her feet were in his hands. "Oh my gosh, I'm pretty sure that's where we parked." She pointed toward the wrecked vehicle, whose flames had engulfed the cars on both sides and shouted, "Will! Will, where are you?"

Though a number of people looked their way, none answered or came their direction. He felt her shift as she surveyed the rest of the lot. "There are ambulances parked at the 7 Eleven across the street. Let's go over there."

She sounded calm, but he knew she really wasn't. She jumped down, and they tried to find a way through the wrought iron fencing that surrounding the lot. Ultimately, he lifted each woman over before vaulting over easily himself. Jogging across the street, Dani started to shout, "Will! Will are you here?"

There was still no answer, but the crowd noise and sirens would make it difficult for anyone to hear.

"Will!" Dani yelled when they were within rock-throwing distance, a distress in her voice that squeezed Steve's heart. He took Tiffany's gloved hand, and the two exchanged worried looks.

Then a man sitting on a cot at the open door of one of the ambulances stood and turned. He looked relatively unharmed although one arm was out of his coat and in a sling, and it looked as though his shoulder had been bandaged. His good arm took Dani in and hugged her to his chest. As Steve and Tiffany approached, Will looked over Dani's head. "Couldn't keep 'em in?"

Steve shook his head. "I did try."

Will nodded with only a slight smile that faded fast. Waving them around the cot, he led them between the two ambulances. "We shouldn't be out in the open."

After they were all in the narrow space, he blew out a breath, his arm still around Dani. "This is getting pretty serious. If it weren't for Roger Bisbee, I'd be dead instead of standing here with a clipped shoulder."

"Roger!" Dani blurted in surprise.

Will pointed to the other ambulance briefly before bringing his arm back to Dani. "He's in that one. He just went down pretty hard, and it didn't help that I went down on top of him. He might have some cracked ribs and a concussion."

Tiffany asked what they all wanted to know. "Why was that rude dude back again?"

Will looked to Dani. "It seems he wanted the engagement ring. And bomb scare or not, he was determined to get it."

Dani's mouth dropped open. "You have got to be kidding!"

"But like I said, if it weren't for him making me so goddamned mad that I got out of the car, I would have been in it when the bomb went off." He looked to Steve and Tiffany. "Or we all might have been." He squeezed his lips together as though thinking for a moment before going on. "So I think we need to fill the cops in on what you suspect Tiffany."

She started to protest, but he put up a hand, shaking his head. "I know all your arguments, but you need to be under police protection." He wiggled the gloved fingers sticking out of the sling. "And I'm officially impaired."

They were interrupted by an EMT. "Mr. Yarnel, you really need stitches in that shoulder, but seeing that it's not a life-threatening emergency, your friends could drive you." He held up a clipboard. "I'll just need your signature here for insurance purposes" —he flipped the page up— "and here, if you are refusing an ambulance ride to the hospital."

Will grimaced as he tried to sign his name left-handed. As soon as the EMT was gone, Tiffany chimed in. "But what about our plans for tomorrow? If we can't catch the embezzlers, I'll be running all my life."

Will looked torn. "If we can get you there safely, then maybe, but right now, I don't know how to get you anywhere safely. These people seem to be right behind us wherever we go, and they are getting more desperate, as tonight they obviously didn't care who else they hurt to take you out."

"So they will assume we will move from here," Tiffany said. "Let's fool them and just stay." She unbuttoned her coat and pulled out the brunette wig she'd draped over her shoulder. "We take you to the ER and buy some different hats and scarves in the gift shop, and I'll wear my wig. Then we take four different rides back."

Will looked more than skeptical, and Steve felt the same. "We haven't gotten an all-clear yet to go back in."

"Yeah, but I bet we will before you're stitched up." She was starting to sound desperate. "Just give me one more day, Will, before we bring in the cops. I just know they'll screw it up by tipping them off somehow."

Steve couldn't help feeling there was something Tiffany wasn't telling them—a reason why she didn't want any help from the police. "Tiff, it's not like they'll send in the Keystone Cops or even raid the place. They will probably just turn over your testimony to the kind of investigators that look into corporate fraud and corruption. They'll do an audit and—"

"And give them plenty of time to hide the evidence," she insisted.

"And what makes you think they haven't already hidden the evidence?" Will's voice was kind, yet firm.

Tiffany's voice was not; she was close to hysterical. "Because I'm being stalked and stolen and shot at and bombed! If they were done milking the company, and all their fingerprints were wiped clean, they wouldn't be worried about a paranoid schizophrenic!" She paused for just a moment. "And besides," she said more quietly, "if Owens was responsible for sending me to a Brazilian brothel, I want to be the one to take him down."

Any rebuttal was interrupted by headlights shining between the ambulances. "That's our ride to the hospital," Dani said as she attempted to turn Will around.

"What?" he said confused. "When did you call a ride?"

"While you guys were farting around," she said emphatically. "Somebody has to take care of you."

Steve felt the same about Tiffany, but he wasn't sure she could let anyone do that for her just yet. He stuck an elbow out to her with a smile, hoping to bring her back to a calmer place. "My lady?"

She took it the same way she had on their walk—a careful slide with her gloved hand. "It's kind of funny that you've gone all medieval on me," she said as they followed Will and Dani to the car, moving quickly so they wouldn't be "out in the open" long, "when I haven't seen a dragon all day."

Steve grinned and opened the back door for her. "Dragons or not, I'll still be your knight."

She climbed in beside Dani, and Steve got in the front. She leaned forward behind him and whispered. "A black knight with a shining heart."

Steve smiled and buckled his seatbelt. He didn't care how long she needed to recover from Brazil. He could wait.

* * *

Dani had often heard jokes about "hospital time" but hadn't had much experience herself. Even more annoying than waiting for Will to be seen, evaluated, and stitched was waiting for the paperwork to be all taken care of after. It all was made more complicated by the Stafford Investigations health insurance plan that spanned several countries, and the fact that Will's primary care physician was back in São Paulo. The hospital needed the space, so they were sent out to the lobby to wait, even though Will had gotten the all-clear message from the motel an hour ago.

Tiffany didn't let the time go to waste, however, as she continued making the case for her Pragnalysis plan to go forward. In spite of all, Will had eventually agreed, but only after she promised that if they didn't find what they wanted, she'd give up and let him bring in the police.

He also had a few safety measures that he wanted implemented. First, they were not to walk anywhere. They would need to be dropped off and picked up right at the door. They also had to be out in ninety minutes. He doubted he could keep the men occupied longer than that. Dani would accompany them and make sure they didn't get so lost in computer hacking that they lost track of the time.

Dani was kind of surprised by that. She had assumed he would want to keep her with him. She hoped it meant that he was starting to loosen up a little bit and trust her more.

"Oh, that's perfect!" Tiffany clapped her hands together. "She can be part of my entourage!" Then she leaned forward to see Dani around Will. "You've got a great dress for you, right?"

Dani was almost embarrassed to say how many expensive designer dresses she had in her bag. "Yeah, I've got one or two." She couldn't help the grin that came to her face with her next thought. "And I just happen to have a big old diamond ring I could wear." She looked to Will's raised brows. "One more time—just for show."

"If you want to risk losing it," he said, looking weary.

"Remember how hard it was to get off. I doubt I'll lose it if I can get it on again."

Steve chuckled. "Maybe Keith's dad will be back at the motel, waiting, when we get back."

Dani cringed at the thought. She wanted to think that was absurd, but she didn't actually know. From what Will said, she doubted that his injuries warranted being admitted to the hospital, but she hoped a concussion would at least keep him from driving for a few days.

At long last, a tall, broad man in scrubs appeared carrying a clipboard. "I think we've got the info we need for your insurance. Just need another signature, and you're good to go."

Will scrawled his name again as best he could, and when they were alone, he said, "All right. So Steve's going back first and will wait in the lobby for Tiffany. Then we'll arrive about twenty minnies later. I've already talked to the front desk about moving to different rooms on another floor using Dani's name instead of mine, but wait until we get there to do that." He sighed. "I should have moved you all to another hotel, no matter the cost. Motel room doors are so—"

"Out in the open," the other three said together, and Will just blinked. Dani grinned and gave him a kiss on the cheek.

Steve's phone dinged. "That'll be my ride." He tugged on the tan stocking cap, that when pulled over his face under a hood, might give him the look of a white man in the parking lot lights. He rose and laid a gentle hand to Tiffany's hair. "I'll text you when I'm there."

She looked up and nodded, and Dani smiled at the obvious caring that flowed between them. She looked over to Will to see him still blinking, but this time to stay awake. Good thing they were riding together or she'd probably find him right here in the morning. She laid her head against his unhurt shoulder, feeling worn out herself. She decided to set an alarm on her phone or else they both might wake up in the ER waiting room in the morning.

* * *

"Oh, Keith, I can't tell you how good it is to see you awake!"

His mother held up a stack of folded clothes. "You don't seem to have a suitcase, so I bought you an outfit for your release."

Keith looked between his mother and his sister, feeling like his head was full of oatmeal.

"The doctor said you've been improving steadily once they switched antibiotics," his sister was saying, "so you should be feeling much better in the next day or two."

Keith gave a weak nod. "I... I don't remember what happened... The accident."

"You went off the road," Heather explained. "Do you know why—"

"Let's not trouble him with the details right now, Heather," his mother interrupted. "He should only be worried about getting better."

"Yes," Heather said with familiar irritation, "but the... man in the hallway will be asking questions soon anyway. It might be good for Keith to... work out his answers first."

Keith was lost. "What man?"

His mother let out a sigh and turned from the bed. Heather took a step closer to his head. "There's a policeman out there who wants to ask you questions about the accident. Why, for instance, you were driving a car that didn't belong to you in the mountains in the wee hours of the morning."

Keith blinked. Nothing in that sentence made sense to him at all. Maybe his brain was truly damaged, hearing something completely different than what was being said.

When he didn't respond, Heather laid a hand on his arm. "Keith, don't you remember anything?"

He licked his dry, chapped lips and decided to just go with the flow and hope that things started making sense to him. "I remember some things, but none of that." He would have laughed if he had any energy. "Where would I find mountains?" Heather looked back at his mother, now sitting, her face lined with concern. "Well seriously, we've got hills close to Kansas City, but nothing you'd call a mountain."

Heather brought her gaze slowly back to his. "You're in Colorado. Denver. We're not sure of all the details, but we think you came out here because of Dani."

"Dani! What's she doing in Colorado? She's supposed to be in Brazil."

Heather shook her head. "Not anymore. Instead of flying home to Kansas City, she flew here. We don't know why. Dad made it impossible to get to the bottom of anything."

"Dad's here too?"

His mother returned to his bed. "Of course he is. . . . He's just not here now because—"

"Because he was being his usual jerk self and got himself into trouble," Heather railed. Disagreements between his dad and Heather had always been a part of every gathering.

"It was that Australian!" his mother insisted with flaming eyes. "He's why your father is in the ER!"

"What?" With every word that came out of their mouths, Keith felt more confused. "Why is Dad in the ER, and what Aus—" He got a sudden image of a tall man with a red beard. Still shots. Pictures. That man by Dani's side. Strolling with her, hand in hand. Kissing her. "Oh, God," he whispered, as the memories rolled in like a tide.

He'd lost her.

He'd had a bad feeling about that Brazilian trip from the start, and he'd been proved right. She'd been seduced by a scruffy guy with an accent that frankly made him cringe.

His mother put a hand to his knee. "Keith, I'm sorry, we shouldn't have burdened you with this. It's too much when you're trying to recover."

"What did he do to Dad?"

"He shoved an old man to the ground!" his mom declared, suddenly unconcerned with "burdening him."

"That isn't the whole story, mother. Dad said Will shoved him, but the doctor said that the car bomb was most likely responsible for throwing them *both* to the ground."

"Car bomb?" Keith didn't know whether to laugh or cry. The sheer lunacy of this conversation made him start to question reality.

Heather's expression shifted quickly to apologetic. "I'm sorry Keith, I can see this is too much." She patted his arm. "We should go back down and see if they've released Dad anyway."

He grabbed her wrist. "You can't just leave me hanging. What car bomb?"

"He was just at the wrong place at the wrong time, and a car bomb went off as he was apparently discussing your engagement ring with Will, who refused to go back into the Days Inn to get it because there was a bomb threat to the building."

And that was the moment that Keith was certain that he was still in a coma.

Chapter 25

Will woke up with a pain in his shoulder, and it was a moment or two before he remembered why.

The car bomb had been surreal and totally unexpected. These people were playing for keeps, and in the middle of the night he had regretted his promise to Tiffany to let her and Steve try to break through Pragnalysis security from the inside.

And his idea to send Dani with them.

Had he been high on pain pills when he came up with that plan? Whoever was after Tiffany had been just a step or two behind them for days, and they all came within an inch of dying last night. If they had all trooped to the car together, chances were good that they'd be in pieces today.

Dani turned over to face him, and even though he knew he should get up and take some Tylenol for his shoulder, he rolled to his side to look at her sweet sleeping face.

He lived a life that was often dangerous, but this woman didn't have to. She could have played it safe back in Kansas City with Keith. If he had just sent her home and hired someone else to chaperone Tiffany, that's where she'd be now. Maybe not with Keith, as they were already having problems—and he wouldn't wish that father-in-law on anybody—but she wouldn't be here in this mess.

And now she wanted him to train her to work with him. When she'd brought it up, it had pulled on something inside him—a team spirit thing that now just seemed dimwitted. He knew women did the kinds of things he does—Val had worked with them in Brazil for years—but could he really see Dani that way? Let her get into the kind of trouble Val had?

His mind moved to the day's agenda. Could he keep Morrow and Owens talking long enough for Tiffany and Steve to get the evidence? He had no idea. How was he going to draw out a jolly long lunch when the main thing he needed to do was grill Owens on his Grand Prix and the sexual harassment of Tiffany while she was a Pragnalysis employee? Was he likely to keep scarfing down escargot, or whatever hoity toity tidbits they'd get at the fancy restaurant Morrow picked out, with that line of questioning, or would Owens get up in a huff and head straight back to work?

His phone buzzed on the night stand behind him, and he turned to grab it before it woke Dani, bringing another sharp pain to his shoulder. She shifted, however, and slipped out of bed, trotting to the bathroom. Will saw Logan's name on the screen and almost didn't pick up. What was he going to think about everything happening here? With a sigh, he answered the call. "G'day, Logan, you're up early."

"Oh, sorry, I keep forgetting you're an hour earlier than we are… I uh, just happened to hear about a car bomb in Denver on the news this morning… No one killed, but some minor injuries from flying debris near a Days Inn… You wouldn't happen to know anything about that, would you?"

Will let out a breath. "Yeah. I was one of those minor injuries." He heard the shower start running and launched into everything the man didn't already know—from Keith's accident in the stolen car and his oldies showing up to Tiffany's Pragnalysis plan. When he was finished, there was a long stretch of silence. "Logan, you still there?"

"Yeah, I'm just trying to figure out how a simple delivery job turned into a major criminal investigation slash soap opera."

Will ran a hand through his hair. "You and me both. Is it crazy to let them go through with their computer hacking scheme today? I'm really having second thoughts about it."

"You know better than me, and I'm willing to trust your instincts, but I do agree with you that if it doesn't work, it's time to turn it over to the police."

"Yeah. Defo." He now heard the hair dryer in the bathroom.

"Call me later and give me the news."

Will flipped the blankets back and moved to sitting on the edge of the bed. "I will. I hope your days with Rita have been… more fun."

Will could hear the smile in Logan's voice when he said, "More fun than I could have ever imagined. I'm in deep, my friend."

"Good for you. I'm stoked for you, mate."

"What about you and Dani? Are you still… hooked up?"

A corner of Will's mouth twitched. "In theory. We haven't had much time for… fun."

"I see. Well wrap this thing up today and get on with your life. Unless Tiffany wants to actually hire you, I need you back on the job. Rod reports that cases are starting to stack up down there."

Dani came out of the bathroom wearing one of his flannies she'd worn to bed, and an easy smile came to his face. "Yeah, I will. I'll yak at ya later. Hooroo."

Rising, he tossed his phone to the bed and came up behind her in nothing but his boxer briefs as she shifted stacks of clothes in her suitcase on the ratty bureau, and slipped his left arm around her waist. "Whatcha looking for?"

"Well, I was hoping to find clean underwear."

He nibbled the edge of her ear. "You don't want to get dressed just yet, do you?" He moved down her neck, kissing a row to her collar. He unbuttoned her top two buttons as her breathing picked up speed and swept the shirt off her shoulder. "I'm thinking of a non-clothes activity." He laid down more kisses on her now-bare skin.

She turned and looked up at him. "Are you sure you feel up to it? I mean, your shoulder has fifteen stitches in it."

It was throbbing, and he could use some pills, but he didn't care. "I'll manage," he whispered, lowering his lips to hers. He kissed her slow and sweet and tender, waiting for her to catch up to his mood.

It didn't take long.

* * *

The Uber ride pulled up to the Pragnalysis building, and the three dressed for success got out and walked speedily to the front doors, thankful for an unseasonably warm day since they hadn't really thought about expensive-looking outerwear.

Tiffany had on her brunette wig while Dani had French-braided hers around the crown of her head. Both wore big sunglasses, and although it had taken some twisting and a fair amount of lotion, Dani had gotten Keith's diamond ring back on her finger. She was wearing a slim-fitting, bright floral dress that she probably bought in Brazil.

It was more difficult to change the appearance of a black man, but the suit, sunglasses and fedora, together with the very serious expression that Tiffany had had him practice, gave him a certain air that she could never have imagined.

They had arrived back at the Days Inn the night before in their three separate cars without incident, and Tiffany hoped that they had truly confused their adversaries by staying put this time.

She glanced around before going through the door that Steve was holding for her. It didn't seem that they'd been followed, but who really knew?

Amy greeted them as if they were expected but unknown guests just as they had plotted together by phone. Then she rang Tiffany's father's office to tell him that his twelve o'clock appointment had arrived. To security footage, it would look as if nothing was unusual, but Tiffany knew her "I'll show you the way" meant that no one had answered the call.

Because of their time constraints, she bypassed the wide, curving stairs in favor of the elevator. There was a brief, tense moment when the elevator stopped on the second floor, and Mitch from Accounting was waiting to get on. Tiffany had worked pretty closely with him, but he stepped back when he saw their group, saying he'd take the stairs.

They sailed past the third floor—the home of Research and Development, which was the heart and soul of Pragnalysis—to the top floor. They stepped into the large, airy room whose ceiling was two floors up. This was where company-wide meetings and training was held. This was where company parties happened.

This was where she'd met Aaron McCain.

She tried not to think about that as they moved through the space. The other half of the floor was divided up into conference rooms and a few other offices, including one belonging to the Morrows' personal secretary.

Another dramatic set of stairs led to a hallway of executive offices above the conference rooms that couldn't be reached by the main elevator. A few years ago, before Tiffany had started to show the signs of schizophrenia and her mother started having migraines, her mom had had an office right next to her dad's. Both rooms had a gorgeous view of the mountains.

The conference rooms were deserted at the moment, which was a bit of a disappointment considering all the work they had put into their costumes and practicing their Portuguese accents, but she supposed it really was for the best.

Her father's personal secretary was on a lunch break that Amy had made sure would last the rest of the day. According to Amy, Carol had left fifteen minutes ago due to "gastric issues." Tiffany didn't ask—she really didn't want to know—but Amy was her new hero.

As soon as they were in, and Amy was gone with a "good luck," Steve sat behind the desk and got to work.

* * *

Close to 11:30, Will made his way quickly across the Days Inn property to another parking lot across the street. He hated being so exposed for this long, despite everyone making fun of his "out in the open" remarks, but the whole motel lot was still cordoned off by the police as they went through the exploded car parts looking for clues to the type of bomb used.

He was grateful they didn't have to comb through body parts, as well.

While the women were primping and planning, and Steve was pacing, Will had gone out to rent a new car, glad he had purchased good insurance on the one that had been blown to bits. With no snow in the forecast for the next ten days, he decided he didn't need an SUV and had rented a ubiquitous white Honda Accord. At least he hoped he still wouldn't be in Denver after ten days. He'd also gotten a new secure case for his handgun.

He was feeling more confident in the day's plans since spending time with Dani that morning. She was spesh—amazing in so many ways—and it was time he stopped trying to micro manage her life. She was here with him because she wanted to be, and after going undercover in Brazil, she certainly understood the danger involved with his life and work.

Still, he couldn't help worrying at least a bit about the three that had already left for Pragnalysis. Will had never had any children, but he imagined this was how it felt when they first started to drive or left for college. At some point, though, every parent just had to let go and hope for the best.

He wondered how this meeting with Morrow and Owens would go. He absolutely had to keep the men there long enough for Steve to have a decent shot at getting through the Pragnalysis security. It was going to be a tricky balance, but if nothing else, he could probably keep them entertained for a while with stories of his trade in finding trafficking victims. Then in the last half hour, he'd get down to the bizzo about the stolen car.

As he approached the rental, he dug the car key out of his pocket and hit the trunk button, then snugged the small gun case into the cargo net to keep it from sliding around. A scuffling sound had him turning, but he didn't see anyone else in the crowded-with-cars lot. A smashed pop bottle skidded along the pavement with a sudden breezy gust.

Closing the trunk, he quickly moved to the door and slipped behind the wheel. After starting the car, however, the trunk ajar button was lit up on the dashboard. Getting back out and walking to the back, he could see that a bit of that cargo net was sticking out, keeping it from closing all the way. He pressed the button on the key fob again as he lurched forward into the car, a sharp pain radiating from the back of his head to the front. Thrown off balance, his knees hit the hard asphalt. Blinking and breathing through the pain, he tried to pull himself up by that bit of net that his fingers were tangled in, scanning the lot with blurred vision.

Another blow, and he saw nothing at all.

Chapter 26

Dani wished she knew anything at all about computer hacking. Steve was tapping away at the keyboard with Tiffany by his side, the two speaking a language as foreign to her as Swahili.

She spent most of her time looking out the window at the magnificent view and down at the parking lot, wishing she knew what kind of car to watch for. She imagined that Morrow, and maybe even Owens, drove something high class. A Lexus might be good enough for Owens, but Morrow probably drove something like a Porsche, a Mercedes, or a Bentley.

"Do you see that?" Steve asked excitedly, while pointing at the monitor.

"Yeah," Tiffany replied with near awe in her voice.

Dani strode to the desk. "What? Did you get through?"

"Not all the way," Steve answered without looking up, his fingers still at work.

"But it was a major breakthrough," Tiffany said, also still glued to the screen.

"Well, good, it's been nearly an hour." Dani hoped Will could really keep the men out for another thirty minutes. He was supposed to text her when everyone was leaving. She looked to the doors of Bret Morrow's private elevator and hoped he wouldn't forget.

With Will now on her mind, she went back to the window, thinking about the morning's surprise return to bed. Wow. It had been so worth the messed-up hair. That man knew just what to do and how long to do it. But it wasn't just about the physical—although the man was darn good at that—it was the way he made her feel like a cherished treasure. Brazil, Australia, Kathmandu… she knew she'd follow him anywhere.

Another whoop of victory from the two hackers gave her hope that they were almost done.

"That's it, Steve! Oh my God, that's an account number, although it's not the one I remember."

Dani knew she was referring to the long number she'd repeated over and over on the flight back and had hidden under a corner of the carpet in her dorm room. She had been "right stoked," as Will would say, to learn that he had found the carpet pulled up in the corner, suggesting that someone had taken it. Dani wondered who would do that. As neat as everything had been in her room, it seemed the police would have put it back where they found it and just taken a picture or something if they thought it might be important.

"Last October, I found receipts for consulting firms, computer tech labs, and manufacturing companies charging three to four times the current rate with way more invoices than you'd expect. They were being paid individually, but a bit more digging showed that all the money was actually being rerouted into that account that I memorized." She seemed to lose confidence. "I wish it was the same number, so I'd know for sure we were on the right track."

"You said yourself they probably changed things up after you nearly caught them," Steve reminded. "And," he said with a huge grin, never taking his eyes off the computer monitor. "This account is definitely where large deposits are being made." His hands unexpectedly sprang up from the keyboard and hung in the air. "And there's the name of the owner of the account."

Tiffany moved in closer, and Dani moved around the desk to look over her shoulder. "Chase Owens." She looked to Steve. "We got him."

She stood and pulled a memory stick out of her pocketbook and handed it to Steve, shaking her head. "Mitch or someone else in accounting has to be in on this. There's no way Owens could have pulled this off alone."

Steve plugged it into the computer, and Tiffany moved in closer to look at the monitor. "What's that symbol in the corner?"

Steve moved in as well. "Looks like a camera. Probably has to do with the security cameras in the building."

Tiffany moved the cursor and clicked to find two folders labeled "Pragnalysis" and "Home."

Dani looked around the space. "You said your dad didn't like cameras in his office."

"He doesn't. And if there were any, I'm sure Security would have been up here long ago." She clicked on "Home" to bring up a whole screen of pictures.

A few Dani recognized as being rooms inside the Morrow mansion. "Wow. That's kind of creepy."

"It must be something new," Tiffany insisted. "Evidently he's gotten as paranoid as he accused me of being."

Dani saw movement in one frame and zeroed in on Min Morrow making her way slowly across the spacious master bedroom in a flowing robe, obviously not yet dressed for the day by afternoon. Was the man keeping tabs on his wife while he was at work? Was her health that shaky? She was about to ask Tiffany what she knew of her mother's health, when a low rumble had them all looking to Morrow's private elevator.

Someone was heading up.

* * *

Will woke slowly, his head pulsing with pain, his knees practically up to his chin. He tried to stretch out but didn't get far before running into something solid. Despite the throbbing in his head, he opened his eyes. At least he thought he did. All he was seeing was black.

He could feel the movement of transportation, and although he didn't have Rod's famous nose, he didn't need it to easily identify odors associated with a car's interior. Especially the interior of a trunk.

He was able to reach the back of his head to find it sticky with blood, the blow he'd received still fresh and painful.

He wondered what time it was. How long had he been out? Did he miss the tee up with Owens? *Maybe this is the tee up with Owens.* He struggled to move his wrist in front of his face and pressed the button to reveal the time. *12:32.*

More maneuvering and groaning got his hand to his back pocket, but he couldn't feel his phone. He couldn't call 911 to save himself—couldn't text Dani to get out of the office. He reached out to feel every inch of the cargo net but didn't find his gun case. His assailant had that as well.

Or else this wasn't his rental car. That's something his nose couldn't differentiate.

His watch said they'd been driving for about forty-five minnies, and with all the turns, he'd bet they were heading into the mountains. Whoever had walloped him in the head and stuffed him in a trunk could easily just pop it and shoot him once he had him in a remote locale. Will had to be ready for that moment somehow, although he wasn't sure what he could do. He had no weapons of any kind, and a painful search of the interior hadn't come up with a crumb to grab onto.

He was up a gum tree.

A sudden bump created a hollowish sound below him, and Will got a picture of what lay beneath him. The spare tire.

And maybe, if he was lucky, a tire iron.

* * *

Dani took two steps toward the elevator, her mind flying before turning back to the stunned computer geniuses. "Get down!" she hissed. "I'll… stall him somehow."

They both slipped out of their chairs and under the huge desk. With her heart pounding, she crossed the room to wait. The door opened to a startled Bret Morrow. She quickly stepped in, making him step back.

"How did you get into my office?" he sputtered, as she turned to press the ground floor button.

She faced him with a smile, wondering if he could hear her heart galloping. "Mr. Morrow, I'm so glad you finally got here! I've been waiting such a long time! Your secretary wasn't feeling well and had to leave quite suddenly. Will Mr. Owens be going with us to the restaurant, or will we meet him there?"

The man looked at her with narrowed eyes that gradually opened wide. "Ah, now I remember you. You're Mr. Yarnel's associate. Miss…"

"Harley," she supplied, not knowing where that name came from at the moment. "Danielle Harley."

He looked her up and down. "I'm sorry, I didn't recognize you out of jeans and snowboots." His eye caught on the engagement ring. "I do remember that, though. You had it on the first time we met, but not the second."

Leave it to the rich to notice riches. "The altitude has made my fingers swell, I'm afraid, so sometimes I just haven't been able to get it back on after my shower."

"Well, it looks like you both hit the jackpot."

Dani thought that an odd thing to say, but maybe Morrow felt as awkward as she did.

They hit the ground floor, the doors opened, and Dani didn't know what else to do but keep this charade going. She stepped out, and the man followed her into a small alcove that probably opened to the parking garage. "Soooo, Mr. Owens?"

Morrow slipped his hands into his slacks pockets. "I'm afraid there's been some mix up. I understood we were to meet Mr. Yarnel at The Capital Grille at noon, but he never showed. I tried calling him, but he didn't pick up. Then Chase called to tell me he wasn't feeling well—this is actually his day off—so I ate lunch and returned to work."

Dani didn't have to fake surprise. *Will didn't show? And neither did Owens?* "Oh, well, I guess there has been a snafu. Mr. Yarnel had something come up and handed the meeting off to me, but I guess I got the meeting place wrong. I'm so sorry."

"No harm done." He smiled. "I just ate a better lunch than usual."

"I… I guess we'll have to reschedule," she stammered, trying to focus on finishing this up while part of her brain started fretting over Will in earnest. She turned toward that door at the end of the hall.

"You actually can't get out that way. It just goes into my personal garage."

"Oh, I see, so…"

He pushed the button and the elevator doors opened immediately. "You'll have to ride up to go back down."

Dani blinked. "Oh."

She walked back to the elevator and stepped in, and once again, he followed. There was a moment or two of awkward silence, then Dani blurted. "How is Mrs. Morrow?"

His face fell. “Not very well, I’m afraid. Her headaches are just about taking over her life.”

“Migraines?”

He nodded. “Yes. They’re very debilitating.” He looked to the floor for a moment, then back up as the doors opened at the top. “I hate burdening Tiffany when she has her own… difficulties, but when you see her, will you ask her to give her mother a call? I think it would help her a lot.”

They stepped into his office, and Dani hoped he wouldn’t be able to tell Tiffany himself. The chair she’d been sitting in had been moved back to in front of the desk, so Dani assumed she and Steve were gone. “I’ll give her the message,” Dani said, as she headed to the office door. “Again, I’m sorry for the mix-up, and I… Well, I’ll talk to Mr. Yarnel about rescheduling.”

He nodded. “I did talk to Chase myself about all this, and he still insists he was… tied up with a woman when the theft occurred. It’s unfortunate that she refuses to corroborate his story.”

He opened the door for her, and she walked out, trying to put a pleasant smile on her face. As soon as it was closed, she kicked off her heels and ran down the short hall and down the stairs, then past Carol’s desk to the elevator. While she waited for it, she slipped back into her shoes and dug her phone out of her purse to call Will, but like Morrow, she was sent to voicemail. She almost decided to take the stairs clear to the bottom, when it opened, and she charged forward, nearly running into Amy coming out.

She backed up again, and Dani got on. “I came up to see if you were all right. I called a cab for Tiffany and Steve, and it’s waiting for you out front.”

“Thanks. Did they get what they needed?”

Amy nodded. “Tiffany thinks so.”

Dani stepped out at the bottom and didn’t pause for any more pleasantries. She threw a “Thanks again” over her shoulder and hurried out, not sure what to do if Will wasn’t at the motel.

* * *

With some difficulty, Will had managed to get into the spare tire storage area without creating such a ruckus that whoever was driving would just shoot him through the back seat. He really didn't want his abductor to know he was awake and possibly ready for him.

With the passage of time came a clearer head and the reminder that all trunks had a safety release on the inside. If he popped out as soon as the car came to a stop, how fast could he get out of shooting range? It was a complete unknown, and he came to the decision that it would be better for his assailant to make the first move on the trunk.

The car turned onto a rough road with plenty of winter ruts. He was jostled mercilessly even though the car was not exactly speeding. After a while, it slowed even more for a right turn and came to a stop. Will's heart sped up. He thought of Dani and her fierce spirit, soft curves, and sweet kiss, hoping he'd get back to her with minimal damage. Nothing else mattered to him in the moments after the car door opened and closed than that—being back in her arms.

He heard footsteps scuffling through rocks and pictured a gravel or rock road. His shoulder put him at a serious disadvantage. He had opted to lay on his left side, but that meant he had to swing the tire iron with his injured right. He would probably tear open his stitches, but that beat a bullet hole in the head.

The trunk suddenly popped up an inch, indicating the key fob button had been employed. Will wasn't about to push it up more. His plan only worked if the guy got close enough to open it himself. After a tense thirty seconds, it flew up, and Will was temporarily blinded by the extra bright Colorado sun. He squinted but couldn't see anybody in his field of vision. The guy was being as cautious as Will, putting them in a kind of backwards standoff where neither could see the other.

Something hit the back of the car, and Will jumped, levering himself up and swinging the tire iron in a wide arc. He hit nothing but air, but now he could see his foe standing a good five meters away. He was in a black parka with a fur-trimmed hood framing a face covered by a ski mask and sunnies. The most important thing, however, was that he was holding Will's handgun.

He didn't say a word—just flicked his wrist with the weapon, indicating he'd like Will to get out of the trunk. He didn't suppose he had a choice. With the tire iron still in hand, he unfolded his tall, stiff frame in an awkward climb out.

"Drop it," came out of his incognito kidnapper, and Will let the cold piece of iron fall from his hand to the ground with a thud. If it wasn't locked in the trunk, he might have a chance to get ahold of it later.

Confident that the man didn't intend to kill him immediately, he looked around. About seven meters in front of him was the rough dirt road, whose every rut he'd felt acutely. They were surrounded by a thick grove of pines that obscured whatever view there might be. The chill in the air compared to just an hour ago confirmed that they were at a higher altitude.

He brought his gaze back to the man holding the gun who, now that he had Will out of the trunk, didn't seem to know what to do with him. Will turned to see a rustic looking cabin between the trees with a cockeyed roof that would seem to indicate a loft or attic on one side but not on the other.

"Get everything out of the back seat," the man barked his direction.

Will didn't move, however. "What is it you want from me?"

The man in black took a menacing step forward. "Move!"

Again, Will felt he had no choice. He'd have to wait for a better time to make a move on that gun.

The back seat held a couple of plastic grocery sacks with supplies. More than a snack, but not enough for days. Will pulled them out and moved ahead of his kidnapper toward the small abode.

The snow was mostly melted in Denver. Here it was still in abundance, although it was torn up by man and animal tracks in the path leading to the cabin. An empty soda bottle lay in the snow, as well as a scrap from a bag of chips.

He stepped up onto the low porch, took a couple of steps past a rocking chair, and tried the door. It opened into a small space containing smooth branch furniture padded with red plaid cushions in front of a fireplace on the right—a small table, an old iron stove and a few cupboards to the left. A ladder led to a loft over the kitchen where Will assumed he'd find a bed. A small bathroom sink could be seen through an open door on the other side of the room, next to the kitchen.

All in all, it seemed tidy, and from the smell of the hearth, used fairly recently.

He set the bags on the table, then moved across the living space and sat, hoping to put the man at ease and off his guard. "Who are you?"

There was no answer. Instead, the ski-masked man sat in the chair opposite him and messed with an electric heater Will hadn't noticed when he'd first come in. He had the gun in his left hand now, which didn't seem to be his dominant, but he could still be ambidextrous enough to shoot with his left, should Will make any sudden moves.

The fireplace looked recently used, although there didn't seem to be any available firewood nearby, and Will was glad for the heater. Will noticed the guy's shoes—expensive slip-ons, hardly suitable for tromping around in snow. The leather was already stained. Was this a spur of the moment abduction? It couldn't have been too spontaneous if he bought groceries first.

The mystery man looked back to Will and shifted the gun back to his right hand. Will grew impatient. "Are we going to just sit here and stare at each other? What's your plan, man?"

He sat back in the chair, his arms on the armrests and stared as though deliberating. "I just want to know why," he said with a voice that sounded a bit hoarse.

Will fought to place it, but he couldn't really make it fit with anyone he knew. "You're going to have to be more clear, mate."

Whatever he said seemed to infuriate the man. He clenched his free hand into a fist, and his whole body seemed to go stiff.

"I can't answer your question," Will said slowly, "unless I have a context. Why what?"

The man pushed up out of the chair in a slow, careful movement, as if he had injuries of his own, and all of a sudden, Will twigged who was hiding behind the mask and sunnies.

Chapter 27

Dani's phone rang again.

It was Heather.

Again.

She simply could not deal with that family at the moment. She had traded in her "schmick" dress for jeans and a long-sleeved t-shirt in a near panic. She had to figure out what had happened to Will. He wasn't answering any calls and wasn't in their motel room, and since the parking lot was still blocked off, she had no idea where the man had parked the new rental car to see if it was missing.

Tiffany and Steve were concerned about Will too but had no idea where to look for him, so they were in their room, looking through what they'd downloaded at Pragnalysis.

After an hour of calling, waiting, pacing, and staring out the window, she was more than ready to call Capt. Rand to report a new missing person, and she wondered if they were safe at the Days Inn after all.

She didn't have his name in her phone like Will did, so she had to go through normal citizen channels to get to him. Several tried to waylay her and take her information, but she knew no one would take her seriously about a man missing for a few hours but Rand.

At last, his voice came on the line. "This is Capt. Rand. How can I help you?"

"Oh thank God. I finally got through to you! This is Dani Harper, and I've been working with Will Yarnel on finding Tiffany Morrow."

"Yes, I remember you. She was found, correct?"

"Yes. In fact, she's with me. But now Will is missing."

"How long?"

"He had a meeting at noon that he never showed up for. And he's not here at our motel, and he's not answering his phone."

"I see. Well that really hasn't been very long. We usually wait at least—"

"Captain, that car bomb at the Days Inn last night was Will's rental car."

There was a pause. "Oh. I hadn't heard that. Was he hurt?"

Dani was drawn to the window to look at the scorched pavement. "No, thank God. I mean, he has stitches in his shoulder, but he wasn't actually in the car when it went off."

He let out a sigh. "That does change things."

"I was hoping it would. There's something else. Chase Owens didn't show for the meeting either. Will had wanted to talk to him about his stolen car and his supposed alibi. I'm concerned that he might have something to do with Will's disappearance."

"Where are you staying? I can't get away myself, but I'll send someone in my department out to talk to you and look around the area. How was he getting around today? Did he rent another car?"

"Yes, but I never actually saw it, and I don't even know what kind or color or anything?"

"Do you know the rental company?"

"Enterprise was where he got the one that was destroyed. I don't know if they would rent him another one or not. He didn't take me with him this time, and we… we just didn't talk about it." Dani was realizing how important even trivial facts were in this line of work.

"Where are you staying?"

She almost told him, then stopped herself. Someone always found them. How? "There's really not much more I can tell you. Shall I call Enterprise to find out if Will rented another car from them?"

"I'll do that. They aren't supposed to give that information out to just anybody."

"Thank you."

"When I find out, we will want to look around your motel and see if the car is anywhere around… We'll have to know where that is."

Dani felt trapped and as paranoid as Tiffany was supposed to be. She didn't see any way out of telling him what he wanted to know, though. "I'm sorry… it's just that we seem to be followed wherever we go…"

"I tell you what. I'll move a few things around and come myself. Would you feel better about that?"

Dani let out a relieved breath. "Yes, I would. We're staying at the Days Inn on Colfax." There was silence again, so Dani said, "What time should I expect you?"

Sudden shouting out in front of the building had her walking to the window again. It almost sounded like her name…

"There was another missing person report that came across my desk this morning that is also weirdly related to Tiffany," Rand, said as though searching. "Let me find it…"

Dani looked down to see Heather walking back and forth in front of the motel. "Dani! Come out and talk to me! This is important!"

Capt. Rand was back. "Ah here it is. The man that wrecked Chase Owens' Grand Prix. Keith Bisbee. You knew him, right?"

"Keith!" Now she knew why Heather kept calling and was now shouting outside. "But he's in the hospital! How could he be missing? When we were there, he was in a coma!"

"According to the report, he came out of it sometime last evening, and sometime this morning, he walked out of the hospital without anyone seeing him go."

"Oh my god." Dani felt weak in the knees. How could this be a coincidence, though? She moved toward the door to go down to talk to Heather. "Call Owens. See if he was really sick this morning."

"What?"

She continued to talk as she moved quickly across the balcony to the stairs. "If he's really sick, then Keith may be responsible for Will's disappearance."

"Why would you think that?"

"Because Keith was my fiancé until I met Will. Keith flew out here to win me back."

"I'll be at the Days Inn as soon as I can get there."

Dani ended the call and ran down the stairs. Heather was waiting on the other side of the metal screen door at the bottom. "Dani, don't you ever answer your phone?"

* * *

"The 'why' has eluded me, too," the Australian said without the context he had said he needed, as Keith moved slowly to the kitchen for a drink of water.

"Huh." He turned to look at him. It was obvious he knew who he was, so there was no point keeping the ski mask on any longer. It was starting to drive him crazy anyway. He took off the sunglasses and pulled the mask over his head, then tossed them to the table. "I guess you really are a P.I." He got a glass out of a cupboard and filled it with water from the tap. "And yet somehow you don't know why Dani chose you over me."

When he turned around, his bruised and stitched face registered in Yarnel's expression. "You should be in a hospital bed, Bisbee. Not driving on curvy mountain roads. God, you could have put another car in the ditch!"

With the mention of the car, he pulled out a chair at the table and sat. "That car… I only have… vague feelings and…"*–confusion, panic, anger–* "sketchy memories of it."

"What do you mean? You don't know Chase Owens?"

He drank half the glass, wondering how he was being pulled into an interrogation when he was the one who wanted answers. He supposed that's how he'd confused Dani. "I've been over and over it, and it simply makes no sense that she would give up life with me to… to… to take up with the likes of you."

Yarnel raised an eyebrow, but Keith made no apologies. What could this guy give her that was better than he could?

"I'll admit," Yarnel began, "I don't have your money, your position, or your political ambition. All I can give her is respect and love and—"

Keith pounded the table with his fist. "I always gave her respect! And I love her more than you do! She was with me for eight months, not just a few weeks! She loved me. She said she wanted to marry me, and then you came into the picture. What did you do to her? How did you turn her against me?"

"Whoa now, I stayed clear of her," Yarnel said with fire in his eyes. "I never touched her until she said she was done with you. I had sensed there was trouble between you two, but I kept my hands off until she took the ring off."

Keith wasn't buying it. Yes, they'd had a few disagreements while she was in Brazil, but didn't that happen in every relationship? She had never been one to run from a challenge before. For heaven's sake, just take that horrible little shop as an example. She would have stuck with that forever if he hadn't given her a better offer.

Yarnel abruptly changed the subject. "Whose cabin is this? I was under the impression you'd never been to Colorado before, but now you've got a cabin? Or did you steal this like the Grand Prix?"

There was the damn car again. He'd given himself a headache trying to remember why he'd been driving it. It didn't help that he'd been drunk at the time. He was usually one to be sensible about not driving when completely soused, but... God, he wished he could remember.

"Bisbee, how did you happen to be driving that car, and who does this cabin belong to?"

Keith at least had the answer to who owned the cabin, but he wasn't really in the mood to talk about how he had hoped to make things right with Dani and bring her here. He refused to tell him that the whole idea of coming up alone to "prove something" had been a disaster until he'd found the bottle of Captain Morgan in a cupboard.

He could tell this Oz dog that, but he wouldn't. He still didn't have his explanation. "You must have offered her something. What was it?"

Yarnel rolled his eyes.

Keith rose and took a step toward him. "Did she love Brazil so much that she'd give up being a congressman's wife for it?"

Yarnel laughed. "If you think Dani ever wanted to be a congressman's wife... well, that just shows you don't know her at all."

He raised the gun, unwilling to admit that she'd asked him to give up his bid for the House.

Yarnel lost his sudden mirth. "If you have any desire to be a congressman, you'll put that down. Most politicians are snakes, but for the most part, they're not murderers."

It was Keith's turn to laugh. "My political career was already over with the DUI, and apparently, I learned this morning, that damned Grand Prix was stolen, so no, Yarnel, you no longer need to worry about my political ambitions."

"Do you care about Dani at all?" he shot back.

"Of course I do! That's why we're here!"

The man had the gall to shake his head. "I don't know why Dani cares for me, but she does. Would you kill someone she cares about? Do you really think that's the way to get her back?"

Keith slowly lowered the gun. That was the problem; he didn't know how to get her back. But he knew one thing with certainty—this idiot didn't deserve her. And Keith was a smart man—he'd turned his corporation into a fortune 500 company. He'd figure it out. He just needed more time. He sank into a chair slowly, trying not to jar his aching head, not really hearing the Australian's continued rant.

* * *

"So when do we take this to the police? I kind of thought we'd head there right after lunch." Steve pulled the memory stick out of his laptop and handed it to Tiffany.

"I don't know." Tiffany got up from the small table and pushed it into her jeans pocket, then stopped, looking blank.

"Tiff?" She'd been doing so well—made it through the stress of nearly being caught in her dad's office without incident. He snapped fingers in front of her. "Tiff, are you there?"

She blinked. "Yeah, I just… had a spark of a memory. A déjà vu. It was when Owens caught me before and took the memory stick from me. But weirdly, right now that memory has no face. All I can see is a black dragon." She moved to the bureau and dug in a grocery sack, pulling out a bag of M&Ms.

"Probably because it's a bad memory."

"Is my face a bad memory? Is that why I can't see it in the mirror?"

Steve cocked his head. "When did that start?"

She sank to the edge of the bed, crunching on the candy. "Sometime in Brazil, after a couple of weeks. It had never happened before."

Steve was no psychologist, but he could imagine it as a kind of protection—her brain's way of letting her off the hook. If she couldn't see herself, maybe she wasn't really the one doing the unthinkable. He'd leave that to a therapist, however. Instead, he smiled at her. "I bet it will all go back to normal soon."

She'd changed into jeans and a t-shirt and lost the wig, but she still had the excess make-up on. It didn't look bad on her; he just wasn't used to seeing it on her. "So back to my question. Why aren't we contacting the police? With Will missing, it seems like we should."

She looked reticent, and Steve was getting a bad feeling. He rose and took a step toward her. "Tiff, you've been kidnapped, shot at, and nearly bombed. Why don't you want to take it to the police?"

"I'm just not sure we can trust them. How is it that someone keeps tracking us down? I blamed Will for setting me up at the Moxy because he had that information, but he told it to us in front of two cops. Who knows how deep this thing goes?"

Steve shook his head. "Then what did we do all this for? You are not going to confront Owens on your own. Who else can help beside the cops?"

She finished off the small bag of M&Ms, wadded up the wrapper and tossed it in the trash. "I don't know yet."

He rose from the table and came to sit across from her on his bed. "I've only got a few more days, and then I need to get back to real life. And I'd rather not do it afraid someone was coming after me."

She looked at him then. "I'm sorry. It was so selfish of me to drag you into all this."

He smiled and leaned toward her. "You didn't twist my arm." His smile got bigger. "And I have to admit, that was pretty exciting today."

She smiled back. "It was, wasn't it?"

"And I noticed that you sat pretty close to me. Did that… bother you?"

"No," she said without hesitation.

"Do you think that's because you were… distracted?"

She looked thoughtful. "Maybe."

Steve knew he should leave it at that.

But he didn't.

"Do you… want to try it again? Just as an experiment," he added.

She gave him a demure smile and rose, stepping across the space to sit down beside him just a few inches away.

"I think," he said with his hands clasped in his lap, "that your arm even brushed mine occasionally."

"Did it?"

He nodded with a hope that almost left him breathless. She leaned in until her arm touched his—white skin to black from elbow to shirt sleeves.

"Are you… okay?"

She nodded without looking at him. "It's the hands, I think, that will take longer. Hands can trap and hold and… hurt."

Steve thought a moment, not wanting to push her too fast, but dying for another kiss. "What about lips?"

"I don't know."

He nodded. The last thing he wanted was for her to go all catatonic on him. For now, this was good. This was enough.

They sat that way for a while before a sharp rap sounded on the door. "Hey, guys, it's Dani." She sounded urgent. "I've got to talk to you."

Chapter 28

When Rand arrived, Dani convinced Tiffany that he was one of the good guys, and she turned the memory stick over to him.

After Steve made a back-up on his laptop.

Then Dani went with Rand while Heather drove her vehicle, splitting up to cruise all the nearby parking lots and garages for a white Honda Accord. They found several but not with the right license plate.

They met up with Heather back in the motel lot that had finally been opened back up to parking. She jumped out of her car as they parked and rushed toward them, her phone in hand. Dani lowered her window. "I didn't find the car, but I did find out something that could be important. I've been working on Keith's campaign, so I thought I should check in with his campaign manager and let her know what is going on." She paused for a quick breath. "She told me that she had offered Keith the use of her cabin in the mountains, thinking you and he were going to take a little vacation when he got out here."

Dani sucked in a breath. "Well that at least explains why he was driving in the mountains, even if it doesn't explain the car."

Heather nodded. "And it also gives us somewhere to look for him."

Dani couldn't wrap her head around Keith spending time in a cabin at all, let alone escaping the hospital to go there when he probably wasn't feeling all that well. "So what about Will? Does it make any sense that Will would be with him?"

"Would he miss an important meeting to go with Bisbee?" Rand questioned.

"No," Dani said emphatically. "If he went with him, it wasn't willingly."

"Now just wait, Dani," Heather said with overstated calm, "you know Keith wouldn't hurt or threaten anyone, and I don't think he could have moved Will without one or the other."

"I'd like to think that, Heather, but his behavior and attitudes have shocked and surprised me over and over in the last month, and he was very derisive of Will." She knew driving up to that cabin could be a complete waste of time, but at the moment they had no other leads, especially since Owens was found at home in his bathrobe. "What's the address of the cabin?"

Heather reluctantly looked back to her phone. "I'll text Marion."

Dani looked to Rand. "Are you okay with driving up to this cabin?"

He nodded as he ran thumb and forefinger down the sides of his mustache. "I think we have to check it out. And if Bisbee is having some kind of breakdown, it would probably help to have you and his sister along."

"Okay. I hate to leave Tiffany and Steve, though. I really don't think this is a safe place for them."

He reached for his radio. "I'll call in someone to watch the motel."

"All right." She blew out a breath as frantic crazy thoughts started to form into worst-case scenarios. "I'll go up and fill them in."

* * *

Steve came out of the motel bathroom to find Tiffany sitting in the middle of her bed near the pillows with her knees pulled up under her chin, staring into space. If he didn't know they had just made off with all the evidence she needed to nail Owens in an exciting close call, he'd say she was sulking.

He studied her as he picked up his suit that had been draped over a chair and hung it up on the rack near the door. She moved every now and then and blinked, so she hadn't gone catatonic. "Tiff, are you okay?"

She tried for a smile, but it seemed forced. "Just thinking about what Dani said earlier about my mom. How she is suffering with migraines because of me. And now Will is missing while helping me."

Steve sat on the side of the bed. "That's quite a talent you have—hearing what people don't say."

She straightened her legs and leaned back against the pillows. "She didn't have to. I know when my mom's migraines began. Not long after I started going crazy." She shook her head. "She just worries so much, I guess." She looked to him, near tears. "And I haven't so much as sent her a text since I've been back. All I could think about was myself and Pragnalysis and catching Owens." Her lip trembled. "I never considered how it all affected her." She threw her hands up. "And Will. How did I not see from the beginning that he was one of the kindest men around?"

Steve so wished he could wrap her up in a hug, but he kept his arms to himself. "Tiff, a lack of empathy—and even the ability to read people—is classic schizophrenia. You can't be so hard on yourself when you weren't on your meds. You—"

A tear broke free and ran down her cheek, then she abruptly put her hands over her face and began to shake as the tears spilled out. "I don't want to be this way, Steve," she sobbed, "dependent on drugs to act normal, to feel normal, to think clearly!"

Steve had no idea what to do. He scooted closer to the head of the bed. "What can I do for you?"

She looked up then, her make-up a real mess, and flung her arms around him. He was shocked and scared she'd go stiff, but she didn't. She just cried on his shoulder. He hesitantly placed his hands lightly on her back. "It's all right," he whispered.

She shook her head against him. "No. It's not. I'm not right. The world's not right." She sobbed all the harder, as if the proverbial dam had broken. "Oh, God, Steve, what they did to me! They hurt me, they… they raped me. They stole everything from me."

Steve's eyebrows flew up. She was no longer crying about her mother. He dared to slide his arms around her and hold her a little bit tighter. "Not everything, Tiff. You still have your family. And… you've got me."

A deep guttural sound started in her throat, and he tried to let go, but she hung on tighter. "Go away!" she yelled, and Steve hoped there was no one in the neighboring room to call the cops on them.

"I can't go away if you hang on to me. I won't touch you if you'll let go."

"It's not you," she whispered. "It's the beast."

He wished he could see it. "How can I help?"

"Just don't let go. Though he rips me limb from limb, don't let go!"

He tightened his hold again and began to whisper in her ear. "You are a strong woman, Tiffany. You can defeat this thing. And you *are* empathetic and kind and caring. You've just been shut off from your feelings because of what you've been through. And I've been the same. I couldn't think of you as a potential girlfriend because I let my family and society tell me who I needed to stay away from." He chuckled. "And rich white girls were on the top of that list."

She started to shake, and he started to panic. "Tiff, are you sure this is what you need?"

She nodded vigorously against his neck.

"All right then." An old story passed down through the Elway family came to mind. "I know you've been hurt and used. Bought and sold like an animal. And while I don't know a lot about that personally, my people do. My great great great grandmother Tillie was a runaway slave who made it to the North to start a new life. She met a free black man named Seymour Elway, and they fell in love.

"When the slavers found her and tried to steal her away back to Alabama, Seymour shot one and horse-whipped the other. Then he packed up and moved farther north into what was basically a wilderness to keep her safe." He paused as she drew back, breaking his hold, her makeup now evidently a part of his shirt. She looked as if she'd just been through a war. He wiped a smudge of mascara off her cheek. "And that's what I'll do for you, Tiffany Morrow. I will fight for you." She looked up at him, still breathing hard. "Is the beast gone?"

"I think so."

"For good?"

"Who knows?" She put a hand to his leg. "Thank you."

He smiled and started to speak, but she surprised him by leaning in, her lips brushing his in a whisper of a kiss. His breath caught, but she was already scooting off the bed and heading to the bathroom.

A screech had him leaping to his feet and at the still-open door in three long strides. She caught his eye in the mirror. "It's me."

* * *

By late afternoon, Bisbee finally let Will eat something, which helped his ability to think a lot. He knew the man could not hold out forever. He was looking damned tired. The question was if he had enough brain cells firing to tie Will up before he conked out.

Will had heard him talking to himself several times, muttering about Dani, about his campaign, and even about Doritos that apparently he'd fed to bears? This rich man seemed to be coming unglued. He seriously doubted that he'd been released from the hospital, so he was missing out on some of those drugs they had been giving him to reduce brain swelling and infection.

The sun was gone, and while several days ago he hadn't given Dani's worry a thought, today, it was practically all he could think about. He hated that she had to fret over him for even a minny, but he was also hoping she would do more than fret. He hoped she'd call Capt. Rand, although he had no idea how anyone would find them in this cabin that Bisbee refused to talk about.

The red curtains attached to rings were made of a lightweight fabric that glowed with the sunshine in the day and did not hide headlights going past at night. He saw some filtered through the trees right now, going slowly past. There had been a few other SUVs bouncing over the rough road, and every time it happened, he hoped for a rescue or even a distraction of someone lost coming to the door that would let him make a grab for the gun. But so far, no one had stopped. This time was no different.

The wind had picked up, making Will grateful for the electric heater in what would certainly feel like an ice box without it. His gaze went back to his captor who was staring into space at the table, sipping a mug of coffee. Will's gun was laying on the table too near his right hand to even think about trying to get it. The man took to muttering again, his eye twitching.

Will was damned tired of this whole thing. "Speak up, Bisbee."

The man's gaze shifted to Will. "She lied to me."

"When?"

"The whole thing was one big lie. She just used me for my money— to get fancy clothes to go to Brazil to meet other men."

Will snorted. "If you really believe that, you're more fool than I thought."

He rose, looking wild-eyed. "No, think about it. I saved her from her wretched little life. She was practically homeless, wearing rags, and I took her in and gave her everything she wanted. She played me like a… like a…" He put a hand to his forehead and grimaced.

Will leaned forward. "Bisbee, you're not thinking straight because of your head injury. If all she wanted was what you could give her, why leave you now for someone with far less? I doubt she'll be coming back to take the clothes, and she tried to give back the ring, but you—"

"She still has it!" He walked around the table. "What a fool I was! She knew I wouldn't take it back!"

"Now how would she know that!" Will interrupted, noticing for the first time how much the man was sweating. The heater had made the cabin comfortable, but it certainly wasn't hot.

Bisbee acted like he didn't hear. "She's probably pawned it by now."

"Bisbee," —he pointed to the chair across the room– "sit down and let's talk about this rationally," he said calmly, hoping to lure him away from the gun.

A knock on the door had Bisbee spinning around, and Will leapt for the Glock, not expecting the dizziness that hit him when he did. He swerved as he reached for it, his hand hitting the table instead of the weapon. Pain shot through his shoulder, and before he could recover, Bisbee had the gun again.

"Get back!" His hand was shaking.

Will put his hands in the air and retreated several steps.

A knock sounded on the door again, this time followed by a voice. "This is the police! Open the door!" It was Rand. Will felt relief, but he also knew that with Keith's irrational thinking, this could all go downhill in a split second.

Keith seemed frozen for several moments while the knocking and admonitions to open the door continued.

"Bisbee, it's over," Will tried to appease loud enough for Rand to hear. "Just put the gun down so you can get help for your head."

The knocking stopped, and heavy footsteps were heard leaving the low porch. Bisbee's face took on an unattractive sneer. "See, Oz dog, I'm not the only one who hates your accent."

Will blinked, hoping Bisbee wasn't this much of a jerk when he hadn't been knocked loopy with a fever. They stood staring at each other for several long moments, then Keith stepped back to the side of the window, trying to peek behind the curtains. He couldn't do that easily and keep the gun pointed at Will. Ducking down, he moved quickly to the other side to try again.

He had barely gotten into place when a log came crashing through at an angle in front of him, tearing the curtains down in the process. He fired wildly, just barely missing Will as he lunged toward the fireplace, toppling a chair in the process.

Keith stumbled back against an empty firewood rack, and Will made his move, grabbing his wrist and forcing his hand and the gun's aim toward the floor.

Bisbee reached his left hand behind him, and the next instant he was swinging a fireplace poker at Will's head. He dodged, but that just meant the hard iron rod came down on his shoulder.

Enraged by another shot of pain, Will shoved him hard against the wall close to the window, then pushed him toward the log. He went down over it, but he had a grip on that gun like a son of a bitch, and his momentum pulled it out of Will's grip. The man rolled and had Will back in his cross hairs faster than any man in need of a hospital bed should be able to move.

"Keith, stop!" was yelled through the window as he got to his feet, and Will's heart plunged. *Dani.*

"Get back, possum!" Will yelled. "He's not in his right mind. I don't know what he'll do!"

Bisbee snorted. "Possum! Is that what you want, Dani? Someone to call you quaint critter names?" He smirked. "I'm sure I could come up with some. How about skunk or weasel?" His face turned ugly. "Or rat."

"Keith Montgomery Bisbee, you stop this right now! If this is how you have been acting, I don't blame Dani for breaking up with you!"

Evidently Heather was out there as well. Where was Rand?

Keith seemed to explode with a new fury. "Go ahead, tell Dad all about Keith's bad behavior! Isn't that what you always do, Heather? Get Keith in trouble one more time!"

Will's brows rose. Was the man reliving some past family squabble now? He didn't like how he was arcing up to a temper with a gun in his hand.

He pointed it at Will once more, breathing like a mad bull. "It's all over. You've stolen everything from me."

"Now wait just a minny, Bisbee. Dani is her own person. Nobody stole her. You pushed her away. And nobody forced you to fly to Colorado, get yourself drunk, and drive a car that wasn't yours. That was all you, mate."

Keith stood staring, his gun hand shaking while the women outside kept up their pleas for him to put down the weapon. His arm sagged, and Will thought he might do just that.

Then he turned it on himself.

Chapter 29

"Hello?"

"He knows about us."

"In what way?"

"Us! The affair!"

"Calm down. What did he say? Does he know about anything else?"

"Nothing else. At least I don't think he knows about the money. Or Tiffany. I don't know how he would. He certainly didn't hear about it from me."

"It won't matter much longer. They can't pin anything on us. I've made sure of that... Why don't you come over?"

"No. It's too danger—"

"I'll take care of everything. I miss you. Come in the back. I'll leave the door unlocked."

"I can't now. It'll have to be late."

"I'll be waiting."

* * *

Both Heather and Dani gasped at Keith, framed in the broken window as he turned the gun to his own head, and Dani flashed back to Miranda in the jungle, doing the same. That man had seen himself and his future clearly and had decided the payment for his crimes was more than he could bear. Will had implied that it was the coward's way out. Was that what Keith was doing?

"Keith!" both women yelled in unison. "Stop!" Dani continued. "There's no reason to take your own life! Things are not that bad!"

He squinted into the dark. "Aren't they? So I suppose you'll tell me that you've given up on the Australian, and that you can magically fix my campaign. That I've still got a shot at being president."

President! Was he really that delusional, or was that his long-term goal all along? She shivered as the wind whipped through the trees. "Keith, you can… start again." Hadn't she said the same to Miranda? And he had done much worse. "Everyone can begin again."

Keith laughed. "So now you're a comedian. Yarnel's right; I didn't know you at all." As if a switch were flipped on his emotions, he grew somber. "Just come home with me, Dani, and *we* can begin again. I promise. Thing's will be different." He walked toward the window, the gun lowering somewhat. "I love you, Dani."

Heather jumped in with no patience left. "Keith, face the facts! You've lost Dani! Now put the goddamned gun down so we can get you back to the hospital! It's freezing out here!"

Dani wasn't sure that was the best approach to take with someone on the edge, and she wondered what had happened to Rand. After finding a ladder out back, it had been his idea to break the glass in an upper window at the same time they crashed through the front.

All at once, Keith jumped and turned, and she saw Will make a sudden dive to the floor. Then two shots rang out. Keith went down, and it took Dani a moment to realize that she had too, her knees sunk into a snowdrift. Heather's screech sounded far away as she looked down to see the snow turning red.

* * *

Tiffany couldn't sleep. It was nearing eleven, they still had no word on Will, and now Dani wasn't answering her phone. Was their trust in Rand misplaced? Had he driven them up into the mountains and left them there, or worse, killed them all?

She swept off her blankets and sat on the edge of her bed. She couldn't see Steve in the dark, but she could hear his quiet whiffling snore in the other bed. She knew he would tell her she was letting her imagination run away with her, but someone in the police department had to be on the take. That was the only explanation for constantly being found wherever they went.

She tiptoed around the bed to the window and peeked through the ancient draperies. The police car was still there, parked out front, supposedly keeping them safe. But Rand had called that man in. If the captain couldn't be trusted, then neither could he.

She let the drapery drop and turned to the dark motel room. If she had to wait any longer for news, she was going to flip out. Who could help if she couldn't go to the police? Would her dad believe her about the embezzling if she showed him what they'd found at Pragnalysis? And what of her mother? If Tiffany could make her see that she'd been taken in by Owens and that Tiffany wasn't quite as paranoid as she thought she was, would her own health improve?

A great longing to make things right for her mom hit her hard, and she made her way across the room to the bathroom, pulling the scrubs top over her head as she went. Finding the clothes she'd worn the day before hanging on the back of the door, she quickly got dressed in jeans and a t-shirt, then went back out to find her socks and shoes by the bed.

Steve hadn't moved a muscle.

She knew he would be shocked at her idea to go home in the middle of the night, and she supposed he'd be right, but she simply couldn't sit here and do nothing. Her mom was rich. Her mom had resources. She could help find Will and Dani. She felt in her pocket for the second memory stick that Steve had made her as a backup. And now her mom and dad would both have to believe her about Owens.

She wrote a note to Steve, even though she would most likely be back before morning, and slipped into the bathroom to quietly call an Uber with instructions to pick her up behind the motel. When her ride was a few minutes away, she called 911 about a robbery at the 7 Eleven next door.

* * *

"Dani!" Will's shout echoed Heather's after retrieving the gun and getting up off the floor. The cloudless sky and nearly full moon gave him a clear view of Dani on her knees in the snow with Heather trying to pull her to her feet. Rand's marksmanship could not be faulted. He'd hit Keith's gun hand squarely, but it had caused him to fire wild. Had Dani been hit?

Will kicked out a chunk of glass at the bottom of the frame and stepped through. The cold had permeated the cabin as soon as that log had shattered the window, but it was even colder outside in the wind. He shivered but kept moving, his eyes, his heart, his very soul focused on Dani as Heather got her to her feet, only for her to yell out and stumble, going down in the snow again.

Will tromped through the drift and squatted down in front of her. "Dani, what is it? Were you hit?"

"It's her leg, I think," Heather volunteered. "She's bleeding."

Will noticed the red snow. "Oh, God, Dani!" He rolled her to her back to get a better look at the leg she'd fallen on. Blood was pouring out of a bullet wound in her thigh. "Rand!" he yelled as he looked to her face. She was out. He stood and pulled on the sides of the dress shirt he'd worn for Morrow's fancy restaurant pick, buttons popping off all over the snow. "Call an ambulance!" Yanking it off his arms brought fresh pain to his shoulder, but he didn't give it a second thought.

"I'm on it, Will," Heather said, pulling out her phone. "Is Keith…"

"He's fine. Rand just shot his hand." He wrapped the shirt around Dani's leg wound, starting to shake in just his undershirt. "Unless his head injuries take him out, he'll live." He ground his teeth as he pulled the fabric tight. "If Dani dies…"

Heather's eyes went wide as she put the phone to her ear, and Will could hear a tremble in her voice as she made the report to the dispatcher.

Will knew he needed to get Dani warm. The cabin was no longer an option for that. Ignoring his own pain, he scooped her up and was met in the yard by Rand. "Is she alive?"

Will nodded. "But she needs some heat. Your car?"

Rand strode forward and opened the back door for him, then got in the front and started the engine. Will moved in with her, hoping there was some warmth left in his body to help heat hers.

Rand turned on the overhead light and pulled a first-aid kit out from somewhere. "Did you wrap her leg?"

"I just tied my shirt around it."

He opened the kit and took out a roll of gauze and handed it to him. "Just in case you need it." He nodded toward the cabin. "I better wrap Bisbee's hand." He looked back to Will, who was trying to maneuver the gauze around her leg in the cramped space. "Hold tight Yarnel, help will be here soon. We're not as far from civilization as it seems."

Will gave a short nod, unable to speak for the lump in his throat. Rand got out and jogged to the cabin, leaving the interior light on. He looked down at Dani's face. She was so pale. "Oh, possum," he whispered, "stay with me. Don't open up that hole in my heart. I don't think I'd survive again."

Heather showed up with blankets from the bed, as well as his coat, and he quickly finished wrapping Dani's leg, then gladly pulled them in to cover her. "Keith's devastated," she began. "He—"

"I don't want to hear about Keith right now," Will interrupted.

She nodded and backed out, then closed the door. Will knew he shouldn't be short with Heather— she seemed to be a different breed from the rest of her family—but he could only handle so much. If he let himself dwell on Keith, he would miss something here in this moment. Maybe his last moments with this woman he loved.

This was what he'd been afraid of, but ironically, the danger had come from outside the case they were working on. From a goddamned jealous ex. He knew he should be cutting him some slack too—he was as crazy as a frog in a sock right now—but he couldn't help thinking that maybe his injury, infection, and fever had just brought out what was deep inside him.

Dani moaned, and he kicked himself for letting his mind wander to that bastard for even a second. "Dani. Love. Help is coming. Hold on."

"Will? I'm so cold."

The car had warmed up to the point that he had stopped shivering. That she was cold, even though held against him in her coat and under two blankets was not a good sign. "I'm trying to warm you up, love. I'm trying." A tear slid down his cheek.

At last, he heard a siren and choked on a sob. Damn it, he hadn't cried in years.

"Will."

"Yes, love," he sputtered.

"I won't leave you. I promise."

He prayed to God it would be true.

* * *

Tiffany hadn't thought about the fact that the route home would take them past Owens' house. It was nearing midnight, and lights were still on. Her heart started racing at the thought of the man that most likely was responsible for her being trafficked, and she wanted nothing more than to slap his face. Slap him the way Perigosa had slapped her the first time she ran. Did she dare? If she was right, he'd tried to kill her several times since being back, but would he try anything in his own house with a car waiting out front for her?

She leaned forward to speak to her driver. "Would you mind a little detour before we head to my house? I promise you a big tip." She had him drive around the block and park right in front on the too-big-for-one-man Victorian. "Please don't leave until I come back," she implored before getting out. "And if you hear screaming or gunshots, call the cops."

She closed the door on his wild-eyed, "What? Wait!"

Running up the sidewalk, all the reasons this was a really stupid idea flooded her brain. She expected lectures from all sides later, but just like she needed to face that beast earlier with Steve, she needed to face this one.

She ran up the steps to his big front porch and rang the bell. She waited, trying to peek through the sheer curtains on the door, but didn't see or hear any movement. She rang again. This time she heard footsteps on the stairs, and the porch light came on.

"Who is it?" came from a speaker somewhere she couldn't see. *Probably Pragnalysis security.* Then "Tiff?" So he could *see* her too. Locks were undone, and the door was pulled open, and there stood her nemesis in a thick terry cloth robe, looking flabbergasted. "What are you doing here? And at this time of night?" He looked past her to the street. "Do you have a car?"

"That's my Uber driver, and I've told him to call the cops if you so much as lay one finger on me."

The shock on his face would have won him an Emmy. Then it turned into his usual smirk. "So you show up at my door in the middle of the night and warn me about touching you?" He shook his head. "God, Tiff, I'm so sorry the docs can't do more for you." He made to close the door. "Now go on home. Your parents are worried about you."

She stuck her foot in the door. "Why did you do it?"

He glanced back toward the stairs, and Tiffany wondered if he was entertaining someone. *Perfect.* She'd let this poor woman know what she was dealing with before she ended up on a plane to Brazil. She shoved on the door, and a surprised Owens stumbled back a step. Pushing in, she ran around him and raced up the stairs. "I guess you weren't so sick today after all."

He ran after her. "Tiffany, stop or I'll be the one to call the police. I won't let you—"

She turned at the top of the stairs to face him coming up behind her, now nearly eye to eye. "She needs to know who you really are. That she could be sold to sex traffickers at any moment."

He looked as though slapped without her ever raising a hand. "Why would you say that?"

"Chase?" A woman's voice sounded down the hall, and Tiffany turned to go find her.

Owens grabbed her wrist. "You're not going anywhere until you explain that comment."

Tiffany laughed. "Well, aren't you quite the actor." Her smile fled. "You introduced me to McCain. He sold me to someone who shipped me to Brazil to work in a sex slave brothel in the middle of the Amazon rainforest." The hurt and confusion on his face was not what she expected.

The voice came again. "Chase, what's going on?"

"I'll just be a minute, darling," he yelled past her. "An old friend just dropped by." He lowered his voice. "McCain. I don't even remember someone named McCain."

She rolled her eyes. "Come on, Owens, surely you can do better than that. You introduced me to him at that impromptu Pragnalysis reception in October for record sales or some such B.S. You seemed really eager for him to meet me." Owens just looked at her blankly. "He had brown hair and a barely-there beard… a pretty sharp suit and those blue wire rim glasses with the pink tint. Gees don't you watch the news! He was arrested for kidnapping me!"

A light slowly came on in Owens eyes. "Ah, yeah, now I remember him." A real scowl spread over his perfect face, making the midnight shadow on his jaw look ominous. "He was that guy?" His eyebrows flew up. "And you think I had something to do with it? Or him? I just met him myself at that reception—he said he was a sales rep or something—and as soon as he… McCain… got a look at you, he wanted to meet you. I just obliged."

"You really expect me to believe that? You caught me on the company computer a few weeks before. You obviously set me up with McCain to get me out of the way. And once I confronted you about the embezzling—"

"What? Embezzling? When did that happen?"

Tiffany was tired of his games. "Good grief, Chase, will you even deny you took the memory stick from me in my dad's office?"

The man blinked and shook his head. "Oh honey, they said you'd been off your meds. I'm sorry. I'm sorry that any of this happened to you, and I'm sorry you would think I could do such a thing as… as… sell you." He ran a hand around his face. "Jesus."

Tiffany felt steam rising inside her. He would not use the "crazy card" on her. Pushing him aside, she charged back down the stairs. "It's all going to come out soon, Chase." She stopped and turned at the bottom. "I got that evidence again, and now it's in the hands of the police."

He shrugged and spread his hands. "Well, that's just super, Tiff. I look forward to finding out where all my money is."

She slammed the door on her way out, furious with him and with herself for thinking he would ever admit to anything. He was a snake. A snake with too much to lose. It was good that he had someone in his bedroom. That had probably kept him from killing her on the spot.

She stopped halfway down the walk with a furious breath out.

Her ride was gone.

* * *

Will paced the waiting room of the hospital, refusing any kind of treatment for his head and torn stitches until he got word on Dani. They had stitched up her leg wound and were giving her blood, but she wasn't out of the woods yet.

Will had never been much of a praying man. It was hard to have much confidence in some kind of supreme being when the world was full of depravity that that being didn't seem to care about fixing. But he found himself praying now. Maybe because he could do nothing else for his sweet blonde, and if he didn't do that, he'd always wonder if it would have made a difference.

He had learned the Lord's prayer as a kid, so he'd started with that, but after a number of times through, he'd branched out, expanding on that whole "kingdom come" line. What would that look like anyway? Jesus was supposed to have been a healer, so he figured that if his kingdom were to come to earth—to this hospital on the edge of Denver, Colorado, in good old God bless America—he'd heal Dani. He wasn't sure why anyone needed to pray for it—why didn't he just do it—but he supposed that was too big a question for someone who hadn't been inside a church since he was twelve, and only on Christmas and Easter for the first dozen years of his life.

His phone, that Rand had returned to him from Keith's effects, sounded an incoming text, and he saw that Heather had sent one from Keith's room asking him about Dani. He shot back a quick "fairly stable, but not awake yet," then noticed how many had been sent by Dani over the course of the afternoon, as well as a couple from Morrow.

He looked up and blinked. He didn't know anything about what happened at Pragnalysis. With their lunch probably canceled or at least cut short with him not showing up, did they have time to get the evidence? He supposed he should call Tiffany and Steve. They were probably worried too.

And then it hit him. They were alone.

He looked around, his tired brain already strained, his head and shoulder aching. *Did Dani leave those kids completely unprotected to find me?*

He looked back to his phone and made a decision Tiffany probably wouldn't like. He was going to call her dad.

He picked up pretty quickly and with some urgency in his voice, probably thinking it was some bad news about Tiffany. "Mr. Morrow, I apologize for the lateness of the hour and for missing our meeting today." How much did he want to go into? "But I was… detained." He ran a hand through his hair. "And everything went south from there. What I'm calling about, though, is that I'm rather far away from being able to protect Tiffany right now. Steve Elway is with her, but I'd feel better if someone else were watching out for them. I know it's the middle of the night, but—"

"Of course I'll go. It was the Days Inn, right?"

"Yes. Thank you."

"I should be thanking you," he insisted, "for taking such good care of my daughter."

Will didn't know what to say to that. He had failed everyone he knew today.

"I assume that Miss Harley is with you then?"

Will didn't know where he got the name Harley, but it hardly mattered. "Yes." He couldn't bring himself to get into the details. "I'm not sure when I'll get back to the motel, but I'm hoping by morning."

"No problem. It's been a while since I've been called on to take care of my daughter. I'm glad to do it."

Will thanked him again and said goodbye. He slid the phone into his back pocket and froze, blinking. *How did he know she was at the Days Inn?*

Chapter 30

Will found Rand on the fourth floor, filling in the policeman who would be guarding Keith's room. He looked to Yarnel with brows raised as he strode toward him. "How's Dani?"

"About the same. Captain, I think I know who has been hunting Tiffany."

"Oh?"

"Bret Morrow."

"What? Why would he—"

"I don't know the why, but he just let slip that he knows where we were staying, and he should not know."

Rand didn't jump on his theory. "He's a rich man with friends in high places. He may have just tracked her down for his own peace of mind."

Will supposed that could be true. He hoped it were true, but he still couldn't just let it go. "I've got to go back and make sure. Will you be much longer here? Shall I get a taxi?"

Rand gave a few parting words to the jack at the door then moved with Will down the hall toward the elevators. "I do have a man watching the place."

"Will he stop Bret Morrow? What if some of those men in high places are cops?" The elevator doors opened, and two people stepped out that he unfortunately recognized. Grabbing Rand's sleeve, he pulled him into a side hall to stare at a dedication plaque.

"Well I certainly hope this hospital is better than the last one," Roger was saying as they passed by. He was moving slower than the last time Will had seen him.

"I just don't understand what has happened to our son," Lillian answered.

The man had more to say—as he always did—but as soon as they were gone, Will urged Rand back out into the main hallway.

"Someone you know?"

"Keith's oldies. Believe me, you do not want to get waylaid by those two."

They got on an elevator, and Will pulled his phone out of his pocket. He decided on calling Steve rather than Tiffany. She had seemed more rational lately, but he didn't want to set her to running again.

It took several rings, but eventually a very weary sounding Steve answered. "Will, where are you? Are you okay? Is Dani with you?"

"I'll explain later. Right now, I just need you to…" What? What did he want them to do? Would it be better to get out or stay put? "Just don't answer the door for anyone, okay? Especially not Tiffany's dad."

"Why not her—"

"I've got some suspicions, but don't tell Tiffany unless he actually does show up. Don't wake her. We should be there in about a half hour."

Steve didn't answer.

"Did you get that?"

"Will… she's not…" He paused again. "Will, she's not here! Let me just get the light."

Will leaned his head back against the elevator wall, holding his breath.

"She's not in her bed, and she's not in the bathroom." The man was panicking. "I don't know where she could be… Wait! Here's a note!"

"What does it say? Where is she?"

"Oh, God, she was feeling guilty earlier about not talking to her mom! She's gone—"

"Home," Will said along with him, then turned and pounded the elevator wall.

* * *

After getting another Uber—and giving the previous one a very bad review—Tiffany eschewed the stone stairs that curved to the front door for a little jaunt beside a stepped wall that ran along the front of the property and one of the secluded patios. At the lowest point in the wall, she pulled herself up and dropped down, being careful not to slide right into the koi pond that curved along the other side.

With her dad's new love of security cameras, she was probably now appearing on a Pragnalysis security monitor, alerting them that there was an intruder, but she didn't care. If the key was still where she had hidden it, she'd be in the house in a matter of seconds.

Just like her dorm room, she had wedged it behind the door's trim. She pulled Steve's jack knife out of her pocket, glad she had thought to bring it along, and pried out the key. She blew out a held breath as the key turned in the lock. It still worked.

She turned the knob slowly and moved into the lower level on light feet. Without cameras everywhere, her parents never knew about some of her comings and goings her last year at home. It was one of the reasons she had moved to a downstairs bedroom. They had fussed over her entirely too much after her schizophrenia diagnosis.

After moving through the rounded sitting room with the green furniture she abhorred, she peered enviously into the dark home gym, looking forward to when she could get back into shape. When she had enrolled at the university, she had hoped to join their track team in the spring. Now she was so far behind, she'd probably have to drop out of the current semester and re-enroll in the fall.

She moved on toward her bedroom, slowing her pace when she thought she heard voices. She paused and determined that they weren't inside her head. *Did Mom and Dad move into my room?* She wondered what they would be discussing in the middle of the night. She edged closer. She didn't want to scare them to death; she had hoped to just look in on her mom. They didn't always sleep in the same room, which Tiffany thought was weird, but her mom claimed that when she had a migraine, her dad's snoring nearly split her head open. She had to admit, it was pretty loud.

There was no snoring going on now, however. It was a rather spirited discussion that was coming from behind the closed door. She put her ear to it.

"Bret, we need to just stick to the plan. We've set him up. All we need to do is let him take the fall."

Tiffany moved her head away in surprise. That was not her mother's voice. With her heart racing, she moved in again to hear more.

"She's muddled now without her drugs. We need to take advantage of that. She'll figure out eventually that the money we've put into Owens' account is only a fraction of what's missing. She'll never let it go."

"Then have her kidnapped again, and don't hire Will Yarnel to find her. Send her to the Congo this time. Just don't… just don't hurt her."

"Amy, dear, it can't be helped. There won't be any rest for us—any starting over—while she is alive."

"Well, we won't have any rest in prison if you kill her! Your men on the force won't look away forever."

"Money talks, sweetheart; they won't say a word. And I fully intend to make it look like a suicide. With her mental illness, it won't be questioned. I just need to convince her to come home." He chuckled. "And Yarnel's given me the perfect opportunity."

Tiffany stumbled away from the door, trembling. Her father and Amy Reynolds were discussing her fate, and it was her work buddy—not the man who had been her dad since she was three—who was begging for her life.

Like being sucked through a wormhole, her mind flew to the night in his office when Owens had caught her, although it wasn't Owens she now saw. It was Bret Morrow. It wasn't this father she had intended to give the evidence to, it was her real father in California. Like dominoes, the memories of Bret Morrow tumbled, each one revealing a darker side and the real reason she had moved to a bedroom with a lock on the door.

The lingering touches that had never felt quite right when she was thirteen. The times she had caught him leering at her as she reached sixteen and beyond. The outright lust she'd seen in the midst of her undiagnosed mental issues. That kiss he'd pressed to her lips before she could make her escape after stealing her memory stick. When she'd finally told her mother, it had been too late—no one believed her anymore.

She now saw that she really had created memories while in Brazil—a façade that hid the truth of her dad's—her *step*dad's—debauchery. She'd created the dad she'd needed, not the dad she had.

The door opened, and both Tiffany and Bret Morrow jumped. "Tiffany! What are you doing here?"

There was an audible gasp behind him, and he stepped out, pulling the door smoothly closed. "Your mother wanted to try out your mattress. She's been uncomfort—"

"Oh good," Tiffany said, her eyes blazing with a fury she'd never felt before. Even in Brazil. "I won't have to climb two flights of stairs to see how she is."

She made to move past him, but he put out his arm. "She's resting."

"Does she have whole conversations in her sleep? You were clearly talking to someone a few minutes ago. And do you go to work at 2 a.m. now? No wait." She took a few steps back, making a show of looking him up and down. "You usually wear a suit to work. What is this outfit? Black jeans, black t-shirt—kind of a clandestine look for you, isn't it?"

The man licked his lips. "I couldn't sleep, and I just threw something on." He waved a hand toward the steps. "Let's go upstairs. I'm sure you have a lot to tell me, and you can speak with your mother in the morning."

"So is that where you keep your gun and your car bombs and your kidnappers?"

He gave her that thin smile he always pulled out to show how indulgent he was of her flights of fancy. This time she wasn't having it. Taking a step forward, she slapped him with every ounce of her strength.

His head snapped to the side even as his hand grabbed her wrist. The look he gave her was far from indulgent, and he changed before her eyes into the black dragon of her hallucinations—the black dragon in her artwork.

More dominoes tumbled in her mind to reveal the black dragon sneaking into her room when she was but a child. The black dragon standing over her. The black dragon in her bed.

She pulled against his grip, but he held on tight, dragging her toward the stairs.

* * *

Steve knew he could very well die tonight. Black men creeping around mansions usually didn't live long. But he had to make sure Tiffany was all right. He paused a moment looking at the huge, modern Morrow mansion. What a kick. Tiff had mentioned that it was unusual. She didn't lie. So now that he was here, what should he do?

It was a little after two in the freaking morning, but maybe he should just ring the bell. He walked up the long set of the curving steps to the monstrous front door, his heart in his throat. After a deep breath, staring at the security doorbell that was no doubt taking his picture, he put his finger to the task.

The resounding bell was like a cathedral or something, and he stepped back, looking around, hoping he wasn't waking the whole neighborhood.

A loud thump inside had him stepping forward again, listening. A frantic, muffled sound came from within, and he reached for the knob. As expected, it was locked. He started to knock, calmly at first, then with more power. He knew he was treading a fine line. If he woke a neighbor, he would have the cops called on him.

With no one answering, he jogged back down the steps and began to look around for other possible ways in, trying to ignore the fact that these people owned Pragnalysis, a company known for its security systems.

Headlights had him stepping behind a tiny forest of now-bare trees next to a curving wall. He'd find no real cover there. He dropped to the ground, laid out flat. A car stopped at the curb, and Steve pushed a rock to the side so he could see. It was a police cruiser.

He held his breath as two officers walked up the sidewalk, talking all the way. "I doubt he's going to appreciate being roused from bed at this time of night."

"I've got no intention of ringing the bell."

Their voices faded as they started up the stone stairs, and Steve got on all fours and crept forward to the steps.

"Just fake it," one of them hissed, "Morrow will back up whatever report we make. If we say we talked to him, he'll say he answered the door."

Steve's brows disappeared under his stocking cap.

"And what if the daughter really is here? Won't she have a different story?"

A snorty snicker floated over to Steve. "That's the beauty. The girl's a nutcase. Nothing she says will be believed."

The two waited a few more moments, then Steve heard footsteps coming back down again. "Civic duty done."

Steve quickly backed up and flattened out again along the wall.

"Easiest grand we've ever made."

Steve was in shock. *Damn, Tiffany was right about the police.* He watched through the branches until they were inside the car. *At least some of them.*

He felt several rocks under his stomach and pulled them out from under him, an idea forming. What if he made these guys do what they came to do? Even if he died trying.

Getting to a squatting position, facing the yard, he launched up and out of the trees into the open, then spun and lobbed one of the rocks at a window. He noted the cracking sound as he plunged back into the trees.

The slamming car doors told him his show had been seen. He easily vaulted the stuccoed wall, landing with an unexpected slip, crack, and splash on the other side. He squelched the shocked yell that wanted to come out of him with the freezing water above his knees.

He scrambled out of the narrow pond, cursing in his head, and sprang for the French doors as he heard the cops. He was ready to smash the glass with the rock he still had in his hand to reach in and unlock it, when he decided to just try the handle. To his surprise, it pushed down easily, and he stepped in, locking the door behind him.

He found himself in some sort of sitting room and made his way in the dark through the furniture, dripping and shivering to the door on the other side. A crash somewhere in the house had him moving faster, although he really had no idea where he needed to go.

As he neared a closed door, it unexpectedly opened, and a woman he recognized but couldn't immediately place, gasped. Steve waved his hands in front of him. "Shhh, I'm a friend of Tiffany's. She uh… she invited me over." He pointed over his shoulder. "She left the door open for me."

The woman clutched her shoulder bag, her eyes fixated on the rock he still held, panic in her eyes.

He dropped it to the thick, plush carpeting, and it barely made a thud. "I swear I'm not here to rob you. I—" His eyes went wide. "Aren't you the receptionist from Pragnalysis?"

That ridiculous doorbell sounded again, and he wondered if the cops had given up looking for him outside and decided they needed to chat with Mr. Morrow after all.

There was a loud crash upstairs, then, "Help! Help me! Amy, he's going to kill me!"

Steve's eyes met Amy's a split second before she turned and ran the way he'd come in. She was obviously not going to help. He sprang for the white, curving stairs, taking them two at a time.

What he saw at the top almost didn't compute as a family home, but he put off analysis of the strange, sterile space for the moment. He needed to find Tiff. The room was lit only by a single lamp on the other side of the room, but he spotted her red hair on the floor. The head moved, but he couldn't see through the furniture enough to know why she wasn't getting up.

He heard Morrow talking to the cops at the door and tiptoed across the raised platform to peek around the corner to his right. He found himself looking into a wide entryway at Morrow's profile. It would be nearly impossible to reach Tiffany without being seen.

As Morrow nodded with concern about the prowler that was probably still lurking around the house, Steve noticed the weird front door, and wondered if that was the future of home security—a solid stainless steel door that looked like it could open to a walk-in freezer rather than the outside.

Steve brought his attention back to Morrow as he seemed to be wrapping up with the police. "Thanks, boys, don't worry about the window. It's only cracked. I'll have it looked at tomorrow."

Tiffany started in again. "Don't leave! He has me tied up! He's going to kill me!"

Morrow gave an irritated glance to the living room, then smiled at the cops. "It's a pretty exciting movie I'm watching tonight." He started to close the door. "Thanks again."

Steve panicked. He would look like a black lamp post against snow just about anywhere in this house, even in the dim light. He made a hasty sideways move and ducked down behind a big barrel chair that was one of two on this weird landing, a small table between them.

Tiffany was still yelling, although she was now trying to reach a different audience. "Mom, wake up! He's going to kill me!"

Steve watched Morrow stroll back across the space, pick up a roll of duct tape off the coffee table and tear off a chunk. He knew where it was going to go.

It killed him to watch Tiff's step-dad sit on her and fight to put that piece of tape on her mouth, but what could he do? He didn't have any kind of weapon, as he seemed to have lost his knife somewhere.

All at once, Morrow rose and strode from the room. Steve got up and quickly moved down the three steps to the living room, ducking down again behind the sofa. He crawled to the end and looked through the furniture grouping, trying to see past a massive stone coffee table. Morrow returned and squatted down with what looked like a syringe.

Steve didn't think. He rose and vaulted over the sofa, jumped onto the table, and used it to dive for the guy, toppling him to the floor.

Tiffany had told him about the home gym that rivaled Planet Fitness for equipment, and now he knew the man used it. He sent an elbow into Steve's gut that rolled him off. He struggled to gain his feet even as the older Morrow sprang up like a rabbit and focused on Steve's face.

He saw the moment he figured him out. "Tiffany's tutor." He relaxed somewhat and waved a hand at Tiff on the floor. "She attacked me, Steve. I hated to do this to her, but she was completely out of control." He pointed to a broken vase on the floor. "And I can't have her breaking her mother's things."

Steve looked to Tiffany's frantic eyes, then back to the lying douchebag who pretended to be a father. "Was that before or after you shagged your receptionist in the downstairs bedroom?"

Morrow's cavalier attitude disappeared. "Min has been ill for so long, and I—"

"Save the performance!" He took a step toward Tiffany. "Since you hate doing this, I'm sure you won't mind if I take Tiff out of here now."

To Steve's surprise, Morrow took a step back and spread his hands. "Please." Bending down he picked up the duct tape and set it on a side table. "It kills me to see her like this. I hope you can get her the help she needs."

Steve walked around to her back, thinking to unwrap the tape so she could walk, but Morrow had other ideas. "I think you better leave those restraints on," the man said as if she were a pitbull in need of a muzzle.

Maybe that is the best plan. Just get her out of here. He squatted down to get his arms under her, but as soon as he started to lift, the man moved in on them both, that syringe back in his hand he must have picked up with the tape.

Steve took several steps back and ran into that immovable coffee table. He sat down hard, still holding Tiffany. As Morrow moved in, Steve brought up his legs, giving the man a kicking shove backward, then got to his feet and ran for the door.

With his hand under Tiff's legs, he tried to pull on the weird handle to this even weirder door, but it didn't budge. Tiffany might be able to tell him how it worked, but he'd have to put her down to get the tape off of her mouth, and there wasn't any time. Morrow now had them cornered in the entry.

And this time, he had a gun.

Chapter 31

Leaving Dani at the hospital had been one of the hardest things Will had ever done, but at least he'd gotten a good report on her before he left, and he knew she would want him to protect their runaway ranga rabbit.

Rand pulled up to the Morrow residence just as a police cruiser was pulling away. Will assumed it was the one the captain had sent to check on Tiffany.

"Hold on, boys," Rand said, winking his lights at them. "I want to ask you a few questions."

The cruiser pulled back to the curb, and Rand pulled in behind them. He and Will got out and walked up to the driver's side.

"Any sign of Tiffany here?" Rand asked after the driver lowered his window.

He shook his head. "Mr. Morrow says he hasn't seen hide nor hair of her, and he was right ticked off to be gotten out of bed at this hour."

"That's right," the other jack put in. "I wouldn't bother the man again."

Will looked to Rand with brows raised. "Morrow told me he'd be right stoked to stake out the motel all night. Seems to me he shouldn't even be here."

Rand nodded, and the two jogged around the cruiser, across the lawn and up the curving steps to the door. Rand pounded with his fist. "Morrow, open up, it's Capt. Rand." Muffled shouts from inside had Rand drawing his weapon. "Morrow, open the door."

A moment later, it opened, but it wasn't Morrow looking out. It was Steve, pointing frantically behind him. "He ran through the house. I assume to get out another way."

Rand waved Will to go around the house one way while he went another, even as he was calling for backup. Will paused just a moment. "Is Tiffany okay?"

Steve nodded and opened the door wider. She was trussed like a calf at the fair, but looked to be sound. "He was going to shoot me up with some kind of drug!" she said with wide eyes. "Will, what if he's been doing that to my mother?"

"We'll catch, him," he said, already evaluating the jump from the stairs to a sunken private courtyard. "Get her out to the car, Steve."

"Watch out for the Koi pond," Steve yelled after him.

Will's jump down was thankfully not a splashdown, and he had no sooner thought how grateful he was for adequate security lighting, than it all went off. Sunk below ground level, with high walls and a lot of ornamental grasses, it was now as dark as a dog's guts.

Which was, he assumed, exactly what Morrow had wanted.

Will moved as quickly as he dared, not wanting to miss the man if he was hiding in this mini jungle, and damn if he didn't almost step right into a pond. A shout out of Rand somewhere on the other side of this massive house had him jumping over a corner of the water and moving faster.

He came upon a spiral staircase. What it went up to, Will couldn't see, but he could imagine it was a deck that went over the courtyard. As he moved past a set of French patio doors, he heard what sounded like a chair being knocked over on a hardwood floor. Had Rand scared Morrow back inside? He tried the handle but found it locked.

With cops at the curb, it would be stupid to go out the front. The mongrel would want to get to the garage. Will tried to see what was on his right. It was no longer a wall, but a building. It seemed too big for a garage, but everything about this place was too big.

The structure above him seemed to attach the main house with this somewhat smaller building. Could one get to the roof of the other building via this route? Was there a way in to that building from the roof? Will remembered the day Morrow had seemed to enter from upstairs and backtracked. Before he went up the spiral staircase, he grabbed a piece of driftwood he might be able to use as a weapon in a pinch.

As he neared the top, a door opened, and Will moved into the shadow of the house. The light was a bit better up there where the streetlights could reach—good enough to see that more than one person trooped out in front of a man dressed in black holding his hand as if it held a gun. Will's jaw clenched as he twigged who the two were.

They moved across the large deck, and Will climbed the last four steps to the top, hoping Rand was somewhere nearby and wishing he had the handgun the captain had insisted he turn over as evidence against Keith.

From this vantage point, he could see the place was now surrounded by cop cars that had come in quiet, but whose lights were flashing a silent warning of their presence. He hoped there were a couple blocking the garage doors.

A voice amplified by a bullhorn sounded. "Morrow, we have the entire place surrounded. There's nowhere to go. It's time to give yourself up."

"Ah, but there *is* somewhere to go," he shouted back, "when I have hostages. Let them know you're here, honey." When Tiffany didn't answer, he jammed the gun into her back.

"I'm here, Captain," she yelled, "and so is Steve. My dad— my *step* dad— has a gun."

Will had had enough of gun standoffs for one day. Coming out of the shadows, he decided on using some good old fashion Aussie bullshit. "Morrow," he yelled, holding the driftwood at his side. "My AR-15 trumps your Glock. Throw it down."

He turned and stepped back, keeping the gun on the kids. "I'll take them out first, Yarnel."

Will caught movement on the roof next door. "I don't think so."

A shot rang out, and Morrow spun and hit the deck floor. Steve jumped to sweep up the weapon that had launched out of his hand and pointed it shakily at the downed man. Morrow levered himself up on his left hand with a groan, and Tifffany, behind him, kicked his wounded shoulder with the flat of her foot. He collapsed again, doubled up in pain, and Will couldn't help the smile that pulled at his lips as he strode forward and put the end of the driftwood to his head. "Bang."

The man opened his eyes, then closed them again, his whole expression reflecting a kind of ugly defeat.

Rand ran across the garage roof, carrying a rifle, as two more jacks burst out of the French doors on the house. "You kids all right?" the captain projected toward Tiffany and Steve as he approached.

Steve handed Rand Morrow's gun as they both nodded weakly.

Will caught Steve's eye. "What happened to getting her to the car?"

Steve shrugged, throwing up his hands. "She wouldn't leave without seeing her mother."

Tiffany made no excuses for her actions. "I had a hard time finding her, and then I couldn't wake her. Will, I think this bastard drugged her."

Rand turned to the two who had cuffed Morrow and were pulling him to his feet. "Tell a paramedic to get in here and see to Mrs. Morrow."

"She's in one of the smaller bedrooms," she threw after them. "Down the back stairs."

Will saw the moment the captain noticed his piece of wood. A smile spread under the man's mustache "I was wondering where you found an AR-15. That was the stupidest brave thing I think I've ever seen."

Will set it on a nearby table. "Well, it's been a damn long day." Will nodded to Rand's rifle. "That's twice you've hit your mark tonight."

He cradled it across his forearm. "I was a sniper in the army. It's a skill that comes in handy every now and then." He shook his head. "More today than in a long while."

The two coppers almost had Morrow to the French doors when Tiffany yelled after them, spreading her hands wide. "Why wasn't this enough for you? A mansion, running a successful corporation, a garage full of luxury sports cars, trips around the world—why wasn't that enough?"

Morrow turned, pain etched on his face. "None of it was really mine," he said through clenched teeth. "It was all hers."

Tiffany strode forward, and her voice broke when she spoke. "Why wasn't *she* enough? Why wasn't it enough to have a beautiful, loving wife? Why did you have to *own* everything?" Her voice went high and tight. "Even the daughter?"

The man seemed to have no answer, and after a silent moment, the jacks got him moving into the house.

Will slid an arm around Tiffany's shaking shoulders as tears ran down her cheeks. "I'm sorry, ranga. Some people don't deserve the gifts the universe gives them."

Steve came up on her other side, and to Will's surprise, took her hand. "I may not deserve them, but I appreciate them." Turning out of Will's hold, she slipped into Steve's. They were evidently not avoiding touching each other anymore. Their long, passionate kiss nearly made him blush.

His phone rang in his pocket, and he took it out, the name on the screen bringing a smile to his weary face. He answered and brought it to his ear. "Possum, you missed a hell of a chase. It turns out that Morrow, himself, was our bad guy."

"Seriously?" she said, her small voice like heavenly music to Will's ears. "And I missed it? Dang it."

He thought about her spunk and knew that, like Tiffany, nothing would keep her from doing what she wanted to do. Renae had been like that. Strong women were like that. And the men who loved them wouldn't change them even if they could.

He followed Tiffany and Steve into the house, hoping it wasn't just the knock on the head and lack of sleep talking when he heard himself say, "Don't worry, sweetheart, there will be plenty more adventure when you're my partner in Brazil."

She didn't miss a beat. "When do we leave?"

Chapter 32

Dani woke to find Will asleep in a recliner in her hospital room, and her eyes filled with tears, remembering his whispered words to her before the ambulance arrived. Yes, she'd only known him a couple of weeks, and yes, she loved everything about him. Even that crazy toothpick he often gnawed on like a hillbilly.

He stirred, as if he felt her watching him, and smiled when he saw her open eyes. "How do you feel?"

"Still kind of tired, but I guess that's normal. How about you?"

He winced, operating the recliner's lever to lower the foot rest. "Never better," he ground out.

Dani laughed. "I thought you promised not to lie to me."

He put a hesitant hand to the back of his head and winced again. "Who's lying? Any day with you in it is a better day."

She put out a hand toward him. "Come here."

He pushed up out of the recliner with his left hand and was by her side in two strides, bending to slide his arms around her. She caught him up tight. "Better and better," he murmured, his bearded cheek next to hers.

After a long hug where neither spoke, Will pulled back slightly to give her a tender kiss. "I love you, Dani Harper."

She looked deep into his hazel eyes. "I love you, Will Yarnel."

She had a sudden remembrance of Keith's maniacal expression with a gun pointed first at Will, then at himself. She shook her head. "I still can't believe what Keith—" She bit her lip, wondering what the man might have done if they hadn't shown up. Would he have killed Will? Or himself?

Will straightened out of her embrace and took her hand. "I know, but what we don't know is how much of his actions were him and how much were his brain injury."

"He didn't have a brain injury when he hired a man to follow us and take pictures," she reminded him.

"True," Will admitted. "All I'm saying is those tendencies were probably amplified."

"Maybe. Probably." She didn't have any idea what she might say to the man if she ever saw him again. She felt as if she didn't know him at all.

Will reached over to the side table and picked up a hospital cafeteria menu. "It's nearly noon. Are you hungry?"

Dani laughed. "Are you ever not hungry?"

His eyes scanned the offerings. "I missed a couple of meals lately."

There was a knock on the door, and Tiffany poked her head in. "You guys awake?"

Dani grinned, opening her arms. "Get in here, you crazy ranga!"

Tiffany moved in for a quick hug with Steve pushing in after her. "I'm so sorry about… everything," Dani said with sincerity. She was still hazy on the details, but Will had told her that Bret Morrow was the embezzler and responsible not only for Tiffany's kidnapping, but years of taking sexual liberties with his young step-daughter. He'd also been slipping his wife pills that made her feel ill to get her out of her leadership role at Pragnalysis. "How is your mother?"

Will's phone rang, and he answered with "Rand, what's the news?" as he slipped past everyone to go out in the hall.

After he was out the door, Tiffany answered. "Improving, although she's still in denial over what Bret was doing to both her and the company. I'd bet my life that whatever he was giving her for her headaches actually caused them. I think his plan was to kill her eventually and make it look like a suicide. At least that's what he planned for me. I heard him and Amy talking about it." She gave a tiny shake of her head. "I haven't told her everything yet. She didn't believe me about so many things… The truth, if she'll ever accept it, is going to be hard to take."

"So she really loved Bret."

Tiffany nodded. "She was utterly blind to his… dark side. And he was very good at playing her. What I didn't see coming was Amy."

Dani knew Tiffany had to be in shock as well, even though she was doing a good job of being stoic at the moment.

Steve slipped an arm around her. "Well, their secrets are out. He and Amy are two bad apples that are going to do some time."

"Was Reynolds caught?" Dani asked as Will came back into the room.

It was Will who answered. "At the airport. She was planning a little Tuscany vacay." Tiffany shook her head as Will went on. "And there's more. I've been wondering why McCain wouldn't spill who had hired him. Turns out it was her. At Bret's direction, of course, but she was the one playing McCain." He lowered his voice. "Sleeping with him. Making him promises. Evidently, he was so smitten he refused to implicate her." A corner of his mouth quirked up. "According to Rand, she, however, cracked like a dollar store figurine, turning on both men for a plea deal."

Tiffany looked to Steve. "Turns out you were right. Amy couldn't be trusted." She turned back to Will. "They both knew exactly what we were doing at Pragnalysis, and they set us up to find the evidence pointing to Chase."

Will nodded solemnly.

Another knock had them all looking to the door. When it didn't open, Dani yelled, "Come in." She wished she had a picture of all of their faces when it turned out to be Chase Owens.

"I hope I'm not intruding. I just stopped in to see Min and found out that you all were here as well. I just want to offer my wishes for a speedy recovery to you, Miss Harper and you, Mr. Yarnel."

His eyes locked on Tiffany with more contrition than Dani might have thought possible for the man. "And to tell Tiffany how deeply sorry I am for what Bret did to her and Min. Just yesterday, I suspected something was going on between Amy and him, but she denied it when I confronted her about it." He gave a sad smile. "And she was right, I was no saint to be accusing anyone else of 'indiscretions.' " He held up a folded piece of paper. "Your apology for last night was completely unnecessary."

Tiffany shook her head. "I was wrong, and I needed to say so."

He stuck out a hand. "Can we begin again, then?"

Tiffany hesitated. "Can I expect a bit more respect than you gave me last summer?"

He dropped his hand as his forehead creased. "I'm not sure there's a woman on the planet I have more respect for right now." His voice grew intense. "Your parents were more than my bosses. They were parental figures and mentors to a young man who had lost his parents." He seemed to wrestle with something for a moment before speaking again. "Finding out this morning what Bret did to you and Min tore me up." His tall frame straightened. "Not to mention what he was trying to do to me. And I decided I don't want to be like that—using women, or anyone, for my own… gain." He put out his hand again. "And I'd appreciate it if you'd keep me in line."

This time she took it with a sly smile. "I'd be happy to."

Dani hoped he was being sincere. Could a man like Chase Owens turn his life completely around that quickly, or was he only concerned with his position at Pragnalysis now that Bret was gone? *I guess time will tell.*

Tiffany looked back to Dani as if struck with a sudden thought. "So what was the deal with your ex-fiancé?"

Dani looked to Will. "I wish I knew."

* * *

Will felt a thousand times better after some ibuprofen, food, a whole night's sleep on a real bed—even if that bed was the lumpy Days Inn variety—more food, and a shower.

Steve and Tiffany had checked out the day before in favor of Steve's apartment, so he had packed up his and Dani's stuff as well, bringing it all to the hospital as the sun was peeking through the clouds, mid-morning.

He wondered that the two would opt for Steve's little apartment rather than the Morrow mansion, but he supposed the sterile monstrosity held too many unpleasant memories now that she was seeing Bret Morrow clearly again.

As he neared Dani's room, pushing her luggage set and his duffle bag on a hospital cart, he heard voices and expected to find her doctor within. *Good. I want to know when she'll be able to fly.* Pushing the cart past the room, he leaned on the door, pulling the load in backward. The voice he now heard quite clearly stopped him in his tracks.

He turned into the room, letting the door fall shut as he instinctively reached for a weapon inside his coat that wasn't there. He pulled it out again slowly, unconsciously forming a fist.

Even though the man was in a wheelchair with Heather standing beside him, Will could feel his blood pressure rising. "Bisbee, what are you doing here? Haven't you caused enough trouble for Dani?"

Keith lifted his hands from his lap in a weak surrender, one of them bandaged. "I'm not here to make trouble, and I. . . " He let out a breath as his hands dropped to his thighs again. "I know it's over between Dani and me. I just needed to... explain... the unexplainable."

Will looked to Dani to see if she believed him. "And did he?"

She gave him a tight smile and didn't really answer. "Did you bring the ring?"

Will dug the small box out of the side pocket of his camo cargo pants and offered it to Keith, who took it without meeting his gaze, looking instead to his ex-fiancée. "Dani, I know you don't believe me about the car, but I swear I had nothing to do with that shooting." He looked to Will. "A lot came back to me this morning about the Grand Prix."

Will arched a brow. "Let's hear it."

"After spending most of the afternoon in that damned cabin drinking whiskey, I convinced myself to drive back to Denver to try one last time to talk to Dani. How I made it down the mountain drunk, I don't know, but once back in the city and almost to your hotel, I slammed on the brakes for something—maybe a cat or a squirrel. Anyway, I was rear-ended. I looked in the rearview mirror at that black Grand Prix."

"I turned into a parking lot, thinking they'd follow to discuss the damages, but they didn't. They just drove on by. I went back out the next exit and followed them, honking. I should have been happy that I wouldn't be charged with a DUI, but," –he shook his head— "I was so drunk, I didn't even think of that.

"Finally, they pulled into another lot and parked, and I stumbled to meet them as they got out. Before I knew what was happening, the driver slapped car keys into my hand, and they jumped into my SUV that I'd left running. They took off. I didn't know what to do, so I jumped in the Grand Prix and followed. I wasn't so lucky on the mountain road the second time."

Will didn't really want to back Bisbee up, but his story matched Rand's recent report. "Your rental was found last night in the railroad yard with some damage to the back bumper, so at least that part fits." Will looked between the Bisbee siblings and Dani. "Using Owens' car was just part of Morrow's attempt to frame him should the car be seen—when you think about it, it was plain stupid to pick up the shooter so close to the scene of the crime—but Morrow wouldn't want to get caught in it himself."

Heather lit up with a new thought. "So Keith put a kink in his plans to just return the car to Owens' garage."

Will nodded. "That's completely possible. Morrow must have known about Owens' hook up with the married woman that gave him time to use the car *and* making his alibi suspect."

Dani seemed skeptical. "Seems a pretty crazy coincidence to me."

Keith nodded. "It does, and if I were you, I wouldn't believe it for a second. But I'm not a car thief, Dani, and I don't own a gun." He waved a hand at Will. "I used his at the cabin." His forehead puckered with the memory of it. "And if I could take all that back, I would."

Heather put a hand to his shoulder, blinking back tears.

Will wouldn't push a reconciliation on Dani for anything in the world, but he also knew that not forgiving Bisbee at least for what he'd done while not in a right state of mind would end up hurting her more than him.

"Bisbee, there were times in that cabin when I wondered if Dani had been plain loco to ever hook up with the likes of you." A corner of his mouth ticked up. "And while I think she was still wise to cut you loose, I can see that who you were there is not really who you are." He put out his hand toward Keith's uninjured one in a gesture of peace. "I wish you all the best." Keith hesitantly took it, and Will gave him a firm grip. "Do the opposite of whatever your father would do, and you'll be okay."

Keith snorted and shook his head. "God, that man." He looked to Heather. "Please tell me I'm not like him."

She gripped his shoulder. "No, you're not, but… well, we'll talk later."

Keith put his hand to his bowed head in a look of despair. "Oh, God."

Will looked to the sister he hoped Keith would listen to. "I'm sorry I was short with you after—"

"No need to apologize." She took hold of the grips on Keith's wheelchair. "We were all under a lot of stress." She gave Dani what seemed like a look of regret behind a thin smile. "Well, I guess we should be going."

Keith nodded, and Heather moved him toward the door. Will was all too happy to hold it open for them, but Keith found more to say before they reached it. "Dani," he began, and Heather paused. "I hope that someday we can… talk."

Dani gave a slight nod. "Someday."

After they were in the hall, Will let the door close and moved to her side. She looked to him with a worried brow. "Do you think I was too hard on him?"

"Only you know the answer to that." He bent to kiss her forehead. "But I think, like Tiffany, you need some time to process."

She slid her arms around his neck and pulled him down to her lips. "Process this, Will Yarnel."

Will smiled and gladly gave in to analyzing all the ways this hard-headed woman would change his life for the better.

* * *

"We're going to miss you guys." Tiffany swiped at a tear, and Dani pulled her into a hug.

Will looked at his watch. They had just a few minnies to say goodbye before boarding their flight back to São Paulo.

"We will be back for a visit." She released the young woman who seemed better every day. "I promise."

Will shook Steve's hand. "I know you'll take good care of her, mate—keep her moving in the right direction."

Steve cocked his head and smiled. "I will try." He looked to his redhead with a hitched brow. "She doesn't make it easy, though."

Tiffany linked her arm with his. "Don't worry, I'll make sure Steve stays out of trouble." She gave Will a smile. "And I already have a call in to a therapist and an appointment with Dr. Schmidt."

Steve leaned to kiss her head, and Will almost cried himself. This trip had turned him into a blubbering drongo. He remembered the gift Dani had for Tiffany and gave her a nudge as she stood smiling at their young friends. "Don't' forget the—"

"Oh! Yes!" Reaching into her big shoulder bag, she pulled out the small white box, tied with a red ribbon and presented it to Tiffany. "This is just a little something for you."

She seemed reluctant to take it. "You guys already gave me more than I can ever repay you for."

"It's a gift," Steve admonished. "By definition, you don't repay a gift, or it's not a gift."

"I suppose you're right." Tiffany smiled, pulled on the bow, and lifted the lid. "But still, you didn't have to..." She paused as she swept the tissue paper aside, then gave a little gasp. She pulled out a small carved cherrywood jackrabbit, her eyes shining with appreciation. It was standing tall on its hind legs as though looking at something in the distance.

"Will and I saw it in the hospital gift shop and just had to buy it," Dani explained.

Tiffany looked from Dani to Will. "It's amazing." She studied it closer. "I love it." She looked to them again. "So you obviously looked through my high school yearbook, but... this rabbit's not running."

"That's right, ranga," Will said, "because now you only need to run if you want to."

Her smile grew, and she stepped forward for a three-way hug. Dani pulled Steve in to make it four. Love was like that. There was always room for more.

Will knew Renae would be proud.

Epilogue

"Oh Will! Oh Wow! That was… amazing!"

Will seemed frozen in complete shock. "That was… really good. Much better than I was expecting." He smiled down at her. "You may be a natural."

Dani couldn't stop grinning at shirtless, sweaty Will. "Let's go again."

Will shook his head as he strode to the tree stumps at the edge of the rain forest clearing to set up the cans for a second rain of bullets.

He'd brought her to a cabin that he said Rita had stayed in for a few days before Formosa caught up with them, and they had moved on to the next safehouse.

As soon as he was walking back, she raised the Glock and took aim.

He waved a hand. "Move back about three meters this time."

She did, hoping that wouldn't make a difference. After having to explain her decision to go back to Brazil with Will over and over to different family members, knocking every one of those cans off their perches was like a sign from heaven that she'd made the right choice—that she really could help him with more than paperwork.

Will crossed his arms. "All right, av a go."

She fired at the cans again, missing only one.

"Are you sure you've never shot a gun before?"

"I have played some tap room darts in my day, but no, I've never even picked up a gun before today."

He scratched the side of his beard. "Well, you've certainly got the knack for it."

"So what else do I have to do to be a private investigator?" She could hardly contain her excitement.

Will chuckled as he strode back to set up the cans one more time. "Hold on, possum," he called over his shoulder, "there's a bit more to being a P.I. than just knowing how to shoot a gun." He set two cans back on their tree trunks. "In fact, that's probably the least of it."

"So how long do you think it will take?" she called across the space.

Will turned with a grin. "Slow down, sheila. We've only been back in Brazil a week."

And what a week it had been. Will said their "courtship" had gone too fast, and he wanted to "win her."

Dani had called him a nilwit, but he wouldn't be dissuaded. He'd put her up in the guest room of his apartment and acted as if they were next door neighbors. Then he asked her out every evening and sent her flowers, chocolates, and other Australian treasures while he was out working with Rod during the day.

Some nights they took in a movie or listened to live music. Other nights they strolled on the beach. Last night, they had danced in the living room that served as a ballroom in a black tie/designer dress affair, then sat out on his balcony holding hands and sipping champagne while gazing at the stars. Will said he was starting to like the bubbly stuff. After an hour, he'd walked her "home" and gave her a goodnight kiss that quickly turned steamy.

She watched him now swaggering back toward her in his camo trousers, his impressive pecs and biceps on display, and couldn't help thinking about what happened after he'd asked her if he could come in to "her place" for a nightcap after their evening of star gazing.

He caught her expression and smiled. "You're having a ripper of a good time, aren't you, firing that thing like some kind of Annie Oakley?"

She didn't tell him about the good time she was really thinking about. "Yes! I'm good at this!"

He slipped an arm around her and pulled her against him. "You're good at a lot of things," he said in a sexy growl.

He bent his head to capture her lips, giving her the kind of kiss that usually led to… a ripper of a good time. After thoroughly heating her up, he broke it off. "We could spend the rest of the afternoon knocking cans to the ground, or…" He put his lips to her ear and whispered an alternate plan. Then he looked down at her with eyebrows raised.

She grinned. "I think you're jealous. I think you don't want me to show you up with my wild west gun skills."

He smiled back. "That's a fair dinkum. But," he said, looking toward the cans, "they'll still be here later, and" —he brought his eyes back to hers, full of mischief— "I should also teach you some one-on-one physical maneuvers, not to mention other… investigative skills."

Handing him the gun, she pulled him toward the cabin. She wanted to learn it all—the job and the man.

And there was plenty of time for both.

Thank you for reading *Red Rabbit on the Run*. I hope you enjoyed it! If you liked this book, please consider reviewing it at Amazon or Goodreads. Your reviews help other readers find new favorites. Thanks for your support!

About the Author

I live with my husband and several spoiled cats in beautiful Colorado Springs where we get to look at Pikes Peak every day!

I've worn many hats in my life, but I spend most of my creative talents these days on writing and art. You can read more about what I do at jodibowersox.com. You can also follow me on BookBub, Goodreads, Linked-In, Pinterest, Etsy (Pikes Peak Unique), Facebook (jodibowersoxartistry), and Twitter.

In addition to romance, I have published a short Bible commentary and a compilation of plays and skits. I also have children's books published under the name J.B. Stockings. I'm available for school presentations on art and writing.

Book four in the Anonymous series *Blue-Eyed Devil* is available now for pre-order!

Read on for a sample of another one of my romances, *Interiors By Design.*

Chapter 1

It's too bright—impossibly bright.

The little red-headed girl in overalls and a white t-shirt is running through flowers—sunflowers, daffodils, daisies. She stops to pick one. She lifts it to her nose, and a baby starts to cry. The little girl searches among the flowers but can't find the baby.

"Where are you, baby?" she yells.

"It's over here!"

The girl looks up to see an old man motioning for her in the distance. She starts toward him, but a purple flower catches her eye. She stops to pick it, and when she looks up again, the man is gone.

She climbs a hill to get a better view of the meadow. There is a flock of chickens at the top scratching and pecking around. As she surveys the meadow below, the chickens surround her. A rooster comes over the hill and stops when he sees her. The little girl sees the rooster and freezes, her heart pounding. The rooster cocks his head to one side and stares for a moment then charges. He jumps with spurs headed toward her chest and wings flapping at her face.

Amanda Billings sat straight up in bed with a gasp, her long red hair plastered in a sweaty mass to her head. Looking frantically around the room, she could just make out jungle leaf wallpaper by the light of the street lamp shining in her window, and her breathing began to slow.

"Another friggin' nightmare," she grumbled as she whipped off the sheets and pulled her sweaty night shirt over her head. Feeling around the corner of her closet, she grabbed a robe and slipped it on as she stumbled to the kitchen, flipping on her bedroom light on the way out. She opened the freezer and pulled out the Peanut Butter Panic ice cream. Touching the box to each cheek before opening it, she then popped off the lid and dug in with a spoon from the dish drainer.

Is this my life now?

She stood a moment staring at her white cupboards by the dim light coming from the lamp post in her backyard, then carrying the ice cream box with her, she left the kitchen and walked purposefully to the mantle in the next room. She turned on a small lamp and picked up a picture of herself in a black graduation gown, arm in arm with an older gentleman—the one from her dream. Putting it down, her eyes came to rest on a school picture of a teenage boy with a devilish grin.

She ate another spoonful of ice cream.

Spying her cell phone charging on a table by the front door, she grabbed it, pushed speed dial #1, and plopped down on the sofa beside her two cats, Buffy and Fiddlesticks, who were curled up together.

Buffy was a blue-eyed moggy chocolate-point with a chocolate beard and half-mustache. Fiddlesticks was a grey and black striped tabby with a mostly white muzzle and underbelly, although tabby patches adorned her white legs in various spots. Disturbed from their slumber, they stretched, yawned, and trotted out to the kitchen.

"Hello, my friend," sang a young man accompanied by a ukulele, "thank you for calling me, but I'm not here right now..."

Amanda smiled through the song, and at the beep, she left her message. "Yeah, it's me. I just wanted to listen to your song—needed a laugh. Talk to you soon, Bro." She ended the call but didn't move from the sofa.

I wish grandpa were really here.

She ate several more spoonfuls of ice cream until she had scraped out the last of it, sighed, and forced herself up. She put the phone back on the table and headed to the kitchen to deposit the empty carton in the trash and the spoon in the sink. Then she headed back to her bedroom and turned out the light.

Five seconds later, she turned the light back on.

* * *

"What's all the fuss about autumn, anyway?" Mick half said this under his breath as he clutched the collar of his grey wool sweater just a little tighter against the winds that swirled leaves bedecked with the usual fall garb around his shoes. *These are just the colors of impending death.*

Mick didn't say this out loud as a group of children were pushing past him in after-school exuberance, seemingly unaware of the wind, the chill, the steady march to bare trees and a lifeless world.

Mick Thompson had put the finishing touches on the ad campaign he had been working on for three months not two hours ago, and already his excitement was lagging. He'd left work early to celebrate but realized during his trek home that he really had no one to celebrate with except his sister, Clarisse, and her family, and he knew she worked late on Thursday evenings. *Maybe tomorrow night.*

The overcast sky was in no more of a celebratory mood than he was, and all alone on the cracked sidewalk in front of a row of townhouses, he once again took to mumbling out loud. "How does she stand this place? I'm driving tomorrow even if it takes me an hour to find a parking space."

Mick's sister was a detective with the Kansas City Police Dept. and had talked him into moving to KC from California after his fiancée walked out on him two weeks before the wedding. This had been nearly a year ago, and he still knew practically no one and didn't really care that he spent most of his evenings alone in front of the TV, a mindless lump of depression.

Turning the corner, his medium build was met with the full force of the wind, which blew whatever small spark of good feeling still remained in him out his back and down the street.

Why am I still here? He thought this last, as saying anything aloud proved difficult. He tucked his head down and pressed forward through the gale. *Now that this project is finished, maybe it's time to go home.*

Clare was wrong. Leaving didn't help.

Mick turned and climbed the stairs to his apartment building, making a mental note to dig his wool topcoat out of storage. He reached for the door, but it suddenly opened, revealing a petite redhead who was struggling to get out, her arms loaded with large, cumbersome books.

He quickly moved to hold the door for her, and she threw him a smile and a "thank you" as she hurried out, her long hair flying both from the wind and her speedy departure. He watched her sail up the street until she unlocked the trunk of a sky blue Mustang parked half-way up the block and dumped the books inside. He was still standing there staring as she drove away, the wind mercilessly tousling his brown hair.

* * *

"Oh my gosh, girl, how much candy did you buy?"

Amanda, carrying two loaded grocery sacks, was making her way through the furniture displays of her interior decorating show room toward the tall, slender blonde with short, spiky hair sitting behind the counter. She grinned as she plunked the bags down in front of Sally, her friend and co-worker.

"I get a lot of Trick or Treat-ers at my door," Amanda defended, "and you know the crap that most people give out—that awful taffy stuff." She pulled a snack-sized Snickers from one of her sacks and held it high. "I will not let children go home without chocolate."

Sally, dressed for Halloween in a green sweater and short orange skirt, tapped her temple with the tip of her pencil. "And there's no point in having any leftovers that you don't like, right?"

Amanda grinned and tore open the wrapper. "Exactly."

Sally turned back to her customer worksheets. "You better watch your weight, girl. Look around. It's not difficult to end up looking like a hippo."

Amanda took off her long grey trench coat, revealing a red button shirt atop an almost ankle-length black skirt and short boots, and stashed her bags of candy under the counter before plunking down in her chair to check her afternoon appointments.

"I'll watch it later," she mumbled, her mouth full of chocolate.

Amanda Billings was the owner and chief designer of Interiors by Design, and Sally Winters had been working for her as long as she had been in business—about three years. Having gone through college together, Sally was Amanda's dearest friend and confidant.

The show room was full of the colors, fabrics, and styles currently popular for windows, furniture, and walls. The displays were constantly changing, partly to keep their customers excited about the possibilities but mostly to keep themselves from becoming bored with the show room they worked in every day.

As Amanda looked through her appointment book, Sally handed her a post-it note. "Mrs. Taylor called while you were out. She would like you to bring more samples—today, if possible."

Amanda sighed and threw the candy wrapper in the trash under the counter. "I was just there yesterday with a million samples, and she didn't like any of them. I'm not sure what else to take."

Sally lowered her voice and did her best Mrs. Taylor imitation, complete with hand gestures, "I'm not sure what I want, love, but I'm desperate for something on my windows! The whole world can look right in!"

Sally yawned, stretched, and went back to punching numbers in her calculator. Both decorators had more clients than they could handle with the holidays approaching. Amanda had to figure out something for Mrs. Taylor and fast.

Amanda stared at her desk—piles of fabric samples on the left, piles of decorating estimates on the right, a bottle of Mylanta in the center. She took off the cap and downed a big swig.

* * *

"Mick, great job on the Harris account," congratulated a short, stocky man with a receding hairline. "I heard they were very happy with it."

Mick, who had been heading to the break room, stopped when Ted from Accounting intercepted him from a connecting hallway. "Thanks. They were a hard sell, but I think we finally ended up with something they liked."

"We?" Ted questioned then lowered his voice. "I mean, did Janine really contribute anything? I heard—"

Mick cut him off. "I'll have to talk to you later, Ted. I'm late for my own party."

With that, he turned and continued toward the break room of the Henry Martin Advertising Agency. As he opened the door, there were cheers and cups of punch held high. The table held a cake with "Congratulations" scrawled across it in light blue icing, and red balloons had been taped at random spots around the smallish room. Mick smiled self-consciously and headed for the punch bowl.

A slender black-haired woman strode across the room with a knife and spatula. "Now that Mick is here, let's cut the cake!" She slipped past him. "What took you so long?" she pouted. "We've been waiting forever."

"I got tied up with the big guy," he lied. "He wanted to discuss our next project." He knew that meeting was coming, but it really hadn't happened yet. The truth was he just couldn't make himself get out of his desk chair. Social events just hadn't been the same for him since Tammy left him. He felt awkward and alone.

"Oh, let's not think about the next big project just yet!" put in a plump woman in a bright blue pantsuit helping herself to a piece of cake. "I'm still having nightmares about the last one!"

When she was out of ear-shot, dark-eyed Irena leaned in. "You need a new partner. Janine is so lazy." Then she grabbed Mick's arm and stood on tip-toe, her lips practically touching his ear. "Put in a word for me with Mr. Martin," she whispered. "You and I would make a great team."

He half smiled, and pretending to notice someone he needed to talk to across the room, excused himself and headed toward a young man in a well-tailored suit. Mick had no idea who he was, but he knew that Irena was watching him, so he decided to find out. Mick offered his hand to the young man who turned out to be a student intern. Mick chatted until Irena was involved in a conversation herself then excused himself, downed his punch, and headed for the door.

He was met yet again by Ted, who, although from a different department, had decided to crash the party. "So, Mick, some of us are hitting the bars after work. You want to join us?"

Mick knew he should say yes. Wasn't that what he wanted yesterday—somebody to celebrate with? But he knew Ted's crowd and the bars they tended to frequent—singles bars and exotic dance clubs. That just wasn't his style, and he couldn't bear the thought of it becoming his style. "I'm sorry, Ted, I've got other plans," he lied again. He wondered if he were forming a habit. "Maybe another time."

Ted grabbed his sleeve before he could make his escape. "Hey, there's Irena.," he said, ogling her across the room. "She is so. . . ." He let out a slow breath. "Do you think she'd go out with me?"

Mick looked over at the dark-haired beauty in a tight, bright floral dress, now chatting up the intern and flirting indiscriminately then back at Ted—balding, overweight, and easily fifteen years older than her.

"Sure, go for it, Ted."

While Ted was daydreaming his approach, Mick slipped out the door.

What is wrong with me? Irena's gorgeous. Why don't I ask her out? He pondered this question as he headed back to his office to get his coat and all the way to his car. Driving home, he tried to picture them together as a couple strolling arm in arm around the Plaza.

He shook his head. It just didn't fit. They didn't fit.

Tammy and I fit.

He shook his head again. Tammy had left him, so evidently this feeling of "fitting" was subjective.

* * *

"Oh, yes, Halloween. I'm sorry, I forgot," Mick apologized into the phone. "No, no, it's no big deal. . . Of course you have to take the kids out...No, don't worry about me. I'll just have this champagne all to myself. In fact, maybe I'll go out... Well, you can stop by if you want, but I'm afraid I don't have any candy to hand out, just the champagne..."

Mick, standing in the middle of his practically bare apartment, was still in the dark grey suit he had worn to work.

"Thanks, Sis... Yes, it was a long project—a long, tedious project...No, I'm fine, really. Like I said, I'll probably go out on the town. I'll talk to you tomorrow. Bye."

He hung up the phone and immediately kicked off his shoes, loosened his tie, and pulled the champagne out of the ice bucket. *Go out?*

Like hell.

He popped the cork, poured a glass, and sank into the sofa.

* * *

Amanda stood waiting in the hall outside Mrs. Taylor's apartment, again loaded down with fabric sample books. She loved the ornate woodwork of this old building—the crown molding, the sconce lighting—even the worn oriental hall rugs made her smile. She had tried to persuade Mrs. Taylor to choose a fabric for her draperies that blended with the style of this grand old building, but Mrs. Taylor had proved to have a different style altogether, and Amanda was having a hard time pinning it down.

The door opened, and Mrs. Taylor ushered her in with, "Oh, here you are, Love! I'm so glad you came!"

The door closed as the Bride of Frankenstein ushered Princess Peach and Buzz Lightyear up to the door across the hall and rang the bell.

* * *

The doorbell rang, but Mick didn't hear it over the blender. He'd finished the champagne and had moved on to making margaritas. His mood had gone from bad to worse, and he had convinced himself that nothing short of a weekend bender would help. He did hear the loud knocking that followed immediately after hitting the off button and was just tipsy enough to think offering a blender of margaritas to Trick or Treat-ers a splendid idea.

He swung open the door with a cocky smile that faded as soon as his eyes locked with the Bride of Frankenstein, a.k.a. Detective Clarisse Whittington, a.k.a. his sister. Her family called her Clare.

The Princess and Buzz yelled, "Trick or Treat!" and held their hollow plastic pumpkins aloft.

"I told your mother I don't have any candy, just champagne."

Clare pushed the kids in past Mick and closed the door.

"What's champagne?" asked the Princess, who on other days went by Lilly.

Mick continued this line of thought despite the stern look his sister was giving him. "Well, I guess I don't even have the champagne anymore. Who's up for a round of margaritas? How 'bout you, Mr. Lightyear?"

Four-year-old Patrick nodded with excitement, his helmet's face mask clattering up and down.

Clare took the blender unceremoniously out of Mick's outstretched hand and marched it to the kitchen where she poured it down the sink.

He knew better than to protest. She was, after all, a police detective, and the Bride of Frankenstein look was fairly frightening as well.

"So where is Frankenstein this evening?" Mick called toward the kitchen as six-year-old Lilly twirled, and Buzz flew around the room.

"Working late," she called back.

Clare re-entered the room, her lady Frankenstein garb not really hiding the fact that she was seven months pregnant. The sternness had left her face, leaving only a kind of sadness.

"If you're going for Dean Martin, I think the drink was a martini, not a margarita."

"Right."

Mick rocked back and forth on his heels uneasily as his sister seemed to size up his state of mind. Finally, she turned and eased herself down on the beige sofa. Other than the TV, it was the only piece of furniture in the room.

"I knew you wouldn't go out. Mick, what are you doing? You just finished the campaign… you should be out celebrating with friends. Not sitting here alone, getting drunk."

Mick grabbed the hands of the two children, who were making him dizzy running round and round him, and led them to the kitchen and sat them down at the table.

"What friends, Clare?" he called back as he searched through the cupboards for snacks. He finally plunked a box of croutons on the table for the kids and returned to the living room.

"I don't really know anyone outside of work, and they are just too…too…"

"Happy?"

"No, not happy. I can live with happy. You're happy." He turned toward his bare window and looked out at the costumed kids scurrying below. "They're clueless, vacuous. It's like they're made of fluff. If I blew on them, they'd blow away."

Clare started to get up, and he quickly offered assistance. She gave him a hug then held him by the shoulders. "That substance you're looking for is life. It's hardship. It's pain. Those who have never experienced it seem less weighty. But give them time, little brother—no one gets through life without it. It will catch up to them eventually."

She stepped toward the door. "Come on, kids. We didn't get all dressed up for croutons. Mama wants some chocolate."

Lilly and Patrick grabbed their pumpkins and headed for the door. Clare took their hands and turned back to Mick. "And some people are just good at hiding their real selves. Sometimes you have to dig a bit for substance in a relationship, Mick. Not everybody wears their emotions on their sleeve like you. Give people a chance. Learn to see beyond the obvious."

He smirked. "Is that Detective Whittington talking?"

Clare paused then nodded. "Yeah, I guess it is. When you're looking for evidence, you have to see what's there and see what's not. Looking a second, or even a third time, usually brings something to light you didn't see the first time."

She made to leave, and he held the door open for the costumed troop. Frankenstein's bride waddled a bit as Lilly and Patrick pulled her down the hall.

Mick was feeling suddenly sober but not so much that he refrained from calling after them, "Sorry about the croutons. I wish I had some chocolate."

Just then, the door across the hall opened, and there was that redhead he had seen the day before. Even though she was once again carrying a pile of large books, she managed to reach into her pocket and pull out a KitKat. She handed it to Mick with a smile and headed down the hallway.

Chapter 2

Amanda is wandering from room to room in an expansive house, arm in arm with her grandfather. She's wondering how she missed seeing all these different rooms in her own home. Exploring the richly ornamented architecture and furniture and marveling at the elaborate window treatments, she points out features to her grandfather. Going to the window, she fingers heavy velvet draperies in a rich purple, green, and gold floral design.

Next to this, there is a doorway to a room that is devoid of all furnishings save a small lavender flowered swimming pool. She enters, and her grandfather is no longer with her. An orange kitten is in the pool mewing and trying to swim to the edge. A rooster is perched on the edge watching it. Suddenly it jumps on the kitten in the water and holds it under. Amanda screams.

Amanda's eyes opened with a start, and she clutched her pillow with a sharp intake of breath.

* * *

Mick sat at the mahogany bar and turned the card over and over in his hands wondering if the redhead had given it to him on purpose, or if it was mere coincidence that it had been stuck to the chocolate bar she had handed him the night before. Due to the entire bottle of champagne he had consumed, the whole event was a bit blurry. But he remembered the hair.

And the smile.

The front of the card said "Interiors by Design" in turquoise with gold swirls. The back said Amanda Billings, Interior Designer.

She had come out of the apartment across the hall. What was that woman's name—the one that always called him Mick, love? Sylvia? Or was it Cynthia? Thomas? Tomlin? *I don't know. I'm not good with names.*

"Hey, Mick!"

He was suddenly assaulted by a slap on the back that nearly made him choke on the peanut he had just popped in his mouth.

"Chuck," Mick coughed, "what's new?"

Chuck, who was easily fifty pounds heavier than Mick, with slightly thinning black hair, sat on the stool next to him and ordered a beer. "Same old, same old," Chuck singsonged his usual reply. "The kids are growing, and so is my wife." Chuck patted his own pudgy belly with both hands. "But I guess you saw her yourself last night. She said she stopped by your place with the kids. I'm beginning to wonder if she's got twins in there."

Mick squinted his hazel eyes in thought. "Really? I guess I hadn't noticed."

"Hadn't noticed?" Chuck paused to down half a mug of beer. "Oh yeah, Clare mentioned you had been drinking just a bit."

"I did see that she was pregnant—I wasn't so drunk that I didn't notice that—she just didn't seem overly pregnant. Maybe it was the costume."

"Hmm, she went as the Bride of Frankenstein, didn't she? I had to work late, so I didn't see it." Chuck paused for a moment and his eyes widened. "That outfit isn't too far from the truth these days. Clare does not like being stuck behind a desk."

Mick pushed his empty glass toward the bartender for a refill. "Behind a desk? What is she doing behind a desk? Is she in some kind of trouble?"

Chuck cocked his head at Mick. "You are in your own world, aren't you? Do you really think pregnant detectives should be out on the street tracking down criminals?"

Mick shook his head, feeling foolish. "Of course, I just hadn't thought about it, I guess."

Chuck noticed the business card lying on the bar in front of Mick. "What's that? Thinking of sprucing up your place a bit? God knows it needs it." Chuck took another gulp of his beer.

"No, not really," Mick fumbled, picking up the card. "I mean, maybe. Maybe that would be a way to uh—no, I uh, don't think so."

Chuck grabbed it out of his hand and flipped it over. "Amanda Billings. Anybody you know?"

"No." Mick snatched it back. "I mean, I've seen her around my building a few times, but we've never spoken. She just…just…smiled." Mick nervously picked up his drink and took a swallow.

Chuck grinned and downed the rest of his beer. Rising, he pulled out his wallet to pay his tab. "Well, I think you should call her. Your place is about as sterile as a hospital. It's depressing." He slammed a ten dollar bill on the bar. "And sometimes a smile dresses up the place better than anything." Chuck winked and gave Mick another slap on the back before turning to head out the door.

Made in the USA
Monee, IL
24 September 2021